Splatterpunks II

OVER THE EDGE

Splatter-punks II

OVER THE EDGE

EDITED BY
PAUL M. SAMMON

TOR®

A Tom Doherty Associates Book
New York

This is a work of fiction. All the characters and events portrayed in this book are fictitious, and any resemblance to real people or events is purely coincidental.

SPLATTERPUNKS II: OVER THE EDGE

This book is printed on acid-free paper.

A Tor Book
Published by Tom Doherty Associates, Inc.
175 Fifth Avenue
New York, N.Y. 10010

Tor® is a registered trademark of Tom Doherty Associates, Inc.

Library of Congress Cataloging-in-Publication Data

Splatterpunks II / Paul M. Sammon, editor.
    p. cm.
"A Tom Doherty Associates book."
ISBN 0-312-85786-1 (pbk.)
ISBN 0-312-85445-5 (hc.)
    1. Horror tales, American. I. Sammon, Paul. II. Title:
Splatterpunks two.
PS648.H6S64   1994
813'.0873808—dc20   94-12929
                                        CIP

First edition: April 1995

Printed in the United States of America

0 9 8 7 6 5 4 3 2 1

ACKNOWLEDGMENTS

This one, finally, is for
SHERRI SIRES SAMMON
Partner in the Quest

A dead woman bites not.

    —Patrick, 6th Lord Gray

CONTENTS

14   CONTENTS

PERSONAL
ACKNOWLEDGMENTS

Some books are like pregnancies; long and difficult, needing the assistance of many midwives. Some evolve so smoothly you wonder what all the fuss was about.

Splatterpunks II was an easy birth. First, thanks to all the writers, agents, and editors whose work is represented herein. You not only helped bring this book to term, you're its parents, and I'm proud to have drawn on such a twisted gene pool.

I'd also like to thank Martin Amis and Clive Barker for their generosity and understanding. *Kudos* to John Skipp, who cares. And keeps surprising me. *Merci* to David Dodds, who I know is pestered by far more important folk than I. *Gracias* to the many readers of my "Rough Cuts" column, in *Cemetery Dance*, who submitted dozens of potential submissions; y'all made me realize that, conventional wisdom to the contrary, the art of literature is alive and flourishing.

Further thanks to Malcolm and Christine Bell of the Mystery and Imagination Bookshop in Glendale, California, who supplied me with necessary materials. You can extend my gratitude by visiting the Bell's well-stocked establishment at 515½ E. Broadway, Glendale, CA 91205, (818) 545-0206.

Appreciations to my agent, Lori Perkins, and my editor at TOR, Natalia Aponte. Their patience during a personally difficult period made this sucker flow.

All love and respect to Sherri as well; this one was easy, eh? But I do miss the voodoo doll. . . .

I'd also like to thank Shulamith Firestone, Dr. Helen Caldicott, Kate Millet, Oriana Falachi, Pat Califia, Mother Teresa, Janet Reno, Bella Abzug, Germaine Greer, Kelly Nichols, Gloria Leonard, Sinead O'Connor, Madonna (begrudgingly), and the countless other women whose heroic refusal to become cultural or economic slaves continues to further the necessary advancement of their sex.

Conversely, may scum-sucking swine like Ronald Reagan, Nancy Reagan, Dan Quayle, Marilyn Quayle, George Bush, Barbara Bush, Patrick Buchanan, Randel Terry, Phyllis Schafley, Jesse Helms, and Pat Robertson—plus any others of their ilk determined to keep women second-class citizens—find themselves bankrupt, sickly, and without hope.

And since there never will be any justice meted out to these criminals here on Earth, may they also, after death, rot in the agonized eternities of their own private hells.

—Paul M. Sammon

INTRODUCTION

They're bad.
They're back.
They're women.
The first *Splatterpunks* showcased seventeen bold talents. Raw, uncompromising visionaries—mostly male—whose unflinching eyes gazed deep into the abyss.

Clive Barker. John Skipp. Joe R. Lansdale. Richard Christian Matheson. Card-carrying members of what Stephen King has tagged "the most vital, visceral coalition operating in horror today."

An outlaw band with one philosophy:

There are no limits.

Now, *Splatterpunks II* continues that tradition.

But this time, the emphasis is female.

Stories by women. Stories *about* women. Gender-twisting dispatches from the front lines of the cutting edge, hot-wired to your skull.

Kathe Koja. Nancy A. Collins. Roberta Lannes. Poppy Z. Brite. More than a dozen renegade femmes joining forces with rogue male counterparts like Martin Amis and Clive Barker to create twenty-eight cage-rattling exercises in literary terrorism.

What to expect?

Homicidal shoe fetishists. S&M pain angels. Paranoid baby-eaters. Shit-crazy comedians.

Plus a nonfiction examination of cult director Brian DePalma, an interview with High Satanist Dr. Anton Szandor LaVey, and a look at the adrenalized connection between horror and rock 'n' roll.

High-octane splatterpunk, all.

What *is* splatterpunk?

Not a movement, but a method. An attitude. A state of mind.

First remove the barriers society and "good taste" impose on fiction. All the barriers. Add a healthy dose of shock, plus the influ-ences of schlock movies and the screaming guitar licks of the world's greatest heavy metal bands.

Now stir in courage. Honesty. A strong awareness of pop culture. Add hot, steaming issues—real-world concerns—and season with a no-bullshit attitude.

To serve up some of the best *writing* in the field today.

So prepare yourself.

The female contributors you are about to meet are not babes, broads, or chicks. Not bimbos, stereotypes, objects, or toys.

They are *women*.

Strong. Independent. Fiercely intelligent.

Outraged, uninhibited, and dangerous as hell.

Who never, ever flinch.

Why?

Because they are—

Splatterpunks II.

Paul M. Sammon

Splatterpunks II

OVER THE EDGE

Accident d'Amour

WILDY PETOUD

"I live in Switzerland, have absolutely no children of any kind, and loathe needlework in any way, shape, or form. This story is my way of telling what it's like not to be the right fuck when you're on the wrong side of the dick. No one has, so far. They need to know.

"Because it hurts."

That's only part of the remarkable biography WILDY PETOUD enclosed with her grim little parable, although it does summarize "Accident d'Amour" more succinctly than I could. A small word of caution, however:

This "Accident" hurts.

Wildy Petoud (love that name!) is in her midthirties. She's been writing fiction for the past eight years, the majority of it seeing print in France. Past efforts include science fiction shorts for such anthologies as Superfuturs *and* Univers 89. *Wildy recently completed an experimental SF novel and is currently working on "a space opera potboiler" entitled* The Word Galaxy.

"An Accident of Love" (to give Petoud's tale its English translation) was originally published in early 1992, in the French anthology Territoires de l'Inquiétude 4. *It was subsequently awarded the 1993 Grand Prix de l'Imaginaire (the French National Fantasy & SF Award) and the Prix Rosny Aine award.*

According to Wildy, this "is the first horror story I ever wrote. There will be others. I like the medium, just as I like Kathe Koja, Poppy Z. Brite, that bunch. The only kind of horror that truly grosses me out is if something gruesome happens to a cat (I have three of them)."

While no cats figure in "Accident d'Amour," something definitely gruesome happens.

Which reminds me—
Splatterpunks I *opened with a disclaimer by an author who wanted the readership to know he* wasn't *a splatterpunk. Well, no such caveats apply this time out.*
"I don't mind the splatterpunk label at all," Petoud tells us. "This story definitely belongs under it. As far as I'm concerned, splatterpunk is the only honest way to write horror—no lies."
Just as "Accident d'Amour" is no better way to introduce the heavy female artillery which bombards this book.

The world isn't the way it used to be, and I hate. It's a world of hurt now, and I—

He was making love to me, finally, finally, after all those months of lying stiff and still against the wall, avoiding my touch—but he was inside me now and I heated deep, the sun of him, and then he, he *screamed*—"Not you, never, it never was you, I don't want it to be you, it's her I want, only her, I want to come into her, she's so much lovelier than you are, always it was her ..."
And he babbled her name over and over, bucking moaning coming calling *love my love.* Weeping for desire of her.
Driven into me.

I hate.
I stumbled blind out of bed, down the stairs, dirtied deep, and his loathing of me ran down my thighs, the filth and dark of it: eternal damnation, inside me forever. I vomited kneeling on the cold, blue tiles, blood, bile, the truth of my life with him ... Heard him come down, heard him walk out, and I knew where he was going, knew where. She is so much lovelier than I.
With bleach and metallic brush I scraped and scoured my sex, digging deep. As long as I could stay conscious. Long enough to kill the skin, the yawning flesh where anything can come in. No more. No more *not you, not you, never you.*
I came to amidst the slaughter, and watched the bleeding torn

sniggering lips between my legs, and decided I didn't like them laughing at me. I decided I finally had some use for the sewing kit my grandmother gave me long ago, "for your hope chest, you know." Well, it's not hope in my chest now. She said always use the toughest thread on thick material. She said the three-sided needle is for leather.

Right.

Stitching, I screamed. Knot it. Double it. Choke on the screams, sweating cold so cold, the skin weeping to say good-bye. I don't like to be laughed at. Shut your forever hungry maw, pussy. Forever.

Afterwards, I cleaned up the bathroom. More bleach.

That was three months ago. Thread rots quickly, and I get to practice my sewing. How glad Grandma would be. But she long ago died and rotted away. Lucky old bitch. My own rotting is more localized. The infected, infested flesh tears and gives, drooling ooze and evil-smelling, black blood. It's hard to walk. That doesn't matter, since I don't go anywhere, except down the street to the market. Bread milk and eggs, "Is that all, miss?" Yes it is. Thanks, have a nice day. The kind lady tells me I look a little sick. Oh, some fever. Flu, or something. No big deal. And she winces a bit, not saying anything, being polite, but I know: the smell.

Once a week I go driving through the night, looking for morphine. It's hard to find. Heroin is more popular.

The heroine: that's me. Not so popular—but tough? You bet. Hurting oozing stinking, but dying? No way. Not yet.

Him I didn't see again. Heard rumors, though: he's very happy now. Everybody's glad to say so, everybody likes him a lot. He's such a nice man, isn't he? And they make such a lovely couple.

My snatch and me, that's a lovely couple too. We fit so well together. Happy making—of a slightly different sort.

I don't go to work anymore, of course. The colleagues would, ah, smell a rat. I live on my savings, luckily large ones: morphine's expensive on the black market.

I hate.

And I wait. It must needs end somewhere.

* * *

"Nothing is as pregnant as cruelty." I read that once, back when I read. Cruelty's not alone.

Today in the mirror—I don't like mirrors too much, as can be guessed, but how to use the sink without catching glimpses of oneself? One's yellowish, thin-lipped, black-eyed, unkempt self, fat cheeks, bad skin, bloated neck, straggling hair ... Long live the queen! Today, then, in the mirror, gazing into said ancient and fabled eyes, and them burning with variegated fevers, I saw brownish, horizontal lines, cutting straight across the sclera from corner to corner of them.

Pregnant.

The love given her had given me a child, and I won't here disclose his name, or hers, or mine either.

I hate.

Gangrenous and pregnant, this the portal of love that I sealed ever so tight. Good job of needlepoint, jobbing it good. Blindstitch. And he wasn't making that child with *me*. Nothing is mine.

I hate.

I gave up dressing, feeding, washing, or lighting myself.

I didn't on the needlework.

Losing weight. My belly's bloating with black, viscous liquids, wet sores bursting open. Hurts. If the little bastard wants out, he'll have to do without my help, and he'd better hurry: no way will I last another six months. I stumble through the darkened, smelly house, shuffling between what debris are too large to crush under-foot, obsessing on a whisper of love, my love.

My hate.

The shards of glass: on those I step. I like to leave signs of my passing. Means I exist. I say that a lot: I am, I am ...

But what am I? To be so discounted. It follows I'm a bad number. Number hate on his account. With interest.

The doorbell rings, time and again. I don't react. Before pulling the plug on the phone, I called: the post office (hold the mail, I'm going on a trip), the bank, and paid six months' rent in advance.

I'm absenting myself, you see.

*   *   *

Honeypot, apricot, pink box black box, piggybank ever so stuffed.
Garden of sweet delight. Dear blight.
  How fertile thy decay. My love. My.

Four months.
  Five.

When I was a child, we had this skipping-rope rhyme. It went:

> *Fudge fudge*
> *Call the judge*
> *Mama's got a brand new baby*
> *Wrap it up in tissue paper*
> *Put it up the elevator*
> *First floor*
> *Stop!*

(Every *stop!* was the signal for this complicated step-and-stop
routine—musn't stumble.)

> *Second floor*
> *Stop!*

(And if you did:)

> *Third floor*
> *Kick it out the door*
> *Mama doesn't wanna brand-new baby anymore!*

Then it was someone else's turn.

Sixth and last floor. It's someone else's turn now.

The pain came in the middle of the pain, hideous, total pain, my
hair hurt, my teeth, nails, my eyes hurt, red hot—white heat in my
belly, black, gurgling, nauseating, alive, up and down like waves.
The skin lifted, something sharp underneath poking, pushing, a
reptilian beak slashing at the soft shell.

My belly exploded in a splatter of rotten flesh and curdled liquids, and she emerged, leaning on the ruined meat, her sharp-clawed, thin arms coated with slime and pieces of me. Her huge, black-scaled head turned to watch me. A single eye blazed in her face where the nose should have been, round and red. She opened a wide, flabby, many-toothed beak, and gobbled all the carrion she could reach, to strengthen herself.

My daughter.

My hate.

She climbed out of me on her own two legs, wobbling a little, but very strong already. She looked at me. I was dying in a splash of rot, but I smiled at her. I told her:

"I'm your mommy. Your name will be Khate. Mommies don't make babies all by themselves, you know? They get help starting them. Go, Khate. Go fetch Daddy. Go. We three shall have fun between us, shall we?"

She even knew how to open the door. Her arms are incredibly strong and elastic. She will know where to go. I trust her. She's a good kid, and very bright for her age. Hope I can hold on till she's back. I should maybe try and clean up? But the girl's got to have some sweets. Let it lie.

I'm proud of the child. She was smart enough to wait until the small hours before she came back. Heard sounds behind the door, scraping, of something heavy being dragged. A present? For me?

I struggled to open my eyes.

Good, good girl. She was already bigger, stronger. She was towing him, gripping his arm. She had eaten some of him, an eye, a few fingers, a big chunk of leg, but not enough to kill him.

He had fouled himself. That disgusted me a little, a man of principles like him, who had convinced me so thoroughly of the necessity of stoicism. Maybe he meant the stoicism of others about what he did to them, and not the reverse? But Khate *is* what he did to me. An act of love. Love my love.

I crawled to him, leaving a wake of corruption behind. I smiled, and used my nails to caress his missing eye. Such lovely eyes, limpid and blue. Looks that you can't but trust.

"Hi, you . . . I'm so glad to see you. So glad you met your daughter. She's a very . . . *special* child, isn't she? Kiss me. I love you. I forgive you, because I want you ever so much since last time. It was . . . an unforgettable moment."

He started yelling, and hasn't stopped yet. Khate saw what I was trying to do, and she helped. That was so sweet of her. Now I feel good about him again. I won't die in hate.

I kept pulling, pulling, but I was so weak it came to nothing. So Khate came close, and castrated him with a single snap of her beak. She took the thing in her hand and gave it to me. How nice.

It was a little difficult, sticking it into me, there's nothing very definite between my legs anymore, and the penis was of course soft. But I made it.

He still screams at intervals, and his remaining eye radiates horror—the impossibility of registering that such nightmares can be. There's something shared between us at long last.

I almost don't hurt anymore. I'm almost happy. In a little while I will be. Khate will clean up, won't you, sweetheart?

It's good to be loved . . .

—Translated by Wildy Petoud

Impermanent Mercies

KATHE KOJA

Let's say this straight:
  KATHE KOJA is one of today's best Serious Authors.
  Yet at the moment, she's suffering from The Curse of the Deadly Label.
  You know the one.
  "Horror Writer."
  Nothing could be a more criminal misrepresentation of the truth. Koja's dense, smoldering prose, her tough eye for detail and dialogue, her smarts and skepticism and complex, disaffected characterizations clearly mark her as a major mainstream *talent.*
  But here comes that label again:
  "Horror Writer."
  What's wrong with the people who come up with these things? Didn't they read The Cipher, *Koja's unnerving first novel? A stylish tour de force that raked open the art world's rotting underbelly and launched a hot new career? Haven't they heard of* Bad Brains, *Koja's brilliant 1992 follow-up, a visceral, hallucinogenic descent into alcoholism and delusion? What about her powerful, unclassifiable short stories (which have appeared in anthologies like* Still Dead *or* A Whisper of Blood*), or the buzz surrounding recent novels like* Skin *and* Strange Angels?
  "Horror Writer," indeed.
  Obviously, the people who invent such tags are mere pus and pimples.
  Or hail from The Village of Pimples, at any rate.
  Kathe Koja lives in Detroit with her husband, artist Rick Lieder, and her son. Further details are hard to come by; we've never met, and Kathe seems to like a low profile. I have spoken with her over

the telephone, though. The woman comes across a bit like her
fiction; tough, wary, intelligent.

But it's always the work that's more important, no? And
Kathe's output obviously exhibits two of what perhaps are the
most important traits of any serious writer.

One's a consistent theme. Kathe's involves messy, self-destruc-
tive artists. Failed or minor-league creative types who forever
stumble along the fringes while personal weaknesses screw up
their work.

Kathe's other strong suit is a coherent worldview. Which, as
you'll soon experience yourself, is neither a safe nor a pretty one.

Koja's twin concerns appear once again in "Impermanent Mer-
cies," a typically outlandish piece. This genuinely crazy nightmare
features yet another artist, a photographer, who, while clicking
through a seemingly normal day—

Well, let's just conclude by pointing out a third Kojian trait.
Kathe enjoys fucking with a reader's head.

Don't say I didn't warn you.

Oκ," Ellis said. "Now pick up the dog."

"True," the boy said. His name was Andy. Ellis had met him at
the 7–11.

"OK, pick True up," and Andy did, smiling, sun in his eyes,
summery squint and the dog almost smiling too in that half-asinine
way of the quintessential mutt; a boy and his dog, shit yes it was
cute. Shot after shot after shot, as sweet a stock photo as anyone
could want, head a-tilt and happy sweat on his back, OK, uh-huh,
and behind the boy the long stretch of railroad tracks, summer and
infinity, the beginning of boyhood's journey; you bought it, you
name it. "OK, great." Shot and shot, enough. "I think we're done
here." Kids were such great models. Cheap too.

Walking back, Andy's questions—little-boy gory, you ever take
any pictures of dead stuff? Any dead people?—high voice punctuated by the low gaining sound of a train, infrequent on these tracks.
Ellis looked over his shoulder: almost too far away to see, there it
was. True ran a loping zigzag on the tracks, Andy on the slope
beside glancing up at the dog from time to time.

"You ever *seen* any dead people?"

The train was closer now. "You better call your dog," Ellis said.

"True, c'mere," pausing, one bare foot on the gully's rise. "True." True paused too, looked at Andy with what seemed to Ellis a particularly stupid grin, snuffle snuffle along the steel of the tracks, lift of small scrawny leg.

"True, come *on*," voice raised in the louder pitch of the train, approaching now as the boy approached the slope, Ellis's hand a warning on his shoulder. "True!" Andy's voice very high, he seemed to lose years in his sudden fear, a littler boy than he had been and *"True!"* Ellis's bellow, best man-to-mammal voice, pure authority that True chose, in his pure doggy way, to ignore. Snuff snuff, yum, more pee.

"True!" And Andy broke for the tracks, almost too fast to stop but Ellis did, startled reflex grab of the skinny elbow, yanking him back as the train ran on, and all at once True turned his head, the look on his face the essence of surprise: *What is that?* and off, four legs in quantum motion, running down the center of the track, Andy jerking and bucking in Ellis's grip, Ellis yelling something, who knows what into the vortex of the train's momentum, gaining and gained all in a second and True disappeared beneath, now you see him, now you don't. Ellis yelling still, how if True stays still, he's a small dog, if he only doesn't move and in the speaking the word's negation for, without any blood at all, a small round rolling thing spat out from under and down the slope as neatly as a softball. True's head.

Man and boy and silence, the sun all at once so hot and a full-born headache springing free and Ellis thought, illogical inner laughter, Now True he's got the big headache; what a shitty thought. Funny though. "Stay here," he said to Andy, who stood as if he might never move again, and up the gully Ellis went, to stand in the train's faraway wake and bend to the small headless body. As he picked it up air rushed into the body cavity with a bizarre sucking sound, ugly, he almost dropped it. Back down, and Andy was gone. The head was gone too, presumably with Andy, wasn't going anywhere itself now was it, stop it where's the kid. Ellis saw weeds, dipping and parting, called a few times but no reply; he gave it up, found he was still holding the body, let it fall beside the warm wood of the tracks which he walked beside, but studiously not on, all the way back to his car.

The pictures came out great.

Smoking the last of his cigarettes, coming out of the 7–11 with a new pack in hand, and "Hey." Andy. Trueless Andy, not smiling. Ellis stopped, stepped back, false guilty smile on his face which he at once replaced with some other kind of look, who knew. "Andy," he said. "Where'd you go, that day? I was worried about you."

"I took True home." Small bare feet, so bottom-black they left sidewalk prints when he shifted. "Want to see?"

Want to see. Hell no, I don't want to see. "What—you mean his, where you buried him?" Little boy grieves at doggy grave. Poignancy of collision, youth with death, innocence with sorrow. How much film did he have. "All right."

Home wasn't far, befitting a boy on foot, lucky Ellis had stopped again at that particular 7–11. Shitty little ranch house, flats of flowers wilting in their plastic containers, oil spots all over the driveway. No car. Andy led him through the back gate into the yard, more sagging flowers, somebody at least was trying, and into the house through an unlocked screen door. The house was hotter than the day outside. "Where's your folks?" Ellis asked, suddenly uneasy at being here, alone with the boy in an empty house.

"My mom's not home," Andy said in that same flat voice. "He's back here," down the skinny hall, he who? Oh shit, not the dog, the dog's head in all this heat, seeing without noticing the badly framed snapshots, Andy and little Andy and baby Andy, one or two with presumably Mom. And True. The *before* pictures.

"Here," in Andy's bedroom, unmade bed hand-me-down to death, and beneath it, oh shit. A saltine box. A *wet* saltine box. Ellis took a big step backwards, hand on the doorframe. "Andy," reasonable adult voice thinned a little by possible pukedom, "maybe I should just—"

"What's the matter, motherfucker? Squeamish?"

From inside the box.

Oh come on, come on this is *not* happening, the kid's a pissed-off ventriloquist, and Andy said, "I told you he wouldn't like it," and at the same time that deeper voice, "Oh he likes it all right. Hey you," and the box rocked, just a little, just enough to make the first hot pissy dribble squirt onto Ellis's jeans. "Take a picture, it'll last longer." Everybody but Ellis laughed.

"You thought he was just a dog," Andy said, and smiled, thin proud stretch as he patted the box. "He's not. He can do stuff. He always could."

"Like talk?" He hadn't meant it as a question but the quaver was there.

"No," shaking his head. "Not out loud."

"But I can now," from the box, and a sudden booming laugh, incredible TV voice: "And it was *worth it!*"

That's it, that's it right there, I'm out of here and he was, pushing the door so hard it nicked the wall, True's voice yelling after him, "But what are you going to tell Sheila?" and he was out of the house and the driveway and down the street, shaking at the stop sign and grabbing for his cigarettes when the words took hold and he cracked the cigarette in two. Sheila, right, Sheila his ex-wife, hide nor hair for what, eight months, even though he'd stopped sending the checks. Sheila, hell of a guess. By the time he got home he had persuaded himself that it was all so very improbable that it was probably stupid to even believe it had happened, and the ringing phone was a pleasant diversion, he picked it up before the machine could, let's have some human contact, hello.

"El, it's me."

His first black thought was that it was somehow the fucking dog, and Sheila's voice, hello, hello until he finally spoke and yes indeed it was the genuine article, just calling to ask if he would get that box of camping stuff out of the garage, she and Richard were going to Padgett Park and they needed the Coleman and it would be nice if he could see his way to a check or two. Thanks, and bye, and Ellis there with hands too cold to sweat, wondering if, there had to be, a way to find the house again. The 7–11, of course, and of course Andy was there, sucking on a slurpee, the unbearable smugness of a child in the right. "Hi," he said before Ellis could speak, and when Ellis did a cool moment of silence, letting Ellis know that he stood on the sufferance of a nine-year-old boy, and that he, Andy, knew it too. But he was nine, after all, there was no way he could say no.

"He told me a bunch of stuff about you," Andy said, matter-of-fact swing of bare ankles, Nikes worn white over the toes. "Some other stuff too."

"Will he," very careful, now, "let me take his picture?"

"I don't know. Ask him."

Say cheese, Mr. Dog Head. Pulling into the afternoon driveway, empty as before. "Does your mom know?"

"Know what," but with indifference, no leverage there; apparently Mom was no mover and shaker in Andy's world. "I clean my own room, and besides she's hardly ever home anyway. Come on," pushing in the screen, you always leave the house wide open, kid? Oh, that's right, you have a watchdog.

The bedroom had a ripe odor that was suspiciously free of decay, but the saltine box was wet to the trademark, wet to the worn yellow carpet beneath. Andy handled the box with priestly care, turned it so the open edge faced Ellis. The damp gray flaps peeled open, and True, big doggy grin, tongue twisted the way no dog's ever should: "How was Sheila?"

"Not funny," forgetting everything but the face before him, Andy behind him, hands clasped in happy calm. True, speaking, a bunch of stuff indeed; they used to call it prophecy. Not so much world "events," stock market tips or sports bullshit, but things in Ellis's own daily life: the guy from *Watersports* will call, the woman from the Sunday supplement won't, your air conditioner's going to hell and it'll get there a week from Wednesday, and Ellis mesmerized by the inscrutable flow, his day-to-day laid bare, so weird and oh, so compelling. Finally True stopped, made a sound it took a second to recognize as a bark.

"I'm thirsty," rolling his eyes to look not at Andy but Ellis. "Get me a drink."

"There's a glass in the bathroom," Andy's faint malicious smirk. "On the sink."

Shit. But he got it, filled it halfway, came back to kneel in awkward crouch before True, long tongue lapping sloppy and water on Ellis's legs, on the floor. True blew some water out of his nose.

Now, Ellis thought. Ask him now. But True was a step ahead.

"No," showing his teeth, blunt tartary fangs. "No pictures."

"Why not?" Grim frustration, keeping his voice even, thinking I could just grab the damn box and be out of here, but the thought of actually touching it, hefting its wet weight, would it sag in the middle—"Why not."

True and Andy, a look shared, and "I got a train to catch," ha ha, they laughed their stupid asses off at that one and all at once Andy was giving him the bum's rush, you gotta go now, my mom's going to be home. "Maybe I'll stay," firm, let's not forget who's the grown-up here. "I'd like to meet her."

Andy, smiling, cheeks still faintly sweet with babyfat. "I'll tell her you tried to touch my dick," and that was the end of that, the best he could get was a vague promise from Andy to meet him the next day, the 7–11, yeah, right. But he came, and so did Andy.

It was a ritual, irregular but not to be missed, and though Ellis was constantly disappointed, no pictures, still he could not stay away. True's voice, its rolling gravel amusement, and oh the things he said—not only tales of Ellis's humdrum days (which always came true, so much so that Ellis had begun without conscious decision to rely on them) but real prophecy, world news of a world Ellis had not even suspected, a universe so black and yet so grayly probable that he believed these stories, too, relied on them: grotesqueries and pains and distortions, people in Switzerland who drank each other's urine and cast runes from the mingled flow, a man in Pittsburgh who saved discarded surgical clamps and what he did with them, the daylight flourishing on a neighborhood cult unique in its blue-collar sophistication and blunt brutality; True the Scheherazade of the ugly and ultimate, Andy his acolyte, and Ellis, what? The skeptic, no, nor just the listener, for at night alone these tales had begun to grow not on him but in him, wreaking changes so gradual yet so acute that, wild-eyed in the mornings, he thought it some subtle form of vengeance, a cool rot like a ticking bomb in the space between his ears. But there was no staying away, and besides True had promised to let Ellis take his picture. When, there was no saying, and Ellis would not chance a miss, so back to that strange bedroom temple, on his knees before them both.

He had never told Andy where he lived, but one night, coming back from putting out the trash, he heard above the sound of crickets a faraway bark, burlesque, then a mingled laugh that froze him, hands clenched in the silence of sinister insect music and Andy, calling him, soft. He let them in, absurdly excited, was it time, should he set up or what. Andy cradled True's box, its bottom bowed and soggy, some viscous fluid dripping with majestic irregularity onto the living room carpet; Andy spoke little and True not at all, and when they left he saw the Rorschach stains, horrible trail all the way to the door.

That night he lay bedbound, staring sick and gratified, and when by dawn he did sleep woke soon after in a turmoil of arousal, behind his eyes a dream of Andy, small hairless penis and his own mouth grasping to close over it, and the fierce immediate throb of his orgasm, slick wet all over and he sat in it and wept with terror, what is happening to me. He thought of Andy's absentee mother, a vague impression from the hallway photos, blonde hair and a worried smile, a *nice* woman, yes certainly, and in his delirium he thought of holding her, spending himself in her, knowing somewhere beneath that what he really wanted was to cry on her tits about her monster son and his even more monstrous pet. He must never go back there, "Never, never, never" moaning into his cupped hands, the words as thick and warm as vomit in his mouth.

He tried, oh surely he did, was it nearly a week? True's snicker, Andy's cold smile: "Should I let him in, True?" and True considering, asking through the closed bedroom door how'd he liked his dreams lately, pretty wild, huh? Hands clenched on his neck strap, Ellis sweating, I will *not* cry, sweating till at last Andy opened the door. "Taken any good shots?" True said, and howled, coyote scream to make his ears ring in the square hot silence of the room, banshee noise that went on and on. Finally and at once it stopped, and True, his eyes somehow a twin to Andy's: "If you want to take my picture, you have to bring me what I need. Andy can't do it anymore."

"Why?"

"Because," growl, yes, like a dog, "Andy's just a kid. There are things a kid can't do, shithead, don't you know that?"

"Like what?"

At first, No, no I will not, I *will not* do these things; but he didn't get far, did he, did he, no. Because after and above all Ellis must have that picture, must hold it in his hands, not even sure any longer why he must but feeling its necessity like a disease.

So he did as he was told. Once, and twice, and by the fifth time it got if not easier—it could never, never be easy, as it could never be safe—then less ugly, or perhaps he was already so mad that another dollop of poison could do nothing but churn his madness to a finer boil. Perhaps part of him was hoping somehow to be caught, he told himself that, sitting at red lights with a torn paper bag beside him, or an object wrapped in plastic, wet plastic, a certain smell infused forever in the atmosphere of his car; he woke at night with that smell in his nostrils, wondering if it was that he hated most, that smell, or what True made him do, sometimes, with the things he brought, or was it the things themselves, wet and smelly and inert, what was it he hated most? Finally he did not speculate, he found he no longer cared to and in fact did not care at all. It was ugly, yeah, and so was he, and so what. All that could bring meaning was to get that picture and in the meantime, why not just roll with it, get belly-deep and deeper, put your *face* in it and suck it in.—And then the mornings, weeping and gagging at the look on his own face, the smirk of the afterglow; maybe other people saw it too. What if they did?

He asked True about it, got a laugh for an answer, and he laughed too. Because it was funny, wasn't it, even True's demands, the sicker they got the funnier they were. It was like feeding a throatless mouth, no end in sight, ha ha ha, wasn't that the third time tonight he'd seen that blue Buick? Wasn't it? He shifted, nervous on the seat, and something warm, sticky-warm, sagged against his thigh, where had he gotten that? He didn't remember, didn't know for sure even what was in that bag there, look at this for me please Officer, I think it might be icky. Definitely he had seen that Buick before. Slewing down a side street, tricky negotiation till he saw the Buick's taillights and back, fast, all the spy movie bullshit like driving without lights, he almost hit a parked car and laughed out loud. The bag broke. His ass, his legs were drenched, he stank, the car stank, he trotted stinking into the house waving the half-wrapped thing by one jaunty corner. "Hope you're hungry," wide chortling grin that sickened and died as he saw their faces, and when True at last raised his lip it was no smile he showed.

"I don't want that," bright bony sneer past Ellis to what he carried. "You're getting useless, you know that? Useless," on a growl, and Andy said, "If you can't bring True what he needs, you can't come here anymore."

No sound at all, more and less than vacuum and his heart somehow gone silent too and he said, "Take me then," and no words
came out and he forced them, loud, "Take me," and Andy's face
wrinkled, refusing pout, but True's growl turned upwards into giggle and he said, "You finally had a good idea, asshole. Andy, pull up
that shade." And the box jiggled, its tearing sides trembling as True
shook his head, hard, the way a dog shakes off from water. "Take
off your clothes, Ellis."

A working in him like an elixir, a pulse, rich and rapid and too
strong, and like a dance he stripped, stinky jeans and smelly shirt
and socks stiff and thick between the toes, stood naked at last with
his hands at his sides and his vision newly narrowed; no, *focused*,
and he understood, he knew and almost cried with the knowing
that he was the camera, the blinkless eye, perfect observer of his
own immolation and he was not going to miss a moment, not a
second's worth as he went crawling to the box, the carpet worn
and sorry on his knees, True suddenly panting and Andy smiling,
there, behind the box, smiling like Christmas morning.

One Flesh:
A Cautionary Tale

ROBERT DEVEREAUX

The publication of Bret Easton Ellis's American Psycho *in 1991 was a cultural earthshaker. Universally reviled at the time of its release, Ellis's novel dealt with a handsome, intelligent Wall Street stockbroker who spends his days earning fortunes and his nights slaughtering women.*

Yet this deeply ironic work was grossly misinterpreted. Which isn't surprising; the same people who condemned Ellis's satiric savaging of the Reagan Era as nothing more than sadistic sexist swill would probably also think that the word "Swiftian" means "a quick read."

If one looks beyond the controversy, though, it's easy to pinpoint American Psycho *as the moment when splatterpunk polluted the literary mainstream. I won't belabor how long that pollution took (five years, at least, since the term "splatterpunk" was coined in 1986), but it is worth mentioning that* American Psycho *prompted the same negative criticism most often leveled against splat.*

Namely, that splatterpunk exploits women. Hates 'em, even. Rapes and kills and slices and dices 'em.

Well, OK; immature splatterpunk might. In fact, while editing this book, I couldn't help but notice that a few potential submissions—whose ugly common denominator consisted of baring a breast before cutting it off—all had the same suspicious smell.

Something like a microwaved cat's.

Anyway, splat's misogynistic tag has become one mighty tired *cliché, and ROBERT DEVEREAUX realizes this. To prove it, he's taken that same cliché, amped it to the max, and turned it on its head.*

The result is "One Flesh."

Devereaux's first novel, Deadweight, *will appear from Dell Abyss in 1994. However, at this point in his career, Bob's better known for writing tour de force short fiction. Things like "Bucky Goes To Church," where God is revealed to be an insane black woman. Or "Ridi Bobo," a tale of clown adultery. Which comes complete with rubber chickens, floppy shoes, and bicycle honkers.*

According to Devereaux's biography, "When Robert's not writing, he loves to sit naked in his room doing absolutely nothing. And though het to the bone, he considers himself an honorary bisexual. A pansexualist, really. Friend to all consenting adults of whatever stripe they may discover themselves to be.

"Like Chance the gardener, Robert also loves to watch."

The act of watching plays a key role in "One Flesh," a punchy civics lesson with a marvelously original hook.

A hook which satirizes this whole violence-against-women thing. While forcing us to realize that yes, once again,

Some men never learn.

W e admit it. There's a right way and a wrong way to bring one's loving lady into conformity with the image of womanly perfection that burns bright in every man's heart. Dad and me, we went about it the wrong way. That's clear to us now, after all the grief that came pelting down into our lives when half the Sacramento police force jackbooted their way through our front door and kept us from further satisfying our desires, modest as they were, on the naked limbs of our composite wife.

But it's our feeling that before the state—that vast motherless bastion of rectitude and righteousness—unlocks our cell to dead-march us along its sexless corridor, then to mumble piety into us from the mercy-thin pages of its Holy Bible, cinch us down snug and secure, and hiss open its gas jets to pack us off to the next life, we owe it to the rest of you idolatrous cockwielders out there to pass on the lesson we learned. Does that sound agreeable to you, Dad? Dad, I'm talking to you! He says it does.

It began with a birth, nearly nineteen years ago, on the night of February 15, 1970. My dear wife Rhonda was all of twenty-one then, amber of eye and huge of breast, vivacious, fun-loving, ever faithful to me in spite of my shortcomings and the handful of cunt-hungry mongrels that always seemed to be sniffing about her skirts. Lovely as life itself was Rhonda, and carrying our son.

My folks came down from Chico in mid-January to help with last-minute preparations; they were radiant with love for us both and just itching to be grandparents. Rhonda's mother, Wilma Flannery, flew in from Iowa to be with "her precious baby" in her finest hour. She was one eccentric biddy, my mother-in-law, old and wizened at fifty. Her husband had left her soon after Rhonda was born, never to be heard from again. That didn't surprise me, and I don't think it surprised Rhonda, either. Although I wished Wilma had stayed in Oskaloosa, I did my level best to ignore her high-pitched demands and irritating ways and focus all my attention on Rhonda.

My wife's projected delivery date was Washington's birthday, and around a quiet dinner one night at Mario's, my mom and especially my dad—Oh, come off it, Dad, you know you did!—teased us about it, threatening to call their grandchild George or Georgina in honor of the man on the dollar. Rhonda's mother sat hunched over her plate, wolfing down tortellini. Good food always seemed to shut dear old Wilma up for a while.

As it happened, the baby arrived ahead of schedule. On the afternoon of the fifteenth, Rhonda and the two older women, wanting some girl-time alone, talked me and Dad into a night on the town. Before they booted us out into the light drizzle that had begun to come down, I pinned a hastily scrawled itinerary on the kitchen corkboard, just in case: dinner and drinks at California Fats, then a late-night showing of *Psycho* at the Tower. Dad and I were fond of Hitchcock movies back then. And after the accident that brought us together, we loved them even more.

The call came halfway through dinner. We'd done more drinking than eating, a lot more. Three swallows of wine to every forkful of food, I'd guess. Ordinarily we'd have thought twice about taking to the highway with that much alcohol in our veins. But I was determined to be right there by Rhonda's side when my baby was born, and judging from Mom's babbling over the phone from the hospital, we had no time to waste thinking about what was safe and what wasn't. So we threw some bills on the table, staggered together to my VW van, ramped up onto Highway 50, and five minutes later— in a passing maneuver that would have meant certain death at high noon on a bone-dry road with a teetotaling priest behind the wheel—we rammed into the back end of a screeching Raley's truck and felt for one mercifully brief instant the twin agonies of metal-mangled flesh and bone from the front and the whomp and sizzle of a fireball engulfing us from the rear.

If the notations of the hospital staff present at my son's delivery were correct, our precise time of death was 7:41 P.M. There was tightness everywhere and a painful sliding and then suddenly the chill of freedom. We were somehow nakedly intertwined, my dad and I. When the shock of the cold was blanketed away and sweet warm milk filled our mouth and soothed our belly, we bleared open our eyes and were astounded to see a gigantic Rhonda-face beaming down at us. We tried to call out to her, but our mouth was full of nipple and our body throbbed and the blankets felt so warm and cozy around us that we soon drifted off. When we awoke, nothing but baby sounds came out of us, no matter how carefully we tried to speak. When Dad saw his wife Arlene (my mom) smiling down at us, I couldn't help but feel his sadness and his frustration, and we wailed with our whole being and fisted our tiny fists and did our best to squeeze every cubic inch of air out of our little lungs with each scream. But just when we thought merciful death might reclaim us, the air came rushing back in and the cruel joke continued.

Our name was Jason. I'd picked it out myself, not because it was popular—the J-names were only starting to catch on back then—but from a love of Greek mythology. It hadn't been high on Rhonda's list, but she relented in exchange for my agreeing to the name Amy Lou if it was a daughter. Yes, Dad, I know, you've told me many times how glad you are we weren't born female.

The newspapers call us Jason Cooper, of course. But Dad and I kept up the use of our old names with each other while we endured the long frustration of babyhood, waiting for my son's body to develop the motor skills to support intelligible speech. For the record, my name is Richard and his is Clarence. The state can believe it's gassing somebody named Jason if it wants to, but I'm telling you there never *was* any such person, leastways not one with an identity separate and distinct from me and my father. We suspect that most reincarnates, being singletons, forget who they were and simply fall for the new identity their mom and dad foist upon them. But we, as doubles, were able to keep Richard and

Clarence alive inside the putative Jason we might otherwise have become.

After word of the accident reached them, Arlene stayed on longer than she'd planned with Rhonda. The two women comforted each other in mourning our deaths, but their joy in Jason's upbringing brought his mother and grandmother even closer. Arlene eventually sold her home in Chico and moved in with Rhonda. Wilma, on the other hand, was spooked by death. She gave her daughter a motherly thump on the brow, glared down at baby Jason, shuddered, crossed herself, and boarded the first plane back to the Midwest.

We're telling you all this because there's no way you can understand why we did what we did unless you know who we are and what it was like growing up this way. But for our own peace of mind, we'll spare you those details. Suffice it to say that we did not like being dictated to by the women we loved. By the time we were able to talk, we realized that no one was going to believe our story and that even if they did, some agency would take us away from Arlene and Rhonda for a lifetime of cold scrutiny. So we kept mum—and thereby kept Mom and Grandmom too, if you'll pardon our humor. Our greatest challenge was chasing away erectile manfriends, but a bit of strategic mayhem beyond our years and one or two well-calculated glances from hell kept the motherfucking to a minimum.

Our infancy and toddlerdom and childhood weren't the worst of it by any means. When puberty struck, we nearly went crazy. We'd both forgotten—given the sleep of the hairless genital in childhood—what it feels like when the hormones surge up for the first time, raging and roaring like typhoons through an adolescent body. And it was even worse for *us* because we understood from the outset what it all meant. As for girls our own age, our grown-up manner fascinated adults but kept our peers ever adversarial; besides which we neither of us felt much propensity toward pedophilia. So their chests filled out and their thighs went soft and curvy and they got that self-conscious wary look about their tender faces, but Dad and I paid them no mind. Understand our dilemma: The women we loved we'd already married. They lived right down the hall from us, growing no younger as the clock stole away moment after moment. And our enthusiastic young cock—sprouting thick curls of brown hair all around and popping up far fatter and longer, we were pleased to note, than either of us had been in our truck-crushed, fire-whomped bodies—took to them like a compass needle takes to magnetic north.

It was touch and go for a while, learning to feel okay about jacking Jason off. I'd hidden that sort of thing from Dad, and he never talked to me about the ins and outs of lovemaking and the rest of it except when I reached ten and he muttered something about "sex rearing its ugly head" and tossed some bland, vaguely Presbyterian book of cautions and platitudes in my lap. And we *were* father and son after all, engaging in what felt, the first couple of times, uncomfortably like homosexuality. But we made the necessary adjustments in our thinking—one always does to get what one's body craves—and relaxed into it like the old hands we were.

But ever and always, Arlene and Rhonda moved through the house, and we had to be on our guard not to be caught leering at them and not to demonstrate anything more than filial and grandfilial affection. We buried ourselves in bookishness, skipping over the stuff we recalled from our previous schooling and delving into new areas of knowledge with a depth that astounded our teachers and made us the loathed bespectacled pariah of the class of '88. With our stratospheric SAT scores and the enthusiastic support of the Hiram Johnson faculty, we wowed our way into Berkeley and began work toward a degree in twentieth-century history—we had, after all, lived through most of it, and current affairs had always been our strong suit.

It was in American History that we met Lorelei Meeks, she of the owl eyes and large glasses, breastless, thin as a rail, blank of face, and devoid of personality. Lorelei was a nonentity, a vacuum of need, a woman who faded into every background. Her body begged to be written upon and we, with our fat fountain pen full of sperm, scribbled all over her. Whatever it struck our fancy to do with her she gave in to. Dad and I divvied up her holes. Every pinch of flesh was ours to caress and lubricate and shackle up and slap until it blushed or bruised or bled. And in the morning, after a shower, she'd be wiped clean again like a newly sponged chalkboard, empty as Orphan Annie's eyes and yearning to be used anew. Our grades suffered, for which we made Lorelei pay in welts and cigarette burns, and in enemas of ice-cold Coors.

At Thanksgiving we brought her home.

We thought we could divert our river of rage onto our wispy girlfriend. We thought that having a receptacle we could empty our lust into anytime we liked would lessen our desire for our former spouses or at least allow us to keep it under control. But we were wrong, as wrong as a Bible thumper. We found out just how wrong when the front door swung open and our two beloved soulmates, all smiles, welcomed Jason and his dear Lorelei into the home Rhonda and I had built in the spring of '71.

While we sat in the living room, going through the maddening ritual of "introducing the girlfriend to the family," all sorts of bells and whistles were going off inside our head. My dad stole glances at Arlene, her hair gone white now, dignified lines of age making more lovely the face he hadn't caressed as a lover for nearly twenty years. She seemed genuinely spritely in her deep blue dress and her pearls, and her short white hair hugged her head just so. But I was in agony over Rhonda, looking sexier than ever at forty, stylish in her washed-out jeans and bulky breast-defining sweater. Her hair tumbled long and blonde down her back, soft and springy and natural in a way that brought to mind her blonde pubic softness and the sweet pink labia so long denied me. Thank God they ignored Jason, choosing instead to pour their endearments into the smiling nullity that sat, legs crossed, nervously beside him on the couch.

But inside us, an idea was gathering bits of itself together. The location of rope and tools in the garage, of clean dust rags in the closet, of scissors and carving knives in the kitchen, suddenly took on grave importance. It was as if the house itself was shoving Dad and me into some inevitable sequence of bloody dancesteps.

We heard Jason's thin voice fielding inane questions. From the way they received his answers, it seemed that our facade of calm was somehow being maintained. And when we moved into the dining room, watching the maddening thighs of our proper wives sway this way and that, we heard Jason announce that he had a special surprise for his three most favorite women in the world. You'd think the odds against one man subduing three women would be pretty high. And in most cases you'd be right. But people become surprisingly compliant when they're in a festive mood and someone they trust—a son or grandson, for example—sets down the rules of playful bondage they must submit to in order to receive an unexpected gift. In no time they were blindfolded with their hands tied tight behind them, a predicament our dear Lorelei was used to.

Not so Arlene and Rhonda. They complained, playfully at first, then more vociferously, about the chafing of the ropes. But their protests really began in earnest when we tied their ankles to the chair legs—right to right, left to left—and removed their shoes. People tend to be funny that way about their feet.

We let them sit there complaining into unresponsive air while we lowered the blinds and gathered tools. Some of the things our hands lifted off the garage pegboard or dug out of the drawers in the kitchen astonished us at the time, made us worry we'd gone off the deep end, though in hindsight they all made perfect sense. Once we had them laid out on the rug, our first order of business was the unclothing of our women. Because garments are not easily stripped from bound limbs, we used Rhonda's pinking shears for most of it. Arlene freaked when we scissored away her stockings, maybe from the feel of the cold metal moving up along her thighs, I can't be sure. Her shrieks spiked out into these absurd high-pitched bursts that sounded like a jackal in a trap. So hard were they on the ears that we decided to remove her blindfold and gag her with it. We did our best to ignore the look in her eyes; it was too painful to dwell on for any length of time. Dad was a little bit ashamed of her, weren't you, Dad? I mean at that point we hadn't so much as broken skin, we hadn't even *hinted* that that's where things were headed, yet already Arlene was huffing and going all red in the face like McMurphy being electroshocked in *One Flew Over the Cuckoo's Nest*.

Rhonda was a lot cooler about things, asking her son what he was doing, keeping her voice as calm and soothing as she could. When we felt like answering her, which was seldom, we kept our responses brief and noncommittal. We preferred letting our Fiskars do the talking for us. We liked their unrelenting ways, the steady rise and fall of the alligator mouth, the steel bite of perfectly zig-zagged teeth, the falling away of fabric, and the slow, hypnotic unveiling of forbidden flesh. From the look of Rhonda's private parts, a bit puffy and vaguely gleaming, we half suspected our perversity was turning her on.

You can imagine the effect all this snipping away of blouses and bras and panties was having on us. But mixed in with the arousal was a sadness, a bitter sorrow at the ravages of time on human flesh. Here, emerging one sharp snip at a time, were the beloved bodies of our dear wives, hidden away for nearly twenty years. Our idle fantasies at childhood's end, our torrid love affair with onanism in adolescence, our imagined substitutions of these two women when we squeezed shut our eyes and eased into Lorelei—all of that had been erected on memories two decades old. We were ill-prepared to witness the accumulated assaults of age on their flesh: the sag, the flab, the withdrawal of vibrancy and resilience and muscle tone.

We dimmed the lights.

When we finished denuding our women, we took Rhonda's suggestion and turned up the thermostat. I was able to convince Dad, despite his initial resistance, that we too ought to disrobe. His preference was to unzip, reach into our shorts, and bring out into the open Jason's erection only; but I argued that we were, after all, going to be doing more than simply fucking the odd vagina and that it would be far easier to shower blood off our skin than to remove it from our best suit, and he, inordinately fond of that suit (his taste, not mine), could only agree. So we removed Rhonda's and Lorelei's blindfolds, not wanting to limit our display to Arlene only, and slow-stripped for our three naked mates. It's fair to say we surprised ourselves—wouldn't you agree, Dad?—with our prowess as ecdysiasts. I sincerely believe we turned the ladies on, even Arlene gasping behind her gag; I can testify that we surely turned ourselves on.

Not to put too fine a point on it, we pleasured them, our wives and the vapidity they flanked. If they played at resistance, which one or two of them did, we read their coyness as a come-on, and came on. At one point, Rhonda, acting the castrating bitch, snapped at our penis, but we had matters well in hand and snatched it free of her cruel jaws, backhanding her for her naughtiness and clamping our own choppers on her left nipple until she screamed out an apology profuse enough to satisfy us. Even so, we steered clear of her mouth thereafter, though memories of my lusty young spouse feasting at my groin during our married life drew me back to her lips again and again, and Dad had to intervene several times for the sake of our manhood.

Finally, when we'd gotten as close to our women as we were going to get without breaking skin, Dad and I began our failed—

albeit noble—experiment. Looking back, it astounds us that we never once questioned the fundamental wisdom of what we were doing. But in this short, sorry life, one moment often leads to the next without time to entertain consequences. There seemed an inevitability in operation at the time, a passionate surging forth which no attempt at mere reason stood a chance against. Maybe all of our synapses weren't firing properly that day, or maybe something inside of us snapped. Whatever the reason, we forged ahead.

From the way Arlene and Rhonda were behaving, it was clear they would never consent to the group marriage idea that had occurred to us first. The very gathering of the tools—the saws, the screwdrivers, the staple gun—was surely our subliminal recognition that that scenario was not about to play itself out. To our unsettled minds, that left but one option: the scavenging of our wives' bodies and the bold reconstitution of what we liberated from those hallowed grounds into as near perfection as we could get on the blank canvas of Lorelei's body.

We began with the teeth. To our surprise, Lorelei resisted. But a small clamp at either corner of her jaws rendered her struggles pointless. Although our first extractions were bumbling and amateurish, before long we were uprooting her stubborn molars with all the élan of any DDS out there. When only gums remained, we found some cotton balls in the medicine cabinet to plug our ears with. Lorelei's gurgled screams were no joy to listen to, and we suspected that Arlene and Rhonda, once we began on them, would be no less merciless in their protests.

I hated what came next. Each of us, as you might imagine, was partial to his own wife's dentition, so we decided, after heated debate, to alternate extractions, taking the odd-numbered teeth from Arlene and the evens from Rhonda. To keep them in their proper sequence, and to counter our worries that teeth, like seedlings, might require immediate transplant to remain viable, we followed each tooth's removal with its immediate insertion into Lorelei's gums, tapping them in as gently as possible so as not to injure their roots. What I hated about all of this were the heartrending screams of my wife and mother. I wasn't prepared for the way their distant cries tore through my innards, making my brain beat with pain.

It grew worse when we began on the fingernails. Dad cursed

me for a coward but I hung back and let him perform the slicing, and pliering, and supergluing on his own. I felt bruised and blistered everywhere inside.

Still shaken, I joined Dad in shaving Lorelei's head, removing her ears, and stitching Arlene's on. But when it came time to scalp my dear sweet Rhonda, I couldn't bring myself—in spite of my lust for her lovely blonde hair—to help him grasp and guide the X-Acto knife and the scraping tools. Instead, I tried, over the static of my father's anger, to soothe Rhonda's torments. I assured her, though I'd begun to doubt it myself, that once she left her own body and moved into Lorelei's with Arlene, she'd come to appreciate the diligence with which we had harvested her hair and understand that the agonies we were putting her through were worth the final result. She did nothing but scream bloody murder and strain her abraded limbs against her bonds.

I wept openly then, while Dad bent, grim-faced, to his bloody task and pressed the blonde skullcap down onto Lorelei's bare, glue-smeared scalp.

Next came the mammaries. There was little point in giving our lovely new bride long tumbling blonde tresses if what they tumbled down onto was a couple of flat nubs rather than the breathtaking swell of two hefty kissable lickable squeezable suckable breasts. Dad and I were used to that kind of pleasure, given the endowments of our old wives. But we found ourselves once again at loggerheads, and it was worse now because Dad had by this time lost all patience with me. Rhonda and Arlene both sported superb knockers and we were not about to break up a set by taking one from each woman. Yet Lorelei barely had room on her chest for *two* decent-sized tits, let alone four. In the end we decided to fasten one pair to her front and another to her back. I lost the coin toss, but I don't think it's sour grapes to say that I got the better of the bargain, because our first mastectomy came off rather badly and in my opinion—You just keep still, Dad!—in my opinion, we botched Arlene's breasts badly. When it came to Rhonda, who was pleading like a little girl at this point, I was ready to refuse the carving knife again, but Dad jammed an awl into my left arm. Then he gave me a powerful talking to, really chewing me out good— "The next time it's your balls, boy!", that sort of thing. I *know* you meant it, Dad; just shut your yap. Anyway, partly because of what Dad said and partly because I wanted the job done right, I helped with the second operation, which I believe we carried out with a greater sense of professionalism and pride. What did I care about having to go behind our new woman's back to get to Rhonda's breasts as long as they retained their full loveliness?

We were in the midst of the arduous task of making a vulval triptych across Lorelei's stretched inner thighs, parenthesizing Lorelei's pussy with the harvested quims of our wives, when there came a distant pounding at the door, and a trio of faces filling one windowpane briefly with ugliness, and then a loud intrusive sound like crunching wood. One pair of arms grabbed us from behind and another handcuffed us, and the rest of the night was nothing but sirens and naked rides and cold baths and damp blankets and question after question after question. You know the rest. Aside from discounting our reincarnation story and sensationalizing out of all proportion what we did, the *Bee* and the *Union* did a fair job of reporting the truth.

What did we learn from all this?

We learned that happiness can't be forced. It's not something that yields to a desperate scheme and a crosscut saw. It's not something you can construct. We tried to piece it together bit by bit and we failed. Those of you out there whose minds may be starting to warp the same way ours did, take my advice and forget it. If kind words and gentle persuasion don't get you what you want, then cheese graters and electric drills and large knives with serrated edges aren't going to do it either. We tried. We failed. And we're going to pay for it. Next time, whoever's body we end up in, we're not even going to think about doing anything like this again.

At least I won't.

Dad tells me *he's* planning to major in premed.

Rant

NANCY A. COLLINS

NANCY A. COLLINS was born in 1959 and raised in rural Arkansas. Her first story was produced in 1963. According to the author, it concerned the love of a taxicab for a bus.

In 1982 Collins moved to New Orleans. While there she wrote and sold her first novel, 1989's Sunglasses After Dark. *A hip, outrageous novel featuring female vampire Sonja Blue,* Sunglasses *developed a cult following, and she produced a sequel, 1992's* In The Blood. Wild Blood, *a werewolf novel, will appear in summer 1994.*

Collins's short fiction has appeared in such anthologies as Shock Rock, There Won't Be War, *and* Still Dead *(with the notable "Necrophiles"). She is now married to underground filmmaker Joe Christ. Both live in New York. If you dial their Greenwich Village apartment, the answering machine informs you that "Neither the Antichrist nor the Whore of Babylon are in right now."*

But that's just a bare-bones bio (reads like one, too). Nancy Collins is steadily gaining recognition as a top-tier practitioner of the darkest sort of fiction, a visceral, strongly imagistic writer who—to use the language of a book jacket—"blends a hip-hop sensibility with a bleakly mordant wit."

Actually, Nancy's pretty damn funny. Gleefully morbid, in fact. As witnessed by the following true-life story:

Early in her career, Collins was stuck in a welfare hospital. In the bed next to her was a woman dying of lung cancer. And throughout Nancy's stay, this terminal patient kept gasping out the same word, over and over again.

Collins eventually deciphered this as a request. A maddeningly monotonous one. Endlessly repeated as a whine, a growl, a shriek.

The woman was saying, "Cigarette."

That sort of humor permeates "Rant," a blackly comic look at a pathological Second Coming. But unlike "Freaktent," which was Collins's contribution to Splatterpunks I, *"Rant" isn't a Southern Gothic.*

Let me explain.

Nancy claims, "I've always produced two sorts of work. Southern Gothics and the other stuff."

Which means the ensuing sick joke must be an example of "the other stuff."

"Rant" makes cancer *look funny.*

*T*HEY will never understand. THEY will see my actions from the outside, sitting in their breakfast nooks, yawning over their newspapers, wrapped in floral pink housecoats, fake dead animals on their feet and frozen orange juice cans wrapped in their tinted hair. Stupid cows.

THEY dare to judge me—me!—the savior of their petty, useless, pitiful lives!—and revile me as a monster! Just like THEY did Hitler, Manson, Torquemada, and King Herod! THEY will pass judgment on me and dismiss me from their memories by the time THEY reach the funny papers. But I will not strike them down for that. I am a merciful god. I will not reach out and swat them like the flies they are. I shall bear my cross as my elder brother did before me. No one understood his actions, either.

I will bide my time until I decide it is right. Then I will shed my mortal guise as a lizard does its skin and stand revealed, horrible in my wrath. My face will split, the glory of my divine beauty bursting forth, and their eyes will melt in their sockets. No handcuffs will hold me. I will have too many hands. No jail will contain me. I will be bigger than the Sears Tower. THEY will scream and point at me, cowering like extras in a Godzilla film. I will crush a hundred with each step. I will drown whole suburbs in a scalding baptism of piss. When I walk the world will tremble and all living things will bow down before me and sing my praises or I will destroy them with a single glance. But not yet. Not yet.

I will wait and play their games. I will look at their inkblots and talk about my mother. It will do them no good. My motives are beyond their understanding. THEY will find long Latin words to describe what their hobbled minds perceive as the method of my "madness." I will not lie. I will not deceive them, although it would be pathetically easy to do so. I will tell them the Truth. THEY will hear my words but their brains will not comprehend what I say. THEY have been programmed from birth to believe what the International Jewish Conspiracy wants them to. THEY see the Truth every day and their Conspiracy-conditioned logic circuits edit out all reference to "forbidden knowledge."

When I finally elect to reveal myself to the masses, the scales will drop from their eyes and the synaptic blockades will collapse and centuries of Truth will flood their grey matter. THEY will realize that THEY were played for dupes, sold into slavery by the filthy, scheming Jews who killed my brother and tried to divert the wrath of the righteous by spreading the Lie that he was born of a Jewess. THEY took all the evidence that he was an Aryan, born of a White mother, and sealed it in the Ark of the Covenant along with the *real* Ten Commandments, the ones that say *None Shall Suffer A Jew To Live* and that fornication between the races is an Abomination in the eyes of the Lord. The Truth shall set them *free! I* will set them free! And the gutters shall run with the blood of the moneylenders and the sky will once more grow black with their ashes!

I'm getting ahead of myself. How is it that I, the Second Coming, the Messiah Reborn, am in prison, watched by cold-eyed Jews in white coats? I was protecting myself from the Anti-Christ, that's all.

I wasn't born aware of my godhood. Now that I look back on my early years, the signs were everywhere for my childish eyes to see. But I was still too young to grasp their implications. I did not understand how impossible it was for two squat, swarthy trolls to produce a tall, fair-skinned boy. I never felt comfortable with my "parents," and when my "father" took to beating me, I realized I wasn't their natural son. I was adopted. I first became suspicious when THEY destroyed my collection of World War Two comics, claiming THEY were saving me from brain rot. The cow that claimed to be my mother said I was morbid. That I had unhealthy interests. When THEY found the cache of clippings about the so-called Nazi war crimes I'd culled from various men's magazines, the man who called himself my father beat me until I bled.

While I was unconscious I had a vision. It revealed to me the exact nature of my conception and birth. My mother was a beautiful, Aryan virgin with long blond hair and blue eyes. My father was God. But not the fierce, storm-eyed God of the Old Testament. He was far older and much weaker now. The Jews and their master, Satan, have made great progress since the Second World War, wringing sympathy from bleeding-heart dupes of the Conspiracy by convincing the world that six million Jews were exterminated in the camps. God is now a senile old deity who drools in His beard. He is disgusting to watch and really quite pathetic. The first thing I will do after revealing myself to the multitudes is depose the old fool. I will banish Him to a suitable limbo. I won't kill Him, like Jupiter did Saturn, although that would be the prudent thing to do. But, after all, He *is* my father.

Anyway, my Divine Father had become forgetful and after I was born I was stolen from my real mother by Jews, who placed me amongst their own to raise, hoping I would remain ignorant of my birthright. Ultimately, THEY failed and I came to manhood aware that I was the Second Coming foretold in the Book of Revelations.

My older brother made the mistake of trying for the hearts and minds of the cows by becoming mortal. He told the parables, performed low-key, tasteful miracles, and ended up nailed to a stick for his troubles. I know better than to follow in his stigmatized footsteps. Benevolence, humanitarianism, and tolerance are the tools of the Conspiracy. THEY mollycoddle the cows into believing that the Lord doesn't mind what you do as long as you keep it to yourself. When I ascend to my rightful inheritance, I will be a god washed in blood and tempered by fire. The Righteous shall be spared while the Communist Jew Humanist Slut Whore Niggers erupt into flame, their skins crackling like bacon in the pan!

Soft words do not work. The only way to get a cow's attention is to goose it with a cattle prod. My brother tried it before me and failed. I shall not fail. My success is secured.

The Anti-Christ. I must tell you about the Anti-Christ!

The Jew bastards were upset when I saw through their mind games. THEY were unprepared for the immensity of my intellect. THEY are crafty, I'll give them that. Seeing that I would one day ascend to my father's throne, THEY got to work creating their Anti-Christ.

I have known for years what THEY were planning, but I was

uncertain as to where to begin my search. The Holy Land? Hyperborea? Des Moines? The possibilities were endless. I used my X-ray vision, scanning the bellies of all the pregnant women on the street. I knew that their Anti-Virgin would be a Jewess, but THEY might use cosmetic surgery on her nose and bleach her hair to throw me off the track. As much as it disgusted me, I stared into the pelvic cradles of thousands of lumbering, milk-laden cows, seeking my ancient enemy. I knew my future would be in doubt for as long as the Anti-Christ lived. It took me three years, but at last I found the Beast!

I was at a McDonald's, toying with the idea of turning my strawberry shake into wine, when a grossly pregnant woman waddled past with a Filet-O-Fish and a large order of fries. She wore a bright pink sweatshirt and matching running pants. Across her bloated belly was printed BABY. An arrow stabbed her uterus.

Out of habit, I turned on my X-ray vision and followed the arrow, peering into the red darkness of her womb. There, curled in its cage of bone and flesh like a hibernating toad, was my adversary. The Beast. The Anti-Christ. The Son of Satan. The King of the Jews.

Its head was bulbous, the flesh a sickly white. It had no nose, only fleshless slits set under two sunken jaundiced eyes. Its mouth was lipless and full of tiny, needle-sharp teeth. The mouth of a moray eel. And it was grinning at me! I could make out the fabled "666," the Mark of the Beast, traced in fire on the corpse-pale expanse of its bulging forehead. Its body was folded under the malformed head like a Japanese lantern. The arms were long, like those of an ape, and its tiny hands were complete with yellowed talons. Its legs were the crooked, hairy shanks of an infant goat. I was revolted by the glimpse of unnaturally large genitals. I noticed the Abomination sported an erection. I nearly gagged on my strawberry shake.

I knew the unholy fetus was aware that I had recognized it. And it was laughing at me from within the Anti-Virgin's unhallowed womb. I felt hate and fear boil inside me and the voices of the Archangels—broadcast from their secret staging base within the Hollow Earth—raged in my head. By the time Satan's whore finished her meal I had decided on my course of action.

I followed her home.

*   *   *

She lived in one of those bland, pasteurized suburban mushroom colonies the Conspiracy-controlled lies of the television and radio have conditioned the cows to want. Let them numb their minds with useless consumer goods. *Let* the cows sate themselves with split-level ranches, wall-to-wall shag, microwaves, Jacuzzis, food processors, and remote-control VCRs! THEY have pulled the wool over their own eyes, blinding themselves with animal comfort, ignoring the signs traced in fire and ice, semen and blood that I Have Come and their time is at hand!

I wandered the neighborhood, making sure I would be able to locate the Anti-Manger after dark. I had little doubt that the Anti-Christ Child's aura would be a beacon, even without my infrared vision. But it doesn't hurt to make sure. All those clapboard hellholes look alike, especially at night. Just like the soul-less cows who live in them.

I had a couple of bad minutes waiting for the bus to take me back to the city. I was certain the Men In Black, the Conspiracy's elite secret police, were watching me. I have never been able to really *see* them. THEY manifest themselves as the dark flickerings at the corners of my eyes. Just when I turn my head to try to get a better look at them—they're gone. I pretended not to notice them and began reciting the Lord's Prayer under my breath. THEY hate that and usually don't hang around to hear me finish.

I rode home on the bus, contemplating my next move. I hate city buses. Hate the smelly old crones in their faded shifts, hairy warts sprouting from their chins. Hate their flaccid lips, their liver-spotted talons wrapped around the handles of ancient shopping bags overflowing with meaningless Conspiracy-approved junk. Just like their huge, overinflated bosoms.

I hate the niggers, especially the slut drug addict mothers with their gaggle of pickaninny bastards who go out to the malls and let their little Tyrones and LaTonyas run wild, just like fucking animals. Bad enough THEY chased the Whites out of the city; now they're spilling into the suburbs. Dragging everything down to their level.

I hate the giggling, pimply-faced little teenaged girls who ride the bus because their daddies won't let them drive the 280Z. THEY sit in clumps like heifers, giggling at me when THEY think I'm not looking because of my hair, my clothes, my complexion, the tape on my glasses. I try to ignore them, shut out the smell of their Baby Soft body perfume, the sound of their caged-bird twittering, the sight of their pert young breasts straining against their blouses, their rounded buttocks sheathed in skintight designer jeans. I know that soon—oh, so *very* soon—I shall stand Revealed and all the high school princesses and prick teasers in the world will be mine. THEY will flock to me, fighting like cats in heat for the privilege of tasting my sperm. Even though my mighty penis shall disembowel them like pigs in a slaughterhouse, still they will writhe and yowl in delight and beg for more!

I felt safe at home. I knew the Men In Black could not see me once I entered my room. I disappeared from their demonic radar as soon as I set foot inside the door. That was because I papered the walls of my room with pages torn from the Bible. But not *all* the Bible. The Old Testament is useless trash, nothing more than Jew propaganda. The New Testament has been tampered with and is untrustworthy. No, I papered my apartment with pages torn from a hundred Bibles: King James, New King James, Revised Standard, St. Joseph's Edition, The Good News for Modern Man . . . Pages torn from the Book of Revelations.

I prayed for two hours, scourging myself with the cord from a steam iron whenever visions of designer jeans intruded on my devotions. My earlier anxiety had passed, leaving a confidence that glowed like a hot coal. My Father was with me. I had nothing to fear. I felt the mantle of my power crackling about my shoulders and sparking from my fingertips. I was eager to go forth and slay my enemy. Still, it could prove fatal to be overconfident. I was going up against Satan, the Anti-Christ, and the International Jewish Conspiracy, not a gang of lunchroom toughs.

It was dark when I left. I caught the last bus out to the suburbs. It was empty, for once. I was pleased. I did not need any further distractions from my holy mission.

I found the neighborhood easily enough. I needn't have worried. The Anti-Christ's aura spilled from the windows, an infernal lamp-light the color of a ripe bruise. I hunkered in the shrubbery, watching the sickly purple-black glow flit from room to room. It would be a long wait, but I couldn't leave even if I wanted to. I was caught up in the machinery of Destiny. I had taken the first step toward godhead and there was no turning back.

The bruise-light finally moved into what my X-ray vision revealed to be the bedroom. I followed the side of the house, keeping in shadow. I found the window I was looking for. I polarized my magnetic field, the energy leaping from my fingertips in a shower of emerald sparks, and the window latch sprang open silently.

I started creepy-crawling back in high school. I enjoyed walking through houses while the owners were away, looking through their private lives. Secrets were laid bare to my all-seeing eyes. The gin bottles hidden in the Greers' planter. The bundle of magazines featuring nude boys squirreled away in Reverend Sanderson's study. The diverse collection of sex toys in Widow Maynard's dresser. It was like being God. I saw it as a form of on-the-job training. Then, during my senior year, I began creepy-crawling while the owners were home, asleep in their beds of sin.

I eased up the window, levering myself over the sill and slithering into the house on my belly and elbows. Creepy-crawl. Wall-to-wall shag brushed my stomach. Creepy-crawl. Energy coursed through me. I felt it building up in the pit of my stomach and radiating throughout my body. When I exhaled a fine mist of golden light escaped from my nostrils. My hair stood on end, sparks snapping from every follicle. As my fingers closed on the doorknob, tiny lightning bolts the color of blood shot from my palm. My skin felt impossibly tight, as if barely able to contain my divinity. The bruise-light oozed from under the doorframe and washed my face in its unholy glow as I opened the door.

I saw the king-size bed and the two figures curled within the covers. I had not expected a husband. For a heartbeat I was confronted by my own doubt, tempted by Satan to entertain the possibility I had made a mistake. The sickly, unwarming light pulled me back to Reality. I knew then how my older brother must have felt, standing on the mountaintop while the Father of Jews whispered in his ears. I was sweating and trembling like a man in the grip of malaria. I had to get it over with before my resolve weakened and I fled.

Ghosting along the edge of the mattress, I reached out and

touched the bedside lamp. Heavenly choirs sang in my ears, urging me onward to my destiny. One hundred watts lit the bedroom and the dark blots that swam before my eyes had the wings of bats.

The Anti-Joseph started awake as if doused with water. His eyelids flew open, the eyeballs jerking about wildly in their sockets. He saw me standing next to the bed and the fear that radiated from him was the sweetest thing I have ever known. The Anti-Virgin mumbled something from inside her blankets and was still.

The Anti-Joseph gained his footing, his sleep-stupid face showing fright and anger. I stepped back, uncertain as to whether he was mortal or some form of incubus watchdog in charge of protecting the unborn Anti-Christ. The bald spot and junior executive's paunch hanging over the waistband of his underwear looked human enough, but you can't be too sure about these things.

He made a clumsy lunge for the nightstand, clawing at the drawer. The heavy blade of my machete bit through his wrist and tasted the wood underneath. The Anti-Joseph recoiled so fast it was like running a film backward. His right hand remained on the nightstand.

He stood holding the stump of his wrist before his horrified eyes, his left hand clamped around the severed ganglia. The blood was redder than the heart of the sun. Each beat of his heart covered the eggshell-white walls in ideograms proclaiming my divinity. Shock glazed his eyes and he collapsed onto the wall-to-wall shag. Satan had erred in his choice of a guardian for his heir apparent.

I kicked the body to make sure the Anti-Joseph wasn't feigning unconsciousness. He rolled onto his back, as slack as an oversize bag of suet. His skin was white, bordering on blue, and his eyelids fluttered in shock. The eyeballs, rolled back in their sockets, were bloodless. I tugged at the waistband of his shorts and pulled the soiled underwear down around his knees.

Even though he had not shown the strength and wiliness of an incubus, I couldn't take a chance. I'd seen those movies where the heroes turn their backs on supposedly "dead" vampires and werewolves.

The Anti-Joseph shuddered once when the machete sliced off his penis. Like all servants of the Lord of Hell, he was circumcised. I thrust my fingers between the dying Jew's blue lips and pried open his jaws. There was something close to sentience flickering in his eyes, but it fled when I stuffed the slippery wet redness of his sex into his mouth. He died with his own blood and semen pooling in his lungs, all hopes of resurrection crushed.

The Anti-Virgin was sitting up in bed, flattened against the headboard. Her eyes were huge and mouth a wide, trembling O. Her swollen belly was crisscrossed with pale blue veins. A roadmap to Hell. She stared at her false husband as he died on the floor. Her thin, tight screams were ultrasonic, the frantic shrieks of a bat. I wasn't fooled by her display. I knew who the *real* husband was. I knew who'd fathered the Beast inside her. In my mind's eye I saw her offering her loathsome, hairy sex to the Black Goat of the Wood. I saw his mammoth, foreskinless member, engorged with venom. Whore. Whore of Babylon.

She scuttled off the bed as I moved for her, her eyes never leaving me. Her mouth moved spasmodically, but no sound came out. One hand was raised in a feeble attempt to blot me out of her world. She was crying, the tears streaming down her face. The tears of a witch. If I licked the tears from her face I would taste no salt. But I had no need for such crude witchfinding, I already knew *who* and *what* she was. She was working a spell, attempting to conjure forth her lover's minions. Had to work fast. Not much time. Had an erection. Her work. Devil's work. Had to stop her. Stop the Anti-Virgin.

My fist slammed into her mouth and I felt teeth shatter and abrade my knuckles. It was wet and red and warm. She fell, and I heard her cry out for the first and last time.

"My baby!"

I stood over her, staring at her pale face and blood-smeared mouth. Painted mouth. Whore of Babylon. Red laughing mouths. Designer jeans. Floral print housecoats. I saw the Anti-Christ struggling within his mother's pelvic cage, shrieking the foulest obscenities. His tongue was forked and covered with fur. The pale loop of the umbilical cord had become a hangman's noose, throttling the unborn demon as he clawed at the pink walls of his uterine prison. I began to laugh.

The machete had undergone a miraculous transformation. It was a burning sword. Not surprising, considering it was forged from a sliver of the original Sword of Righteousness my Father used to chase those ingrates from the Garden. It sent shock waves of ice-cold heat up my arm and into my brain.

She screamed when I slit her open, totally ruining the moment. Her scream jarred against the bones of my inner ear like a dentist's drill bit, rattling my teeth in their moorings. Bitch. Cow. Purple-pink entrails unraveled onto the carpet like party streamers. The odor of bile was strong. The Anti-Virgin stared up at me, still alive and conscious. Even though she was beyond speaking, I knew she was asking "why." As if *I* had to justify my actions to the whore of the Prince of Lies! I was disappointed. It had been too easy. Satan's wife was just another cow, ignorant of the malignancy she carried in her womb.

In answer to her silent plea, I reached into her and pulled out my nemesis.

The thing I removed from the Anti-Virgin's belly was not what I had expected. Gone were the horns, the crooked shanks and pinioned wings. What I held in my hands did not look very human, but neither did it resemble the Abomination I had glimpsed earlier.

Tiny matchstick legs jerked in feeble protest and something inside its brittle rib cage shuddered. It was soft and squishy, like an octopus, with rubber bones and skin as translucent as rice paper. The eyes bulged in the oversize head and opened wide enough for me to glimpse colorless irises and a dark-adapted pupil. I was overwhelmed by a desire to hurl the half-formed thing against the wall. I had been cheated.

The Host spoke unto me then, their crystalline voices melding into one. The Host told me I was being deceived. My faith was being tested to its utmost. To turn back now would extinguish all hope of achieving my divine inheritance. I had to prove that I was stronger than my rival. I had to take his dark power and make it mine.

I looked into the Anti-Virgin's dumb, uncomprehending eyes as she died. I knew that she would take what she saw to Hell. It made me feel better knowing that.

I was reminded of a poster I used to have as a kid, before my so-called "father" found it and tore it to shreds. It was called *Satan Devouring His Children*.

It was a lot like veal.

*   *   *

THEY tell me I was apprehended walking down the street, laughing and crying at the top of my lungs, and that it took six policemen to subdue me. I really don't remember.

THEY've kept me in this damn straitjacket ever since I was arrested. THEY don't even take it off during mealtimes. A burly orderly—a flunky working for the Conspiracy—feeds me spaghetti with a plastic spoon.

When THEY aren't asking me questions, I'm left alone in a room without windows or furniture. It doesn't matter, since I can sleep on the heavy padding as easily as I could on a bed.

I have endured these indignities because I must marshal my energies for the Transfiguration. The time is near. Very near. I can feel my musculature restructuring under cover of the canvas. Soon I will burst my restraints like a butterfly its cocoon and the Archangels shall emerge from their secret staging bases deep inside the Hollow Earth and drive their flaming UFO chariots across the night sky.

Rebirth—like birth—is a painful process. I was not aware just how agonizing it would be. My teeth ache constantly, especially the canines. My eyes feel hot and dry and it's a struggle simply to blink. My spine feels like it's turning into a question mark. Sometimes I suffer immense, painful erections that threaten to tear the seams of my pants.

I have been visited by the Host on at least two occasions, its multitude of voices begging me to have patience and wait out the Transfiguration. I shall bear my agony in silence, as befits a god on earth. But even a god incarnate has moments of doubt, and this is one of them. The pain that attends the discarding of my mortal form has weakened me.

I've begun to wonder if I was mistaken, after all. Not about the unborn thing being my nemesis. Of that I'm certain. But maybe . . . just maybe, mind you . . . I got my wires crossed concerning my origins . . . about who, or what, my Father *really* is . . .

I wish I had something to drink. The fur on my tongue tickles something awful.

Lacunae

KARL EDWARD WAGNER

*Among the most profound biological achievements of this sick
and shining century is the medical community's ability to alter
our own sex. Women trapped in men's bodies can be surgically/
hormonally "adjusted"; to a lesser extent, the inverse is also true.*

*However, this raises a question: After a gross remodeling of
the body, what subtle changes may have been wrought upon the
mind?*

KARL EDWARD WAGNER attempts to answer that.

*Wagner is a former psychiatrist who early on discovered his
true vocation was writing. But for a long period, Karl's fine editorial talents (reflected through his ongoing YEAR'S BEST HORROR
STORIES) seemed to reduce production of Wagner's equally fine
fiction. Thankfully, that situation has recently changed; Wagner's
literary efforts have reappeared with a vengeance.*

Wagner's latest books include Tell Me, Dark, *a graphic novel
with artist Kent Williams, and the novels* At First Just Ghostly
and The Fourth Seal. *Three Wagnerian short-story collections also
exist:* In a Lonely Place, Why Not You and I?, *and* Exorcisms and
Ecstacies.

*But the Karl-creation I'm most fond of is his immortal, enig-
matic Kane. An ambiguous antihero, Kane's exploits virtually
span the centuries. Appearing as everything from a prehistoric
mercenary (in novels like* Bloodstone*) to a twentieth-century record producer (in the short story "Deep Within the Depths of the
Acme Warehouse"), Kane can pop up as devil or angel, good guy
or bad. On either side of the law.*

*"Lacunae" is another Kane story. Karl tells me it's partially
based on the strange death of famed seventies comic book artist
Vaughn Bode, who accidentally killed himself while entangled*

*within an autoerotic mechanism quite similar to the one de-
scribed by Wagner.*

*The inclusion of said sex machine forces me to append this
warning:*

Do not *attempt this stunt at home.*

Unless you're a trained professional, of course.

They were resting, still joined together, in the redwood hot tub,
water pushing in bubbling surges about their bodies. Elaine watched
as the hot vortex caught up streamers of her semen, swirled it away
like boiled confetti, dissipating it throughout the turbulence.

I'm disseminated, she thought.

Elaine said: "I feel reborn."

Allen kissed the back of her neck and brushed her softening
nipples with his fingertips. "Your breasts are getting so full. Are you
stepping up the estrogens?"

His detumescent penis, still slick with Vaseline, tickled as it
eased out of Elaine's ass. Allen's right hand moved down through
the warm water, milked the last droplets of orgasm from Elaine's
flaccid cock. Gently he turned Elaine around, kissed her lovingly—
probing his tongue deep into her mouth.

"Here," said Allen, breaking their kiss. He pushed down on
Elaine's shoulders, urging her beneath the foaming surface. Elaine
let her knees bend, ducked beneath the water that swirled about
Allen's hips. As Allen's hands cupped her head, Elaine opened her
mouth to accept Allen's slippery cock. She tasted the sweet smear
of her own shit as she sucked in its entire length. Suddenly swelling,
the cock filled her mouth, hardening as it pushed deep into her
throat.

Elaine gagged and tried to pull back, but Allen's hands forced
her head hard into his pubic hair. Water filled Elaine's nostrils as
she choked, bit down in an uncontrollable reflex. Allen's severed
cock, bitten free at the base, wriggled inward, sliding past the back
of her throat and down into her windpipe.

Elaine wrenched free of Allen's hands. Blood and come filled
her lungs—spewed from her mouth in an obscene fountain as her
head pushed toward the surface. But her head could not break
through the surface, no matter how desperately she fought. There

was a black resilient layer that separated her from the air above, closed like wax over her face, pushed the vomit back into her lungs.

A vortex of blood and semen sucked her soul into its warm depths.

The first thing she heard was a monotoned *shit-shit-shit*—like autumn leaves brushing the window. She became aware of an abrupt pressure against her abdomen, of vomit being expelled from her mouth. She was breathing in gasps.

She opened her eyes. The layer of clinging blackness was gone.

"Shit goddammit," said Blacklight, wiping vomit from her face and nostrils. "Don't ever try that alone again."

Elaine stared at him dumbly, oxygen returning to her brain.

Beside her on the carpet lay the black leather bondage mask—its straps and laces cut. The attached phallus-shaped gag, almost bitten through, was covered with her vomit. A spiked leather belt, also slashed, was coiled about the mask.

"Jesus!" said Blacklight. "You OK now?"

He was wrapping a blanket around her, busily tucking it in. There was a buzzing somewhere, in her head or in her pelvis—she wasn't sure. Memory was returning.

"I dreamed I was a man," she said, forcing her throat to speak.

"Fuckin' A. You nearly dreamed you were dead. I had a buddy from 'Nam who used to do this kinda shit. He'd been dead two days before they found him."

Elaine looked upward at the chinning bar mounted high across her entrance-hall doorway. The leather mask with its padded blindfold and gag—sensory deprivation and sensual depravity—cutting out the world. The belt, looped around her neck, free end held in her hands as she kicked away the stool. The belt buckle should have slipped free when she fainted from lack of oxygen. Instead its buckle had become entangled with the complex buckles of the bondage mask, not releasing, nearly suffocating her. Friends who had shown her how to experience visions of inner realities through this method had warned her, but until now there had been no problems. No worse than with the inversion apparatus.

"I heard you banging about on the floor," Blacklight explained, taking her pulse. He had been an army medic until he'd Section-

Eighted—no future for a broad six-foot-eight medic in the paddies. "Thought maybe you were balling somebody, but it didn't feel right. I busted in your door."

Good job through two dead bolts and a chain, but Blacklight could do it. Her neighbor in the duplex loft had split last week, and the pizzeria downstairs was being redone as a vegetarian restaurant. Elaine might have lain there dead on the floor until her cats polished her bones.

"I dreamed I had a cock," she said, massaging her neck.

"Maybe you still do," Blacklight told her. He looked at his hands and went into the bathroom to wash them.

Elaine wondered what he meant, then remembered. She reached down to flick off the vibrator switch on the grotesque dildo she had strapped around her pelvis. Gathering the blanket about herself, she made it to her feet and waited for Blacklight to come out of the bathroom.

When she had removed the rest of her costume and washed herself, she put on a Chinese silk kimono and went to look for Blacklight. She felt little embarrassment. Between cheap smack in 'Nam and killer acid in the Haight, Blacklight's brain had been fried for most of his life. He was more reliable for deliveries than the Colombians, and old contacts supported him and his habit.

Blacklight was standing in the center of her studio—the loft was little more than one big room with a few shelves and counters to partition space—staring uncertainly at an unfinished canvas.

"You better look closer at your model, or else you got a freak." The canvas was wall-sized, originally commissioned and never paid for by a trendy leather bar, since closed. Blacklight pointed. "Balls don't hang side by side like that. One dangles a little lower. Even a dyke ought to know that."

"It's not completed," Elaine said. She was looking at the bag of white powder Blacklight had dropped onto her bar.

"You want to know why?"

"What?"

"It's so they don't bang together."

"Who doesn't?"

"Your balls. One slides away from the other when you mash your legs together."

"Terrific," said Elaine, digging a fingernail into the powder.

"You like it?"

"The thing about balls." Elaine tasted a smear of coke, licking her fingertip.

"Uncut Peruvian flake," Blacklight promised, forgetting the earlier subject.

Elaine sampled a nailful up each nostril. The ringing bitterness of the coke cut through the residues of vomit. Good shit.

"It's like Yin and Yang," Blacklight explained. "Good and Evil. Light and Dark."

One doesn't correct a large and crazed biker. He was wrestling his fists together. "Have you ever heard the story of Love and Hate?"

Across the knuckles of his right fist was tattooed LOVE; across those of his left: HATE.

Elaine had seen *The Night of the Hunter*, and she was not impressed.

"An ounce?"

"One humongous oh-zee." Blacklight was finger-wrestling with himself. "They got to be kept apart, Love and Hate, but they can't keep from coming together and trying to see which one's stronger."

Elaine opened the drawer beneath her telephone and counted out the bills she had set aside earlier. Blacklight forgot his Robert Mitchum impersonation and accepted the money.

"I got five paintings to finish before my show opens in SoHo, OK? That's next month. This is the end of this month. My ass is fucked, and I'm stone out of inspiration. So give me a break and split now, right?"

"Just don't try too much free-basing with that shit, OK?" Blacklight advised. He craned his thick neck to consider another unfinished canvas. It reminded him of someone, but then he forgot who before he could form the thought.

"Your brain is like your balls, did you know that?" He picked up the thread of the last conversation he could remember.

"No, I didn't know that."

"Two hunks rolling around inside your skull," Blacklight said, knotting his fists side by side. "They swim in your skull side by side, just like your balls swing around in your scrotum. Why are there two halves of your brain instead of just one big chunk—like, say, your heart?"

"I give up."

Blacklight massaged his fists together. "So they don't bang together, see. Got to keep them apart. Love and Hate. Yin and Yang."

"Look, I got to work." Elaine shook a gram's worth of lines out of the Baggie and onto the glass top of her coffee table.

"Sure. You sure you're gonna be OK?"

"No more anoxic rushes with a mask on. And thanks."

"You got a beer?"

"Try the fridge."

Blacklight found a St. Pauli and plinked the non-twist-off cap free with his thumb. Elaine thought he looked like a black-bearded Wookie.

"I had a buddy from 'Nam who offed himself trying that," Blacklight suddenly remembered.

"You told me."

"Like, whatever turns you on. Just don't drop the hammer when you don't mean to."

"Want a line?"

"No. I'm off Charlie. Fucks up my brain." Blacklight's eyes glazed in an effort to concentrate. "Off the goddamn dinks," he said. "Off 'em all." There were old tracks fighting with the tattoos, as he raised his arm to kill the beer. "Are you sure you're gonna be OK?" He was pulling out a fresh beer from behind the tuna salad.

Elaine was a foot shorter and a hundred pounds lighter, and aerobicised muscles weren't enough to overawe Blacklight. "Look, I'm all right now. Thanks. Just let me get back to work. OK? I mean, deadline-wise, this is truly crunch city."

"Want some crystal? Got a dynamite price."

"Got some. Look, I think I'm going to throw up some more. Want to give me some privacy?"

Blacklight dropped the beer bottle into his shirt pocket. "Hang loose." He started for the door. The beer bottle seemed no larger than a pen in his pocket.

"Oh," he said. "I can get you something better. A new one. Takes out the blank spots in your head. Just met a new contact who's radically into designer drugs. Weird dude. Working on some new kind of speed."

"I'll take some," said Elaine, opening the door. She really needed to sleep for a week.

"Catch you later," promised Blacklight.

He paused halfway through the door, dug into his denim jacket pocket. "Superb blotter," he said, handing her a dingy square of dolphin-patterned paper. "Very inspirational. Use it and grow. Are you sure you're gonna be OK?"

Elaine shut the door.

Mr. Fix-it promised to come by tomorrow, or the next morning after that, for sure.

Elaine replaced the chain with one from the bathroom door, hammered the torn-out and useless dead bolts back into place for her own peace of mind, then propped a wooden chair against the doorknob. Feeling better, she pulled on a leotard, and tried a gram or so of this and that.

She was working rather hard, and the airbrush was a bit loud, although her stereo would have drowned out most sounds of entry in any event.

"That blue," said Kane from behind her. "Cerulean, to be sure— but why? It impresses me as antagonistic to the overdone flesh tones you've so laboriously mulled and muddled to confuse the faces of the two lovers."

Elaine did not scream. There would be no one to hear. She turned very cautiously. A friend had once told her how to react in these situations.

"Are you an art critic?" The chair was still propped beside her door. Perhaps it was a little askew.

"Merely a dilettante," lied Kane. "An interested patron of the arts for many years. *That* is not a female escutcheon."

"It shouldn't be."

"Possibly not."

"I'm expecting my boyfriend at any minute. He's bringing over some buyers. Are you waiting for them?"

"Blacklight contacted me. He thought you'd like something stronger to help you finish your gallery collection."

Elaine decided to take a breath. He was big, very big. His belted trenchcoat could have held two of her and an umbrella. A biker friend of Blacklight's was her first thought. They hadn't quite decided whether to be hit men for the Mafia or their replacements in the lucrative drug trade. He was a head shorter than Blacklight, probably weighed more. There was no fat. His movements reminded Elaine of her karate instructor. His face, although unscarred, called to mind an NFL lineman who'd flunked his advertising screen test. His hair and short beard were a shade darker than her hennaed Grace Jones flattop. She did not like his blue eyes—quickly looked away.

"Here," said Kane.

She took from his spadelike hand a two-gram glass phial—corner headshop stuff, spoon attached by an aluminum chain.

"How much?" There was a can of Mace in the drawer beneath the telephone. She didn't think it would help.

"New lot," said Kane, sitting down on the arm of her largest chair. He balanced his weight, but she flinched. "Trying to recreate a lost drug from long ago. Perfectly legal."

"How long ago?"

"Before you'd remember. It's a sort of superspeed."

"Superspeed?"

Kane dropped the rest of the way into the chair. It held his weight. He said: "Can you remember everything that has happened to you, or that you have done, for the past forty-eight hours?"

"Of course."

"Tell me about eleven thirty-eight this morning."

"All right." Elaine was open to a dare. "I was in the shower. I'd been awake all night, working on the paintings for the show. I called my agent's answering machine, then took a shower. I thought I'd try some TM afterward, before getting back to work."

"But what were you thinking at eleven thirty-eight this morning?"

"About the showing."

"No."

Elaine decided it was too risky to jump for the phone. "I forget what I was thinking exactly," she conceded. "Would you like some coffee?" Scalding coffee in the face might work.

"What was on your mind at nine forty-two last night?"

"I was fixing coffee. Would you like some . . . ?"

"At nine forty-two. Exactly then."

"All right. I don't remember. I was flipping around the cable dial, I think. Maybe I was daydreaming."

"Lacunae," said Kane.

"Say what?"

"Gaps. Missing pieces. Missing moments of memory. Time lost from your consciousness, and thus from your life. Where? Why?"

He rolled the phial about on his broad palm. "No one really remembers every instant of life. There are always forgotten moments, daydreams, musings—as you like. It's lost time from your life. Where does it go? You can't remember. You can't even remember forgetting that moment. Part of your life is lost in vacant moments, in lapses of total consciousness. Where does your conscious mind go? And why?

"This"—and he tossed the glass phial toward her—"will remove those lost moments. No gaps in your memory—wondering where your car keys are, where you left your sunglasses, who called before lunch, what was foremost in your mind when you woke up. Better than speed or coke. Total awareness of your total consciousness. No more lacunae."

"I don't have any cash on hand."

"There's no charge. Think of it as a trial sample."

"I know—the first one is free."

"That's meant to be a mirror, isn't it?" Kane returned to the unfinished painting. "The blue made me think of water. It's someone making love to a reflection."

"Someone," said Elaine.

"Narcissus?"

"I call it: *Lick It Till It Bleeds.*"

"I'll make a point of attending the opening."

"There won't be one unless people leave me alone to work."

"Then I'll be getting along." Kane seemed to be standing without ever having arisen from the chair. "By the way, I wouldn't shove that. New lab equipment. Never know about impurities."

"I don't like needlework anyway," Elaine told him, dipping into the phial with the attached spoon. She snorted cautiously, felt no burn. Clean enough. She heaped the spoon twice again.

She closed her eyes and inhaled deeply. Already she could feel a buzz. Trust Blacklight to steer her onto something good.

She was trying another spoonful when it occurred to her that she was alone once again.

*   *   *

Blacklight secured the lid of the industrial chemical drum and finished his beer. The body of the designer drug lab's former owner had folded inside nicely. Off to the illegal toxic waste dump with the others. Some suckers just can't tell which way the wind blows.

"Did you really land in a flying saucer?" he asked, rummaging in the cooler for another beer.

Kane was scowling over a chromatogram. "For sure. Looked just like a 1957 Chrysler 300C hubcap."

Blacklight puzzled over it while he chugged his beer. The prettiest girl in his junior high—her family had had a white 300C convertible. Was there a connection?

"Then how come you speak English so good?"

"I was Tor Johnson's stand-in in *Plan Nine from Outer Space.* Must have done a hundred retakes before we got it down right."

Blacklight thought about it. "Did you know Bela Lugosi?"

Kane jabbed at the computer keyboard, watching the monitor intently. "I've got to get some better equipment. There's a methyl group somewhere where it shouldn't be."

"Is that bad?"

"Might potentiate. Start thinking of another guinea pig."

At first she became aware of her hands.

It was 1:01:36 A.M., said the digital clock beside her bed. She stepped back from the painting and considered her hands. They were tobacco-stained and paint-smeared, and her nails needed polish. How could she hope to create with hands such as these?

Elaine glared at her hands for forty-three seconds, found no evidence of improvement. The back of her skull didn't feel quite right either; it tingled, like when her mohawk started to grow out last year. Maybe some wine.

There was an opened bottle of Liebfraumilch in the refrigerator. She poured a glass, sipped, set it aside in distaste. Elaine thought about the wine for the next eighty-six seconds, reading the label twice. She made a mental note never to buy it again. Stirring through a canister of artificial-sweetener packets, she found half a 'lude, washed it down with the wine.

She returned to *Lick It Till It Bleeds* and worked furiously, with total concentration and with mounting dissatisfaction, for the next one hour, thirty-one minutes, and eighteen seconds.

Her skin itched.

Elaine glowered at the painting for another seven minutes nineteen seconds.

She decided to phone Allen.

An insomniac recording answered her. The number she had dialed was no longer in service. Please . . .

Elaine tried to visualize Allen. How long had it been?

Her skin itched.

Had she left him, or had he driven her out? And did it really matter? She hated him. She had always hated him. She hated all that she had previously been.

Her body felt strange, like a stranger's body. The leotard was binding her crotch. Stupid design.

Elaine stripped off her leotard and tights. Her skin still itched. Like a caterpillar's transformation throes. Death throes of former life. Did the caterpillar hate the moth?

She thought about Allen.

She thought about herself.

Love and hate.

There was a full-length mirror on her closet door. Elaine stared at her reflection, caressing her breasts and crotch. She moved closer, pressed herself to the mirror, rubbing against her reflection.

Making love to herself.

And hating.

Pressed against her reflection, Elaine could not ignore the finest of scars where the plastic surgeon had implanted silicone in her once-flat breasts. Fingering her surgically constructed vagina, Elaine could not repress the memories of her sex-change operation, repress the awareness of her former maleness.

Every instant remembered. Of joy. Of pain. Of longing. Of rage. Of hatred. Of self-loathing.

Of being Allen.

Her fists hammered her reflection, smashing it into a hundred brittle moments.

Blood trickled from her fists, streamed along her arms, made curling patterns across her breasts and belly.

She licked her blood, and found it good. It was shed for herself.

Gripping splinter shards of mirror, Elaine crossed to her unfinished painting. She stood before the life-sized figures, loving and hating what she had created.

Her fists moved across the canvas, slashing it into mad patterns. Take. This is my body. Given for me.

Blacklight was finishing a cold anchovy-and-black-olive pizza. He considered his greasy sauce-stained hands, wiped them on his jeans. Stains were exchanged, with little disruption of status quo. He licked his tattooed knuckles clean.

It was raining somewhere, because the roof of the old warehouse leaked monotonously away from the light. He watched Kane. Maybe Lionel Atwill's caged gorilla on the loose in the lab. Maybe Rondo Hatton as Mr. Hyde.

"So what are lacunae?"

Kane was studying a biochemical supply catalogue. "Gaps. Cavities. Blank spaces."

"Spaces are important," Blacklight said. He knotted his pizza-stained fists and rolled their knuckles together. "Do you know how atomic bombs work?"

"Used to build them," Kane said. "They're overrated."

"You take two hunks of plutonium or something," Blacklight informed him. "Big as your fist. Now then, keep spaces between them, and it's on safety. But"—and he knocked his fists against one another—"take away the spaces, slam 'em together. Critical mass. Ker-blooie."

He punctuated the lecture with an explosive belch. "So that's why there's always got to be spaces in between," Blacklight concluded. "Like the two halves of your brain. Id and Ego. Yin and Yang. Male and Female. Even in your thoughts you've got to have these gaps—moments to daydream, to forget, to be absentminded. What happens when you fill in all the lacunae?"

"Critical mass," said Kane.

The mirror was a doorway, clouded and slippery with the taste of blood. Clutching angry shards of glass, Allen and Elaine waited on opposite sides, waited each for the other to break through.

Heels

*The recent women's movement in horror fiction (many of whose
members are represented in this book) has pressed some satisfying
new wrinkles into otherwise worn fabrics.*

*One's the long-overdue payback on that old woman-as-victim
crap, a weary contrivance which dominated the endless cycle of
slasher films. You remember—male psycho sees bimbo, male
psycho gets horny, male psycho kills bimbo. And on and dreary
on . . .*

*Leave it to the splattercunts, though, to throw a homicidal foot
fetishist into the mix.*

*LUCY TAYLOR is a widely published journalist and short story
writer whose travel articles have appeared in* International Living,
Boca Raton Magazine, *and* Caribbean Travel and Life. *Lately, she's
been billed "The Queen of Erotic Horror." Her fiction has been
published in such anthologies as* Women of the West *and* Bizarre
Sex and Other Crimes of Passion, *while two of Lucy's short story
collections include* Unnatural Acts and Other Stories *(to be published by Masquerade Books) and* Close to the Bone *(from Silver
Salamander Press).*

*Finally, Lucy Taylor lives in Boulder, Colorado. She enjoys
hiking, horseback riding, and traveling.*

As well as curling hairs. Through nasty little tales like Heels.
Whose rather blunt message goes something like this:
Don't fuck with the wrong shoe, fellas.

*T*he shoe was burgundy suede, size six and a half, made in Spain.
On the outside, it was soft as foreskin, velvety as the pelt of a mole.

Inside, the sleek interior gleamed like soft lips unfurling between female thighs.

The heel wasn't as high as Theo would have liked—a mere three inches—but the toe was rounded, allowing him to fit the whole head of his cock inside, probing, pushing, ravishing the silky, pink interior.

He imagined the woman's foot inside the shoe, her toes lined up like sausages, nestled beneath his cock, which was fucking the shoe now, hard and painfully fast, and he tried to stop himself, because he hated to spew all over such pristine loveliness, but it happened anyway—again—and Theo spasmed over and over and as he did, moaned out the name Felicia.

Felicia would be number five, the first one in Florida. So far, there had been two in Oregon, one in Iowa, and one in Arkansas.

Theo caressed the befouled shoe, pressed it to his nose. He reminded himself that killing wasn't something he enjoyed, although with practice, as with most things, it got easier. He wouldn't even need to do it if the women would cooperate, just let him take what he must have. But he'd learned, with numbers one and two, that people will fight desperately over a scrap of flesh no bigger than a pencil eraser if it's a part of their own bodies, and even forfeit their lives in the process.

So it was really their own fault the women died, Theo told himself. His mother had been wrong; he wasn't a bad boy, nor had he grown up to be an evil man. He just had—needs.

"I got more shoes for you," said the pretty Puerto Rican teenager. "Can you fix these good as last time?"

Theo examined the heels on the bright red fuck-me sandals, then smiled at Felicia across the counter. She had a pink-dyed mohawk, and both ears were pierced in half a dozen places, right up into the cartilage, where gold hoops gleamed like the ritual adornments of some Micronesian tribeswoman.

"I know it's not my business and I hope you don't get mad, but why would a lovely girl like you do that to her hair?"

"You're right. It's not your goddamn business, and you don't wanna make me mad. You gonna fix these shoes or what?"

Theo flashed his warmest, most Young Republican smile. Even though he was well past thirty, he still had the disarming charm of a young zealot soliciting charitable contributions door to door, and his voice held a seductive, lulling quality that, had he chosen to pursue a career in medicine, would have given him a splendid bedside manner. He was the kind of man women felt comfortable riding in an elevator alone with.

"They'll be ready Tuesday afternoon. That be okay?"

"I guess so."

"I hope I didn't offend you, miss, what I said about your hair. I guess I have a conservative streak."

"I don't," she said and flashed a smile that was part dare, part invitation. He knew then for sure that she was number five, even though, for his taste, she was too young, too foul-mouthed. He hadn't even seen her feet close up yet, but he'd seen those strappy shoes. That was enough.

"You lost my fucking shoes! I don't believe this, you lost the fucking shoes!" The way she was carrying on, you'd have thought she had hundred-dollar bills cached underneath the soles.

"This is so embarrassing," said Theo. "I fired a new girl the other day and I believe she stole them—"

"I want to see the manager."

"I'm the manager."

"Shit!"

"Look, you'll be reimbursed, of course. What did you pay for the shoes?"

"How the hell do I—shit, a hundred bucks, a hundred fifty, I don't know—"

"Tell you what," said Theo, "I feel terrible about this. Let's go over to the mall tonight and I'll buy you any pair of shoes you like, forget the price, and then take you out to dinner."

She chewed on her lower lip, as if an inner dialogue was taking place. That bad girl's gleam flashed in her eyes, and Theo thought, *She shouldn't look at men that way, she'll give them bad ideas.*

"Look, pal," she said, "before you hustle me, you oughta know what you're in for. I like women just as well as men and my favorite things are crack and three-way sex. How does that grab you, Mr. Conservative?"

"Right here," he said and squeezed his crotch.

She giggled. He knew he had her.

She was eighteen, it turned out, and worked the late shift dancing at the Cheetah Lounge in Hallandale. She liked to drink, so he took her first to Mr. Laugh's on Federal Highway. After a few tequila shooters got her talking, she confessed she didn't think it was politically correct to be bisexual, she wanted to choose, cocks or cunts, pricks or pussies, so many hormonal excesses to delight in, make up your mind, her lover had demanded, what'll it be, estrogen or testosterone tonight, the hard or the wet or a dildo with studs, but she was confused, this little sepia-skinned stripper with the tufted punk hair and antelope eyes, so Theo offered to help her decide.

Felicia drank so much, it turned out, that they never got to the Galleria Mall, which disappointed Edgar because he'd've loved to see her feet squeezed into Frederick's highest, although, in the dim light of Mr. Laugh's, her feet did look slightly larger than a six and a half. But then again, maybe she bought her shoes too small; some women, masochistically inclined, did that.

Felicia began to loudly debate the merits of cocksucking versus pussylicking. The bartender was starting to snicker, so Theo suggested they go to her place and work on deciding if homo or hetero was the better choice, orgasmically speaking.

It was all so easy, really, so unbelievably simple, that he thanked God and Jose Cuervo. In her apartment, Felicia slithered drunkenly out of her T-shirt. Her nipples, small and dark, looked up at him like a second set of eyes, and her bare feet scarcely indented the carpet as she padded toward the bedroom.

Theo slid into the waterbed beside her and told her she needn't bother taking off the rest of her clothes, because from the ankles down would do nicely, thank you.

She got mad, she thought he meant he only wanted a blow job, that she wasn't good enough to fuck, so he apologized and told her that he never fucked anybody, that wasn't his thing, and while he was explaining that, he strangled her.

Afterwards, he anointed her feet with jism and carefully, with great attention to severing the bone as cleanly as possible, amputated her big toe with a kitchen knife. He kissed the severed digit, noting that the nail was ragged and would need trimming once he got it home. Then he popped the keepsake into a sandwich Baggy and tucked it in his pocket.

This little piggy went to market, these little piggies stayed home . . .

Theo squatted in his closet, surrounded by racks of women's shoes, and admired his trophy necklace. Five victims, but only four keepsakes. That first time, in Portland, he'd been too frightened and excited to do anything but satisfy himself and flee, so he'd missed a trophy-taking opportunity. But now, thanks to Felicia, his necklace had gained a pleasing symmetry, the four toes dangling from the thread like small, shriveled fish reared in a lightless cavern.

With the acquisition of Felicia's keepsake, Theo decided it was time to leave Fort Lauderdale. He'd never felt safe staying in one place, even before there was any reason for anyone to be hunting him, and the South Florida sleaze scene was beginning to depress him: the drunks passed out in the alley behind the AA Clubhouse when he came to work, the hookers on the Strip, who might as well have had "HIV positive" tattooed on their eyelids but still got plenty of business, the dope deals going down behind the 7–11 day and night.

He was thinking of the Carolinas, of an aunt he had in Charlotte, when the little bell above the door jangled and number six walked in.

"Walked" was actually not an adequate description for this woman's gait. She swayed, waddled, undulated. Her breasts, melonous as those of a Paleolithic Venus, bulged under a bright scarlet blouse; a print skirt that could have provided shade for several toddlers encased her hips. Most fat women wouldn't wear clothes like that to their own funerals, Theo thought. The old cliché went through his mind: she'd be one great-looking woman if she'd just lose weight.

But then she put three pairs of shoes up on the counter, and he stopped seeing her as a fat woman. He saw her now as Feet.

"What do these require?" He lifted up a pair of black five-inch stilettos while his cock began to stir like a reptile disturbed from hibernation.

"I want them accessorized," the woman said.

"Accessorized?"

"The sign outside says you do that. You know, black bows, sequins. I was thinking of a design in seed pearls for these ivory ones. I own Jules' Dance Studio," she added. "My shoes must always have that extra touch of glamour."

"You're Jules?"

She must have known what he wanted to ask, because she said, without any rancor at all, "I gave up dancing years ago, but I still attend all the studio galas and the monthly showcase."

Theo lifted up an ostrich-skin pump with a heel thin as the stem of a champagne glass. He'd never seen heels this high outside of catalogs for leather fetishists. He couldn't even imagine how such shoes supported a woman of Jules's weight—her heels must leave a trail of puncture marks in every floor and carpet she traversed.

"These need to be resoled," he said. "Look here, they're wearing down."

"I've only worn those once but—I guess I do wear heels down fast."

She pushed back blond hair that was threatening to tumble into one eye. Her wrist was slender, her mannerisms girlish. Theo could see her meticulously drawn-in eyebrows and the line of demarcation where the peach blusher ended against a paler patch of skin along her cheekbone.

"These'll be ready Thursday," he said, handing Jules a claim slip.

"Thanks."

"Oh, ma'am?"

She turned. "Hope you don't mind my saying this, but that blouse is really great. Nothing quite as pretty as a blond wearing red."

There was a moment when Theo feared he had miscalculated, that she might be so accustomed to male rejection that she'd take his words as sarcasm, but then she smiled, a lush smile, crimson and kissable, before tottering out the door on her five-inch spikes.

Christ.

Theo couldn't get Jules's feet off his mind. Nor did he try too hard, because he now had in his possession, until Thursday, three pairs of her shoes. Each pair more sexually charged, more outrageously erotic than the next. He sneaked a pair of her shoes home and made love to them wearing a condom, because he knew he couldn't control himself. By Thursday, the head of his scraped and battered cock felt as pointy as the inside of Jules's pumps.

The problem, though, as Theo saw it, was that Jules might take time. He'd have to proceed slowly. He couldn't just jump in the way he had with number five, who basically had been a slut with a serious drinking problem, he now realized.

The papers had reported the murder of stripper Felicia Lopeno a few days earlier. Several neighbors were quoted as saying she was a quiet young woman who kept to herself, which, Theo observed, was virtually the same thing the neighbors of his previous victims had said. No mention was made of the missing toe, although one paper did hint of mutilation. A day later, though, a sixteen-year-old crack addict blugeoned his father to death with a tire iron, making Felicia's murder pall into the category of merely humdrum carnage.

He decided to stay in Fort Lauderdale long enough to take a trophy from Jules.

Theo knew about big women who went on shoe-buying sprees because footwear was the only part of their apparel that stayed a constant size. Jules seemed to be this type. She came in often, bringing in shoes made of exotic leathers with towering harlot spikes, most of them with heels worn down from supporting her great bulk. Each time, Theo tried to find something about her appearance to compliment. Surprisingly that wasn't difficult. Since his only interest in Jules was her feet, he didn't really see her size as a disadvantage. It was hard for him to understand, in fact, how some men might be repelled by such corpulence, an excess of breast and thigh and calf that decades of centerfolds with twenty-four-inch waists had rendered repulsive to the collective male imagination. What did inches matter, when Jules had lovely petite feet and wore drop-dead sexy shoes?

After a few conversations with her, Theo concluded that Jules was a caring yet clearly lonely woman. He decided he must make her pity him.

The next time she came in the store, he confessed to her his great and secret shame. It was so humiliating, but—maybe she would understand.

"I always wanted to dance, you know, but—I was such a klutz in high school. People laughed when I walked onto the floor. I've never had the nerve to try again."

The disclosure seemed to act on her emotions like meat tenderizer. Tears glimmered in her blue eyes. Here was someone to lick her wounds with, Theo imagined she was thinking, and perhaps her pussy, too, though that thought did repulse him.

"Lots of people are afraid to dance. You just need lessons."

"You'd teach me?"

"Oh, no." The blush extended to the roots of her frosted hair. "I don't dance anymore."

"You used to, though."

"Yes. I was very good."

"What about a private lesson?"

But Jules only laughed, gave him two pairs of shoes to be resoled, and sashayed out of the store, leaving Theo to curse himself for his impatience.

That night, Theo spent another evening in worship of Jules's shoe, caressing, sniffing, fondling, imagining the slope and curve of her dainty foot inside.

Afterwards, he fell asleep with the fetish object pressed against his belly. Perversely, though, when he should have been dreaming happily of Jules, sleep brought instead a banshee reeking of Chanel, her crimson nails raking his vulnerable genitals, screams flaying the small boy like a raptor's talons.

The nightmare blossomed into three dimensions while the witch-mother howled in his head like an air raid warning. He was fleeing on his hands and knees now, scuttling over floorboards, his shoulder banging into something sharp—the corner of a table—then fragrant dark and silence and the touch of velvet and leather, a sensation that, for another man, might have been tantamount to lounging in a seraglio with naked odalisques, all willing, mute, and mindlessly compliant.

In the morning, he was not surprised to find himself inside the closet, legs stiff and cramping, belly crusted from last night's passion.

It was passion, he remembered, the furtive lust for his own boy-flesh that had caused his mother to punish him the first time.

She used to lock him in her bedroom closet for hours, turning up the volume on the TV set when he screamed, but it was there among her shoes that he had learned to get relief, that all the raging vigor of his sexuality had found a focus. Shoes were so possessable, so easily acquired, yet they evoked the smell and image of those rarer objects they enclosed. Theo lay back and closed his eyes, reached for his fetish necklace.

The four toes, like little fetuses, wiggled gently.

The breakthrough came on Friday. Jules dropped by the store looking depressed and puffy-eyed—she hadn't slept well lately, she explained vaguely—and agreed to meet Theo for a drink at Poet's when he got off work. The trendy Las Olas bar was packed with yuppies guzzling happy-hour drinks, but Jules sat at a table in the corner, eating a banana split, when Theo finally found her. She saw the look on his face and laughed. "I'm probably the only fat woman in the world who isn't pretending to be on a diet. I like my size. I miss dancing, but I prefer being fat."

"I like your size, too," Theo said. "I'm still hoping I can talk you into that private dance lesson."

Jules's laughter was high and fluty, full of mirth.

"Why, Theo, I'm beginning to think you're not shy at all."

"Maybe just at dancing." He took her hand and slid one finger into his mouth, sucking off the sticky film of chocolate syrup.

The look on Jules's face told him she was almost as aroused as if he'd slid beneath the table to eat her pussy.

Jules's condo on Galt Ocean Mile turned out to be as spacious and flashy as she was. The bedroom was decorated entirely in pink and royal purple, the living room done in black and gold with one wall mirrored floor to ceiling. The place resembled Theo's fantasy of a brothel for Kuwaiti sheiks, except he'd never been in anything except seedy massage parlors.

On an end table, he noticed a photo of a slender blond in a fuchsia dress being spun above the head of her male partner. Her arms were up and back; she looked like some exotic bird that would be hunted for its plumage.

He picked up the photo. "Wow."

"That was six years and a hundred and fifty pounds ago," said Jules.

She showed him her bookcase full of trophies, silver cups and plaques and ribbons, pedestals topped with figures of dancing couples.

"I was one of the rising ballroom stars, competing my way into the international scene." She sighed almost inaudibly. Her breath came faster, and Theo slid his arm around her shoulder, contemplating her pink and meaty throat.

Suddenly, though, he wanted to *know*. Before he killed her, he had to satisfy his curiosity. She'd been a champion dancer—why would she have let herself become obese?

Jules didn't seem offended by the question. She seemed, in fact, grateful that he'd asked.

"I was dancing at the Southeastern Ballroom Competition in New Orleans, and I was supposed to join some friends for dinner. The restaurant was just a block away, so I walked. A van pulled up. Two men. One dragged me into the back, the other drove. They drove around all night, taking turns, and when the one raping me fell asleep, I jumped out and ran.

"I was wearing a skimpy dance dress and theatrical makeup. The cops acted like I'd asked for it, like if I'd been dressed in something ugly and baggy the men wouldn't have picked me to rape.

"I'd always kept my weight down. After that, I wanted to be big, to keep men away from me. I was right, too. Men never look at me now, except to make fat lady jokes. I don't turn anybody on, so I'm safe. You're the first man who's noticed me in I don't know how long."

He felt awkward now because her story had given him a throbbing hard-on, thinking about what he would have done to her in that van, and he turned his back and pretended to peruse some dance magazines on the coffee table.

"After what happened, I guess you must hate men," he said— just as something crashed against his temple with a sound like a bowling ball scoring a strike inside his skull. The room upended. He felt like a skydiver whose chute hadn't opened.

Just before a second blow ignited an agony of twinkling neon, he heard Jules say, "No, I don't hate men. Just you."

Locked in his mother's closet after a beating. That was his first thought. Darkness, the pain blasting him like buckshot. He must be hurt bad, too, because he couldn't move. Then he opened his eyes and saw a mirrored wall and felt the shag carpet his bloody head was stuck to, and all he could think at first was, *I've been bad. I've been bad again with Mother's shoes.*

He lay on his back next to the gore-smeared dance trophy she'd bludgeoned him with, his wrists and ankles bound with wire that bit into the flesh when he squirmed. He was naked, quaking convulsively with pain and fear. In the mirror, his trussed body looked pathetic, his penis draped across his thigh like a pallid slug. He felt ashamed. He wanted to be someplace dark and silent, someplace no one could see him.

"I once had a pair of burgundy pumps," said Jules from somewhere behind him. "I asked my lover to have the heels repaired, like she'd had some others done for me. But the guy at the shoe repair shop stole my shoes. Worse than that, he stole my lover. Then he killed her."

"You're crazy," Theo said. "You don't know what you're saying."

"I saw Felicia bring you home with her the night she died. I suspected she was cheating on me, and I wanted to be sure. I figured you were fucking her; I didn't know you'd kill her. I could've gone to the police with your description and license number, but for what? Felicia was an alkie stripper. I'm a dyke. I doubt the case would have gotten top priority. And anyway, the way I see it is, Felicia died so I could punish you. I've had six years to plan this. It's what I'm going to do if I ever find the men who had me in that van."

Theo began to scream.

Immediately ballroom music, a lush Strauss waltz, crescendoed through the condo.

"My neighbors work nights," Jules said. "The old lady down below is deaf."

She turned the volume higher. Moved out where Theo could see her in the mirror.

Jules was naked.

Almost.

On her feet Jules wore black sequined pumps with five-inch heels. Above that, her lush flesh rippled in glorious abundance.

Placing one hand against the wall for balance, she walked toward Theo.

Onto Theo.

Bore down.

Her heels stabbed gut and penile shaft and liver. Then onto his spleen, which made a muffled farting sound when her right heel punctured it.

Onto his chest and Adam's apple, cutting short the thrashing and the screams. His left eye she ground out like a cigarette. The other one she spared so he could watch.

"I've got all night," Jules whispered.

She started walking back.

Brian De Palma: The Movie Brute

MARTIN AMIS

I first met MARTIN AMIS in Houston, Texas, while I was acting as computer graphics supervisor/unit publicist on RoboCop 2. *Martin was visiting the set as a journalist for* Premiere *magazine. To my great surprise, we got along famously.*

I use the word "surprise" because this friendly, charming young writer wasn't at all what I'd come to expect.

You see, Amis has a forbidding reputation. Widely regarded as Britain's reigning literary smartass, Martin's a respected serious author whose stinging, surgically precise wit is just as renowned as his work.

This includes prickly novels like The Rachel Papers, Time's Arrow, Dead Babies, Money, *and* London Fields *(a recent bestseller). Said novels are usually nasty black comedies, blisteringly mordant critiques featuring idiosyncratic young antiheroes with a horror of the sham and pretension riddling contemporary England. They are also very hip books, plugged in to modern culture. Beautifully crafted. Lucid and penetrating. Unafraid to portray the occasionally outrageous scene of sex, drugs, or violence. Traits which prompted* The New Statesman *to describe Amis's distinctively sarcastic voice as "somewhere between T.S. Eliot and a pop video."*

Or, to put it another way, as a splatterpunk. A formidably talented splatterpunk.

So it was something of a relief to discover that this celebrated wiseacre was actually a polite pussycat. One who genuinely seemed to enjoy hanging out as we endlessly discussed films, politics, and literature. Talks which uncovered this eccentric footnote to Martin's brief acting career:

"I have a small part in the 1965 film A High Wind in Jamaica,*"*

*Amis explains, "but all my lines were later redubbed by an elderly
female performer. The producers, to their great horror, realized
they'd hired a teenage actor whose voice had changed midway
through production."*

*Which will have to serve as a sloppy segue to the following,
typically skeptical Amis interview with filmmaker Brian De
Palma.*

*De Palma's long been a problematic director. Undeniably tal-
ented, I nevertheless find him (with the distinct exceptions of
his* Casualties of War *and* Phantom of the Paradise*) to be cold,
misogynistic, and overpraised. A technical show-off who's hollow
at heart. Yet this opinion is apparently a minority one; De Palma's
a splatterpunk icon, especially for such over-the-toppers as* Carrie
and Dressed to Kill.

*How refreshing, then, to discover that Martin Amis feels the
same way I do.*

"Brian De Palma: The Movie Brute" was collected in The Moronic Inferno, *Amis's ironic 1987 nonfiction survey of America's
cultural landscape. However, this interview actually first saw
print in* Vanity Fair *magazine, which severely edited the piece.*

*We now present the uncensored version. One I hope you will
enjoy.*

*Just as I enjoyed Martin's saucer-eyed expression, the night we
both found ourselves in that Texas titty bar ...*

*B*urbank Studios, Sound Stage 16. In silent hommage to Hitchcock, perhaps, Brian De Palma's belly swells formidably over the
waistband of his safari suit ... So, at any rate, I had thought of
beginning this profile of the light-fingered, flash-trash movie brute,
director of *Carrie, Dressed to Kill, Scarface*—and *Body Double.* But
that was before I had been exposed to De Palma's obscure though
unmistakable charm: three weeks, twenty telephone calls, and a few
thousand miles later. "I know you've come all the way from London,
and I know Brian promised to see you while you were in LA," his
PA told me at the entrance to the lot. "Well, he's *rescinded* on that,"
she said, and laughed with musical significance. This significant
laughter told me three things: one, that she was scandalized by his
behavior; two, that he did it all the time; and three, that I wasn't to

take him seriously, because no one else did. I laughed too. I had never met a real-life moody genius before; and they *are* very funny.

So let's start again. Brian De Palma sits slumped on his director's chair, down at Burbank, in boiling Los Angeles. It is "wrap" day on *Body Double*, his pornographic new thriller: only two climatic scenes remain to be shot. "Put the chest back on," De Palma tells the villain, played by Gregg Henry. "Okay. New chest! New belly!" This means another forty-minute delay. De Palma gets to his feet and wanders heavily round the set. He is indeed rather tubby now, the back resting burdensomely on the buttocks, and he walks with an effortful, cross-footed gait. "Hitchcock was sixty when he made *Psycho*," De Palma would later tell me. "I don't know if I'll be able to *walk* when I'm sixty." A curious remark—but then Brian is not a good walker, even now, at forty-four; he is not a talented walker. He walks as if he is concentrating very hard on what he has in his pockets.

I approached the sinister Gregg Henry and asked him about the scene they were shooting. It sounded like standard De Palma: "I throttle Craig Wasson to the ground or whatever. I jump out of the grave. I rip off my false belly." The false belly is part of Gregg's disguise, along with the rug, the redskin facial pancake, and the Meccano dentures. As in *Dressed to Kill*, a goody turns out to be a baddy, in disguise. It takes a headlining makeup veteran three and a half hours to get Gregg looking as sinister as this. Presumably it takes the baddy in the film even longer—but this is a De Palma picture, where gross insults to plausibility are routine. The second shot involves an elaborate false-perspective prop (to dramatize the hero's claustrophobia as he is buried alive), like the staircase scene in *Vertigo*. The camera will wobble. "With luck, you'll feel sick," says the amiable first assistant. *Body Double* has gone pretty smoothly, within schedule and under budget. The only real hitch was a "hair problem" with Melanie Griffith. She spent two weeks under the drier and over the sink. "We tried brown, red, platinum—until we got what Brian wanted."

Suddenly—that is to say, after a fifteen-minute yelling delay—the shot is ready to go again. De Palma talks to no one but the camera operator. "Why don't you pull back a bit? Why don't you try to hold him from head to foot?" All his instructions are in this dogged rhetorical style. Action. Gregg Henry and Craig Wasson perform creditably ("Oh, *man,*" says Gregg, peeling off his false belly, "you ruined my whole surprise ending"), but De Palma is unhappy about the camera's swooning backtrack. He should have been unhappy about his surprise ending, which doesn't work "New belly," says Brian, and the delay resumes. A series of delays interrupted by repetitions: that's motion pictures.

De Palma went trudge-about "I think this would be a good time for you to be introduced to Brian," said Rob, the unit publicist— also likable "He's in a receptive mood."

"Are you sure?"

"Yes. Very receptive."

We walked over. I was introduced. De Palma wearily offered his hand. Rob explained who I was. "Uh," said De Palma, and turned away.

"Is that as good as it gets?" I asked as we walked off.

"See him in New York," said Rob. "He'll be better, when he's wrapped."

And so an hour or two later I left him in the lot, which was still doing its imitation of Hell. Gaunt ladies lurk near the catering caravan. Fat minders or shifters or teamsters called Buck and Flip and Heck move stoically about. The place is big and dark and hot, swathed in black drapes, vulcanic, loud with vile engines, horrid buzzers, expert noisemakers. Nearly all the time absolutely nothing is happening. Eight hours later, at midnight, De Palma wrapped.

As a filmmaker, Brian De Palma knows exactly what he wants. Unlike his peers and pals, Spielberg, Lucas, Coppola, and Scorsese (they all teamed up at Warner Brothers in the early seventies), De Palma doesn't shoot miles of footage and then redesign the movie in the editing room. His rough cuts are usually shorter than the finished film. Every scene is meticulously story-boarded, every pan and zoom, every camera angle. Here's a sample on-set interview:

So, Brian, before you make a movie, do you see the whole thing in your head?

Yes.

Do you have problems re-creating the movie you see?

No.

How does the actual movie measure up to what you originally imagined?

It measures up.

He seldom advises or encourages his actors. Michael Caine has said that the highest praise you'll hear from De Palma is "Print." As a filmmaker, Brian De Palma knows exactly what he wants. The only question is: why does he want it?

Always an ungainly cultural phenomenon, De Palma's reputation has never been more oddly poised. He likes to think of himself as over the top and beyond the pale, an iconoclast and controversialist, someone that people love to hate or hate to love—someone, above all, who cannot be *ignored*. In moments of excitement he will grandly refer to "whole schools of De Palma criticism" which say this, that, and the other about his work. Well, too many people have failed to ignore De Palma for us to start ignoring him now. But it may be that the only serious school of De Palma criticism is the one where all the classrooms are empty. Everyone is off playing hookey. They're all busy ignoring him.

De Palma's history forms a promising confection, full of quirkiness and mild exoticism. His parents were both Italian Catholics yet little Brian was reared as a Presbyterian. The Catholic imagery was naturally the more tenacious for the young artist ("that is one spooky religion") and its themes and forms linger in his work: the diabolism, the ritualized but arbitrary moral schemes, the guilt. De Palma Senior was a surgeon—orthopedics, the correction of deformity. Brian used to sit in on operations, often catching a skin graft or a bone transplant, and would later do vacation jobs in medical laboratories. "I have a high tolerance for blood," he says. The cast of *The Fury* (1978) nicknamed him Brian De Plasma. On the set his most frequent remarks are "Action," "Print," and "More blood!" De Palma was tempted by medicine but rejected the discipline as "not precise enough."

He used to be keen on precision, and still sees his work in terms of "precise visual storytelling," streamlined and dynamic, all pincer grips and rapier thrusts. In fact, "precision" in De Palma is entirely a matter of sharp surfaces and smooth assembly; within, all is smudge and fudge, woolliness, approximation. The young Brian was also something of a physics prodigy and computer whiz. At a National Science Fair competition he took second prize for his critical study of hydrogen quantum mechanics through cybernetics. (This is impressive, all right. *You* try it.) One imagines the teenage De Palma as owlish, bespectacled, and solitary, like the kid in *Dressed to Kill*. That solitude is still with him, I would say. Then at university the brainy loner changed tack, selling his homemade computers for a Bolex film camera, "trading one obsession for another."

Born in Newark, raised in Philadelphia, a student of physics at Columbia and of drama at Sarah Lawrence College, Bronxville, De Palma is solidly East Coast in his origins, urban, radical, antiestablishment, anti-Hollywood. He admired Godard, Polanski, and of course Hitchcock, but he entered the industry from left field: via the TV-dominated world of documentary and vérité, low-budget satire and chaotic improvisation, war protest and sexual daring—a product of the sixties, that golden age of high energy and low art. It must be said that of all De Palma's early work, from *Greetings* in 1968 to *Phantom of the Paradise* in 1974, nothing survives. These films are now no more than memories of art-house late nights, student screenings, left-wing laughter, and radical applause. De Palma's first visit to Hollywood, for *Get to Know Your Rabbit*, was a disaster movie in itself. His authority attacked, his star out of control, De Palma "quit" the picture two weeks before its completion—as he would later quit *Prince of the City* and *Flashdance*. The film was shelved for two years. On his own admission De Palma was suddenly "dead" in Los Angeles, where the locals are superstitious about failure; they quarantine you, in case failure is catching. No one returned his calls. They crossed the street to avoid him. "People think—what has he *got* in that can?" In any event, *Rabbit* was a dog. Furtively released in 1974 as a B-feature, it interred itself within a week.

Then two years later along came *Carrie*, far and away De Palma's most successful film, in all senses. By now Brian's contemporaries, his Warner brothers, were all drowning in riches and esteem, and he was "more than ready" for a smash of his own "I pleaded, *pleaded* to do *Carrie*." And so began De Palma's assimilation into the Hollywood machine, his extended stay in "the land of the devil." The sixties radical package was merely the set of values that got to him first, and he had wearied of a "revolution" he found ever more commercialized. De Palma now wanted the other kind of independence, the "dignity" that comes from power and success within the establishment. He is honest—or at any rate brazen—about the reversal. "I too became a capitalist," he has said. "By even dealing with the devil you become devilish. There's no clean money. There I was, worrying about *Carrie* not doing forty million. That's how deranged your perspectives get." Nowadays his politics are cautious and pragmatic: "capitalism tempered by compassion, do unto others—stuff like that." The liberal minimum. His later films do sometimes deal in political questions of the Watergate-buff variety, but the slant is personal, prankish, paranoid—De Palmaesque. All that remains of the sixties guerrilla is an unquenchable taste for anarchy: moral anarchy, artistic anarchy.

What use has he made of his freedom? What exactly are we looking at here? "Mature" De Palma consists of *Dressed to Kill*, *Blowout*, and now *Body Double*. These are the medium-budget films which De Palma conceived, wrote, directed, and cut. (*The Fury* and *Scarface* we can set aside as fancy-priced hackwork, while *Home Movies*, a shoestring project put together at Sarah Lawrence and released in 1980, is already a vanished curiosity.) De Palma's three main credits, or debits, reveal his cinematic vision, unfettered by any constraints other than those imposed by the censors. They also show how blinkered, intransigent, and marginal that vision really is. Such unedifying fixity has no equivalent in mainstream cinema, and none in literature, except perhaps Céline, or William Burroughs—or Kathy Acker.

Each installment in the De Palma trilogy concerns itself with a man who goes about the place cutting up women: straight razor, chisel, power drill. The women are either prostitutes, sexual adventuresses, or adult-movie queens. There is no conventional sex whatever in De Palma's movies: it is always a function of money, violence, or defilement, glimpsed at a voyeuristic remove or through a pornographic sheen (and this interest in flash and peep goes right back to *Greetings*). The heroes are childish or ineffectual figures, helpless in the face of the villain's superior human energies. There are no plots: the narratives themselves submit to a psychopathic rationale, and are littered with coincidence, blind spots, black holes. Like its predecessors, *Body Double* could be exploded by a telephone call, by a pertinent question, by five minutes' thought. Most candidly of all, De Palma dispenses with the humanistic ensemble of character, motive, development, and resolution. He tries his best, but people bore him, and that's that.

Brian has something, though. Without it, he would be indistinguishable from the gory hucksters of the exploitation circuit, the slashers and manglers, the Movie Morons who gave us *The Evil Dead*, *Prom Night*, and *I Spit on Your Grave*. Brian has style—a rare and volatile commodity. Style will always convince cinematic purists that the surfaces they admire contain depth, and that clear shortcomings are really subtle virtues in disguise. De Palma isn't logical, so he must be impressionistic. He isn't realistic, so he must be surrealistic. He isn't scrupulous, so he must be audacious. He isn't earnest, so he must be ironical. He isn't funny, so he must be *serious*.

And so I hung around in damp New York, waiting on the man. Every now and then De Palma's "people" at Columbia would apologetically pass on the odd message: "Brian's probably going to decide tomorrow whether he'll let you have this interview . . ." I had urgent reasons for returning to London. A week passed. Now, there is no reason why celebrities should submit to journalistic inspection, and in fact they are increasingly reluctant to do so—except in the trash press, where publicity is always tilted towards celebration. But having agreed to an interview, they should play by the rules, which are rules of ordinary etiquette: do unto others—stuff like that. A week passed. And then Brian came down from the mountain.

"Mr. De Palma? He's right over there," said the porter down in lower Fifth Avenue. Brian sat ponderously on a bench by the lift with a newspaper under his arm. Always keen to stay in touch with "street reality," De Palma had just staggered out for a *New York Times*. "Hi," I said, and reintroduced myself. De Palma nodded at the floor. "It's kind of you to give me your time." De Palma shrugged helplessly—yes, what a bountiful old softie he was. In eerie silence we rode the swaying lift.

"Coffee?" he sighed. With studied gracelessness he shuffled around his four-room office—televisions, hi-fis, a pinball machine, De Palma film posters, curved white tables, orderly work-surfaces.

This was where Brian did all his writing and conceiving. Wordlessly he gave me my coffee mug and sloped off to take a few telephone calls. At last he levered himself in behind the desk, his nostrils flaring with a suppressed yawn, and waved a limp hand at me. The interview began. *Great*, I thought, after ten minutes. *He really is bananas. This is going like a dream.*

"My films are so filmically astute that people think I'm not good with actors. Actors trust me and my judgment because I'm so up front about what I feel ... I don't make 'aggressive' use of the camera. I make the *right* use. I go with my instinct ... I use Hitchcock's grammar but I have a romantic vision that's more sweeping and Wagnerian ... I have a tremendous amount of experience. I'm not afraid to try new things ... Financially in Hollywood I'm a sound economic given. Three-quarters of my films have made money. Anybody who can make *one* film that makes money is a genius!"

"Casting all modesty aside," I said, fondling my biro, "where would you place yourself among your contemporaries—Coppola, Scorsese?"

"Oh, I don't know. I'm up there, I guess. Time ..." he said, and paused. De Palma is generally tentative about time—aware, perhaps, of what time has already done to much of his *oeuvre*. "Let's face up to it! I'm never going to get a lifetime-achievement award. I never bought those values anyway. In ten years hence they ... I don't know. Time will find a place for me."

On this note of caution, Brian unwound. His mood of frenzied self-advertisement receded, alas, and I have to report that he then talked pretty soberly and fluently for well over an hour—bearish, grinning, gesturing, his laughter frayed by hidden wildness. Of course, the time to catch De Palma in full manic babble is when he is writhing under the tethers of a collaborative project, as on *Scarface*, or tangling with the censors, as he did on *Dressed to Kill*, which barely escaped an X. But he was relatively calm during our meeting, with *Body Double* in the can and another project nicely brewing: *Carpool*, in which he intends to indulge his fascination with rearview mirrors "Steven will produce," says Brian snugly. In January he had told *Esquire*: "As soon as I get this dignity from *Scarface* I am going to go out and make an X-rated suspense porn picture." Later he added, "If *Body Double* doesn't get an X, nothing I ever do is going to. I'm going to give them everything they hate, and more of it than they've ever seen." What major company, you wonder, would finance and distribute an X? I asked Brian about this. He grew sheepish. "No major company would finance or distribute it," he said. So it's an R. "Most frustrating," De Palma muses. "I mean, look at cable TV. Kids can watch anything these days."

Despite such checks and balances De Palma is quick to claim full responsibility for his projects. "It *is* an *auteur* situation out there. You guys, you writers, you got to stop thinking of directors as still living in the fifties. It's not an entrenched power system. There's a lot of free will. No one wants to confront you. No one wants to take responsibility. That's why directors are emergent figures. If the executives lean on you, you just have to say, "Okay, guys, *you* do it.' Either they let you alone, or it's 'Goodbye, Bri! Well, De Palma fucked up!' "

After a little coaxing, however, Brian confessed to moments of self-doubt. "It's an intolerable kind of regime. You wake up at four in the morning, thinking—Who *wants* it! Who *needs* it! It's all so com*plex*. It's like *Waiting for Godot* [this last word stressed oddly too, like *Gdansk*]. Then the rushes, the final mix—that's pleasure. I like to write. My own pace. I basically like to work by myself."

At this point I recalled the morose and taciturn figure at Burbank Studios, in LA. Among all the clamor and clatter, the compulsive wisecracking and bovine bonhomie, there was De Palma, doing as good an impersonation of a man alone as the circumstances could well permit. Occasionally, too, I thought I glimpsed the obsessive and abstracted kid in him, the bristle of a more rarefied talent. Human relations are always difficult for this kind of artist—messy, confusing, "not precise enough." De Palma has been married once, and briefly, to Nancy Allen, whom he had cast as a monosyllabic hooker in three movies running. Informed Hollywood gossip maintains that Nancy wanted a family, and Brian didn't. Well, he's batching it now. Asked why he always equates sex with terror, De Palma says equably, "Casual sex *is* terrifying. It's one of the few areas of terror still left to us." And this is why pornography interests him. It is casual, but safe. And it is solitary: nobody else need come in on the act.

The time had come for the crucial question, made more ticklish by the fact that De Palma's manner had softened—was bordering, indeed, on outright civility. One could now see traces of his man-

management skills, his knack with actors, how he calms and charms them into a confident partisanship. Despite De Palma's indifference to characterization, there are remarkably few bad performances in his films. "I always felt that Brian adored me," John Travolta has said. "He seemed to get pure joy out of watching me work." But perhaps Travolta feels that way about everybody. De Palma is best with the stock types of lowbrow fiction, as in *Carrie*. Elsewhere, he is about as penetrating as the studio makeup girl. Even with an award-winning writer (Oliver Stone), an award-winning star (Al Pacino), and an unlimited canvas ($22 million and three hours plus of screen time), De Palma showed no inkling of human complexity: *Scarface* might as well have been called *Shitface* for all the subtlety he applied to the monotonous turpitude of Tony Montana.

Girding myself, I asked De Palma why his films made no sense. He bounced back with some eagerness, explaining that Hitchcock was illogical too and that, besides, *life* didn't make any sense either. "Hitchcock did it all the time! Didn't anyone look at the corpse in *Vertigo*? In *Blowout* the illogic was immense—but it was in Watergate too! I'm not interested in being Agatha Christie! Life is *not* like a crossword puzzle! I trust my instinct and emotion! I go with *that!*"

Brian De Palma once described, with typical recklessness, his notion of an ideal viewership: "I like a real street audience—people who talk during and *at* a movie, a very unsophisticated Forty-second Street crowd." He is right to think that he has an affinity with these cineasts, who have trouble distinguishing filmic life from the real thing. De Palma movies depend, not on a suspension of disbelief, but on a suspension of intelligence such as the Forty-second Street crowd have already made before they come jabbering into the stalls. Quite simply, you cannot watch his films twice. Reinspect them on video (on the small screen with the lights up, with the sharply reduced *affect*) and they disintegrate into strident chaos. Niggling doubts become farcical certainties. Where? When? How? Why? There's hardly a *sequitur* in sight.

The illogicality, the reality-blurring, the media-borne cretinization of modern life is indeed a great theme, and all De Palma's major contemporaries are on to it. De Palma is on to it too, but in a different way. He abets and exemplifies it, passively. In the conception of his films De Palma has half a dozen big scenes that he knows how to shoot. How he gets from one to the other is a matter of indifference. On some level he realizes that the ignorant will not care or notice, and that the overinformed will mistake his wantonness for something else.

De Palma is regarded as an intellectual. Now it clearly isn't hard to come by such a reputation in the film world, particularly among the present generation of moviemakers. Spielberg, the most popular, is bright and articulate; but his idea of intellection is to skip an hour's TV. And Scorsese, the most brilliant (and the most prescient), is a giggling mute. De Palma isn't an intellectual, though his films, like his conversation, have a patina of smartness. He isn't a cynic either, nor is he the cheerful charlatan I had geared myself to expect. Is he a "master" (as critics on both sides of the Atlantic claim), or is he a moron? He has no middlebrow following: his fans are to be found either in the street or in the screening-room. Occupying an area rich in double-think, De Palma is simply the innocent beneficiary of a cultural joke. It *is* an achievement of a kind, to fashion an art that appeals to the purist, the hooligan, and nobody else.

I Walk Alone

ROBERTA LANNES

ROBERTA LANNES wrote this to me a few years ago:

"I choose to use extremes when they can push a story into the fully sensual, the experiential realm. To create a power in my work that only personal experience could otherwise invoke."

Anyone who's encountered the classically extreme "Goodbye, Dark Love" (an explicit tale of incest and necrophilia found in Splatterpunks I*) will know exactly what Roberta is talking about. Those who haven't, will; "I Walk Alone" is surely among the more sensual, experiential offerings in this book.*

Lannes's short work has appeared in the anthologies Alien Sex *and* Cutting Edge, *plus such magazines as* Iniquities. *Prior to her genre sales, Roberta published in literary reviews and specialty-press poetry anthologies. Personally she's a stylish, intelligent woman who also teaches. Professionally, she's something of an object of devotion; Lannes's work is usually ranked right up there alongside such critical favorites as Kathe Koja and Poppy Z. Brite.*

"I Walk Alone" was originally published in Still Dead, *Skipp and Spector's worthwhile follow-up to their equally fine* Book of the Dead. *Both of these anthologies feature a print continuation of the zombie mythos first propounded by George A. Romero's* Night of the Living Dead.

But that's just a framework. The gimmick. The true worth of the Skipp and Spector books is how they've made contributors realize that Romero's zombie mythology is so much more than explicit flesh-eating ghoulishness.

Because, in the land of the living dead, potent metaphors reside within every corpse.

No one's had to point this out to Roberta Lannes, though.

*One final comment: I do not ever want to make this woman
angry with me. Inadvertently or otherwise.
After this "Walk" you'll see why.*

You're dead. Slow-rotting in the corner of our basement. I sit here
and look at your mummy-wrapped body, your head emerging from
the cellophane and graying pink bed sheets like a dusty bee from a
pale rose, and weep. I've been walking dead on the streets of Manhattan with nary an emotion for over a year. Now that I can feel, I
would wish for joy or gladness, but at the moment I'll take sorrow.
Any emotion at all.

I would have come down here sooner, but for the four months
you've been locked up, hidden down here, my existence has gone
from a zombie kind of hell to walking-dead splendor. If you'd been
alive down here all of this time, you would have gone insane without
your "things to do." That endless litany of exigencies; "needing to
do this, having to do that." What a relief it's been to know you've
just been fucking sitting still all this time and not have to hear
about it.

Keeping you fresh like this was a good idea. One of the half-
dead I've been hanging with, a gourmet chef from Balducci's, told
me that it would preserve you, just in case you came back, sort of.
If any of the "usual" types found you, they would have made off
with you long ago. That's why I covered you with all that junk we
had down here. Even with all the contempt I've found that I have
for you, I still feel committed to you. To your best. To keeping you
close. To an *us*. Love binds even in death.

There's so much to tell you. When you were last alive and we
were still upstairs in number 9, you were scared to death to venture
out, and thoroughly disgusted by my state of decay. That didn't
bode well for the relationship. As I recall, I was too physically cold
and emotionally unresponsive to fuck, and I'd lost my voluptuous-
ness and copper-toned skin to the lean and pale. I didn't know then
what I know now. I look good for being half-dead.

All the time and effort I put into keeping my California-girl
appearance and radiant health before the scourge paid off. Yes. You
thought it was vainglorious and a waste of time. Turns out, the way

one ends up after death is determined by the lifestyle one led prior. The nutritionist, acupuncturist, herbalist, masseuse, personal trainer, detoxing, infusions of BHT and other preservatives with my vitamin supplements, plus the hours getting facials, wraps, and moisturizing gave me the essential foundation for a healthy half-life. I'm not like the usuals with their graying skin, expressionless faces, stiff, ambling bulk, indiscriminately flesh-eating like crazed piranhas, their fingers and arms and ears falling off, groaning incoherently, lost in their pure instinctual being. I'm sort of an elite type.

I can hear you laughing, you bastard. You'd say it sounds snobbish and silly. But fuck it, you're lying there like a piece of beef Wellington, and I'm feeling damned lucky. I'm out there doing things. See, as a zombie, my blood runs like sap, everything is slowed down, except my thinking. Well, even if my mind is plodding, my awareness of it seems to be equally paced and nothing seems different. The only things that come and go are my appetite, my compulsiveness, and my sex drive. My feelings died with me when I killed myself. Or so I thought. Enough stimulus, and the feelings respond. Unfortunately, uncontrollably so.

Agh, here comes the loneliness . . . agony for me sitting here looking at you. You useless fuck! Sorry, it's like this. One second I'm giddy, the next murderously mad. . . .

There are others like me. I found them two days after you died. I wandered over to SoHo one evening. It was during the spring thaw and the usuals were roaming the streets like cockroaches. I noticed a taxi on Houston, turning up Greene. The only vehicles still moving are driven by live ones, so I followed.

Up in a loft that had been left in midrenovation, there was a party going on. I had dressed well and evidently looked as alive as I thought I did, because I was let in without question. There were thirty, forty people there, alive as you and I once were, or so I'd thought.

I was welcomed by a handsome couple. The Doctor, One-Eye, and his girlfriend, Rula.

"You're one of us, aren't you?" He stroked the patch over his missing eye.

"One of us?" My voice is more gravelly than it was before, but very sexy, I'm told.

"*Us*. The not-quite-wholly-dead, zombilina. Fucking purgatory-ette time, dear. Dead, but a hell of a lot better off than the stiffs on the street." He was smug. I didn't think I liked him. Rula hung on him like sweat.

"Do I look dead?" Maybe he was testing me. I'd fooled so many for so long—been chased as live meat by the usuals. I didn't even believe *he* was dead.

"Not so that it's obvious. But I can tell. Took good care of yourself before you went, am I right? Like the rest of us ..." He gestured toward the crowd milling around tables of human delicacies.

"I tried." My appetite was returning.

"How'd you go, suicide? Drugs? You've got that fragile but angry look. And it's not local. You're not a New Yorker, are you?"

Without feelings then, I couldn't loathe him or get indignant at the pushy, ingratiating way he came on. But if I could, I would have.

"California-bred, transplanted for love. Died for it. And you ... I'd guess uptown plastic surgeon, hooked on Xanax, who couldn't stand the thought of eating on and disfiguring the former palette of his work and took his own life?"

He snarled, frowning. "Oooh, you're good. Done this long?" He turned on his heels and left without my answer. Having been a psychologist, I had an edge at determining the less discernible attributes of others. Too, I detected a distinct surge of emotions and got curious.

I stuffed myself with hors d'oeuvres, marveling at the taste of well-prepared human flesh, and gravitated over to the man of the evening, one Sammy Gagliano. He had six gorgeous women around him. He acknowledged me with a wink and a compliment. You'd be proud.

"A blonde! Get over here, beautiful. I need one more adoring girl for my entourage."

I told him, "I'm flattered."

"There isn't much beauty left in this fucking world, but what there is, I want around me, get it?" He grinned. He had a gold tooth. I took him for a drug dealer or a pimp. "So what's your name?"

"Katy. I live in the Village. Tenth Street and Sixth Avenue."

Everyone chuckled. Sammy stood up and reached out a hand.

"Great joke. 'I *live* in the Village.' Well, Katy, welcome. Anybody who looks as good as you has to be part of this thing."

That's how it started. Into the wee hours of the morning we each told stories. I seemed to be the only one there without feelings and my humor was strained, but I told them about you, me. I said we met in California at a party. You were instantly impressed. I was married. Three months later you were sending me a ticket to come to New York as my marriage crumbled. I was sure to tell them the marriage was dead long before. It was passion and romance from the moment I got off the plane, until you ingratiated yourself into my life on the West Coast two months later. I never asked you to come. You moving in, even though I objected, felt like rape. But I didn't tell them that. They wanted to hear the romantic drama. So I told them how, over the next six months, you used hysterical tantrums, suicide threats, and every romantic trick in the book to sway me. And it worked, you fucking pig!

In these bursts of anger, I can see what an utter, unredeemable psychopath you were. Why, when I recall the moments of sweetness, do I imagine you were sane?

I spared no detail in my tale when it came to your ultimatum that I move to Manhattan or we end the relationship, my moving here, and your subsequent emotional abandonment. Everyone "tsked" and shook their heads. I felt nothing. The end, when I explained how I woke up, realized I'd been fooled and found myself estranged in a bizarre and hostile city, then killed myself, garnered applause. It was mystifying.

"How is it you all seem to *feel* things? I haven't got an emotion. Not one." I looked around at them, stoically.

Rula sat pretzeled with Sammy, licking his ear and purring. He shivered. "Well, when you have a half-life full of maximum stimulation, your feelings get cranked. Maxing-out, it's good stuff."

"I miss my feelings. I think about how I would feel, but ..." I shrugged.

"Hey, let's show Katy how we get off, huh?" Sammy gathered everyone together and we filed downstairs.

Oh, no. I'm weeping again. The pain, surging on me now like raging PMS, clenching my gut and bleeding me dry of tears. How I missed them. Like torture now, in the most ironic sense. But there they are. Damn.

If I thought New York was a war zone before this plague, I got to see guerrilla tactics up close that night. For them, a typical evening out "maxing" involves an abundance of activities. The women, as sexist as it seems, act as bait for the usuals, luring them places like the subway stations or the zoo in Central Park. There, expecting to have a bite of live flesh, they find themselves as subjects for "maxing."

Down in the subway, a hidden arsenal of baseball bats, axes, clubs, and knives aids in the restructuring of the usuals into disposable bits. The ultimate high comes when these elite types can get a dozen or more usuals down there and string them up like piñatas. At the zoo, the usuals are lured into cages where they are taken apart in spectacles Sammy likens to early Roman barbarism.

That night I watched it all without noticeable response. The next night was different. We went hunting. I'd wondered where they got the impeccably prepared human flesh at the party, and I found out. They search the living out, lure them with the most live-looking of the elite, by telling them of more secure housing or transportation out of the city. The captured "cunning and ruthless" ones are taken to Balducci's and slaughtered for food. You can't imagine what it's like to have someone who thinks that they are better than you—who are willing to throw you to the wolves first— in your power and watch them wither, humble and sniveling, into pot roast or tournedos of flesh. I watched the whole process. My very first emotion was joy. Then disgust.

The live ones that Sammy's entourage can relate to, or intimidate, are invited to maintain their lives, protected by the elite, in exchange for their useful skills. They become the taxi drivers, subway engineers, beauticians, food preparers, waiters, maids, and the like. The third night out, I found a housekeeper for the apartment. She was so thankful to be spared, she ironed my sheets! The rush as I sensed her palpable fear was intoxicating.

Her name was Anisa, a Jamaican from Queens who was hiding in one of the best source hotels in the city, the Waldorf-Astoria. She didn't believe I was dead until I let her feel my pulse. She screamed for two full minutes, then fell to her knees to pray. We grew close, like friends, but I didn't tell her you were here. My eating habits and hygiene upset her enough, and she didn't want to be reminded that it's easy for me to take a life. I didn't want to lose her.

After the first month of maxing, like the others, I grew complacent with the resurgence of emotion, and then restless. I craved
greater stimulation. Each of us, in turn, came up with new ways to
max-out. One-Eye began performing surgical theater on the living
who were destined for Balducci's, creating bizarre and sometimes
wondrous creations in flesh as the patient howled and writhed on
the table.

A former pimp named Smokey turned us onto "Splatters." We
took the really fucked-up junkies who were too saturated with shit
to eat and not skilled in anything useful and tossed them off the
World Trade Center. Some of us got to heave, some receive on the
ground. It was much more thrilling to throw them off as they
pleaded and fought. Landings were simply messy and gruesome,
unless they had last words or tried to drag their broken bodies
away. Just a mild emotional jolt there, usually revulsion.

For two months, we tried other less stimulating games, but again
we grew dysphoric. When those days of unease grew, I felt rages
that ripped at my barely tethered soul, heartache that threatened
to eat at my bones, gloom at my half-life condition, the killing, flesh
consumption, head games, and endless struggle to keep up my
appearance so that I was good enough to run with Sammy's crowd,
that brought back the urge to snuff out the remaining life I had.

I recalled the utter anguish I knew when you told me time and
time again how much you loved me, that everything you did, you
did for us, yet how you stayed away all day and night only to
crawl into bed exhausted and unwilling to share a word or scrap of
affection. I replayed your hysterical fits of anger when you whined
that I was so needy, that just my looking at you with my big sad
eyes threw you into paroxysms of guilt and remorse for never being
able to love me enough.

I believed you then. That it was all my fault. But now that I've
had a year without emotions, most of it with you still alive and
complaining that *I* was unavailable for *you*, and these last four
months of soul-searching and emotional rescue, I can see what a
fraud and master manipulator you were. My experience as a psychologist made me aware of such things in the lives of others, but
in love I was blind, faithful to your vision. A warped and sick one.
You coward. I've been released.

Damn, I'm crying again. Loss. I've never been tough enough with it.

Then it was my turn to find a maxing sport. I thought of those sex clubs you told me about from one of your seedier relationships. I couldn't remember any places, but as soon as I mentioned the idea to the others, some of them knew of live ones who had traded their lives for servitude in these dens of iniquity. Sammy kicked himself for not having thought of it sooner.

We piled into taxis and headed uptown. Twenty-sixth and Tenth Avenue. Close to the river. Lots of warehouses. As we walked from the corner, a summer drizzle was just starting up. I could smell the asphalt and the heat from the day rising up in the steam as the drizzle hit the street. And the stench of rotting flesh on bones that littered the entrances.

The twelve of us stood around outside this club like a bunch of kids caught out of school. I felt awkward, excited, *naughty*. There was nothing out front but a faded sign that read WHACKERS. The building was three stories tall. No windows. Just an imposing bulk of rusting sheet metal. We glanced over each other's shoulders casually at the odd clientele that seemed to bleed up from the cracks in the sidewalk. Two transvestites, looking like Laurel and Hardy in drag, ambled by. Then some old guys in ragged raincoats. A couple of butch biker babes. Four Upper East Side matrons, one I could swear was your friend Moira's mother. None of us moved as we got wet in the drizzle. We hadn't seen so many elite types in one place before besides us.

Sammy stepped away from us, eyeing a pretty slave girl, alive and not more than twenty years old, her face turned to the ground. She was leashed by a dog collar to a zombie master in an oxford-cloth shirt, polyester slacks, and heavy loafers just like the ones my seventh-grade math teacher wore. Sammy's gravelly voice cut through the quiet of the light rain.

"Whoa, she's what I want."

Her master turned and glared at him. "If I choose to auction her off for the night, you could never afford her." He sneered and pulled the young thing after him. Her coat flapped open in the breeze, exposing lots of living flesh and a smattering of black lace. I have to admit, she even made me hungry.

Sammy snorted. "Never underestimate the incomplete dead, man." We all nodded after him.

Rula yanked on One-Eye's sleeve, pouting. "I want to go in and have some fun. All I feel is bored."

One-Eye nodded. "Enough of this. Let's go on in."

We went in as one huddled mass. I looked up immediately. The ceiling was three stories tall in the gutted warehouse. Half of the wall that lined our way in was the bar, lit up like somebody's backyard barbecue at night. The patrons were drinking and talking, looking old and wrinkled, every facial flaw deeply etched, cast into shadows. Like dead people. A low fake-stone wall on the other side pointed us out onto a huge dance area. Centered there was a raised wooden platform, twenty feet square. Hanging ominously over that was a trapeze and gibbet. We hurried past some dancers as the loud rock music droned on and found ourselves in a circle of the fake stone.

I closed my eyes for a moment. The smells were unfamiliar; cheesy, rank, dusty, sweaty, oil-on-metal blended. The sounds of chains dragging, groaned conversations, and rubber hitting flesh made their way through the clamorous music. The ambience was one of desolation, stark and barren. I could feel it. I looked at the people, amazed at all the blank faces and empty eyes that looked back at me. Eyes of the living. I was awed. So many of us and so many live ones, all in one place and no one was feeding on the other.

Sammy pulled me further into the circle. There was a wooden frame there, where a naked Japanese woman stood chained by her ankles and wrists. Her black lover covered her body from our view as we moved closer. One-Eye was ahead of us. He turned back.

He shouted, "The guy's applying alligator clips to her nipples. This is serious S&M shit!"

Sammy swooned. "Maximum overload! I'm ready for this."

Rula leaned close and spoke into my ear. "I thought I'd seen everything, didn't you?" Her eyes were on the black man as he stepped away, the chain connecting the clips attached to his lover's nipples in his firm grasp.

"Not really." My eyes were riveted on the couple.

The black man yanked on the chain, twisting it, then pulled a rubber strap from his belt and began smacking her backside with it. I actually felt a shot of empathic pain.

Rula smiled wanly, leaning into me. "God, Katy, I'm feeling something. Something good."

Then I felt it, too. Sexual buzz. Sammy and the doctor were rubbing themselves against some of the girls like cats in heat. The black man began deep-kissing his woman. I was getting very turned on. *High.* I looked around, feeling anxious, sudden paranoia oozing from me like pus in a bad sore. Would anyone notice how naive I was? What now? Damn feelings. Things I can't control. Shit. Maximum stuff.

We found seats and watched the drama continue. There were more blank people with empty eyes, cold hearts, strumming each other, beating backsides, twisting, smacking, and humiliating one another. Our group all came alive, our faces growing animated, reflecting the stirring within.

I noticed a troll-like woman beating a beautiful bare ass. When the man in her lap looked up, I recognized him as a regular on a television program I used to watch. The woman's mate stood by passively, his eye on me. He lumbered over.

"You want this?" He had an accent. Swedish. Norwegian. Exaggerated.

"Who, me?" I stared up at him, then past him to a huge mirrored ball suspended from the ceiling. Colors danced off of it like fireworks.

Sammy leaned over. "I do. Let me at the little bitch."

The guy lifted Sammy off of the bench. "She is the mistress. You want to get it, she give it to you. You don't touch her." He pointed to me. "I ask her, not you."

I cocked one eyebrow. "I don't want to be beaten." I shook my head.

"No, you give to live one. Gisella show you. This new for you, yes?"

I nodded. The guy was like a wall of meat with a shock of white hair and small rat eyes. His voice was loud and deep, as if it came up from his bowels. He motioned for his partner to cut short her beating and join us.

She introduced herself. "I am Gisella, mistress of pain. You want to do this?" Her face reminded me of a gargoyle's and her accent was obviously fake. Now I wondered about his.

"Well, I don't know. . . ." Gisella began to turn away. "Yeah, I do. I want to try it." I tried to sound street-eager and worldly-wise. Me. The Vanilla Kid.

"Good." She groaned down at me. Grabbing her mate by the elbow, she shouted up to him.

"Take her to our room. Find her someone. Eric would be fine." She searched my eyes as if she could ascertain whether her choice was appropriate. "Yes, Eric."

The man reached out. "Come. I will take you to a bad boy who needs to be punished and disciplined. Follow me."

I stood. Gisella's gaze took in every pore of me as I turned to follow. She was licking her lips.

One-Eye stopped me as I went to pass him. "Katy, remember they are alive and we aren't aware of our strength. You could kill one. The rules, Katy, the rules."

"The rules?" I was in an emotional surge, unable to form a rational thought.

"Never take the life of anyone who might serve us or feed us. You could risk . . . well, there are stigmas attached. You know."

I did know. This was a tight group with scruples that worked. I was grateful to be a part of them and wouldn't want to lose them. God, no. And be alone again? Never.

I hurried after the master as he lumbered through the club. While we'd been watching the drama behind the wall, the room beyond had become crowded with old men in diapers with handcuffs and ankle manacles on, fat women in latex, *Rocky Horror*–type masters and mistresses, slimy-looking tax-consultant types in three-piece suits, their fists pumping under light wool worsted, and a whole gang of anorexic butch dykes whose tattoos gave their arms the appearance of being covered in black lace. The place now had the ambience of a chic Village club during a bad acid trip.

I could see the others in my group watching as I looked over my shoulder. My fear was growing the farther we got from the security of my friends.

We wended our way down a maze of hallways to a small room. It was occupied, so we turned to leave, but not before I saw the men in the dull neon lighting. Two guys in leather masks and G-strings were sodomizing a third man with the handle of a whip. The victim lay on his back with his knees up, on a concrete block. He made no sound, showed no sign of pain or pleasure, yet he quickly ejaculated over his belly at our arrival. The two perpetrators then argued between them over who was next.

I followed the master three doors down to another small room. Inside, three sweet, young, innocent-looking men stood against the wall smoking cigarettes and drinking. When we entered, the men fell to their knees and crawled to the master's boots and lowered their heads.

"Eric, stand." He was a third-year law-school dropout, bad-boy good-looking and alive. He began to grin when he saw who his mistress was, but the master frowned. "You will obey Mistress Katrina all evening. If she is not pleased, you will feed us, understand?"

Eric nodded nervously.

"You boys come with me." The man turned, walked out, and the other guys followed.

I pulled anxiously on a stray hair. "So, Eric, you come here often?" I stared at the floor, embarrassed.

"I live here, protected, so that I may serve you and others like you. You are . . . dead?"

"You're not sure?" I was flattered. Again.

"Sometimes not. So, how may I serve you, mistress?" He sounded mildly disinterested.

"Well, first of all, you could sound like you're into it. And take off those preppy clothes. Now!" An anger jolt. Appropriate for the moment. He was immediately chastised and eager to please. His clothes came off quickly and he stood before me.

He had a beautiful, youthful hard body. Nothing sagging or bloating or getting funny hairs on it like yours. He wore rings in his nipples and scrotum. They glittered in the single bare-bulb light. He clasped his hands and bowed his head.

"I am yours, sweet mistress. I will submit to any pain or humiliation to serve you, gratify you."

I found a concrete seat and sat down. Behind me were whips and vinyl straps and restraining gear.

"I have to confess. I've never done this before." I was feeling awkward, inept. Not exactly feelings I missed.

He fell to my feet, kissing my red high heels. I grabbed him by the hair and lifted his head. His mouth was open just a bit and I found his lips very inviting. I began to kiss him, then pulled away. "No. You must earn my kisses. Lay down here." I reached up and took some handcuffs, a bit of rope, and a whip as he reclined on the slab of cement beside me.

You would be screaming about now for me to shut up. You wouldn't want to hear a word about my sexual pleasure with anyone else but you. Ha. Pleasure with you ... was fleeting. And not often. How many times can a woman watch a man lose his erection during lovemaking and finish almost every time with him jerking off, his eyes closed, his heart and mind closed, closeted in a fantasy where she is nowhere to be found? And be told it is all her fault. I needed to know it wasn't me. It wasn't me!

I found the anger and will to inflict pain on pretty Eric by thinking of you. I could have killed him if he hadn't begun to cry.

"Eric, what ... what's happening?"

"Oh, Mistress Katrina, I am afraid you're strangling me. I deserve the pain. But I don't want to die." He wept, deeply. I took him up in my arms and held him. When the tears subsided, he told me how he'd held in his fear and anguish now for over a year, but he'd never been so close to dying.

"I must stop. I'm so turned on, I'm out of my mind. So angry, so intoxicated." I wiped his tears from his cheeks.

"I ... I am turned on, also." He lifted his hips. His cock was swollen. "But not here. It's not allowed. Only pain, no release."

"No sex, sex?"

He shook his head. I gave him our address and he met me there in the morning. He had to sneak out. It was so hot. God, I want to feel that right now. Too bad you couldn't perform. Maybe if I just take a look and see if it was all preserved ...

Yes. Your broken middle-aged body and all its parts are intact. Funny, I would have thought I'd still want you. But I don't. Not like the others.

There have been others. Many. That's how I find myself here in the musty basement talking to you. So many. I'll go on.

That first night, Sammy ended up with Gisella while her mate, Wert, watched. Rula found two dykes, One-Eye got the slave girl, and Smokey took the Upper East Side matrons for the rides of their lives. So naturally we went back. Every night. They've all run together. I found a constant high. We all have.

And I crashed. One by one, we reached incredible ecstasy and maintained it, only to find ourselves growing more restless, anxious, surly, hungry. We tried to stay away for a few nights, try other maxing sports. It was no good.

Anisa told me she thought I was looking strung out. I heard her. We weren't just getting our feelings recharged, we were getting hooked. She told me back what I'd told her about you, your becoming a human doing instead of a human being. I remembered how you escaped your feelings of horrible shame and inadequacy in your "stuff." I've been escaping the existence I knew without feelings, then running from the feelings of pain and sorrow I get now that I'm emoting. I thought right then about quitting.

I couldn't stop. Nor could anyone else.

It was five days ago that we all hustled back to Whackers. It was auction night. We'd amassed a huge amount of "cash" over the weeks we'd been going to the club, buying drinks and flesh snacks and getting tickets good at auction as money.

Zelda, a three-hundred-pound Raggedy Ann look-alike in leather, was the emcee. One by one, she announced willing victims and masters or mistresses for sale. Each of them stood on the platform and showed the crowd their bottoms or panties or genitals. I passed on a thirty-year-old computer nerd with a cute ass and the promise that he could take all of the spanking I might administer. I said no to a fiftyish banker type who wanted to be verbally humiliated. I balked on a couple that looked too mean to take orders. Then there was Tio.

Tio was a slight, beautiful Italian man. He danced off his lace panties from under his maid's costume to show all of us his pretty cock and buttocks. He flirted with the crowd, who began counting their tickets. Tio was willing to be a doormat, to lick and suck and pander to any orifice, to be beaten, humiliated, forced to degrade himself in extraordinary ways. He came with a key to the Dungeon. The response was huge.

Sammy saw me drooling, and knew that I would also want to save Tio from the hands of someone harsher and indifferent. He handed me his entire wad of tickets. Tio was mine.

For such a seasoned deviant, I was going to be a disappointment, I feared. Tio followed me obediently to one of the overstuffed sofas in the back of the room. Eric hurried over, excited for me.

"You have a key to the Dungeon! I've always wanted to go there. Mistress Katrina, you're lucky."

Suddenly, the thought of having the security of Eric along lessened my anxiety. "Come join us." I looked at Tio.

"Mistress, I will be a slave to you both. I will eat the cum from you after he has you. I will do anything for you." His accent was slight, charming.

I looked to Eric. "Is it all right to do whatever, the things we can't do here . . . in the Dungeon?"

Eric nodded. "It's in the basement, separate. Its own domain. I'll show you."

Remember the book on the Inquisition we looked at in that strange bookstore in San Francisco? This was a torture chamber to rival that. In the center of the room was a wrought-iron chandelier hanging loosely from the ceiling. On the walls were numerous hooks bearing every form of device I saw in that book as well as others I knew from the Tower of London tour. There were breast rippers, metal pears for any orifice, spiked necklaces and belts, cat's paws, a ladder-type rack, thumbscrews, whips, and gags. A long rack and pillory sat at one end of the room. An inquisitor's chair, scavenger's daughter, and iron maiden filled the main part of the dungeon. An open closet carried clothing, shelves with towels, bandages, and a spigot in the sink by the door dripped rusty water into a pail. With the room dimly lit like an intimate dinner party, I could barely find a place to sit until my eyes adjusted.

Eric knelt before me, stripped himself bare, and offered up a heretic's fork. "I deserve to wear this. I have blasphemed against the higher order."

"I don't know how it works." I grinned at Tio.

"I will show you, mistress." His hands shook as he placed the forked ends, one under Eric's chin, the other on his breastbone, then joined the metal notches on the collar securely behind Eric's head. The metal bar, from fork to fork, held Eric's head up at a sharp angle, stiffly.

"Can you speak?" I could see his eyes tearing up.

He garbled out a no, pulling me to him. He pushed my skirt

up to my waist and took down my panties. With his head in the arched-back position, I had only to step over his face and find ecstasy.

Tio began touching my breasts as I took a step forward.

I was weakened by the orgasm and yet, with the level of addiction I had to the high, I couldn't stop. Tio crawled up onto the rack. Eric knelt beside it, whimpering in pain. I strapped Tio down and pulled a leather mask over his face until only his eyes and mouth were exposed. I rammed a gagball into his mouth, reeling with adrenaline and lust.

I cranked the ropes holding Tio tighter. He squealed around the metal ball. I grabbed two whips, one cat-o'-nine-tails, and a rectal pear. I set the whips down and greased up the metal orb. It slid too easily up Tio's ass. I kept turning the handle of the pear so that it could split into its four segments and fan out to stretch the walls of his rectum. I twisted until it no longer moved. Tio's eyes were wide with a pleasure I still didn't understand.

I began whipping Tio; the anger over your abandonment escalated my furor. I thought of how you made us a home here in New York, introduced me to all of your friends who quickly lost interest in me, went off to work, and never came back. I thought of what I'd given up back home. A husband, a good practice, my family and friends, and my house. For love. For the version you promised and never even got close to. Why? Why! I flogged Tio for the last two years I waited and believed I'd get loved back.

I got hotter and hotter, until I could no longer ignore the turgid product of my efforts on Tio. I climbed on top of him, impaled myself on his flesh, live, warm, pulsing inside of me. I grasped at his face mask, my mouth seeking his lips that were swollen around the ball. I bucked over him until I shouted into another climax.

I fell across his chest and lay my head at his chin. He seemed so quiet, still. I ripped out the gagball and put my lips to his. I noticed immediately how cold they were. Deathly cold.

Turning to Eric, I saw blood running down his chest from the fork in his breastbone. His eyes were huge. I moved off Tio and undid the heretic's fork from around Eric's neck. He let his head fall, working his jaw.

I was shaking now. "He's dead, Eric. I killed him." Fear rose in my gut, claws extended.

Eric stood up, loosened the mask on Tio, and felt for a pulse. He shook his head.

"Oh my God. What am I going to do? The others. They'll know...."

Eric put his arm around me. "Mistress, we're in the Dungeon. It's all right. No one will know. Tio? He got what he wanted. He found heaven in your hands. Now you have to consume him."

"Eat him? Oh, then no one will find—"

"It's the last pleasure in this, his pleasure and yours. No one will know unless you tell them."

I thought of you. *Dead* dead. Soul in heaven. Forever, never to walk on this earth again. And I felt so sad. What if they knew about you, that I've been hoarding you all of this time?

"I can't. He's not prepared. I'm not a 'usual,' slathering over just any body." I slammed my fist on Tio's chest. "Damn you! Why did you have to die on me?!"

Eric took my shoulders in his hands and shook me. "Stop this. Be here with me. I want you to give me what you gave Tio. I've never witnessed such rapture. I am unworthy of anything less now. Give me death. Glorious death."

"What? How could you ask that? Can't you see how I feel?"

"If you don't, I'll tell them. Your friends." He got down on his knees, begging.

I broke down. I heaved sobs into a towel as I sat on the floor, so much built up from so many tiny sorrows over the year, flooding me. The loneliness, the angst, the regret. Simmering all this time, it erupted.

I lost track of time, but when the tears were fewer and quieter, I felt a hand on my head. My face and stomach hurt. I didn't want to deal with Eric's demand now. The hand lifted my face. It was Tio!

Tio, half-dead. A zombie masochist lover, doomed to forever take the punishment of others. For eternity. And I didn't care. All I knew was that Eric was gone and soon the others would know. Soon, once again, I would walk alone. All because I wanted to share some feelings with someone.

Damn, here come the tears.

And there you are, with sunken orbs not seeing, you with whom I wanted to walk always. You, whom I killed in the hopes we would both know the half-life, stay goddamned stone-cold dead in the corner. And some fucking Italian pervert gets a half-life on me!

In my heart that beats stronger, I feel your loss. A cruel injustice I can feel! The guilt, remorse, my misery. And you would tell me I asked for it. That I knew better, but I followed my impulse, anything to cure my despair. "Any act of desperation creates devastation in its wake," or something like that. I may be paying for taking your life, but I'll find a way to make it through. I've learned that I'm better than you made me think I was. So what if I walk alone . . .

I traded what remained of my soul for what I imagined would be sweet passion's return, a little emotional rescue. Some companionship in the name of love. Damn. But there is no love in this half-life. I have you now, you selfish asshole, and I won't find any more love here than I had before.

It's all over. The high life. I may not be able to get served at Balducci's anymore, or go to hot parties, but I'll find another way. Until then, I make do with you, you miserable fuck. Leftovers don't bother me.

Scape-Goats

CLIVE BARKER

Is there anyone who hasn't *heard of CLIVE BARKER?*
I can't see how—he's everywhere. As novelist. Artist. Film-
maker. Interview subject. Philosopher. Talk-show guest.
In fact, Clive seems determined to succeed in all possible fields.
So far, he's done pretty well at it.
Barker's ground-breaking debut came in 1984 with the Books
of Blood, *a three-volume set of uniquely unsettling short stories.*
Graphic, intense, and sexually explicit, these Books *blended killer*
craftsmanship with lyric brutality to invoke a painfully honest
philosophy, one which would soon be articulated as the rallying
cry of the then-nascent splatterpunks:
"There are no limits."
Since that time Clive's generated epic fantasies (Imajica), *art-*
work collections of his own pen-and-ink drawings (Clive
Barker—Illustrator), *and even children's books* (The Thief of Always). *He's probably best known for creating Pinhead, though.*
Cult icon, movie star, S&M zombie from hell, Pinhead has ap-
peared in the three Hellraiser *films which Clive has either directed,*
presented, or produced.
Yet Clive's mutability is far more impressive than his pro-
lificity. He may have first hit the charts using tools of sex and
violence, but he's admirably refused to repeat himself. Instead,
Barker's taken the more difficult course of constant reevaluation
and expansion. Reading something like Weaveworld *(a Tol-*
kienesque fantasy) or The Great and Secret Show *(which, in part,*
reminds me of C.S. Lewis's classic 1943 Christian science-fiction
novel Perelandra) *only underscores how far—and how quickly—*
Barker has grown away from his bloody roots.
Still, those roots remain. "Scape-Goats" is a good example. This

downbeat, explicit tale of shipboard angst *and the uneasy dead comes off like a queasy jam session between Polanski's* Knife In The Water *and Fulci's* Zombie. *With all the psychology and gore that mixture portends.*

More pertinently, "Goats" is a heartening reminder that no matter how large Barker's fame has become, he continues (as in tales like "Jacqueline Ess" and "The Life of Death," or films like Hellraiser *and* Candyman*) to be fascinated by intelligent, independent women.*

Not that those qualities always count for much.

Especially on "Scape-Goats" tight little island ...

*I*t wasn't a real island the tide had carried us on to, it was a lifeless mound of stones. Calling a hunchbacked shit pile like this an island is flattery. Islands are oases in the sea: green and abundant. This is a forsaken place: no seals in the water around it, no birds in the air above it. I can think of no use for a place like this, except that you could say of it: I saw the heart of nothing, and survived.

"It's not on any of the charts," said Ray, poring over the map of the Inner Hebrides, his nail at the spot where he'd calculated that we should be. It was, as he'd said, an empty space on the map, just pale blue sea without the merest speck to sign the existence of this rock. It wasn't just the seals and the birds that ignored it then, the chart makers had too. There were one or two arrows in the vicinity of Ray's finger, marking the currents that should have been taking us north: tiny red darts on a paper ocean. The rest, like the world outside, was deserted.

Jonathan was jubilant, of course, once he discovered that the place wasn't even to be found on the map; he seemed to feel instantly exonerated. The blame for our being here wasn't his any longer, it was the map makers': he wasn't going to be held responsible for our being beached if the mound wasn't even marked on the charts. The apologetic expression he'd worn since our unscheduled arrival was replaced with a look of self-satisfaction.

"You can't avoid a place that doesn't exist, can you?" he crowed. "I mean, can you?"

"You could have used the eyes God gave you," Ray flung back at him; but Jonathan wasn't about to be cowed by reasonable criticism.

"It was so sudden, Raymond," he said. "I mean, in this mist I didn't have a chance. It was on top of us before I knew it."

It had been sudden, no two ways about that. I'd been in the galley preparing breakfast, which had become my responsibility since neither Angela nor Jonathan showed any enthusiasm for the task, when the hull of the *Emmanuelle* grated on shingle, then plowed her way, juddering, up on to the stony beach. There was a moment's silence: then the shouting began. I climbed up out of the galley to find Jonathan standing on deck, grinning sheepishly and waving his arms around to semaphore his innocence.

"Before you ask," he said, "I don't know how it happened. One minute we were just coasting along—"

"Oh Jesus Christ all-fucking Mighty." Ray was clambering out of the cabin, hauling a pair of jeans on as he did so, and looking much the worse for a night in a bunk with Angela. I'd had the questionable honor of listening to her orgasms all night; she was certainly demanding. Jonathan began his defense speech again from the beginning: "Before you ask—", but Ray silenced him with a few choice insults. I retreated into the confines of the galley while the argument raged on deck. It gave me no small satisfaction to hear Jonathan slanged; I even hoped Ray would lose his cool enough to bloody that perfect hook nose.

The galley was a slop bucket. The breakfast I'd been preparing was all over the floor and I left it there, the yolks of the eggs, the gammon and the French toasts all congealing in pools of spilt fat. It was Jonathan's fault; let him clear it up. I poured myself a glass of grapefruit juice, waited until the recriminations died down, and went back up.

It was barely two hours after dawn, and the mist that had shrouded this island from Jonathan's view still covered the sun. If today was anything like the week that we'd had so far, by noon the deck would be too hot to step on barefoot, but now, with the mist still thick, I felt cold wearing just the bottom of my bikini. It didn't matter much, sailing amongst the islands, what you wore. There was no one to see you. I'd got the best allover tan I'd ever had. But this morning the chill drove me back below to find a sweater. There was no wind: the cold was coming up out of the sea. It's still night down there, I thought, just a few yards off the beach; limitless night.

I pulled on a sweater, and went back on deck. The maps were out, and Ray was bending over them. His bare back was peeling from an excess of sun, and I could see the bald patch he tried to hide in his dirty yellow curls. Jonathan was staring at the beach and stroking his nose.

"Christ, what a place," I said.

He glanced at me, trying a smile. He had this illusion, poor Jonathan, that his face could charm a tortoise out of its shell, and to be fair to him there were a few women who melted if he so much as looked at them. I wasn't one of them, and it irritated him. I'd always thought his Jewish good looks too bland to be beautiful. My indifference was a red rag to him.

A voice, sleepy and pouting, drifted up from below deck. Our Lady of the Bunk was awake at last: time to make her late entrance, coyly wrapping a towel around her nakedness as she emerged. Her face was puffed up with too much red wine, and her hair needed a comb through it. Still she turned on the radiance, eyes wide, Shirley Temple with cleavage.

"What's happening, Ray? Where are we?"

Ray didn't look up from his computations, which earned him a frown.

"We've got a bloody awful navigator, that's all," he said.

"I don't even know what happened," Jonathan protested, clearly hoping for a show of sympathy from Angela. None was forthcoming.

"But where are we?" she asked again.

"Good morning, Angela," I said; I too was ignored.

"Is it an island?" she said.

"Of course it's an island: I just don't know which one yet," Ray replied.

"Perhaps it's Barra," she suggested.

Ray pulled a face. "We're nowhere near Barra," he said. "If you'll just let me retrace our steps—"

Retrace our steps, in the sea? Just Ray's Jesus fixation, I thought, looking back at the beach. It was impossible to guess how big the place was; the mist erased the landscape after a hundred yards. Perhaps somewhere in that grey wall there was human habitation.

Ray, having located the blank spot on the map where we were supposedly stranded, climbed down on to the beach and took a

critical look at the bow. More to be out of Angela's way than anything else I climbed down to join him. The round stones of the
beach were cold and slippery on the bare soles of my feet. Ray
smoothed his palm down the side of the *Emmanuelle*, almost a
caress, then crouched to look at the damage to the bow.

"I don't think we're holed," he said, "but I can't be sure."

"We'll float off come high tide," said Jonathan, posing on the
bow, hands on hips. "No sweat," he winked at me, "no sweat at all."

"Will we shit float off!" Ray snapped. "Take a look for yourself."

"Then we'll get some help to haul us off." Jonathan's confidence
was unscathed.

"And you can damn well fetch someone, you asshole."

"Sure, why not? Give it an hour or so for the fog to shift and I'll
take a walk, find some help."

He sauntered away.

"I'll put on some coffee," Angela volunteered.

Knowing her, that'd take an hour to brew. There was time for a
stroll.

I started along the beach.

"Don't go too far, love," Ray called.

"No."

Love, he said. Easy word; he meant nothing by it.

The sun was warmer now, and as I walked I stripped off the
sweater. My bare breasts were already brown as two nuts, and, I
thought, about as big. Still, you can't have everything. At least I'd
got two neurons in my head to rub together, which was more than
could be said for Angela; she had tits like melons and a brain that'd
shame a mule.

The sun still wasn't getting through the mist properly. It was
filtering down on the island fitfully, and its light flattened everything
out, draining the place of color or weight, reducing the sea and the
rocks and the rubbish on the beach to one bleached-out grey, the
color of overboiled meat.

After only a hundred yards something about the place began to
depress me, so I turned back. On my right tiny, lisping waves crept
up to the shore and collapsed with a weary slopping sound on the
stones. No majestic rollers here: just the rhythmical slop, slop, slop
of an exhausted tide.

I hated the place already.

*   *   *

Back at the boat, Ray was trying the radio, but for some reason all he could get was a blanket of white noise on every frequency. He cursed it awhile, then gave up. After half an hour, breakfast was served, though we had to make do with sardines, tinned mushrooms and the remains of the French toast. Angela served this feast with her usual aplomb, looking as though she was performing a second miracle with loaves and fishes. It was all but impossible to enjoy the food anyway; the air seemed to drain all the taste away.

"Funny, isn't it—" began Jonathan.

"Hilarious," said Ray.

"—there's no foghorns. Mist, but no horns. Not even the sound of a motor; weird."

He was right. Total silence wrapped us up, a damp and smothering hush. Except for the apologetic slop of the waves and the sound of our voices, we might as well have been deaf.

I sat at the stern and looked into the empty sea. It was still grey, but the sun was beginning to strike other colors in it now: a somber green, and, deeper, a hint of blue-purple. Below the boat I could see strands of kelp and maiden's hair, toys to the tide, swaying. It looked inviting: and anything was better than the sour atmosphere on the *Emmanuelle*.

"I'm going for a swim," I said.

"I wouldn't, love," Ray replied.

"Why not?"

"The current that threw us up here must be pretty strong. You don't want to get caught in it."

"But the tide's still coming in: I'd only be swept back to the beach."

"You don't know what crosscurrents there are out there. Whirlpools even: they're quite common. Suck you down in a flash."

I looked out to sea again. It looked harmless enough, but then I'd read that these were treacherous waters, and thought better of it.

Angela had started a little sulking session because nobody had finished her immaculately prepared breakfast. Ray was playing up to it. He loved babying her, letting her play damn stupid games. It made me sick.

I went below to do the washing up, tossing the slops out of the porthole into the sea. They didn't sink immediately. They floated in an oily patch, half-eaten mushrooms and slivers of sardines bobbing around on the surface, as though someone had thrown up on the sea. Food for crabs, if any self-respecting crab condescended to live here.

Jonathan joined me in the galley, obviously still feeling a little foolish, despite the bravado. He stood in the doorway, trying to catch my eye, while I pumped up some cold water into the bowl and halfheartedly rinsed the greasy plastic plates. All he wanted was to be told I didn't think this was his fault, and yes, of course he was a kosher Adonis. I said nothing.

"Do you mind if I lend a hand?" he said.

"There's not really room for two," I told him, trying not to sound too dismissive. He flinched nevertheless: this whole episode had punctured his self-esteem more badly than I'd realized, despite his strutting around.

"Look," I said gently, "why don't you go back on deck: take in the sun before it gets too hot?"

"I feel like a shit," he said.

"It was an accident."

"An utter shit."

"Like you said, we'll float off with the tide."

He moved out of the doorway and down into the galley; his proximity made me feel almost claustrophobic. His body was too large for the space: too tanned, too assertive.

"I said there wasn't any room, Jonathan."

He put his hand on the back of my neck, and instead of shrugging it off I let it stay there, gently massaging the muscles. I wanted to tell him to leave me alone, but the lassitude of the place seemed to have got into my system. His other hand was palm down on my belly, moving up to my breast. I was indifferent to these ministrations: if he wanted this he could have it.

Above deck Angela was gasping in the middle of a giggling fit, almost choking on her hysteria. I could see her in my mind's eye, throwing back her head, shaking her hair loose. Jonathan had unbuttoned his shorts, and had let them drop. The gift of his foreskin to God had been neatly made; his erection was so hygienic in its enthusiasm it seemed incapable of the least harm. I let his mouth stick to mine, let his tongue explore my gums, insistent as a dentist's finger. He slid my bikini down far enough to get access, fumbled to position himself, then pressed in.

Behind him, the stair creaked, and I looked over his shoulder in time to glimpse Ray, bending at the hatch and staring down at Jonathan's buttocks and at the tangle of our arms. Did he see, I wondered, that I felt nothing; did he understand that I did this dispassionately, and could only have felt a twinge of desire if I substituted his head, his back, his cock for Jonathan's? Soundlessly, he withdrew from the stairway; a moment passed, in which Jonathan said he loved me, then I heard Angela's laughter begin again as Ray described what he'd just witnessed. Let the bitch think whatever she pleased: I didn't care.

Jonathan was still working at me with deliberate but uninspired strokes, a frown on his face like that of a schoolboy trying to solve some impossible equation. Discharge came without warning, signaled only by a tightening of his hold on my shoulders, and a deepening of his frown. His thrusts slowed and stopped; his eyes found mine for a flustered moment. I wanted to kiss him, but he'd lost all interest. He withdrew still hard, wincing. "I'm always sensitive when I've come," he murmured, hauling his shorts up. "Was it good for you?"

I nodded. It was laughable; the whole thing was laughable. Stuck in the middle of nowhere with this little boy of twenty-six, and Angela, and a man who didn't care if I lived or died. But then perhaps neither did I. I thought, for no reason, of the slops on the sea, bobbing around, waiting for the next wave to catch them.

Jonathan had already retreated up the stairs. I boiled up some coffee, standing staring out of the porthole and feeling his come dry to a corrugated pearliness on the inside of my thigh.

Ray and Angela had gone by the time I'd brewed the coffee, off for a walk on the island apparently, looking for help.

Jonathan was sitting in my place at the stern, gazing out at the mist. More to break the silence than anything I said:

"I think it's lifted a bit."

"Has it?"

I put a mug of black coffee beside him.

"Thanks."

"Where are the others?"

"Exploring."

He looked round at me, confusion in his eyes. "I still feel like a shit."

I noticed the bottle of gin on the deck beside him.

"Bit early for drinking, isn't it?"

"Want some?"

"It's not even eleven."

"Who cares?"

He pointed out to sea. "Follow my finger," he said.

I leaned over his shoulder and did as he asked.

"No, you're not looking at the right place. Follow my finger—see it?"

"Nothing."

"At the edge of the mist. It appears and disappears. There! Again!"

I did see something in the water, twenty or thirty yards from the *Emmanuelle*'s stern. Brown-colored, wrinkled, turning over.

"It's a seal," I said.

"I don't think so."

"The sun's warming up the sea. They're probably coming in to bask in the shallows."

"It doesn't look like a seal. It rolls in a funny way—"

"Maybe a piece of flotsam—"

"Could be."

He swigged deeply from the bottle.

"Leave some for tonight."

"Yes, Mother."

We sat in silence for a few minutes. Just the waves on the beach. Slop. Slop. Slop.

Once in a while the seal, or whatever it was, broke surface, rolled, and disappeared again.

Another hour, I thought, and the tide will begin to turn. Float us off this little afterthought of creation.

"Hey!" Angela's voice, from a distance. "Hey, you guys!"

You guys, she called us.

Jonathan stood up, hand up to his face against the glare of sunlit rock. It was much brighter now: and getting hotter all the time.

"She's waving to us," he said, disinterested.

"Let her wave."

"You guys!" she screeched, her arms waving.

Jonathan cupped his hands around his mouth and bawled a reply:

"What do you want?"

"Come and see," she replied.

"She wants us to come and see."

"I heard."

"Come on," he said. "Nothing to lose."

I didn't want to move, but he hauled me up by the arm. It wasn't worth arguing. His breath was inflammable.

It was difficult making our way up the beach. The stones were not wet with seawater, but covered in a slick film of grey-green algae, like sweat on a skull.

Jonathan was having even more difficulty getting across the beach than I was. Twice he lost his balance and fell heavily on his backside, cursing. The seat of his shorts was soon a filthy olive color, and there was a tear where his buttocks showed.

I was no ballerina, but I managed to make it, step by slow step, trying to avoid the large rocks so that if I slipped I wouldn't have far to fall.

Every few yards we'd have to negotiate a line of stinking seaweed. I was able to jump them with reasonable elegance but Jonathan, pissed and uncertain of his balance, plowed through them, his naked feet completely buried in the stuff. It wasn't just kelp; there was the usual detritus washed up on any beach: the broken bottles, the rusting Coke cans, the scum-stained cork, globs of tar, fragments of crabs, pale yellow durex. And crawling over these stinking piles of dross were inch-long, fat-eyed blue flies. Hundreds of them, clambering over the shit, and over each other, buzzing to be alive, and alive to be buzzing.

It was the first life we'd seen.

I was doing my best not to fall flat on my face as I stepped across one of these lines of seaweed, when a little avalanche of pebbles began off to my left. Three, four, five stones were skipping over each other towards the sea, and setting another dozen stones moving as they jumped.

There was no visible cause for the effect.

Jonathan didn't even bother to look up; he was having too much trouble staying vertical.

The avalanche stopped: run out of energy. Then another: this time between us and the sea. Skipping stones: bigger this time than the last, and gaining more height as they leapt.

The sequence was longer than before: it knocked stone into stone until a few pebbles actually reached the sea at the end of the dance.

Plop.

Dead noise.

Plop. Plop.

Ray appeared from behind one of the big boulders at the height of the beach, beaming like a loon.

"There's life on Mars," he yelled and ducked back the way he'd come.

A few more perilous moments and we reached him, the sweat sticking our hair to our foreheads like caps.

Jonathan looked a little sick.

"What's the big deal?" he demanded.

"Look what we've found," said Ray, and led the way beyond the boulders.

The first shock.

Once we got to the height of the beach we were looking down on the other side of the island. There was more of the same drab beach, and then sea. No inhabitants, no boats, no sign of human existence. The whole place couldn't have been more than half a mile across: barely the back of a whale.

But there was some life here; that was the second shock.

In the sheltering ring of the large, bald boulders which crowned the island was a fenced-in compound. The posts were rotting in the salt air, but a tangle of rusted barbed wire had been wound around and between them to form a primitive pen. Inside the pen there was a patch of coarse grass, and on this pitiful lawn stood three sheep. And Angela.

She was standing in the penal colony, stroking one of the inmates and cooing in its blank face.

"Sheep," she said, triumphantly.

Jonathan was there before me with his snapped remark: "So what?"

"Well, it's strange, isn't it?" said Ray."Three sheep in the middle of a little place like this?"

"They don't look well to me," said Angela.

She was right. The animals were the worse for their exposure to the elements; their eyes were gummy with matter, and their fleeces hung off their hides in knotted clumps, exposing panting flanks. One of them had collapsed against the barbed wire, and seemed unable to right itself again, either too depleted or too sick.

"It's cruel," said Angela.

I had to agree: it seemed positively sadistic, locking up these creatures without more than a few blades of grass to chew on, and a battered tin bath of stagnant water to quench their thirst.

"Odd, isn't it?" said Ray.

"I've cut my foot." Jonathan was squatting on the top of one of the flatter boulders, peering at the underside of his right foot.

"There's glass on the beach," I said, exchanging a vacant stare with one of the sheep.

"They're so deadpan," said Ray. "Nature's straight men."

Curiously, they didn't look so unhappy with their condition; their stares were philosophical. Their eyes said: I'm just a sheep, I don't expect you to like me, care for me, preserve me, except for your stomach's sake. There were no angry baas, no stamping of a frustrated hoof.

Just three grey sheep, waiting to die.

Ray had lost interest in the business. He was wandering back down the beach, kicking a can ahead of him. It rattled and skipped, reminding me of the stones.

"We should let them free," said Angela.

I ignored her; what was freedom in a place like this? She persisted. "Don't you think we should?"

"No."

"They'll die."

"Somebody put them here for a reason."

"But they'll *die.*"

"They'll die on the beach if we let them out. There's no food for them."

"We'll feed them."

"French toast and gin," suggested Jonathan, picking a sliver of glass from his sole.

"We can't just leave them."

"It's not our business," I said. It was all getting boring. Three sheep. Who cared if they lived or—

I'd thought that about myself an hour earlier. We had something in common, the sheep and I.

My head was aching.

"They'll die," whined Angela, for the third time.

"You're a stupid bitch," Jonathan told her. The remark was made without malice: he said it calmly, as a statement of plain fact.

I couldn't help grinning.

"What?" She looked as though she'd been bitten.

"Stupid bitch," he said again."B-I-T-C-H."

Angela flushed with anger and embarrassment, and turned on him. "You got us stuck here," she said, lip curling.

The inevitable accusation. Tears in her eyes. Stung by his words.

"I did it deliberately," he said, spitting on his fingers and rubbing saliva into the cut. "I wanted to see if we could leave you here."

"You're drunk."

"And you're stupid. But I'll be sober in the morning."

The old lines still made their mark.

Outstripped, Angela started down the beach after Ray, trying to hold back her tears until she was out of sight. I almost felt some sympathy for her. She was, when it came down to verbal fisticuffs, easy meat.

"You're a bastard when you want to be," I told Jonathan; he just looked at me, glassy-eyed.

"Better be friends. Then I won't be a bastard to you."

"You don't scare me."

"I know."

The mutton was staring at me again. I stared back.

"Fucking sheep," he said.

"They can't help it."

"If they had any decency, they'd slit their ugly fucking throats."

"I'm going back to the boat."

"Ugly fuckers."

"Coming?"

He took hold of my hand: fast, tight, and held it in his hand like he'd never let go. Eyes on me suddenly.

"Don't go."

"It's too hot up here."

"Stay. The stone's nice and warm. Lie down. They won't interrupt us this time."

"You knew?" I said.

"You mean Ray? Of course I knew. I thought we put on quite a little performance."

He drew me close, hand over hand up my arm, like he was hauling in a rope. The smell of him brought back the galley, his frown, his muttered profession ("Love you"), the quiet retreat.

Déjà vu.

Still, what was there to do on a day like this but go round in the same dreary circle, like the sheep in the pen? Round and round. Breathe, sex, eat, shit.

The gin had gone to his groin. He tried his best but he hadn't got a hope. It was like trying to thread spaghetti.

Exasperated, he rolled off me.

"Fuck. Fuck. Fuck."

Senseless word. Once it was repeated, it had lost all its meaning, like everything else. Signifying nothing.

"It doesn't matter," I said.

"Fuck off."

"It really doesn't."

He didn't look at me, just stared down at his cock. If he'd had a knife in his hand at that moment, I think he'd have cut it off and laid it on the warm rock, a shrine to sterility.

I left him studying himself, and walked back to the *Emmanuelle*. Something odd struck me as I went, something I hadn't noticed before. The blue flies, instead of jumping ahead of me as I approached, just let themselves be trodden on. Positively lethargic; or suicidal. They sat on the hot stones and popped under my soles, their gaudy little lives going out like so many lights.

The mist was disappearing at last, and as the air warmed up, the island unveiled its next disgusting trick: the smell. The fragrance was as wholesome as a roomful of rotting peaches, thick and sickly. It came in through the pores as well as the nostrils, like a syrup. And under the sweetness, something else, rather less pleasant than peaches, fresh or rotten. A smell like an open drain clogged with old meat: like the gutters of a slaughterhouse, caked with suet and black blood. It was the seaweed, I assumed, although I'd never smelled anything to match the stench on any other beach.

I was halfway back to the *Emmanuelle*, holding my nose as I stepped over the bands of rotting weed, when I heard the noise of a little murder behind me. Jonathan's whoops of satanic glee almost drowned the pathetic voice of the sheep as it was killed, but I knew instinctively what the drunken bastard had done.

I turned back, my heel pivoting on the slime. It was almost certainly too late to save one of the beasts, but maybe I could prevent him from massacring the other two. I couldn't see the pen; it was hidden behind the boulders, but I could hear Jonathan's triumphant yells, and the thud, thud of his strokes. I knew what I'd see before it came into sight.

The grey-green lawn had turned red. Jonathan was in the pen with the sheep. The two survivors were charging back and forth in a rhythmical trot of panic, baaing in terror, while Jonathan stood over the third sheep, erect now. The victim had partially collapsed, its sticklike front legs buckled beneath it, its back legs rigid with approaching death. Its bulk shuddered with nervous spasms, and its eyes showed more white than brown. The top of its skull had been almost entirely dashed to pieces, and the grey hash of its brain exposed, punctured by shards of its own bone and pulped by the large round stone that Jonathan was still wielding. Even as I watched he brought the weapon down once more onto the sheep's brainpan. Globs of tissue flew off in every direction, speckling me with hot matter and blood. Jonathan looked like some nightmare lunatic (which for that moment, I suppose, he was). His naked body, so recently white, was stained as a butcher's apron after a hard day's hammering at the abattoir. His face was more sheep's gore than Jonathan—

The animal itself was dead. Its pathetic complaints had ceased completely. It keeled over, rather comically, like a cartoon character, one of its ears snagging the wire. Jonathan watched it fall: his face a grin under the blood. Oh that grin: it served so many purposes. Wasn't that the same smile he charmed women with? The same grin that spoke lechery and love? Now, at last, it was put to its true purpose: the gawping smile of the satisfied savage, standing over his prey with a stone in one hand and his manhood in the other.

Then, slowly, the smile decayed as his senses returned.

"Jesus," he said, and from his abdomen a wave of revulsion climbed up his body. I could see it quite clearly, the way his gut rolled as a throb of nausea threw his head forward, pitching half-digested gin and toast over the grass.

I didn't move. I didn't want to comfort him, calm him, console him—he was simply beyond my help.

I turned away.

"Frankie," he said through a throat of bile.

I couldn't bring myself to look at him. There was nothing to be done for the sheep, it was dead and gone; all I wanted to do was run away from the little ring of stones, and put the sight out of my head.

"Frankie."

I began to walk, as fast as I was able over such tricky terrain, back down towards the beach and the relative sanity of the *Emmanuelle*.

The smell was stronger now: coming up out of the ground towards my face in filthy waves.

Horrible island. Vile, stinking, insane island.

All I thought was hate as I stumbled across the weed and the filth. The *Emmanuelle* wasn't far off—

Then, a little pattering of pebbles like before. I stopped, balancing uneasily on the sleek dome of a stone, and looked to my left, where even now one of the pebbles was rolling to a halt. As it stopped, another, larger pebble, fully six inches across, seemed to move spontaneously from its resting place and roll down the beach, striking its neighbors and beginning another exodus towards the sea. I frowned: the frown made my head buzz.

Was there some sort of animal—a crab maybe—under the beach, moving the stones? Or was it the heat that in some way twitched them into life?

Again: a bigger stone—

I walked on, while behind the rattle and patter continued, one little sequence coming close upon another, to make an almost seamless percussion.

I began, without real focus or explanation, to be afraid.

* * *

Angela and Ray were sunning themselves on the deck of the *Emmanuelle*.

"Another couple of hours before we can start to get the bitch off her backside," he said, squinting as he looked up at me.

I thought he meant Angela at first, then realized he was talking about floating the boat out to sea again.

"May as well get some sun." He smiled wanly at me.

"Yeah."

Angela was either asleep or ignoring me. Whichever, it suited me fine.

I slumped down on the sun deck at Ray's feet and let the sun soak into me. The specks of blood had dried on my skin, like tiny scabs. I picked them off idly, and listened to the noise of the stones, and the slop of the sea.

Behind me, pages were being turned. I glanced round. Ray, never able to lie still for very long, was flicking through a library book on the Hebrides he'd brought from home.

I looked back at the sun. My mother always said it burned a hole in the back of your eye, to look straight into the sun, but it was hot and alive up there; I wanted to look into its face. There was a chill in me—I don't know where it had come from—a chill in my gut and in between my legs—that wouldn't go away. Maybe I would have to burn it away by looking at the sun.

Some way along the beach I glimpsed Jonathan, tiptoeing down towards the sea. From that distance the mixture of blood and white skin made him look like some piebald freak. He'd stripped off his shorts and he was crouching at the sea's edge to wash off the sheep.

Then, Ray's voice, very quietly: "Oh God," he said, in such an understated way that I knew the news couldn't be brilliant.

"What is it?"

"I've found out where we are."

"Good."

"No, not good."

"Why? What's wrong?" I sat upright, turning to him.

"It's here, in the book. There's a paragraph on this place."

Angela opened one eye. "Well?" she said.

"It's not just an island. It's a burial mound."

The chill in between my legs fed upon itself, and grew gross.

The sun wasn't hot enough to warm me that deep, where I should be hottest.

I looked away from Ray along the beach again. Jonathan was still washing, splashing water up on his chest. The shadows of the stones suddenly seemed very black and heavy, their edges pressed down on the upturned faces of—

Seeing me looking his way Jonathan waved.

Can it be there are corpses under those stones? Buried faceup to the sun, like holiday-makers laid out on a Blackpool beach?

The world is monochrome. Sun and shadow. The white tops of stones and their black underbellies. Life on top, death underneath.

"Burial?" said Angela. "What sort of burial?"

"War dead," Ray answered.

Angela: "What, you mean Vikings or something?"

"World War One, World War Two. Soldiers from torpedoed troopships, sailors washed up. Brought down here by the Gulf Stream; apparently the current funnels them through the straits and washes them up on the beaches of the islands around here."

"Washes them up?" said Angela.

"That's what it says."

"Not any longer, though."

"I'm sure the occasional fisherman gets buried here still," Ray replied.

Jonathan had stood up, staring out to sea, the blood off his body. His hand shaded his eyes as he looked out over the blue-grey water, and I followed his gaze as I had followed his finger. A hundred yards out that seal, or whale, or whatever it was, had returned, lolling in the water. Sometimes, as it turned, it threw up a fin, like a swimmer's arm, beckoning.

"How many people were buried?" asked Angela, nonchalantly. She seemed completely unperturbed by the fact that we were sitting on a grave.

"Hundreds, probably."

"Hundreds?"

"It just says 'many dead' in the book."

"And do they put them in coffins?"

"How should I know?"

What else could it be, this godforsaken mound—but a cemetery? I looked at the island with new eyes, as though I'd just recognized it for what it was. Now I had a reason to despise its humpy back, its sordid beach, the smell of peaches.

"I wonder if they buried them all over," mused Angela, "or just at the top of the hill, where we found the sheep? Probably just at the top; out of the way of the water."

Yes, they'd probably had too much of water: their poor green faces picked by fish, their uniforms rotted, their dog tags encrusted with algae. What deaths; and worse, what journeys after death, in squads of fellow corpses, along the Gulf Stream to this bleak landfall. I saw them, in my mind's eye, the bodies of the soldiers, subject to every whim of the tide, borne backwards and forwards in a slush of rollers until a casual limb snagged on a rock, and the sea lost possession of them. With each receding wave uncovered; sodden and jellied brine, spat out by the sea to stink a while and be stripped by gulls.

I had a sudden, morbid desire to walk on the beach again, armed with this knowledge, kicking over the pebbles in the hope of turning up a bone or two.

As the thought formed, my body made the decision for me. I was standing: I was climbing off the *Emmanuelle*.

"Where are you off to?" said Angela.

"Jonathan," I murmured, and set foot on the mound.

The stench was clearer now: that was the accrued odor of the dead. Maybe drowned men got buried here still, as Ray had suggested, slotted under the pile of stones. The unwary yachtsman, the careless swimmer, their faces wiped off with water. At the feet the beach flies were less sluggish than they'd been: instead of waiting to be killed they jumped and buzzed ahead of my steps, with a new enthusiasm for life.

Jonathan was not to be seen. His shorts were still on the stones at the water's edge, but he'd disappeared. I looked out to sea: nothing; no bobbing head; no lolling, beckoning something.

I called his name.

My voice seemed to excite the flies; they rose in seething clouds. Jonathan didn't reply.

I began to walk along the margin of the sea, my feet sometimes caught by an idle wave, as often as not left untouched. I realized I hadn't told Angela and Ray about the dead sheep. Maybe that was a secret between us four. Jonathan, myself, and the two survivors in the pen.

Then I saw him: a few yards ahead—his chest white, wide and clean, every speck of blood washed off. A secret it is, then, I thought.

"Where have you been?" I called to him.

"Walking it off," he called back.

"What off?"

"Too much gin," he grinned.

I returned the smile, spontaneously; he'd said he loved me in the galley; that counted for something.

Behind him, a rattle of skipping stones. He was no more than ten yards from me now, shamelessly naked as he walked; his gait was sober.

The rattle of stones suddenly seemed rhythmical. It was no longer a random series of notes as one pebble struck another—it was a beat, a sequence of repeated sounds, a tick-tap pulse.

No accident: intention.

Not chance: purpose.

Not stone: thought. Behind stone, with stone, carrying stone—

Jonathan, now close, was bright. His skin was almost luminous with sun on it, thrown into relief by the darkness behind him.

Wait—

—What darkness?

The stone mounted the air like a bird, defying gravity. A blank black stone, disengaged from the earth. It was the size of a baby: a whistling baby, and it grew behind Jonathan's head as it shimmered down the air towards him.

The beach had been flexing its muscles, tossing small pebbles down to the sea, all the time strengthening its will to raise this boulder off the ground and fling it at Jonathan.

It swelled behind him, murderous in its intention, but my throat had no sound to make worthy of my fright.

Was he deaf? His grin broke open again; he thought the horror on my face was a jibe at his nakedness, I realized. He doesn't understand—

The stone sheared off the top of his head, from the middle of his nose upwards, leaving his mouth still wide, his tongue rooted in blood, and flinging the rest of his beauty towards me in a cloud

of wet red dust. The upper part of his head was split on to the face
of the stone, its expression intact as it swooped towards me. I half
fell, and it screamed past me, veering off towards the sea. Once over
the water the assassin seemed to lose its will somehow, and faltered
in the air before plunging into the waves.

At my feet, blood. A trail that led to where Jonathan's body lay,
the open edge of his head towards me, its machinery plain for the
sky to see.

I was still not screaming, though for sanity's sake I had to unleash
the terror suffocating me. Somebody must hear me, hold me, take
me away and explain to me, before the skipping pebbles found
their rhythm again. Or worse, before the minds below the beach,
unsatisfied with murder by proxy, rolled away their grave stones
and rose to kiss me themselves.

But the scream would not come.

All I could hear was the patter of stones to my right and left.
They intend to kill us all for invading their sacred ground. Stoned
to death, like heretics.

Then, a voice.

"For Christ's sake—"

A man's voice; but not Ray's.

He seemed to have appeared from out of thin air: a short, broad
man, standing at the sea's edge. In one hand a bucket and under his
arm a bundle of coarsely cut hay. Food for the sheep, I thought,
through a jumble of half-formed words. Food for sheep.

He stared at me, then down at Jonathan's body, his old eyes
wild.

"What's gone on?" he said. The Gaelic accent was thick. "In the
name of Christ what's gone on?"

I shook my head. It seemed loose on my neck, almost as though
I might shake it off. Maybe I pointed to the sheep pen, maybe not.
Whatever the reason, he seemed to know what I was thinking, and
began to climb the beach towards the crown of the island, dropping
bucket and bundle as he went.

Half blind with confusion, I followed, but before I could reach
the boulders he was out of their shadow again, his face suddenly
shining with panic.

"Who did that?"

"Jonathan," I replied. I cast a hand towards the corpse, not daring to look back at him. The man cursed in Gaelic, and stumbled out of the shelter of the boulders.

"What have you done?" he yelled at me. "My Christ, what have you done? Killing their gifts."

"Just sheep," I said. In my head the instant of Jonathan's decapitation was playing over and over again, a loop of slaughter.

"They demand it, don't you see, or they rise—"

"Who rise?" I said, knowing. Seeing the stones shift.

"All of them. Put away without grief or mourning. But they've got the sea in them, in their heads—"

I knew what he was talking about: it was quite plain to me, suddenly. The dead were here: as we knew. Under the stones. But they had the rhythm of the sea in them, and they wouldn't lie down. So to placate them, these sheep were tethered in a pen, to be offered up to their wills.

Did the dead eat mutton? No; it wasn't food they wanted. It was the gesture of recognition—as simple as that.

"Drowned," he was saying, "all drowned."

Then, the familiar patter began again, the drumming of stones, which grew, without warning, into an ear-splitting thunder, as though the entire beach was shifting.

And under the cacophony three other sounds: splashing, screaming and wholesale destruction.

I turned to see a wave of stones rising into the air on the other side of the island—

Again the terrible screams, wrung from a body that was being buffeted and broken.

They were after the *Emmanuelle*. After Ray. I started to run in the direction of the boat, the beach rippling beneath my feet. Behind me, I could hear the boots of the sheep feeder on the stones. As we ran the noise of the assault became louder. Stones danced in the air like fat birds, blocking the sun, before plunging down to strike at some unseen target. Maybe the boat. Maybe flesh itself—

Angela's tormented screams had ceased.

I rounded the beachhead a few steps ahead of the sheep feeder, and the *Emmanuelle* came into sight. It, and its human contents, were beyond all hope of salvation. The vessel was being bombarded by endless ranks of stones, all sizes and shapes; its hull was smashed, its windows, mast and deck shattered. Angela lay sprawled on the remains of the sun deck, quite obviously dead. The fury of the hail hadn't stopped, however. The stones beat a tattoo on the remaining structure of the hull, and thrashed at the lifeless bulk of Angela's body, making it bob up and down as though a current were being passed through it.

Ray was nowhere to be seen.

I screamed then: and for a moment it seemed there was a lull in the thunder, a brief respite in the attack. Then it began again: wave after wave of pebbles and rocks rising off the beach and flinging themselves at their senseless targets. They would not be content, it seemed, until the *Emmanuelle* was reduced to flotsam and jetsam, and Angela's body was in small enough pieces to accommodate a shrimp's palate.

The sheep feeder took hold of my arm in a grip so fierce it stopped the blood flowing to my hand.

"Come on," he said. I heard his voice but did nothing. I was waiting for Ray's face to appear—or to hear his voice calling my name. But there was nothing: just the barrage of the stones. He was dead in the ruins of the boat somewhere—smashed to smithereens.

The sheep feeder was dragging me now, and I was following him back over the beach.

"The boat," he was saying, "we can get away in my boat—"

The idea of escape seemed ludicrous. The island had us on its back; we were its objects utterly.

But I followed, slipping and sliding over the sweaty rocks, ploughing through the tangle of seaweed, back the way we'd come.

On the other side of the island was his poor hope of life. A rowing boat, dragged up on the shingle: an inconsequential walnut shell of a boat.

Would we go to sea in that, like the three men in a sieve?

He dragged me, unresisting, towards our deliverance. With every step I became more certain that the beach would suddenly rise up and stone us to death. Maybe make a wall of itself, a tower even, when we were within a single step of safety. It could play any game it liked, any game at all. But then, maybe the dead didn't like games. Games are about gambles, and the dead had already lost. Maybe the dead act only with the arid certainty of mathematicians.

He half threw me into the boat, and began to push it out into the thick tide. No walls of stones rose to prevent our escape. No towers appeared, no slaughtering hail. Even the attack on the *Emmanuelle* had ceased.

Had they sated themselves on three victims? Or was it that the presence of the sheep feeder, an innocent, a servant of these willful dead, would protect me from their tantrums?

The rowing boat was off the shingle. We bobbed a little on the backs of a few limp waves until we were deep enough for the oars, and then we were pulling away from the shore and my savior was sitting opposite me, rowing for all he was worth, a dew of fresh sweat on his forehead, multiplying with every pull.

The beach receded; we were being set free. The sheep feeder seemed to relax a little. He gazed down at the swill of dirty water in the bottom of the boat and drew in half a dozen deep breaths; then he looked up at me, his wasted face drained of expression.

"One day, it had to happen—" he said, his voice low and heavy. "Somebody would spoil the way we lived. Break the rhythm."

It was almost soporific, the hauling of the oars, forward and back. I wanted to sleep, to wrap myself up in the tarpaulin I was sitting on, and forget. Behind us, the beach was a distant line. I couldn't see the *Emmanuelle*.

"Where are we going?" I said.

"Back to Tiree," he replied. "We'll see what's to be done there. Find some way to make amends, to help them sleep soundly again."

"Do they eat the sheep?"

"What good is food to the dead? No. No, they have no need of mutton. They take the beasts as a gesture of remembrance."

Remembrance.

I nodded.

"It's our way of mourning them—"

He stopped rowing, too heartsick to finish his explanation, and too exhausted to do anything but let the tide carry us home. A blank moment passed.

Then the scratching.

A mouse noise, no more, a scrabbling at the underside of the boat like a man's nails tickling the planks to be let in. Not one man: many. The sound of their entreaties multiplied, the soft dragging of rotted cuticles across the wood.

In the boat, we didn't move, we didn't speak, we didn't believe. Even as we heard the worst—we didn't believe the worst.

A splash off to starboard; I turned and he was coming towards me, rigid in the water, borne up by unseen puppeteers like a figurehead. It was Ray, his body covered in killing bruises and cuts: stoned to death, then brought, like a gleeful mascot, like proof of power, to spook us. It was almost as though he were walking on water, his feet just hidden by the swell, his arms hanging loosely by his side as he was hauled towards the boat. I looked at his face: lacerated and broken. One eye almost closed, the other smashed from its orbit.

Two yards from the boat, the puppeteers let him sink back into the sea, where he disappeared in a swirl of pink water.

"Your companion?" said the sheep feeder.

I nodded. He must have fallen into the sea from the stern of the *Emmanuelle*. Now he was like them, a drowned man. They'd already claimed him as their plaything. So they did like games after all; they hauled him from the beach like children come to fetch a playmate, eager that he should join the horseplay.

The scratching had stopped. Ray's body had disappeared altogether. Not a murmur off the pristine sea, just the slop of the waves against the boards of the boat.

I pulled at the oars—

"Row!" I screamed at the sheep feeder. "Row, or they'll kill us."

He seemed resigned to whatever they had in mind to punish us with. He shook his head and spat onto the water. Beneath his floating phlegm something moved in the deep, pale forms rolled and somersaulted, too far down to be clearly seen. Even as I watched they came floating up towards us, their sea-corrupted faces better defined with every fathom they rose, their arms outstretched to embrace us.

A shoal of corpses. The dead in dozens, crab-cleaned and fish-picked, their remaining flesh scarcely sitting on their bones.

The boat rocked gently as their hands reached up to touch it.

The look of resignation on the sheep feeder's face didn't falter for a moment as the boat was shaken backwards and forwards; at first gently, then so violently we were beaten about like dolls. They meant to capsize us, and there was no help for it. A moment later, the boat tipped over.

The water was icy, far colder than I'd anticipated, and it took my breath away. I'd always been a fairly strong swimmer. My strokes were confident as I began to swim from the boat, cleaving through the white water. The sheep feeder was less lucky. Like many men who live with the sea, he apparently couldn't swim. Without issuing a cry or a prayer, he sank like a stone.

What did I hope? That four was enough: that I could be left to thumb a current to safety? Whatever hopes of escape I had, they were short-lived.

I felt a soft, oh so very soft, brushing of my ankles and my feet, almost a caress. Something broke surface briefly close to my head. I glimpsed a grey back, as of a large fish. The touch on my ankle had become a grasp. A pulpy hand, mushed by so long in the water, had a hold of me, and inexorably began to claim me for the sea. I gulped what I knew to be my last breath of air, and as I did so Ray's head bobbed no more than a yard from me. I saw his wounds in clinical detail—the water-cleansed cuts were ugly flaps of white tissue, with a gleam of bone at their core. The loose eye had been washed away by now, his hair, flattened to his skull, no longer disguised the bald patch at his crown.

The water closed over my head. My eyes were open, and I saw my hard-earned breath flashing past my face in a display of silver bubbles. Ray was beside me, consoling, attentive. His arms floated over his head as though he were surrendering. The pressure of the water distorted his face, puffing his cheeks out and spilling threads of severed nerves from his empty eye socket like the tentacles of a tiny squid.

I let it happen. I opened my mouth and felt it fill with cold water. Salt burned my sinuses, the cold stabbed behind my eyes. I felt the brine burning down my throat, a rush of eager water where water shouldn't go—flushing air from my tubes and cavities, 'til my system was overwhelmed.

Below me, two corpses, their hair swaying loosely in the current, hugged my legs. Their heads lolled and danced on rotted ropes of neck muscle, and though I pawed at their hands, and their flesh came off the bone in grey, lace-edged pieces, their loving grip didn't falter. They wanted me, oh how dearly they wanted me.

Ray was holding me too, wrapping me up, pressing his face to mine. There was no purpose in the gesture, I suppose. He didn't know or feel, or love or care. And I, losing my life with every second, succumbing to the sea absolutely, couldn't take pleasure in the intimacy that I'd longed for.

Too late for love; the sunlight was already a memory. Was it that the world was going out—darkening towards the edges as I died—or that we were now so deep the sun couldn't penetrate so far? Panic and terror had left me—my heart seemed not to beat at all—my breath didn't come and go in anguished bursts as it had. A kind of peace was on me.

Now the grip of my companions relaxed, and the gentle tide had its way with me. A rape of the body: a ravaging of skin and muscle, gut, eye, sinus, tongue, brain.

Time had no place here. The days may have passed into weeks, I couldn't know. The keels of boats glided over and maybe we looked up from our rock hovels on occasion and watched them pass. A ringed finger was trailed in the water, a splashless puddle clove the sky, a fishing line trailed a worm. Signs of life.

Maybe the same hour as I died, or maybe a year later, the current sniffs me out of my rock and has some mercy. I am twitched from amongst the sea anemones and given to the tide. Ray is with me. His time too has come. The sea change has occurred; there is no turning back for us.

Relentlessly the tide bears us—sometimes floating, bloated decks for gulls, sometimes half sunk and nibbled by fish—bears us towards the island. We know the surge of the shingle, and hear, without ears, the rattle of the stones.

The sea has long since washed the plate clean of its leavings. Angela, the *Emmanuelle*, and Jonathan, are gone. Only we drowned belong here, faceup, under the stones, soothed by the rhythm of tiny waves and the absurd incomprehension of sheep.

Cannibal Cats Come Out Tonight

NANCY HOLDER

Splatterpunk, like the mythical hydra, sports multiple heads. While they all share the same body, some of these cranial offshoots have lately acquired names of their own.

One's "new horror"; another, "rock 'n' roll horror."

Which is a shorthand way of introducing "Cannibal Cats Come Out Tonight," a choice representative of the latter head.

"Choice" as in meat, you understand . . .

NANCY HOLDER is a Navy brat who once lived in Japan and dropped out of high school to study ballet in Europe. Since the mideighties, she's produced over three dozen stories for such an-thologies as Still Dead: Book of the Dead II, Borderlands, *and* Women of Darkness. *Holder's most recent novel is* Making Love, *cowritten by Splat II contributor Melanie Tem.*

Nancy's also authored some thirteen romance novels. And if you were to sprinkle some Holderian swoonings over a loin of "long pig," out would pop "Cannibal Cats," a savory black com-edy with a tart aftertaste.

Let's see if we can identify some of the ingredients Nancy's used to make this dish. Hmm—that tastes like "Antimacho." And that's definitely "Woman as Meat." Mmm—do I detect the subtle aroma of "Music Industry Metaphor"?

But enough. Time to close the cookbook and cruise on down to Hollywood, where we'll pick up a couple of rock star wannabes. Two cool cats named Dwight & Angelo (whose adventures con-tinue in "Love Me Tenderized: Or, You Ain't Nothin' But a Hot Dog," a sequel found in my The King Is Dead *anthology). A pair of struggling rockers who've found it's a real dog-eat-dog world out there.*

*Just as Nancy Holder's found a rather tasty way to lampoon
the notion of a woman's "place" in the kitchen.*

Early on, Dwight Jones knew his daddy was not Ward Cleaver.
Daddy liked to drink. Daddy liked to swear.
Daddy liked to hit.
"It's a dog-eat-dog world out there, son. Never forget that. *Ever.*"
These were the first words Dwight could remember his dad
saying to him.

His father started out in a pawnshop and moved into foreclo-
sures. He collected debts for people with Italian last names. Dwight
also suspected he killed people for money, but he was never certain
of that.

One thing he was sure of was that he would grow up to be just
like his old man. There was no way to prevent it, no one to stop
it—certainly not his mother. No kindly teacher at school, no Cub
Scout leader, no priest. He seemed to move in a shadow where no
one saw what was happening to him; no one gave a good goddamn
about the bruises and the missed days of school. He was a beautiful
child, with huge blue eyes and curly red hair—but no one remarked
on it. Even ugly kids were fawned over, adored, made pets of by
old men with wood shops or by doting, childless chorus teachers.
Not Dwight.

He was going to become just like Daddy, unable to love, aroused
only by violence, ruthless and killing cruel, because everyone was
afraid of his father.

And for some reason, they were also afraid of Dwight.

At first he used to cry over the inevitability of his fate. Even as
a little boy, sobbing alone in his room after a beating—"teach you
a lesson, make a man out of you"—feeling the rage build, feeling it
fester and disease him, he understood the hardening process that
was taking place inside. He was not to be like other boys. He was
not to have a normal life. In the innocence of youth, he looked in
the mirror behind the placid face, the clear eyes, and saw a monster.

Daddy was obsessed with the savagery of nature; they spent
hours at the zoo, watching the big cats feasting on meat. Father took
son out to the cornfields on the outskirts of town to watch the
insects in the stalks devour one another.

"Dog eat dog, son," his father would say with satisfaction as insect legs kicked and struggled inside insect mouths. "For them and for us."

Dwight would grimace and clench his fists, not wanting to watch. He hated *Wild Kingdom*, Daddy's favorite show: It was a tarantula-eat-scorpion, snake-eat-rabbit, wolf-eat-doe world on TV. In his father's world, it was men beating on women, young men beating on old men, Daddy beating on everybody.

Daddy liked strength. He lifted weights and worked out at a gym. He hated weakness. He made Dwight go out for sports, and smacked him when he came home with a black eye from the school bully. But Dwight was weak and, as he grew, ugly. And stupid. He was such a loser he didn't blame Daddy for hitting him. He was pretty sure Daddy would eventually kill him.

Then something happened to Dwight.

He made a friend.

He was on the verge of puberty—wet dreams, acne, his hatred of his father spilling out into night dreams of murder and day-dreams of running away. And then he met Angelo, sent by the angels themselves; a tall, dark Italian kid with big brown eyes and curved lips but for the moment zitty, like Dwight. Angelo was hip—he had a garage band, The Tokers, that was already getting gigs at after-school dances. Angelo was smart, he was rich, and he liked Dwight.

Dwight never understood why. Angelo had everything going for him. Everyone at school wanted to be Angelo's friend. The girls all lusted after him. He got straight A's but he was cool. He played the guitar like Hendrix; no, better. Dwight, on the other hand, was a loner, a dildo, a bizarro. The high school pack had cut him out long before—doesn't matter, fuck 'em, Dwight thought—but he longed to be one of the crowd—

—and Angelo Leone wanted to be Dwight Jones's best friend, and so he was.

It was Dwight who suggested they become blood brothers. He never knew why he suggested it; neither of them could remember—had it been after some funky John Wayne movie or some primo Colombian or what? But they pricked their little fingers, grinning sheepishly—Christ, they were almost fourteen!—and touched them together. How stupid, how sticky, how nothing—

Dwight's world changed. He had a best friend *and* a blood brother.

And the following year, they decided to do it the real way, cut their wrists the way the Indians did, make it official.

Only Dwight cut too deeply; at the hospital, they accused him of trying to kill himself. He always wondered if that's what he had tried to do. His old man beat the hell out of him for it.

But they tried again, with the other wrist. Angelo went first—the blood dripped onto the scarred table where they played cards and ferreted out seeds in their dope stashes and worked on music for the band—the blood dripped and Dwight bent down on impulse and licked it up; and gasped and said, "Damn, Angelo, it tastes fucking *good!*"

And it did, both of them agreed on that. And then the next year, Angelo cut the top of his finger off with the paper cutter—just the tip of his pinkie, just a tiny bit, and Dwight popped it into his mouth.

It was so terrific he fainted. It was like the best kind of acid; it was psychedelically delicious. Bullshit that it tasted like chicken—what crap; whoever said that had never tried it. It was incredible. Food from another planet, living human flesh.

Angelo agreed, after Dwight topped off his own little finger for his benefit. It hurt like hell, but Angelo's reaction made it worthwhile.

Meanwhile, the lessons of Dwight's dad had incubated and yeasted and abscessed inside his son. Dwight's mother was buried—fell down the stairs, bruises like rotten apples on her face and breasts—and Dwight found he had nothing but contempt for her. He found himself thinking about digging her up and having a chew.

Then he knew that but for Angelo, he would've been lost by now. Angelo stuck by him; Angelo was always there. Dwight began to worry he was gay on top of being a sicko. He, not Angelo, because Angelo was manly and strong and on the football team.

Dwight's father got meaner after his wife died. When Dwight ran to Angelo's with a bloody nose, Angelo decided it was time to get the hell out of Iowa. They wouldn't graduate with their class; but with Angelo's trust funds and allowances and boss leather jackets, who needed to?

On the road to Los Angeles, they both began to crave another psychedelically delicious snack. They admitted it to each other hesitantly—this was weird shit—and the more they talked about it, the worse the craving grew. The top of a finger was barely a nibble—think what a real man-sized bit would taste like!

"Well, we can't carve ourselves up," Angelo said. "What are we going to do?"

For a few weeks, they pretended they didn't know.

But after they set the band up and got a few gigs, and rented a house near the mansion wherein dwelt their heroes, The Grateful Dead, Dwight and Angelo had a long night of blood-brother talk and drew up two lists.

The first was:

THE PROS AND CONS OF EATING HUMAN FLESH

PRO	CON
1. It tastes good	It's hard to come by
2. It tastes good	It hurts to cut ourselves up
3. It tastes good	It's sick
4. It tastes good	It's wrong
5. It tastes *fucking* good	

They were stuck. How to continue the feed, the delirious, psychedelically delicious feed? It was too beautiful to stop doing it. (Years later, Dwight joked that sushi might have saved them, but he wasn't really serious—there was no comparison.) Yes, it hurt like hell, and it was wrong, but oh, God, God, God, the *taste*.

After a lot of talking, a lot of soul-searching, a few tears, they made a second list:

PEOPLE WE WANT TO EAT

1. Billy Idol

2. David Bowie

3. Madonna

4. Janet Jackson

5. David Lee Roth

Their idols. "Gourmet food," Angelo said, laughing.

Dwight cried all night. He had thought Angelo would save him, but no one could. He blamed himself for dragging Angelo into it— hadn't Dwight been the one to suggest they become blood brothers? And Angelo, dear Angelo, with his innocent offer of friendship, hadn't realized he was befriending a ghoul.

Dog eat dog; insects chomping each other; blood in the water as the sharks circled round—

How had Daddy known? How had the figures of his childhood, who had steered clear of a miserable boy obviously in need of rescuing, how had they known?

Right on, Pop. Right on, old guy. Old dead guy. Dwight didn't go back for that funeral, either, but that was the first night he and Angelo actually stalked someone, just followed her down the alley and took her home to the mansion and into Dwight's room. Sat her on the bed and took off her clothes—

gave her grass, fucked her—

and when she asked if there was anything else, Dwight stared helplessly at Angelo, who said, "Yeah, we want to eat you."

She grinned and lay back.

They killed her first. That was a mistake. For the magic left the flesh with the soul. Angelo theorized it had something to do with circulation, with the beating of the living heart. They also discovered the flesh had to be clean, very clean. Otherwise it was . . . unappetizing.

Dwight swallowed an overdose of Librium. Angelo got his stomach pumped and brought him home. He fed him chicken soup—or tried to. Dwight could eat nothing Angelo offered him.

Except Angelo's little toe.

After that, they took their victims into the shower with them, or suggested a nice bubble bath. They ate only women—Daddy's doing, Dwight figured—and gradually, women were all they ate. (There was enough vegetable matter in the intestines to provide a balanced diet.)

"We're cannibal cats!" Angelo said, posing in his leathers. He wore his hair long and tumbling in curls down his back. He was a beautiful boy, a hot and nasty boy, and the girls flocked to him.

Dwight, on the other hand, looked okay. He didn't think he qualified as a cannibal cat, but he was grateful to Angelo for saying so, anyway.

They went on like this for a year or so.

Then they both fell in love.

Her name was Alice, which was, coincidentally, Dwight's mother's name. She came in for an audition as a backup singer with the band.

Offstage she was shy and sweet, despite her black spiky hair and thick eye makeup, sassy red lips, and leather skirts and corsets and boots that hugged her thighs. A little girl dressed in big girl's clothes. It was clear to Dwight that she dug both of them, and clearer still that Angelo wanted her all to himself.

Listen, he wanted to say to Angelo. Listen, you've been loved and adored. You've been *popular.* But I haven't had jackshit but my old man, who knew I was a freak, or made me into a freak, or I don't know what. Let me have her; she likes me, too. You can have any girl you want. You know it. But all I'll ever have is Alice.

Dwight loved sweet Alice. He cherished her in a way he thought impossible for him. She made his heart crack open, and he wanted to kneel before her and tell her she was a queen. When she sang, she sounded like the sweetest bird in the universe. When she smiled, he had to turn his head because he loved her so much. He didn't care if they ever made love; he wanted to keep his feelings for her pure and beautiful. It was the best thing about his life, except his friendship with his blood brother.

He truly, thoroughly loved Alice.

He agonized over their ghoulish secret, his and Angelo's. What if Alice found out? What if she knew that the lips that longed to kiss her had . . . eaten things?

And he agonized over what to do about his love for Alice, because it was clear that Angelo wasn't going to back off.

Alice, beautiful Alice. "Hi, babe," Angelo would say casually, as if speaking to her were the easiest thing to do in the world. "You're looking good."

Whenever Dwight was alone with her, he couldn't think of anything to say. She'd watch him expectantly, as if she were waiting for him to say something clever, like Angelo. But nothing came out but mumbling and bullshit. He had never been good with girls. Angelo was the one who picked them up when they went stalking. Despairing, he finally let Angelo have her. He played weak, even though he wasn't really weak. He made Alice think he wasn't interested anymore—God, he would have cut off his right arm for her—and Angelo swooped down on her like a hawk.

Well, if it made them happy, it was okay by Dwight.

Only, it wasn't, not really.

And then Angelo betrayed him.

He ate Alice.

By himself.

He ate Alice!

Dwight found him with the remains, bloody and stoned and happy, and he lost his cool. He raged, he screamed, he hit Angelo, his brother. Not since his childhood had he ranted and sobbed as he did that night.

Angelo was contrite. He said he hadn't known the depth of Dwight's feelings for Alice. "I would've backed off," he told Dwight. "After all, you're my blood brother."

After a while, Dwight found a way to forgive him. He, Dwight, had been weak. But Alice had been weaker, falling for Angelo. Trusting him—that was the ultimate weakness. Alice was a stupid, weak, trusting woman. And that was the name of that tune.

And that was the way things stood for another year. The Tokers played all over the country, Dwight and Angelo the two lead singers. Standing together on the stage in front of the lasers and strobes and fog banks of dry ice, in leather and lipstick, shocking, virile boys. Cannibal cats.

After their gigs they tiptoed out of the parties for a psychedelically delicious snack, then popped back, unsuspected and sated. And though the rift between them never quite healed, they were still cool.

Things were still cool.

And then Angelo brought up the matter of the second list.

"We haven't munched any of them," he reminded Dwight. "We've got to get to work."

By that time, their musical tastes had changed. And since they'd decided to eat only women, they had some discussions and agreed on a new hit parade:

1. Tina Turner

2. Madonna

3. Cyndi Lauper

4. Janet Jackson

5. Annie Lennox

Dwight was terrified—these were major ladies—but Angelo insisted. "Don't tell me you're a pussy!" he flung at his blood brother, perhaps sensing that was the equivalent of a double dare to Dwight. Dwight bucked up; they sucked each other's wrists to seal the pact, and began thinking about how they could get closer to Tina.

Then both of them fell in love again, with a beautiful Danish girl named Liss.

Oh, Liss. She was a tough, tall, ultrasexy woman who wore red leather unisuits and leopard skins around her shoulders. On stage she strutted like a panther; she moved slow and sure and dangerous. She was a strong woman, and Dwight warned Angelo that this time, he wouldn't back off.

"Ain't asking you to, man," Angelo said, smiling. "But I'm not, either."

So they both pursued Liss. Since all three of them were in music, it was easy to find out the clubs and parties she went to. The boys were so involved in courting her they forgot about their second list, which might or might not have saved Tina Turner's ass.

Liss noticed them at the Grammys—or was it Angelo she noticed, Dwight wondered. She was friendly to both of them; said, in her charming, halting English, "I know you. You sing with The Tokers."

When she said it, the band's name sounded dumb and kidlike to Dwight, not cool in a retro way the way Angelo insisted it did.

"We *lead* The Tokers," Angelo corrected her saucily.

"It's Angelo's band." Now why did he have to say that?

"Oh, really? But you both sing so well." She smiled. She had dazzling white teeth and deep blue eyes. Dwight felt a pang as he thought of Alice, his sweet, lost love. Liss wasn't a bit like her. She was a bitch-fox. Thank God.

He had a talk with Angelo. For the first time in their friendship, Dwight took the upper hand. "No way do we eat her," he said. And at Angelo's casual nod, he clenched his fist and exposed his scarred wrist, saying, "Swear."

"Aw, come on, man." Angelo started to turn away, but Dwight grabbed his shoulder.

"Swear."

So they cut their wrists and held them together, slurped up the extra. Angelo's eyes softened and he said, "I'm sorry, man. You're right. We're brothers. We don't eat her. Hey, you can have her. It's wrong for me to hassle you over her."

Dwight drew himself up. "No. I want to win her fair and square." He wanted to know he was strong enough to.

So they kept after Liss. They went out, the three of them, to On the Rox and Touch and all the cool Hollywood hangouts. She let them kiss her but they didn't go to bed with her. Dwight thought he would burst with longing whenever he was around her.

Then she invited them to her place in the desert.

"It's miles from anywhere," she said. "We can play music and . . . play." She smiled at Angelo, who winked at Dwight. Dwight tried to smile, but he was too nervous. His moment was at hand. He would do whatever he had to to have Liss.

Whatever.

Almost.

They jumped in the Jaguar and flashed out to the Anza-Borrego Desert. It really was miles from anywhere. They had to bring in food—Dwight and Angelo had already thought of this, and agreed they would have to fast all weekend, faking eating so she wouldn't notice.

It was a two-story stone house in the middle of the desert, off roads and paths—how did the Jag manage it? But it was a fabulous place, stone and glass and rawhide couches and chairs. Indian art and big wood beams. A fireplace and a phone in every room. Jacuzzis and a pool that circled the house like a moat. And the biggest bed Dwight had ever seen.

Angelo nudged him. "I gave you my word, man," he whispered, when Liss bounced on it suggestively and smiled at the two of them.

They made dinner in the kitchen—blood-rare steaks and salads and fries. She ate and they talked, then cleared the table before she had a chance to notice that all the little bits of food cluttering their plates added up to full, untouched meals. They broke out guitars and grass and coke and got supremely high. She gave them things they'd never had before, Danish peyote or pastries or Copenhagen PCP. As they played, Angelo's eyes gleamed and Dwight was terrified he was going to forget his promises; either make love to Liss or eat her.

And then Dwight found himself in bed with her. In bed with Liss, whose glistening thighs and perfect, large breasts belonged to him. Whose pelvis moved in exquisite rhythms as he stroked her. She smiled and sighed and gave him permission to do whatever he wanted. Anything. She urged him on—*take me, do me,* lille skat, *oh, God, I'm yours* . . .

He was making love to a woman, to the woman he loved, and he had never been . . . *more* . . . in his life. He felt almost human. Like the king of the jungle, a real animal.

A real one.

Then as he came, it seemed a nightmare; it seemed someone was biting him, teeth sinking into him, and he was terribly afraid. He fought back; he was Daddy's little man, his strong, little man—

So this was what it was about, he thought, straining and pitching inside her. Grabbing her, holding her. Loving the way she gasped and screamed. This was the thing that saved you.

In the morning he woke and sat up quickly, still battling his dream. It was hot, and he was alone.

The air conditioning was off. He rose naked from the bed and found Angelo in the next bedroom, also naked, asleep. Dwight roused him and he woke slowly, complaining of the heat.

The house was littered with clothes and dope and pills. A broken guitar lay smashed against the stone fireplace. Beside it, the rough surface was flecked with droplets of blood.

The blood brothers searched everywhere, but they couldn't find Liss.

They did, however, find a note in the kitchen: "Forgive me," it said. That was all.

Together they ran naked—

—there was no one around for *miles*—

outside. The Jag was gone.

The electricity had been turned off. The phones were dead. It was as if nobody had been there for years.

It grew blazing hot, inside and out.

The hours passed; the shadows grew and brought chill desert air. They made a fire in the fireplace—Dwight discovered a shred of tattered red leather among the logs of mesquite.

"Someone will come, man," Angelo said.

Forgive me.

A week passed, and no one came. Two. They had plenty to drink because Liss had stockpiled cases of mineral water in the pantry. But they couldn't eat any of the food. It made them violently ill.

Days dragged on. They staggered for hours through the desert, staggered back to the house. They tried to catch rabbits or birds— they had never tried animals before—but nothing showed up in their snares.

"This can't be happening," Angelo said. "We can't die."

Dwight winced when he looked at his blood brother. He was so thin. His eyes were sunken, and his teeth protruded from his gums. He was wasting away, his best friend. His body was eating itself, how psychedelically undelicious.

Another week passed. Still they were alone. They dragged lethargically around the house by night, after the heat had died down; but as the days wore on, they could barely move.

Flecks of blood by the fireplace. Tatters of red leather—

Forgive me.

"Listen, bro," Dwight said, swallowing hard. "You've been so good to me. My old man probably would've killed me if you hadn't come along." He took a deep breath. "I'd be dead by now anyway."

Angelo stared at Dwight. His lips parted. "Oh, no, man, no. No. It's both of us, or nothing. It's . . . someone will come."

Dwight lifted his chin. He had found his strength, his nature. After the years of doubt and hesitation, it was all coming together.

Fucking Liss had done it—she was the real cat, the food from outer space.

He saw that now.

He rose in the moonlight, light and steady on his feet.

"I'll go take a shower, Angelo. There's still water in the pipes."

Angelo became hysterical. "No, man, don't do this. I'm so hungry. Don't tempt me. Don't do this."

"It's okay." Dwight patted him, then fell into Angelo's arms and embraced him. "It's okay, Angelo."

They sobbed together for a long time. Then Dwight stood and walked toward the master bathroom. He could hear Angelo wailing with grief down the hall.

He turned on the shower—he had saved the water, just for this occasion—took off his clothes, and crept back down the hall into the kitchen. He found the biggest, sharpest knife he could; he began to salivate as he carried it back into the bathroom.

Forgive me.

He hoped she had, wherever she was now. Angelo would shit a brick if he knew the Jag was less than two miles away—hidden, well hidden. And the other weaknesses of civilization, obliterated. Phones, electricity, gas—they had taken the Wild Kingdom out of him. But now he was stripped free. Now he was the strong one, the cunning one, the cannibal cat—

"Angelo, hurry! Angelo, you'll never guess what I found!" He tried to sound as excited as he could.

And he was pretty excited, anyway.

"What? Is she back?"

"You'll never guess! Come here!!" To the shower, to be cleansed—

"I'm coming!"

Now Angelo sounded excited. Hope, Dwight supposed, could do that to people.

Dwight stopped his tears and began to laugh. What a twit. What a stupid, weak, trusting twit.

It's a dog-eat-dog world, son.

Wrong, Dad. Wrong, old guy. But thanks for the lesson just the same. You had the idea right, if not the actual details—

—He heard Angelo falling against the walls as he hurried to his blood brother—

—the rift never quite healed—

He had waited until Angelo was so hungry he'd gotten careless; he, of course, had dined more recently—

Eating the weak, Dad, that's what makes you strong. But to take someone strong and make him weak, make her weak with lust, make him weak with greed—and then eat 'em, that is the ultimate, the totality—

—Hatred's better than spinach, as you well know.

It wasn't dog-eat-dog; it was cat-eat-cat.

Dwight clutched the knife. He glanced in the bathroom mirror and saw the placid face, the clear eyes—

—oh yes, you thing they'd all been afraid of—

the monster.

All Flesh Is Clay

JOHN J. ORDOVER

JOHN J. ORDOVER currently works as an editor at Pocket Books, where he edits that company's line of Star Trek books. This profession was apparently genetically coded. According to Ordover, he was born an editor, which caused him trouble right from the start; in kindergarten he was censured for complaining that "Run, Spot, Run! See Spot Run!" was, in his own words, "Flawed minimalism at best. Needlessly redundant at worst."

Ordover has sold several short stories to such publications as Amazing Stories, New Destinies, Pulphouse, *and* Weird Tales *(where "All Flesh Is Clay" first saw print). Additionally, John's coedited an anthology titled* Coney Island Wonder Stories *with Bob Howe. This will be published in 1994 by Wildside Press.*

John also would like it to be known that he doesn't dress nearly well enough to be a splatterpunk.

At the time of this writing, "All Flesh Is Clay" had just made the preliminary ballot for the Horror Writers of America's Bram Stoker Award. And on its most literal level, this is a parable of resurrection.

Yet these analyses only constitute the bare-bones approach.

The meat on this moody, moving little snack is far more savory, as I think you'll soon agree....

Again there is a knock on my workshop door, a dry white sound that scrapes along the wood. The empty figure stands there as always, grinning as always. It moves slowly in; its thinning tendons pull at its yellowed bones.

I have a reputation among the dead. My name is whispered in the graveyards and given to the dying as a sign of hope. I gesture, and moved by love or hate or desperation the skeleton seats itself in my special chair.

I have no sympathy for them; if I were freed of life I would never return. To me there could be no reason strong enough; no lover, no child, no need for vengeance powerful enough to pull me back.

I examine the body carefully, measure the sleeve and inseam, use tiny instruments to check the shape and pattern of the cheekbones and chin. A woman, I see by the pelvis, Caucasian by the arms, Irish by the eye sockets. I speak to her.

"I can do it," I say, "can you pay the fee?" Her jaw opens and her hand comes up. From behind silver-filled teeth she takes a photograph and a money card authorized to the estate of Joan McFarrel. She'd prepared well. Few anticipate the need.

I slide the chair down flat and begin. The remnants of her tendons are useless and I cut them away, paralyzing her. Then I turn to the head.

The textbooks I studied to be licensed for my craft require a layered approach; start with the organs, they say, lash the plastic replicas in place within the ribs; put in the simulated blood tubing, then set the contracting fiber muscles; connect the metal tendons and give motion to the body; then progress to the dermal coverings and finally the head. They condemn any other practice as grotesque and unlikely to be successful.

I disagree.

I bring out a bowl of dull red putty and roll it into long thin snakes. I place them on her skull and circle her empty sockets with them, then flatten them out, spread them, knead them flat. There are still no eyes, and her cheekbones are white and rough. Her teeth still grin at me.

I lay the muscles and tendons into the red mask on her blank face, then cover them with a second layer, then a third, the cosmetic layer that looks like human skin. From a box on my desk I take round white balls, styrofoam, with black buttons glued on. Sculpting carefully, I match them to the sockets, then lay them to one side.

I build the eyelids out of cardboard backed with clay, then anchor them above the empty sockets. I place two saline-soaked pads inside the skull, then reach for the puppet eyes. The first stage is complete and I wait for the soul to merge.

There are many reasons, apparently, to leave your coffin and go walking through the night. Most are better done without flesh: flesh that can hurt; flesh that can die again. Often the reason becomes unimportant when the pain of living returns.

That is why I start with the eyes. The books tell you to finish the limbs and torso first, to work your way backward through the anatomy text. Many of those operations are successful, but the patients, reminded now of life, remain dead of their own choosing.

The full process is lucrative, and the estate pays win or lose. Many of my colleagues consider the fee and follow the book precisely, wasting time.

Her eyes come to life, blinking and staring, salt tears from the pads running down and back into her empty braincase. The styrofoam softens and the black eye-buttons turn light blue. I check the photograph and find blue eyes.

I will continue.

The face is the simplest part, and the part that gets the most praise. I am not a visual artist, but any craftsman can follow a design. I do it quickly, matching her to the picture she brought. Soon her face is staring at me from below a bare bone headcap.

The tone of the flesh, the general appearance—that requires no true talent or genius. But will the skin feel like skin, the muscles feel like muscles, not from the outside, but from the inside, to the wearer?

I run my fingers along soft but muscular arms that hours ago were nothing but bone. The hands require much precision, and I work on them closely under bright lights. Her eyes follow me as I work, sometimes closing in fear, sometimes spreading wide as I trip over a too-soon-functioning nerve; they have dampened further, the no-longer-button pupils contract and dilate in the light.

Her hands are shaped and finished, and her arms and legs and feet, but her ribs are still bone and lie empty, her pelvis fleshless and stark white. I stop for lunch before I move on.

I watch her face as I eat. Without lungs the newly made mouth cannot speak, but somehow with nothing in her skull she can still think, still have emotions that come in waves of silent laughter or lips set in grim, determined lines. The constant use is changing the face quickly, the clay fading into true skin, the eyes already filling with their own tears.

As always, I wonder what reason she has that is worth the pain

I inflict. I have heard many explanations, some trivial or misconceived; many tragic: one man, shot dead by a woman he could not make love him, thought this act of suffering would win his murderess's heart; one rich young woman, strangled by a husband who she did not know would kill her daughter next; when I told her she had no child left behind she slumped back to clay before my eyes. People return to wives and lovers; to hate and pain; to uncompleted follies: swept away by what they think they feel.

After lunch I place the major organs. They are prepackaged yet complex, both boring and difficult. I tear the cellophane wrapping from her lungs and tie them carefully inside her ribs. With air from a tube I inflate them, and check them for leaks or punctures. They work well, and I attach the trachea to the back of her throat. The sound of the air rushing through her mouth is a scream muffled by clay walls.

I put a respirator in her, then watch the inflating lungs change color and become at least somewhat alive. I unblock her throat and speak to her.

"Hello," I say pleasantly. "Things are going well." She tries to speak, then tries again. I think I understand her. "Yes, quite well," I say, then turn back to my work while she breathes deeply and tries to talk. Despite the distraction I secure the heart and stomach and liver, then discover the gallbladder is too wide and trim it back.

Her lungs are working better now. She is crying with the pain, yelling it out, the sound sinking into my padded walls. Her volume lifts and falls, going up whenever I touch her, softening when I step away.

Her pain comes from her own choice. I can see in her eyes that she knows this, that she does not regret the ordeal. How foolish.

I finish inside her, her heart beating slowly, intestines and uterus in place. The law requires that my creations be sterile, but I refuse to be less than thorough and connect her ovaries. She must be complete.

Her arms and legs have motion now, and I cuff them down to keep myself and her new body safe. There is still no skin between her neck and thighs, and there are many nerves to place. An unrestrained reflex could destroy her.

Her screams increase in number as I lay the skin in and the new connections start to grow. If I placed her brain now, it would be far worse. This way the impulses are implied, not sensed, and some of the pain is lost. At least that's what the souls tell us.

The first and second layers done, I start on her breasts. She is clothed in the photo she gave me, but I can guess at the shape her body had and I improve it slightly. I make the men just a trifle longer, too. No one complains.

I build her vulva and vagina carefully, using the standard pattern for her genetic type. I plant the area with scattered hair, slightly darker than the bright red I will use on her head. I feel inside her for a moment, getting the texture perfect and the small glands placed correctly. I stroke her gently until I feel her contract once on my fingers, then I withdraw them and step back.

She looks perfect, and when I run my hands along her she feels perfect, still more like clay than flesh but evolving quickly. I walk around her and put my hands on her head.

Her braincase is still empty. Gently I remove the package from the cool, dark place it is stored, then peel back its wet covering. The grey rubber mass is slippery and must be connected exactly right.

The brain sealed in place, I secure her red hair and sit waiting, coffee in hand, for the true scream.

It comes an hour later, an average time, and she shakes the house with her voice, shouting her pain outward like a baby. She does it twice, then pants heavily. I walk over to her.

I examine her again for texture, ask a few questions about how this or that feels to her. She pants as she answers, her tone reflecting relief and memory of pain. I help her up and go to fetch clothes for her, all part of the service.

When I get back she dresses and asks for coffee. I use it to test her senses; taste, smell, heat, touch, and the numerous small reflexes of drinking and swallowing. She works perfectly, nature and determination again making up for lack of precision, smoothing over any errors in duplication.

She does not now look or feel like clay.

"Was it worth it?" I ask her. No one ever says no; they would look idiotic.

She turns her eyes on me, surprised. "Of course," she says.

"Was being dead so bad?" I ask, watching her face carefully.

She thinks about it while sipping at her coffee. "It was a great opportunity," she begins, "you know, a chance to be forgiven and begin again. But you can't finish what you'd already started."

"And you have something to finish?" I say, a patronizing tone in my voice. "A marriage, a love affair, a child you think needs you?"

"A painting," she answers flatly. "It's sitting on my easel, only half-finished. I tried to forget about it . . ." She sips again at her coffee, then looks helpless and shrugs, ". . . so I came back."

"A painting?" I ask. For some reason the thought upsets me.

She shrugs again. "So sue me, I don't like to stop in the middle of something." She stands up. "My will said to leave my studio alone. Can you call me a cab?"

I do so, and when she leaves I think about my next client, and my next. I work a lot, and there is always the chance that something will happen, that between the lungs and liver my heart will fail, or I will fall, and there will be a canvas on my table that I will never finish, never make whole.

The image chases me and I shake; I think of the pain of merging and I shake again. For most of the night I balance the fears.

In the morning I call my lawyer, then arrange for nude photos to be taken, from many angles. I will be ready, I tell myself, if I become a canvas for someone else. If I become the one strapped empty to a table, desperate for life. I am prepared.

I love my work.

Imprint

NINA KIRIKI HOFFMAN

A prime singularity of splatterpunk lies in its focus on the now. *Call it what you will—realworld horror, urban terror, fractured reality—splatterpunk characteristically examines isochronal kinks. True-life fears like pathological brutality. Bigotry. Sexual violence. And splat usually accomplishes this the same way rock 'n' roll does.*

By playing REAL LOUD, right in your face.

But not always.

Witness "Red," Richard Christian Matheson's contribution to Splatterpunks I. *A short-short story I dubbed* subtle splat.

A tag which could just as easily be affixed to NINA KIRIKI HOFFMAN's "Imprint."

Hoffman is the sixth of seven children who grew up in southern California. Her day job "involves channeling other writers, most of them still living." She presently resides in Eugene, Oregon, with "four cats, a big TV, and a mannequin." The Thread That Binds the Bones, a fantasy novel, was published by Avon in 1993.

Like Poppy Z. Brite, Nina's one of those rising stars whose quick ascension has been dizzying. She first appeared in small-press publications like Grue *and* 2 A.M., *but her unpredictable, off-the-wall talents rapidly moved Hoffman into such professional circles as* Amazing Stories, Weird Tales, *and* Alfred Hitchcock's Mystery Magazine.

One such professional effort, "Zombies For Jesus," is a personal favorite. I enjoy it for the fact that it's a strange, ultimately touching story, combining guilt, evangelical tent shows, and the redemption of the living dead.

But I still thought Nina's "Imprint" was best suited for this book.

Why?
Go back to what I wrote earlier, about reality and subtle splat.
And remember that an all-too-real situation fuels "Imprint"'s little motor.
The same motor which subtly powers the awful, perpetual-motion machine that situation has become ...

*B*ang.
Ten-year-old Sharon was sitting in the living room with her younger sister Caren. Daddy was in the study. He had played with Sharon and Caren for a while, the no-panties game, first him being the horse, then the girls being the horse, each in turn. Then they played the puppy-feeding game. "Put it in your mouth, honey girl," Daddy had said to them, first Caren, then Sharon. Sharon got a mouthful of warm salty white. It was messy, and Daddy told them to go clean up and get dressed. Then he went into his study, but he didn't close the door. He told the girls to be quiet. He said he had a headache. He said he needed to think. So Sharon and Caren sat on the couch, staring at the TV set, which was off.

Sharon made pictures and music come on. It was a school picture, with lots of pretty children in it. The girls were wearing white ruffled frocks and the boys had on white suits with short pants, and they were standing and singing by their desks. The teacher wore a ruffled dress too, and she had waves and waves of beautiful golden hair. She smiled at the children as if she was proud of them, and all the children were singing and smiling. They were happy because they lived at school and never never had to go home.

The bang was awfully loud. It made the picture on the TV screen go away, and left a big gray blank.

The oven door dropped open with a bang.
Sharon was thirty-four.
The boys were due home from school any minute. She stood in the yellow and white kitchen with two oven mitts on. One was shaped like a fish and the other had a picture of a little country house on it in slate blue. Cookies were baking in the oven, and the

house was full of the warm doughy smell of them. Every ten minutes, she took a sheet of cookies out, slid another in.

If only she could keep both oven mitts on all the time, she wouldn't have to see her hands, the image of her father's hands. She could glance away from mirrors, not stare into the ice-gray eyes that looked like her father's eyes, not notice the crinkling around the edges of her eyes that was just like the crinkling on her father's face. But her hands were always there in front of her. And they had a life of their own.

She had first noticed it when Douglas, the younger boy, was in diapers. When she changed him, one of her hands always stroked his little penis before she fastened the tapes. That was when she knew that her father had come back to lead her and lock her into living his life over.

Her hands made fists inside the oven mitts. The timer beeped, and she took a sheet of cookies out and slid the next one in. She had to take the oven mitts off now. Dropping cookie dough from a spoon onto a cookie sheet with the mitts on was just too clumsy.

She drew the mitts off and looked at her hands. There was the tracery of veins, just like she had seen on Daddy's hands, two maps of the same rivers.

She heard the boys shouting outside, yelling to their friend who lived down the block. Her head pounded. The back door banged open. The boys, subdued now, came into the kitchen.

The bang was so loud. Not like guns on television. Caren and Sharon saw cop shows sometimes, but they had to keep the sound low because Daddy got headaches so easily. They had heard guns on television: distant pops like cap pistols two houses away.

Sharon glanced at Caren. Caren was twisting her finger in her hair, the way she did sometimes, over and over until there was a big snarl on the side of her head that had to be cut out and Mommy told her what a bad girl she was to ruin her pretty looks that way.

Caren was staring at the floor. Sharon wondered if the bang had made her jump. Sharon wondered when Mommy would get home. She sat for a while staring at the screen of the TV, but her musical wouldn't come back. She sighed, edged forward, and her shoes thudded on the floor as she stood up.

The back door banged open. "Cookies," said Sharon to her sons, smiling.

The older boy, Arnold, gave her a nervous smile in response. Douglas stared at the kitchen floor.

Maybe this time she could just give them the cookies, let them go upstairs, leave them alone. Maybe this time she could just be Sharon, acting alone. She loved her boys so much, and she hated what she did to them. Still wearing the clumsy oven mitts, she picked up two cookies and turned to the boys. Daddy's voice came out of her mouth, saying what Daddy had always said: "Who wants to be first?"

Douglas kicked the stove.

The house was silent. The only thing Sharon heard was Caren's breathing, loud, through her mouth. Sharon tiptoed across the living room rug. Daddy said their footsteps gave him headaches if they ran around being rough loud children, so they had learned to be very quiet, even if they were wearing shoes with loud soles.

She looked into the study. Daddy had his head on the desk, and his hand. There was a black thing in his hand, and his head was broken and red.

Her knees felt wobbly, and what was in her stomach wanted to come back up. She turned away and tiptoed back across the rug to sit on the couch again. Caren still sat twirling her hair. They waited as daylight faded. When the door banged open and Mommy walked in, it was dark everywhere in the house.

She stopped fighting Daddy. She did the boys and then sent them up to their rooms with lots of cookies. Her head pounded. She went into the bathroom and washed her hands, then went to sit in her husband's study. He was still at the hardware store he managed; he'd be home soon. She got the key out of the trophy cup on the mantel, unlocked the bottom drawer of his desk, and took out the gun.

It was heavy and dark in her hand, more complicated than she had guessed it would be. She had told her husband she didn't want to know anything about guns, and he had respected her wishes.

She turned the gun over, looking at it from all sides. There was a little red button on it. The safety, Daddy whispered in her head. Push it.

She pushed the button. She held the gun the correct way, with her finger on the trigger. What do I do now? she thought, over the pounding in her temples.

Some people hold it up to their foreheads, whispered Daddy, but if you really want to make sure, you have to eat it. Put it in your mouth, honey girl.

She put the barrel in her mouth and sucked on it for a little while. It tasted cold and blank and oily. She thought about the boys upstairs and wondered what they would do when they heard the bang.

Daddy had died when he was thirty-four. She couldn't live on past this year: there was no path for her to follow, none of Daddy's footprints left to guide her. Her hands were his.

Bang.

Twenty-Two and Absolutely Free

JOHN PIWARSKI

If a single word could somehow capture the emotional undercurrent of the 1990's, it would have to be: RAGE. A sullen anger that's particularly apparent in today's twentysomethings.

Yet who can blame them? Yes, each generation may inevitably inherit the proceeding's problems. But Generation X, (to cop the term invented by Doug Coupland in his 1991 book of the same name, a label most twentysomethings don't particularly care for), has been passed the filthy end of a particularly dirty stick.

Frenzied nationwide violence. A bleak economic future. Polluted environments. Corrupt power structures. The death of all beauty, security, and hope.

No wonder the American Dream's become a pointless joke to the very children for which it was intended.

That's nearly as ironic as the notion that splatterpunk's just a bloodier form of old-fashioned horror.

Hoo-boy.

We're all laughing at that *one, folks. You betcha.*

Guys like JOHN PIWARSKI are laughing loudest of all.

"Twenty-four, resident of Syracuse, New York, and recipient of the prestigious Cheese Award for Best Actor in a Musical Comedy—The Man Who Collected Lungs—*Piwarski has been writing dirty limericks since the age of twenty-one, successfully passing them off as stories that have either appeared or are slated to appear in such magazines as* Midnight Graffiti, Abberations, *and* Hardboiled. *Well over seventeen kilometers in length, John is soft and green with a series of finlike ridges riddling his hindquarters and underbelly. Capable of speeds up to and including seventy-five mph, he is a territorial animal that keeps to the trees."*

That's all the biographical information Piwarski sent in. But the more important details are already evident in this work.

"Twenty-Two and Absolutely Free" takes an edgy, absolutely hilarious look at Anytown, U.S.A. And its sarcastic treatment of our culture's mutant fascination with serial killers is only an opening shot; Piwarski's after much bigger game.

Like the nuclear family. Dating. Or what it's like to be a certain type of angry young American female.

One who's honest, confrontational, and loud.

Pissed off, smart, and funny. Very funny.

Sorta like a splatterpunk.

Of which this story is a prime cut.

*I*t says here that he only kills women aged twenty-two. By the way, happy birthday."

"Some present . . . Here, let me see that." She proceeded to read aloud the chronicle of indelicacies committed by a nameless, faceless entity who Kathy referred to simply as a "fuckhead."

"Could be anybody, this guy," Mark said, mussing up his brush-cut Eraserhead style and doing the *Twilight Zone* theme. "Ooo-na-na/Ooo-na-na-na."

"Stop."

". . . could even be me."

"Don't make me laugh," she snapped. "I'd kick the shit out of you any day of the week." She threw the newspaper out of the convertible. The wind carried it away.

"Litterbug," Mark said, his hand on her thigh, his mood ring going bright crimson.

"What's the difference?" she said, cranking Van Halen up another notch and looking for cops as she pulled a small mirror and a razor blade from the glove compartment. "We're all fucked."

"You use the eff word too much," Mark said, rolling a twenty. "But you never put out. Scared to death of the word when *I* use it. You're a walking contradiction."

"Please spare me your notions of delicatessen poetry. There's a murderer out there somewhere. Besides, I'm not entirely comfortable around you just yet. When I am, I'll fuck you comatose."

"It could be your subtlety that draws me to you," he said, doing

his John Malkovich. Turning . . . "Shit! Cops!" and they stashed the
stuff quickly, but just as the police car cruised by the lights started
to flash and up came the sirens. The neighborhood shark was gone
in moments. Mark let out a pent-up breath. "Too close, too close.
He was right on our ass."

"Maybe he got a lead on that fuckhead with the butcher knife
and fishing gear."

"Yeah, or maybe he *is* that fuckhead. Don't forget what happened
to that speeder on camera in L.A. Nobody trusts cops anymore."

"Don't be paranoid," she said serenely, looking up at the stars.
The night was right. Maybe she would have sex with him tonight,
at last. At least it would shut him up for a while. But then again, if
she did go ahead and satisfy him, he would undoubtedly stop trying
to please her; he would stop buying flowers and taking her to Jojo's
and the clubs on Saturday night and calling up out of the blue just
to ask, "How you doing?"

He hadn't earned her trust yet.

No, she thought. *Let him wait it out.*

They finished the coke and went to Sage's and danced until four.
Well, she danced. Mark spent most of the time puking in the john.
On the way home he presented her with a birthday present, then
promptly passed out in the back seat.

"You're the only one I know that coke makes tired," she said
tenderly, touching his face.

She put the top up, secured it, locked the doors and windows,
and left him there. She walked the four blocks home and as she
turned her house key she noticed the light was on and rolled her
eyes.

"Terrific," she muttered.

She opened the door.

There was Mother, passed out atop the kitchen table. Catsup
bottles and salt and pepper shakers and the sugar flask and cream
decanter and candle holders and vase and centerpiece of wilted
roses and tablecloth and doilies and cutlery and all the rubble of an
uneaten, painstakingly prepared dinner were strewn about the floor,
as was an empty Scotch bottle. Not Chivas, she noticed. *Oh Mom*,
she thought, *if you're going to punish yourself, why can't you do
it with decent booze? The cheap stuff should be for good times. . . .*

To make matters worse, it looked as if Kathy's mother had masturbated, or tried to, before passing out. Her skirt was hiked up, her panties were down around her ankles, and her hands were . . .

"One day Dad's going to find you and not me," Kathy muttered, helping the dead weight of her mother up the stairs and into bed. If Kathy noticed that she was crying and going hoarse as she whispered pleadingly, incoherently into her mother's ear, she chose not to dwell upon it.

Dad came home shortly afterward, lipstick forming a layered glaze about the zipper of his rumpled trousers, blood streaming down his nose. "Hi, darling!" He started to make coffee. "Want some? Jesus! What happened to the kitchen?" Dad seemed in most excellent humor. Flushed, in fact. Had been for weeks, ever since his bald spot had started to cloud over.

"I fell," Kathy said, throwing hate rays into his broad back. "Sorry." Icy.

"No problemo, sweetie." He filled a *LOVE YA, PUDDIN'!* mug with coffee and sauntered away. "I'll be out on the veranda admiring this most heavenly of sunrises." He raised his arms exuberantly. "Yell if you need me."

"I'll yell," she said, "if I need you." She shook three Bayer aspirin into her hand and downed them dry as she set about cleaning the kitchen. Mom had broken at least three dinner dishes. Good ones, the china, the most expensive stuff. Of the set, there were maybe three or four dishes remaining. The china had been a wedding present from . . . from who? She couldn't remember. Some divorce lawyer friend of Dad's. What did it matter anymore anyway? Kathy guessed that when the day came when there were no longer any valuables to shatter, enraged, then that day would be the end of Mom and Dad. Which wasn't so bad, actually. Almost all of her friends had divorced parents. All it meant to them was two party houses instead of one. Her friends would be so pleased, but Kathy guessed she would feel bad when the whip finally did come down.

Valium and R.E.M. on headphones with her feet up and Marlboro after Marlboro until Mom knocked on the door at two-thirty P.M. with a black eye and said, "Your father thinks we should have breakfast as a family. One of his nurturer moods again. Please come down."

Mom wore driving gloves in the house.

Breakfast as a family, Kathy thought.

Mom kept her head down like a good little soldier.

Dad hid behind a newspaper folded out like a carnival dome and snapped facts at everyone as if he were the only one in the house who could read. "That maniac fuckhead killed another girl last night," he said, leering around the newspaper, teasing his only daughter. "Twenty-two, like you. By the way, happy belated birthday."

"Some present."

"Potato pancake, anyone?" Mom chanced, ready to duck at the first sign of artillery, cringing at Dad's dramatic silence.

"Just one," he said menacingly.

"I'll take seven," Kathy said. Then: "Who?"

"Who what?" said Dad.

"Who'd this fuckhead kill?"

"Um ... Meyers, Stacy Meyers ... *Saaaaay*, wasn't she at your birthday party yesterday afternoon?"

"Yeah," Kathy said, asking Mom for more potato pancakes but not making a move to eat any. "She came stag. She looked awful."

"That's a damned shame," Dad said. "The bastard chopped her up into little tiny teeny-weeny bits."

"May I have some catsup?" Kathy asked.

Mom jumped, excited; at last she had a chance to *do* something, and was grateful.

Kathy lathered her stack of potato pancakes with catsup and mustard and pickle relish and strawberry jam and asked for another helping. "These are great, Mom," she said, her fork still idle and cold. "Mmm! You never fail!"

Mom beamed, pleased.

"Bystanders say there was blood everywhere," Dad went on. "Police cannot find the toes or vagina. Jeeezus! Was she a good friend, Kathy?"

Kathy shrugged. "She was kind of weird. She spent afternoons helping deformed children gain self-esteem or something. A real do-gooder Just-Say-No Mother-Theresa type who never got any attention from guys. Where'd she die?"

"Near the arcade," Dad said, nibbling the edges of his single potato pancake; Kathy knew from painful experience that he could make it last for hours, and Mom always made such a huge batch. Although Dad's nose was no longer bleeding, he hadn't bothered washing his face or changing his clothes; he never did; he liked Mom to see the evidence; he wanted her to have no illusions whatsoever about the way things were.

Kathy asked pleadingly for another potato pancake.

"There's a cop killer on the loose now too," said Dad. "The car was found upside down. It had been torched and gutted. They can't find the poor guy's head."

Mom piped up, "I heard on the news this morning that the precinct got a ransom note for the head and there are rumors that the cops are actually going to pay the ransom. Now what do you suppose they'd want with a head?"

Dad glared at her for a full minute, until she was a quivering thing, ashamed of herself for ever having opened her mouth. "I'm going out," Dad proclaimed gaily, lumbering heavily out the door. "Don't wait up."

Next came the rev of his Jag.

Mom cradled her head in her hands and began to cry. "Go to your CUNT! See if I CARE!" she shrieked, but by then Dad was three miles away, probably. "I'm going to KILL that man one of these days," she whimpered. "I mean it."

"You're a mess," Kathy said. "Why don't you go to bed, Mom?"

Mom continued to cry and spit useless venom at the four walls. She'd been wearing the same dressing gown for three weeks now. Her pallor was a jaundice yellow; she could no longer tolerate sunlight. The stems of her dancing fingers were burned by filterless Camels, as were her twiggy wrists and forearms. Mom was forty-four.

This is how she gets back at him, Kathy thought. *By humiliating herself, chopping her hair off, burning her arms. He just shrugs and drives away.*

"I'll kill him, I swear I will," Mom ranted as Kathy once again assisted her up the stairs.

"No," Kathy insisted. "That won't solve anything."

"You've been reading the Bible again!" Mom snapped accusingly. "I told you to stay away from that mind poison!"

"I mean you'd get *caught*, Mom. Look at you; you'd never be able to hide what you did, least of all in front of detectives. C'mon, you've seen movies, you know how merciless those fuckheads are; everything's a game to those people; they don't care about anybody's feelings. They'd break you down for good. So stop talking about killing Dad. It's stupid."

Mom made it up the stairs all right, then rushed headlong into the bathroom. Kathy cleaned her up afterward, and forced Valium down her throat by holding her nose, then led her to bed.

"I have to do it," Mom said. "Somebody help me...."

Kathy closed the door quietly behind her.

"What then?" she said aloud. "What if she does kill him and somehow gets away with it? Three months from now I'll read about yet another serial killer and it'll be Mom, running around with a chainsaw in one hand, a Camel in the other. I *know* her; she never knows when to stop. She'll kill Dad's girlfriends, the recycling guy who throws trash on the lawn, the mailman who opens our Christmas cards . . . won't solve anything. . . . Oh great, now I'm talking to myself!"

Kathy gave her potato pancakes to Ether, Shout, and Ichor, her Dobermans. She cleaned the upstairs bathroom with as much energy as the sleepless night of her birthday had allotted her, then used up a whole can of Lysol all through the house, as if anything in a can and bought in a store could ever erase the stench of the pure hatred between Mom and Dad.

The phone rang at six P.M.

"What?" Kathy said.

"Hey, babe," said Mark.

"Hi," she said, watching the evening news with the sound turned low. An infant had been found, dismembered, in a church on West and Forty-ninth. Police said three quarts of holy water had been stolen as well. They also said that it looked like the MO of a serial killer from Washington, DC. *They're all migrating to my hometown*, Kathy thought.

"Do you like it?" Mark asked, trying and failing to sound casual.
"Like what?"

Silence. Three minutes of it. Then: "That hurts, Kathy, it really does—"

"Look, would you tell me what . . ." Then she remembered. "Oh Mark, baby, I was just kidding, don't get upset. Of course your present is wonderful."

She could hear him smile, relieved, over the phone. "I knew you'd like it. It's special, like you. Not another one like it anywhere."

"I know," Kathy said, snatching the tiny, gaily wrapped box from the bedside table and hurriedly undoing the bow. "I can see that; it *is* unique."

She opened her present.

It was, indeed, unique.

"Wear it tonight," he beseeched.

"I will," she said. "Wear it where?"

"I thought maybe we'd go to the movies."

She groaned. "Are you sure it's safe? I mean, I was just reading about a serial killer who brings hedge clippers into movie theaters and cuts heads off, and that's right around here."

"Yeah, I heard about him, too, but he only does that in theaters showing love movies. We'll see the new Scorsese, just to be safe, or maybe a sci-fi thing. That reminds me, you hear about Stacy?"

Kathy fidgeted. "Yeah. Cold meat pie."

"Fucking waste. Pick you up at eight?"

A sigh. "I guess so."

"Don't forget. Wear the brooch."

She hung up.

The brooch was solid gold. Kathy could tell. When she was thirteen years old, her mother had sat her down upon her knee and explained the myriad of differences between real gold and the type of gold you got from guys who only wanted a fuck, a night, not love. And this was real gold, all right. And she guessed Mark really did love her; at least he thought he did. That was good enough for her. She guessed.

It was a mushroom cloud, and at the center there was the shape of a man, a suave silhouette, emerging from the mushroom cloud, his back turned to it in disgust, striding away, untouched, from the devastation.

She squealed as she studied the brooch.

"Wild," she muttered, tacking it to her blouse and inadvertently—"Shit!"—gouging herself.

She studied the bead of blood for a long time.

At six P.M. she watched the news and sang Happy Birthday to herself as she learned of yet another serial killer. This one's known proclivities included strangulation and ...

She turned away from the set. She didn't care about the latest high-tech cutting-edge serial killer. She continued eating her Cheerios and drinking peppermint schnapps.

In the mirrorlike face of the fridge she decided she hated her hair, her face, and especially her nails; she just couldn't get a sharp enough edge to them. She snarled at her reflection.

Turning back to the TV, she saw that the government was planning to bomb certain sections of her hometown. Apparently the serial killer who disliked policemen had gone on a rampage and killed forty-two of them, and that was going too far.

The screen filled with pictures of nuclear missiles and a map of city central, Hometown USA.

Kathy went upstairs to check on Mom.

Mom was blue, still, and very dead.

Overdose. Big time.

The strength left her legs, and she fell to her knees.

Mom wore a blissful smile, loud and surreal, the smile of a slaughterhouse escapee, the smile of one utterly at peace.

Kathy quietly closed the door behind her. She checked the medicine chest and found the empty bottle of sleeping pills. Apparently Mom had been playing possum earlier. She'd developed an immunity to Valium.

Kathy called the ambulance, a little shocked by her own lucidity and appalled by the complete absence of grief or even a quaver in her voice as she flatly told the snotty woman her home address and explained the circumstances.

"How long has she been dead, miss?" A nasal twang made all the more annoying by the snapping of gum. Cow and cud. "Miss?"

"Many, many years," Kathy said, hanging up.

"If I'd have let you kill Daddy," she said to the closed door of her mother's bedroom, "you wouldn't . . ."

Her words, like her thoughts, trailed off into nowhere.

Mark was five minutes late. Kathy left the front door wide open for the ambulance. As she and Mark roared away, she could hear the faraway beginnings of sirens.

"I'll miss you," Kathy whispered.

"Who are you talking to?" Mark asked.

"No one."

The sky was vast and grey. Silent like a predator. There were two half-moons up there, seemingly spaced millions of miles apart. No stars.

As they cruised past the neighborhoods in silence, Kathy decided to tell Mark everything about her day.

"Jesus Christ! You want to go back home?"

"No," she said. "Never."

"I'm really sorry," Mark said, sounding as if he meant it. She studied his horsey features, his horrid haircut, his big, graceless hands, his funny chicken legs and jams.

"You see the news tonight?" she asked, searching the sky for bombs, for mushroom clouds, for UFOs, hell, maybe even pterodactyls, considering what a strange day it had been thus far.

"No," he said. "Why? Should I have? You look worried."

They're gonna bomb us tonight, she thought, hoping he could read her mind, for she found she could not bring herself to say it; she was seized with the urge to say something else, something important. Like an itch demanding to be scratched, she found she *had* to say it, and, touching her doomsday brooch gingerly, she looked over at him, and was about to say "I love you" when her eyes drifted past him toward an alleyway.

Mark had stopped for a red light.

She saw Daddy. He swung an axe viciously into the throat of a motionless derelict. Swung it again and again and again and again and the derelict just stayed put, sprawled out. There were rows of them, waiting. They were not asleep, not soused out of their heads. They were complacent, complying, resigned to the twisted necessity of the axe.

Daddy, it seemed, was more than happy to oblige them. One by one. Endless rows of meat on a treadmill.

"Kathy?" Mark said, waving a hand before her face and bugging his eyes.

Behind them, a trucker's horn blared. *"Move it, asshole!"*

"Kathy?"

She tore her eyes away from the axe, away from the grateful, stained smiles of the derelicts, away from the all-business bearing in Daddy's face and shoulders and swiftness, his tight job-well-done smile, the tongue protruding . . .

"Kathy?"

"C'mon, move it up there!"

"I'm all right, Mark. Just drive. You got a green light. Green lights from here on in. Just go, please."

"You looked at me so hard for a second. . . . You looked like you were about to say something."

She studied his unblinking green eyes.

Behind them, the beefy trucker dropped down from the cab, crowbar at the ready.

"We're going to miss the credits, Mark," she said.

He hit the gas and they were gone. In the distance, Kathy thought she heard Daddy begin to whistle as he worked.

Outside the Ciniplex, police cruisers were stacked like burnt toast, one atop the other, each smoldering and wheezing. Severed heads were scattered everywhere.

"Two, please," said Mark, holding Kathy tightly, protectively, as if she had never seen severed heads before.

"Shouldn't you call an ambulance, lady?" Kathy snapped.

The dainty young woman behind the glass shrugged, tugging at her iron earrings. Below her waistline a man was grunting and lapping. "No ambulances to call," she said. "There's a new serial killer kills only ambulance drivers. You should watch the news."

As Kathy and Mark went in to see the movie, Kathy thought she heard bombs whistling faintly through the sky. But the sound, real or imagined, was quickly swallowed by an ominous silence that hummed faintly, as if manufactured.

"They're gonna bomb us tonight," Kathy said.

"Who?" said Mark.

"Da gubment."

"That's just the Lower East Side. My dad was just made junior partner! They're gonna bomb *him?* The white picket suburbs? Such an idyllic tax bracket? Get Now!"

On the walls, glass-encased one-sheets of bad films were all but smothered with bloody handprints and afterbirth graffiti.

Mark ordered popcorn with cow-flavored mock butter and Pepsi and Corn Nuts and together they got coked up during the previews.

Midway through the slapstick comedy on child molestation, Kathy leaned over and said, "I have something important to tell you, Mark."

He looked over, eyes agleam. "I already know."

"Then you'll help me?"

His face fell. "I don't quite follow you—"

"I thought you said you knew!"

"SHHH!" said the man behind them, the only other person in the theater.

"I know that you love me," Mark said softly.

"Until I say it, you don't know shit. But I need your help with something. Something important."

Mark looked back at the screen for a while. The images flickered dully across his overcooked eyes. His knees went up and down and down and up. A little too much coke. Soon he would be dead to the world. "Good movie," he hiccupped.

"SHHH!" said the man behind them.

Kathy squirmed around in her seat. She could not make out the guy's features. "Fuck you," she whispered, staring.

She looked back at the screen, flustered. The scene currently playing featured heavy daylight, garishly bright. There was no reason in the world why she couldn't see the face of the man behind her.

Turning again, she stared at this figure, trying once again to make out his face. She thought she caught a gleam of very large, very white teeth. She drew back. "SHHH!" he hissed. She went cold to the marrow and turned away, clutching her brooch and feeling the shape of the golden dapper little man upon its face.

He's Death, she thought. *Capital D.*

That's the coke talking!—a stray quip in her head.

"Death," she said aloud. She had only done one line; it was not "the coke talking," as this self-righteous little preacher in her psyche insisted. She turned yet again to face the man who didn't have one.

"I am not afraid of you," she said softly.

Death's smile grew wider. It hovered, faintly swaying, as if disembodied, or dangling by a string. An ice-cold draft hit her full-force in the face. She turned away from Death and ate her popcorn and tried to watch the movie.

"Mark," she struggled. "I'm going to kill my father with or without you. But I need your help. He's big. Yes or no? No maybes or I'll-think-about-its. Give."

She studied her boyfriend.

"SHHH!" Death rattled.

She ignored him, her, or it, and stared at Mark until the whole world, the whole universe was Mark, all Mark and nothing but. He turned, expectant. Although his hands were in his lap, it seemed as if a palm lay outstretched.

"I love you," she said matter-of-factly.

"Then I will help you," he said, rolling his bloodshot attention back to the screen. "I have a gun in the glove compartment. Fully loaded. Semiauto. Kerpow!"

"Why do you have a gun?"

" 'S hardly important, Kath. Guns are a prerequisite, I suppose. So: you distract him and I ice him and then what? This is, after all, your plan." His knees went up and down and up and—

"SHHH!" said Death.

"AWW, GO TO HELL!" Mark brayed, not turning around.

"I'm sure there's a serial killer in the area who favors firearms," said Kathy with a sense of falling. "We could pin it on him. My Dad uses MCI and there's this new serial killer who I guess uses AT&T and kills people he thinks are giving his number to that 'Friends and Family' conspiracy."

"Yeah," Mark said. "Hey yeah! Okay! That sounds good!"

They went back to watching the movie.

Behind them, Death had apparently given up his campaign to have quiet. He drummed his fingers on the back of Kathy's seat. There was a crunch of crackling plastic. "I'm too sexy for my scythe," he sang softly.

There was an icy draft on the back of Kathy's neck. A foul stench got into her hair. Death was blowing rudely into her ear, tenderly whispering sick nothings—"I get lonely sometimes, and cored apples don't cut it like they used to, my little blood muffin"— dropping popcorn pellets down the back of her blouse, popcorn that was greasy from his hands, popcorn stinking of gasoline and dried blood and phony butter flavoring and something else, sickly sweet, some outlaw perfume of madness. Distilled, manufactured, bottled inside the head.

She would not turn and look the jerk in the teeth again and after a while Death left her alone.

Kathy and Mark, their hands clasped tightly, watched the remainder of the film in silence. She wasn't really paying attention, and she suspected Mark wasn't either, but she needed to drown herself, immerse her tumultuous thoughts in imagery, and she forced herself to accept nothing but the movie. The movie was all-important. Timed and rehearsed. It would go away when the lights came up. Death wouldn't.

As the end credits rolled and Kathy was left with nothing to pay attention to but the worms of worry in her guts, she noticed that Mark's grip had slackened, had become quite limp and cold.

She turned to him.

Mark's head was gone, in its stead a stringy stalk.

Her hands were caked with blood. Red, red mittens. They were asleep in their many-layered cakes. She could feel nothing in them save the tingle of onrushing wakefulness.

She was about to scream. It welled up in her throat, a living thing; wailed and crashed and pounded its fists against the lining of her cheeks. It grew in the womb of her mouth. Coming, coming. Death hissed

"SHHHHHHHHHHHHHH!"

behind her.

Kathy whirled around but there was nothing, nothing but the

rusty blood-stained crescent moon of a free-handed scythe. Death's vacated theater seat was a sponge dripping offal.

The credits ended. The house lights came up.

The scream punched its way into the light. It had had time to ferment inside her head. It had matured into a word. The word was: "FUCKHEAD!"

and it shattered the amazing silence.

Running now, running, Reeboks squeaking shrilly against the flypaper floor of Ciniplex Moviebox 9.

She roared toward the beacon of EXIT, certain it would be locked, certain she would have to barrel on through, which she was fully prepared to do. She would not look back; Death would be there, lips puckered like a raisin for a French kiss crammed with maggots and Chuckles. Her heart told her this was so.

Since she'd turned twenty-two, however, she had learned to never trust what was in her heart.

The door was unlocked. She chanced a look back. Death was not there. The door swung wide.

Freedom. Gorgeous, radiant light. Smell of pseudobutter and spilled Cola product. Popcorn and candy. The hum of the bullet-riddled condom machine.

And blood and brains and hair and teeth and eyes.

The zit-faced boy with the cherry beret—the kid who'd sold them the popcorn and Corn Nuts—was dead. His head was all over the place. Laughing patrons spilled from an adjacent Moviebox, oblivious to the blood and carnage, heedless of Death as he flitted and flirted and ingratiated himself into their number, goosing the elderly and buggering children in the skull, cutting off heads and copping cheap feels.

The laughing ones gradually seemed to accept his presence as something natural, something kitsch but compelling, like a weirdly patterned poisonous snake better admired in pictures than eye to eye. They jockeyed for his attentions, a lugubrious indifference upon the faces of some, while on others the blanched, desperate, gleeful gratefulness she'd seen on the faces of the derelicts Daddy's axe was having for din-din.

Death, the overgrown figure in his Hawaiian shirt and rubber apron and muddy army boots and hairless, polished pate, his wide mouth with its wormlike gums and blinding nuclear teeth, his color-less eyes dry and gritty like stones, was a sucker for this kind of thing, and continued exploiting his flock until there was nothing left.

Kathy waited to die. Unafraid.

Death yawned and stretched. "Hey, babe," he said.

"You're a fuckhead," she said, strangely rational.

He stared hard. "Them's fightin' words."

She slid her hand into her pocket and came up with a ring of keys she could use as claws, remembering an old saying that human spirit was bred to challenge hurricanes and earthquakes. But she realized, on closer inspection, that this was just a man, a man whose eyes would squirt like squibs just like anybody else's. No, this wasn't Death. Death didn't lift his leg and fart and giggle afterward like some ill-bred schoolboy. Death, to the best of her knowledge, didn't wear a name tag that said "Earl Niglet" on it.

The man considered her for a long, long time. Then: "Wait in the damned car."

"I want a piece of you. You killed my boyfriend."

"WAIT! IN! THE! CAR!"

She stared him down until a thin line of tobacco drool fell from his lips. She slid her claws back into her pocket and slowly exited the theater. She strode across the parking lot.

Earl Niglet drove a beat-up but souped-up hearse with all sorts of social activist bumper stickers on it. She leaned against the door. The man she'd mistaken for Death exited the theater with a small black box in his big white hands, a plunger at the center of the box. When he was almost to the car, sidestepping severed heads, he depressed the plunger and the world shook and slipped for a moment.

The Ciniplex went up in a roiling white mushroom, with Earl Niglet functioning as the dapper silhouette.

She tore the brooch from her blouse and stared at it, feeling enormously cheated.

She numbly opened the passenger door of the hearse and saw a box of dentifrice on the dash.

That's all she remembered.

* * *

She awoke in Death's admittedly shitty apartment, an ice pack on her head, the brooch still clasped in her left hand, the pin drawing blood. Earl Niglet's apartment was a place of distant drippings and damp, cracked walls. A dinosaur TV on an orange crate, hooked to the nines with VCRs, Nintendo and Sega Genesis games, and cable boxes. There was a bookshelf here, with only two books: *The Anarchist Cookbook* and *The Little Engine That Could.* "Death" was in his dingy underthings, eating pink cereal flakes with a plastic spoon.

Kathy gave herself the once-over. She was fully dressed. Still . . .

The thought sickened her. She rushed headlong for the bathroom. The bathroom sickened her still more. The tub was filled with . . .

She lifted the lid of the toilet, her mouth crammed with vomit.

What was in the toilet was still worse. It stared hard with dead eyes. She whirled around in shock just as Earl entered. She sprayed him with uncontrollable vomit.

"GAWWWWWWD!" he bellowed, clearing the muck from his eyes and nostrils. "Were you born in a fucking barn???"

"I want you to kill my father," she said.

"Is that how you ask me?"

"Why did you bring me here?"

There were three eyeballs in the sink, skewered by syringes. Earl didn't seem to notice as he bent over it and washed the vomit from his smooth white head.

"I felt bad about killing that guy, your little fashion pussy sweetheart there. Shit. I'm not cut out for this. I was born to be a singer."

He went on to say that he was fully prepared to give her a sampling. Had a whole repertoire of Cole Porter tunes in his thrashing grey matter. She passed on the notion.

"I heard you tell him you loved him," he said somberly. "I'm a romantic deep deep down. I felt like a shit killing him, but hey, loud talkers ruin the whole damn moviegoing experience; *somebody* has to get the shit detail, *somebody* has to deal with those kinds of people. You never once raised your voice when addressing me during the picture, and I admired that."

"Uh-huh."

"I mainly like musicals," he offered.

"Why did you bring me here?"

"I'm gonna make it up to you."

"With song?" she snapped.

"I'll help you." He grinned. "With your problem." He moved closer. "I'll help you kill your father."

"And then I'll kill you," she said softly.

Thus began a two-minute face-off, eyes burning like acid into eyes. Earl Niglet killed because he was off his bean. But Kathy had a reason. She had hate. And loss. And, at this moment, passion. Earl decided he was not up to the task at the moment, and would let her wisecrack slide until a better day.

"You can try," he said finally. "But first you have to tell me something. And be honest. This is very important. You prolly think I'm a weak suck but at least I got ethics and a moral code; more'n some assholes out there killin' indiscriminate. I kill one type of person. Here's the thing: Is your father a loud talker at movies?"

"Yes," she said. She looked him straight in the eye. A pregnant pause from drama class. "And," she added, "he also puts his feet up and gives away endings."

"Good Lord . . . I'm gonna enjoy this."

"He's also a serial killer."

"Yeah? Who isn't? What's his name?"

"He never told me," she said.

"What do you call him?"

"A lot of things."

"What's his turf?"

"Grand and Gein. Derelicts. Axe man."

"Freshman, huh?"

She nodded.

"I used to work that route. Sissy stuff. When you first get the sickness you like to get your hands on the product. No art, no style."

"Sickness?"

"Sickness of the soul. Sick of the world going to shit. A man rises up." He pounded his chest.

"Puhleeeeeeze. Don't coddle your emotional problems. You're a fuckhead. There's no sickness."

"You'll see," he said. He plucked a satchel from beneath the fold-out couch and began to put things in it.

*   *   *

Mother's body was at the foot of the stairs, stripped naked, blue and stinking, a mosquito on her bare eyeball, the other eye closed. Wink wink. Dad's axe was perched against the aging newel post, polished shiny with soap and good honest sweat. It waited obediently as its master rested. A-hunting we will go.

"Nice house," said Death.

No. Not Death. Earl. Earl Niglet. Unemployed divorce lawyer and father to festering sores. The image on the brooch Mark had given her, *that* was Death. An elegant image and very probably a lie, but a cool lie. Earl was just a sorry substitute. A vulgar, smelly also-ran.

Gentleman Death would never have said anything as painful and uncouth as: "This place *reeks* of potato pancake batter."

And blood and desperation and hopelessness and lies. Yeah, your olfactory's quick on the uptake, you fuckhead.

She shook her head. "Shut up. Let's complete this transaction and have done with it."

As much as she hated her father, she wasn't about to stand around and watch. All she wanted was her revenge. For Mother and for herself. That was enough. She didn't want to smell his fear, nor the shit that would very probably pulse down his leg. She didn't want blood on her hands. She didn't want to straddle his body and beat his face into raw sewage, because perhaps Earl Niglet had been right, simple as he was. Perhaps there *was* a sickness. Perhaps she could get it.

If she got too close.

She watched the rise and fall of her father's chest as he slept the sleep of the just. He had flung his wife's body down the stairs, caught up in his need for rest and soft sheets. Twenty-five years (centuries) of marriage kerplunked down the stairs without so much as a by-your-leave. She stared at his frosty white eyebrows, thick and overhanging. She looked at his scrubbed-shiny pinkness, the smell of Irish Spring and a faint under-odor of blood and piss.

That was enough. That and the first fall of the ball-peen hammer that barely succeeded in incapacitating the large, robust man. It took four blows to blast him to sleep. It was like clubbing a basketball filled with cement. Although she was as red in the face as a woman in the throes of seizure, although her grip upon the hammer was an intense and unshaking white, although she could feel blue lightning clamber over her skull, she was cold inside, cold and scholarly. She would not get caught up in all this shit. "Besides," she laughed. "I don't have an act! Wouldn't be much good without a tag line! Can't go around killing people unless you've got some spiffy duds and a handle! Maybe I could kill with a squeegee! Any you fuckheads thoughta that???"

No. She wouldn't get caught up in it.

Four blows turned into eight but it was only enough to pummel Daddy deeper into dream. She cracked him one in the crotch for good measure but the blissful smile remained on his face, curled at the corners.

"Be my guest," she said, dropping the hammer, and Earl began hog-tying Daddy with baling wire. She left the room.

And, after a moment, came back.

Leaned against the doorjamb. And watched.

Earl, tongue protruding, sat astride the big man, lost in his labors. He wanted to impress her, it was obvious. He leaned over to secure the legs lest Daddy blunder back through the door of sleep.

She stared into Earl's back and thought of Mark.

And arrived at a decision.

Ether, Ichor, and Shout, her Dobermans, were in the backyard, munching down to nubs the doggie bag Daddy had brought home from the alleyway. They came over to her, stubby tails at the wag, and allowed themselves to be petted.

The window of her parents' room was wide open. There was no screaming, only a series of wet thuds and the sound of the bed pounding up and down (like a good little marriage bed) as Daddy thrashed against the baling wire, only driving the wire deeper into flesh and bone. Earl had promised to take his time.

She looked at the dogs. It had been a long time since they'd had any meat, and stringy, homeless meat was a poor substitute for leathery Jag drivers with potbellies and blisters from wife-beating.

She thought of Daddy's axe.

It was midnight when her parents' bedroom door opened. During the nine-hour period of chopping and cursing she had buried her mother in the backyard, behind the doghouses. Mother had always shared her deepest confidences and darkest secrets with Ether, Ichor, and Shout. Those dogs knew worlds of hurt and shame and degradation yet had never been away from home. Kathy's ear had always been there, true, but as she stood against the doorjamb, axe at the ready, she realized that such horrid stories of abuse and self-hate should only be shared with dogs. A dog couldn't yell at you to wise up and walk out when you had no choice but to stay, because a dog could remember the good times, the old times, could remember when its master had not been a master at all but a friend and playmate. A dog could remember life before its friend went bad and started kicking and screaming.

There had been good times. Seemingly centuries old, but dammit, there had been good times.

Mother had been threatening to kill Father for years.

But she had only bared teeth. Had never bitten. Had never once said she hated him. She died little more than a dog herself.

Daddy had been a dog too, and if your dog goes rabid it's hard to hate him when you remember laughter and sunny days.

It was easy to hate Earl, a man as brutish and stupid as an earthquake.

"With a headful of show tunes," she added.

When he opened the bedroom door and trudged out, stoop-shouldered and dog tired, she swung the axe, peppered the walls with blood and brains and show tunes.

Ether, Ichor, and Shout were asleep in the back of the hearse, bellies full, two corpses split three ways. With a doggie bag for later. The engine grumbled as Hometown USA funneled by at eighty-five per, and Kathy with a Marlboro between her teeth. She drove without music; a first. She avoided eye contact with the murky sun and the white noise of the Heavens.

She could have stayed; she knew that. She could have stayed and picked a pet peeve and started killing people who insisted on crossing the line, like wife-beaters, dinner theater dreamers, and people who talked during movies.

Yes. There were plenty of possibilities. The open road represented them. It felt good not to think, to not know what was going to be around the next corner. Although there was pain and heartbreak still to face over all that had happened, although there were nightmares that would last ages, although there was Mark and Mom, ghosts who hadn't deserved what they had gotten, now, at this moment, it felt good not to think, to be up in the clouds somewhere with the open road all to herself, leading God knows where. It felt good to be twenty-two and absolutely free.

Hooked on Buzzer

ELIZABETH MASSIE

ELIZABETH MASSIE speaks with a soft Southern drawl, has always lived in the Shenandoah Valley of Virginia, and possesses a seriously twisted imagination (a characteristic spectacularly exhibited in "Abed," Massie's ghastly contribution to Skipp & Spector's Still Dead: Book of the Dead 2*). Her short fiction has appeared in such magazines as* Iniquities *and* Gauntlet; *anthology contributions can be found in* Borderlands, Hottest Blood, *and* Women of Darkness.

It is in that last (recommended) volume that "Hooked On Buzzer" first appeared. While "Buzzer" can be read as an attack against the then-pervasive Moral Majority, such a reading addresses only a single level of this story's complexity. For Massie, like the best artists, has a consistent point of view, one which repeatedly resurfaces in both short works and recent novels such as Sineater, Homegrown, *and* Welcome Back to the Night.

Right. But what is *that point of view? Let's let Elizabeth herself tell you, from a revealing little note she appended to the Massie biography which found its way to my desk here at* La Casa Pescado:

"Currently I'm working on another novel titled Small Minds," *Liz wrote. "It's about hatred, jealously, fear, and ignorance. In a southern trailer court."*

Ah-ha.

Hatred, fear, and ignorance. The South.

All prime ingredients of "Hooked on Buzzer," a powerful repudiation of the retroactive Puritanism which infiltrated this country during the hypocritical 1980s.

By the way, Elizabeth—

Just what the hell are they putting into your water supply, down there in the Shenandoah Valley?

*G*lory.

"Glory."

Nubbed fingers stroked the scratched window; lips made tiny, moist patterns in the dust of the glass. Wide eyes panned the street below, waiting, watching.

Feo was late.

Angel took a slow breath. Her throat rumbled. "Glory," she said, and shifted her weight against the radiator. "Praise Him, Amen."

There was movement down on the street, and Angel started. But it was only a cat, a knotted patch of fur winding about the tires of the newspaper delivery truck.

"Glory," said Angel, sighing.

Behind Angel, a child's battered record player throbbed with the wailings of the Savior's Salvation Seven. Angel's thick finger stubs pawed the window in rhythm with the music. She knew the lyrics, they were as much a part of her as Mother or Buzzer, but Mother had never sung and so neither did Angel. Mother had felt her own voice to be poor, and so singing along with the Salvation Seven would have been a blasphemy. Angel was sure that her voice was even more unworthy than Mother's.

Feo was very late.

Angel tapped her stubs and closed her eyes. The music began to pull at her, pushing her legs gently into the vertical ribs of the radiator and then sucking her away. She rode the current, thinking of Mother and of Glory. Hearing Mother and Brother Randolph.

"Angel," said Mother.

Angel said, "Mother." She closed her eyes more tightly, and saw Mother on the sofa in the tiny living room of Mother's trailer. Mother wore a wool shift. There were large sweat rings under her upper arms. Brother Randolph sat beside her.

"Angel," said Mother.

Angel was beside the wall, the tiny toes of her dirty sneakers pointed toward a toy top in the middle of the floor.

"Don't you dare, Angel," said Mother.

Angel took a step and moved slightly from the wall. Mother frowned, the fat around her eyes squeezing them to slits.

"Train the child, Amen," said Brother Randolph.

Angel's hands moved outward for balance as she took another

sliding step. She looked from the top to Mother and back again. The Salvation Seven sang on the shelf.

"Angel!" said Mother.

"Self-denial," said Brother Randolph. "Glory to the child that withstands earthly rigors and temptations and to the mother that leads that child in the way."

"Glory," said Mother. "No, Angel!"

Angel hesitated, then reached out to the top. She picked it up and looked at Mother.

Mother roared from the sofa and grabbed her, shaking the top free. Angel gasped. Mother grappled the prong end of an extension cord from the floor and plugged it into the socket beneath the record-player shelf. The other end of the cord was a frayed mass of wire.

Brother Randolph nodded sadly and said, "Buzz her. Amen."

Mother drew Angel close.

After a moment, Brother Randolph said, "Glory."

Mother dropped the cord. "Amen," she said. The Salvation Seven's gospel cantation cut a piercing, frantic current in the air.

"Put her by the wall," said Brother Randolph. "We'll try again."

"Glory," said Mother.

"Buzzer, Amen," said Angel. She opened her eyes and looked again at the street below. The cat was gone. And Feo was very, very late. Feo was supposed to be bringing the groceries today. He was the landlady's brother. He was nineteen, two years younger than Angel. Angel felt a holy love for Feo. It burned in her when she saw his face through the door. God was in Feo. Feo's eyes were green, like pastures in the Bible.

Angel turned up the gospel music. The voices shook the newspapered walls. Someone next door hit the wall with a heavy object. Angel went into the bedroom and lay down on the frameless twin bed. The music pinned her to the mattress. She looked at the ceiling and drove herself to climax with a Prelude II. Sweaty and panting, Angel rolled off the bed and knelt to give thanks.

Feo sat on the edge of the bus bench and watched as the small assembly of shoppers filed through the door and climbed the bus steps. He turned his face away then, so the bus driver would not wait for him. He held a bag of groceries between his knees. In his jacket pocket was the change from the purchase. He was in no hurry to return with the food.

Goddamn freak.

Lizzie was expecting too much. She was the one who usually got the freak's groceries, but Lizzie had gotten an idea when Feo had gotten the note, and when Lizzie had an idea it was like riding downhill on a snowplow. No getting off until the ride was over.

"Goddamn freak," muttered Feo. He pulled his knees together and something inside the bag gave way. Lizzie had said, "The death of me you don't care to do for your family."

"You see her, Lizzie?" Feo had answered. "You see her face? Her fingers?"

"Blood is thicker than looks."

"She's crazy. They kicked her out of the halfway house, said she's on her own for shocking herself all the time. You heard that."

"I heard that. And I seen her note to you. She wants you. She got money, I know."

"She don't want me." Feo balled the note and shook it in Lizzie's face. "It says here she wants to pray with me. I get the willies when I see her looking through that door crack. Like she wants to suck me in."

"She got money. Lots, I bet. Holed it up all this time, from disability and from when her mama died a couple years ago. Buy her groceries. Pray with her. She got money, Feo."

"Fuck you."

"No, fuck her. Pray with her, whatever she wants. She got money. And we living in this dumphole with nothing but late payments and cockroaches."

Feo threw the note against the wall. It bounced and rolled back to where he stood. He stepped over it and through the apartment door, swearing softly and fiercely.

In the bathroom, Angel switched on the clock radio and worked the knob until she found Reverend Olley of the Truth and Way Mission. Reverend Olley was speaking in tongues and a missioner was interpreting. The radio had been a going-away gift to Angel from one of her many foster mothers. When Angel was six, Social

Services had taken her from her mother. Angel had lived in sixteen foster homes over the next ten years. Most of the homes had quietly requested that Angel be sent elsewhere after several months.

The Ryders, however, had not been as concerned with discretion. Mrs. Ryder had been a religious woman, or so she had told Angel, yet when she caught Angel witnessing at Lisa Ryder's slumber party, she had become enraged.

Nine eleven-year-olds had attended the party. They spread their sleeping bags about the basement floor and entertained themselves with gossip and makeup and ghost stories. Angel was forgotten, alone in the corner on a blanket, until she began to talk about Heaven and Glory and earthly rigors. The girls stopped and stared. Lisa Ryder groaned nervously and said, "Not again." Angel unscrewed the bulb from a table lamp and poised her finger above the empty socket. One girl said, "Oh shit, neat." Another said, "I heard she does stuff like this for God or something." Everybody watched, except for Lisa, who dashed up the steps.

Snorts rippled through the gathering. Angel lowered her finger into the socket.

"Praise Him, Amen," she said.

Angel was thrown back from the lamp with an electric pop. She held up her burned finger and the girls cheered. Lisa and Mrs. Ryder thundered down the stairs.

"Demon-child!" screamed Mrs. Ryder. "You aren't welcome here anymore!"

"Go fry yourself somewhere else!" cried Lisa.

"Buzzer, Amen," whispered Angel.

The girls on their sleeping bags rolled their eyes and giggled darkly.

Angel adjusted the volume on Reverend Olley. She plugged the tub drain and turned on the spigot. Feo was late, but Angel was sure nothing had happened to him. Feo was safe in holy arms. Feo would come. Angel stepped into the water and stretched out her legs; her fingers strummed erratically on the water's surface. Sometimes Angel could feel the entire length of the fingers, and she found that to be a wondrous miracle. Angel lifted the stubs to her face and caressed the scars there. At the halfway house they would not give her lamps or cords or batteries. And so Angel was forced to seek

Glory without Buzzer. She used a plastic knife that came with her
dinner. When she was eighteen, they let her go.

The living room door thumped. Someone was knocking. Angel
climbed from the tub and wrapped herself in her terry robe. "Be
ready for His call!" said Reverend Olley.

"Glory," Angel said.

Feo hit the door again with his boot and looked quickly about over
his shoulders. If anyone in the other apartments saw him going in
with the freak's groceries, he would kill Lizzie. He couldn't believe
he'd wasted as much time as he had already on her. It had been
thirty minutes getting the groceries and an hour and a half sitting
on the bus bench worrying about taking them back. Then he spent
another fifteen minutes telling himself that Lizzie was right. The
freak had to have money stashed somewhere in her apartment. And
braving her looks long enough to gain her confidence would pay
off. If he didn't get the chance to slip anything into his pocket while
she was praying, at least he could get a good idea of where things
were, and he could schedule a late-night visit later on.

"Come on, freak," he muttered.

There was a soft sound behind the apartment door. A voice said,
"Who is it?"

"Feo," said Feo, and in doing so he had a sudden, horrid sensation
that he had offered his soul along with his name. He spit angrily on
the floor.

The doorknob twisted, and the door bucked on its warped
framework. Then it was jerked open, as far as the chain links would
reach. The scarred face was in the crack.

"Feo?"

"Got your groceries," said Feo.

"Ah, yes," said the freak. But she did not move from the crack.

"And I got your note," Feo added. "Gonna let me in?" He cleared
his throat unintentionally.

The face smiled, then withdrew from the crack. The chain came
off. The door swung wide.

Feo stepped in, being careful not to look directly at the freak.
He put the bag of groceries on the dinette table in the kitchen

corner. The bag fell over and two cans of bean-with-bacon soup rolled out. Feo anxiously snatched them up and stuffed them into the bag. Then he felt the freak behind him. He turned around.

She was fat. Her hair was near white, slicked back into a thin, greasy ponytail. Huge blue eyes dominated the ravaged face. She smelled of sweat and imitation chocolate.

"You come to pray with me," she said.

Feo stepped quickly around her and stopped in the middle of the living room.

"Don't clean up much, do you?"

"God asks self-denial, praise Him."

"Yeah, right," said Feo. "Hey, why don't you show me around?"

"What?"

"Show me around. When people come to visit, you show them around."

He turned back to the freak. Her eyes seemed even larger. Her hands were pressed together in a nubby ball.

He nodded cautiously at her hands. "Why you do that to yourself?"

"Is it worthy?"

He blinked. "I . . . don't know. I guess."

The freak took several steps closer to him. Feo flinched but did not step back. She tipped her head as if studying him.

"Show me around, okay?" Feo managed.

"What do you want to see?"

"I don't know. Anything. Everything."

And then the freak opened her robe and let it fall to the floor. Her huge body was slick and damp.

Feo's mouth fell open soundlessly.

"Bless me. Baptize me. All I have is yours."

"Oh, shit," said Feo.

"I have been worthy. You have come to me. Bless me."

Feo watched as she went into the bathroom. He was horrified and transfixed. She climbed into the tub and looked at him. He walked slowly to the bathroom door. She lay back, her giant breasts falling to opposite sides. "Bless me," she said, and closed her eyes.

Feo went to the side of the tub. He wiped his mouth and clenched his fist. "Shit," he said. Her malformity and willingness was terrifyingly sensual.

"Ah," she said softly.

Feo slipped out of his clothes and kicked them aside. He grasped the sides of the tub and carefully climbed in. He thought of how the money would be a breeze after this; he knew she would give him anything. He thought of the old joke about the woman so ugly that you had to put a paper bag over her head to make love. He laughed out loud, thinking this added a new twist to the joke. Paper bag and a pair of work gloves. Feo's hands moved through water, through flesh.

"Glory," said Angel. "Buzzer, Amen." One set of nubbed fingers reached out of the tub and caught the cord of the clock radio. And with a rapturous wail, Reverend Olley joined the holy lovers.

Pig

GORMAN BECHARD

*According to his submitted biography, "GORMAN BECHARD's ca-
reer is conclusive testimony to the fortifying powers of Rolling
Rock beer and pizza from New Haven, Connecticut, the town he
calls home. While most of us were still trying to figure out which
pair of socks to wear with which pair of pants, Gorman was
hard at work producing, directing, and writing B films, including*
Galactic Gigolo, Cemetery High, *and the cult favorite* Psychos In
Love. *Then, having chewed up and spit out the exploitation movie
genre, he turned his attention to novels.*

*"Within minutes, he'd authored one of the most entertaining
and beloved books of 1991,* The Second Greatest Story Ever Told.
*This detailed the coming of a modern-day Jesus Christ, who hap-
pened to be a woman. Bechard's second novel is* Balls, *to be published by Dutton/Penguin in 1995. This one's about a female first
baseman playing for the Manhattan Meteorites; movie rights for*
Balls *have been optioned by 20th Century Fox."*

*Then there's "Pig," Bechard's sardonic examination of that
societal ambivalence known as "law 'n' order." Filtered through
a futuristic lens.*

*Problem is, I'm not altogether certain that the all-woman hit
squad Gorman posits here is actually a fantasy.*

*Because I, like Bechard's deadlier-than-the-male protagonists,
also live in Los Angeles.*

If you're puzzled by that statement, well, you never have.

Lived in Los Angeles, that is.

*T*he moon, man. They blew up the fucking moon. Not that I ever
really saw the thing. I mean, not in person. Los Angeles ain't exactly

known for its clear skies. Fuck, I don't even think I've seen the sun in about five or six years. And that's a hell of a lot brighter than the little ol' moon. I saw pictures, though. As a kid. I remember it had a face, well, sort of a face. Man, that face must have been wincing in agony when those nuclear blasts went off—*ka-fucking-boom!*

I suppose I could have watched it on TV. The "celebrations" were broadcast live. Twenty-four hours of massive partying leading up to the detonation. Our Mr. *Two-hundred-sixty-seven-channels-of-free-cable-TV* President even declared the day a national holiday. But I didn't want anything to do with it. Wouldn't go to any of the parties. Wouldn't watch it on TV—the *Mooncast*, twenty-four-hour coverage on every one of those two hundred sixty-seven channels. (I just know there's an asshole somewhere who hooked up as many VCRs to tape every blasted second.) Wouldn't watch a second of it. Not even to say good-bye. I just went about my life as usual. I mean, what's the use of finally getting to see the moon when the thing ain't gonna be around to enjoy. It's like falling in love with someone who's got a terminal disease, or is moving away. Man, I don't need that kind of heartbreak in my life.

The name's Pandora. But everyone calls me Pandy—got my fill of box jokes at an early age. Even my partner doesn't know my real name. Always asking, "What's that short for?" I tell her it ain't short for nothing. Man, she'd bust my ass but bad!

Her name's Ralph—that's short for Ralphina, which is about the most hideous name I've ever heard. Fuck! I'd have just changed it completely, never mind cutting it down. No matter what you do, you can't make Ralphina sound feminine. There's no way a Ralphina could ever be cute.

Ralph, see, she took the big night off—wanted to see what all the commotion was about. The moon and all. I told her go ahead, I wanted to work. Needed the overtime, y'know? And like I said, I didn't want to see the thing go boom.

It was my usual gig. Ralph and I work the Hollywood beat. That's where most of the problems are now. A lot of white trash drug dealers—baby lords. And with Watts and Compton being nuked out, where else was a PIG to go? That's what we're called, PIGS. Not by the trash, either. They call us *Police Officers*. Sort of to bust our ass. Not that they ever live long enough to razz us bad. But when they find out, right before we pull the trigger, they call us *Police Officers* right to our face. Man, then it's a pleasure to blow the suckers away.

We're a special undercover group. We don't look or act like cops. We certainly don't dress like 'em—you won't find one blue uniform in *my* closet. The government—our fine mayor and cop commissioner—got together one morning and decided they needed to do something about the *drug problem* in the greater Los Angeles area. Another nuclear *accident* was out of the question— the feds were still sniffing around after the last one. Nuclear accidents were no longer looked upon as convenient—guess a few too many of our more influential citizens got burned in the fallout. So, they come up with this idea for us PIGS—a group of pumped-up, pumped-out babes who'd infiltrate the drug dens, and whatnots, by whatever means possible, then open fire.

That's our job. That's what me and Ralph do. We blow away scum—first figuratively, then literally. I mean, sure, it's high risk. There's no backup, or shit like that—the fucking authorities won't even acknowledge our existence. Strictly hush-hush. Just you and your partner out on the street—real hazardous work. But we know that going in. We're well aware. And besides, it's a paycheck.

Well, last night, an hour or so before the old man in the moon winked bye-bye for the last time, I was standing on the corner of Hollywood and Highland. That's where I always hang when I'm working alone. Lots of action—parties, cruising. Y'know, people looking for more than what all those cable channels can offer.

It was hot—thermometers were inching over the one-hundred-degree point. Too hot for my black motorcycle jacket—the staple of any PIG's wardrobe. So, I picked out this leather corset thing that hadn't see the dark of a bedroom in many a—if you'll forgive the pun—moon. I could barely get my boobs into it—either the Frederick's special had shrunk, or my boobs were getting bigger. That's possible, right? I mean, they hurt real bad, like they were expanding—if the universe is expanding, why not my boobs? I also had on these thigh-high boots. Those boots, man, they always work.

This bright glow-in-the-dark yellow stretch limo pulls up. The back window rolls down and this guy named Horatio sticks his head out and yells, "Any specials?" Like I'm some sort of hooker diner with a blue-plate special written out in chalk across my chest.

I pulled aside the matching leather panties and gave ol' Horatio a gander at my just-shaved twat. Man, the way the fucker's eyes bugged out you'd think a telephone pole had just been shoved up his butt. "Smooth," he said.

"Like a crystal ball," I told him.

"If I rub it, will it tell me my fortune?"

"Only if you rub it the right way."

The door to the limo opened and I got in, trying to figure out what exactly there was about clean-shaved twat that drove men crazy. Was it that prepubescent age-of-innocence shit? Or were they just tired of picking twat hairs from between their teeth? Whatever it was, it *always* worked. *Always*. Just scratch off one more notch on the male predictability bedpost. Man, that piece of wood can't take any more abuse.

In the limo, Horatio kept telling me how he liked tall chicks— that's what he called me, "a chick." Though when he said it, it sounded like *cheek*, two syllables, with a couple extra *e* 's.

"You're tall like a basketball player," he said. "A basketball-playing chick."

"Almost," I said.

"But you got better legs than any basketball player I've ever seen."

"Thanks," I said. "I guess."

We finally got to his place. Some sprawling one-story stucco estate high up on Mulholland. He told me a movie star once lived there. Must have been years ago, before they all moved off to Japan, or wherever it is that movie stars now go to die.

Horatio gave me the ten-cent tour, pointing out what he claimed to be an original Van Gogh. *Starry Night*, he called it. Claimed to have bought it off some guys who ripped off museums for a living. "Pretty cool, huh?" he said.

I nodded and shrugged, my way of exhibiting awe.

He led me out into the deck and suggested we hop into the Jacuzzi. *My pleasure!* It felt nice. The hot water and all. But he didn't want to fuck. "Not yet," he told me, explaining that twats don't get wet enough in the Jacuzzi. "You know the wet I mean?"

I nodded and smiled, glad to have some time to stretch out and let the jets of water beat against my muscles. Man, sometimes my muscles hurt so bad.

In his bedroom, after the Jacuzzi, Horatio pulled out some needles. Said he just got a stash in from Ecuador. He showed me these double-lined plastic trash bags filled with smack. "Want some?" he asked.

This was gonna be too easy, I thought. "What the fuck?" I said. And I meant it. After all the shit that's poured through my veins, what harm can a little smack do?

He set up the fix, aimed the hypodermic in my direction, and asked, "Where do you want it?"

I knew this would get him good. Lying back on the bed, I spread my legs real wide—up and back like when I take it up the ass. "My clit," I said. "Shoot up my clit."

His eye went wide again. "Shit!" he said. "You are one fucking crazy chick."

"Got that right."

He leaned over and stuck the needle into me, right into my clit—the fucker had good aim. He jabbed it hard, smiling, thinking he could hurt me. What a joke. Hurt me? Down there? Fuck, I haven't had feeling in my twat for at least a couple of years. Not since the steroids and the tube tying. I guess that's the price you pay for a job nowadays.

Edith, she's the head PIG, the one we report to, the one who gives us our assignments, told me those in charge didn't want to be held responsible for unwanted pregnancies. Like, we were big enough to kill, but not to take our pills on time. And the steroids, well, those were my idea. I wasn't muscular enough for the job— I had the height, but was too damn skinny. Missed the first group by close to thirty pounds. They wanted big girls—lots of muscle. Girls who could take care of themselves. I figured with the local unemployment rate hovering around sixty percent, a good steady job with all the benefits was worth a little steroid abuse. And so I lost the feeling in my twat. Big deal, right? But I gotta laugh—the things we'd fucking do for a little food, a place to live, and some cool clothes. Man, the things we'd fucking do!

Anyway, Horatio shot up and we started to fuck. Like I said, I can't feel anything down there. But he's humping and groaning and sweating and mumbling some shit in Spanish—find the pig in *this* picture. I'm just sort of going with the flow. Y'know, letting the smack take over. And I began dreaming about this guy I once knew—y'know, my one true love. The man of my dreams—all that shit. And then, I don't know—ka-fucking-boom, it happened. Must have had something to do with the moon—like I was on its timetable. I started wanting it. I wanted to feel it. I needed to feel something. Anything. Fast. And real bad. So, I asked Horatio to put it in my ass.

"You're my kind of chick," he said.

"That's good to know," I said, thinking, I bet you say that to all the *chee-eeks*.

Horatio pulled out of my twat, pushed my legs back, then placed the tip of his cock against my asshole and plunged in. I gasped—the biggest pleasure is knowing I can still feel *something* down there, thank God.

"That feel good, chickie?" he asked, a variation on his theme.

"Uh-huh," I said, not exactly in the mood for conversation. But hell, it did feel pretty good. I'll admit it. He wasn't huge, just big enough. Big enough to do the trick. And he had a lot of staying power. Well, more than the usual amount of staying power. And then he got that Chinese look in his eyes, and I knew he was about to come.

So, I reached under the pillow, and got a firm grip. That's where I usually put it. And tonight was especially easy. Horatio kept disappearing into the toilet—he gave me plenty of setup time. And just as he started to come, just as I felt the first squirt of spunk shoot up my shithole, I pulled the pocket .45 from under the pillow and jammed the tip of the barrel under Horatio's jaw. His eyes went wide and he mouthed the words "crazy chick" just as I squeezed the trigger. His head exploded, covering me and the ceiling with blood and brains and guts in a design Jackson Pollock would have been proud to sign his name to. His cock exploded, giving my small intestine a healthy come enema. He fell backwards, his cock slipping out of me. But I wanted more. I needed more. Keeping my legs pulled back, I shoved the thick cold metal grip of my pistol into my ass, and began moving it in and out in short rapid jerks. I could feel the steamy gooey heat of Horatio's blood—the droplets inching their way in fierce pleasure down my sides, onto my belly, and into my eyes and ears. Into my mouth. I could taste his death as I sucked my teeth clean of the deep red gunk. I yanked up on the gun, hard. Harder. I was going over the edge. I was closer. Closer. *FFFUUUCCCKKK!!!*

So, that's what I was doing on May 1, 2030—the night they blew up the moon.

After the orgasm—sure, sometimes it takes a lot for me to come, but it's *always* worth it—I wiped off my gun, got dressed and set Horatio's house on fire. Protocol, just protocol—though I hated having to torch the Van Gogh. Destroys all the evidence and, more importantly, all the smack—keeps the shit from getting onto the street and into the wrong veins. Like there's such a thing as the *right* veins.

Romantic, huh? Sort of touching. Like everything else in my life. Yeah, right. There's nothing romantic or touching about being a PIG—unless you consider a steady paycheck the cream dream ad infinitum.

Anyway, that's what me and Ralph do. Though she's a lot more creative than I am. She likes knives. Says it takes longer for them to die. And Ralph enjoys watching them suffer.

One time, this baby lord was giving her a good ol'-fashion shtupping, and just as he was about to shoot his load, she reaches down and shoves a foot-long blade up his ass. One of those mongo hunting knives. Fuck, she tugged up and just about split the son-of-a-bitch in two. Told me she cut his sack open, and his nuts spilled out. Plopped onto the bed. They bounced around and rolled onto the floor. Said it was the funniest thing she ever saw.

Usually, though, she just whacks off their dicks as they're coming. Then finishes them off with a little slashing action to the throat, or maybe a jab to the chest. Sometimes she'll keep the dick inside her, all night long—brings the sucker home. She's got this collection. There's one mother that's like eighteen inches long. She had it coated with this clear acrylic and mounted on her shower wall. It just sticks straight out—real weird. She loves that thing—calls it her *shower toy*. Says she can fuck it whenever she's in the mood. And Ralph is *always* in the mood.

So, the next day, after me and Ralph exchanged our "So, who'd *you* do last night?" stories over a couple of doughnuts and a cup of java at the Double-D, we met with Edith, like we always do on Monday mornings.

The PIG-sty—that what me and Ralph and the rest of the girls call it behind Edith's back—was located on the top floor of this old warehouse over in Glendale. It's just a few small offices with rusted-out metal desks, a locker room with showers, and this arsenal of guns and knives and anything else we might need to effectively achieve our goals. Edith's always there, seated in her office behind her desk—smiling this shit-eating grin whenever I approach. She's a dyke—I know it. The way she's always staring. And one time when we were alone, she told me I had the best ass of any of the PIGS.

"I beg your pardon," I said.

"Your ass," Edith explained. "Every time I look at it I have this amazing desire to spread your cheeks and dive in tongue first." She licked her lips. "I'll bet your asshole tastes just like sweet and sour chicken."

"It might," I said, not having a fucking clue as to what else I should say. I mean, it was sort of a compliment—I guess. Though it put my craving for Chinese food on permanent hold.

I mean, doesn't that sound like a dyke thing to say? And it's not like I'm gorgeous or anything. I'm okay. Just okay. But I just couldn't imagine doing it with another woman, especially Edith. She's, well, let's just say she's not the most attractive creature on the face of this here earth. If you catch my drift. She's got a mustache, and I don't think she shaves her legs, or anywhere else for that matter.

Ralph? Well, that's another story. She's a couple years younger than me—twenty-one, I think. She's short, only five seven, but real muscular. And, man, she's got the best hair—wild and red. Down there, too. I know because she's always walking around the locker room naked. It looks real cool—sort of like funky cotton candy. "Wild cherry flavored," she says.

Me, I'm just a brunette—ugly brown, I call it. Root flavored. *That's* why I shave.

I'd probably consider doing Ralph. If I was fucked-up enough. Or if she ever asked. I mean, she *is* my partner. And if your partner can't fuck your face, then who can? Y'know?

So, anyway, we're in Edith's office. There's this man standing there. He looks familiar. Edith introduced him as the Reverend

Joseph Bolton. I kept saying his name over and over in my head, examining his face. Where had I seen that mug before? And then it hit me. He was Reverend Joe—the guy with the TV show—a bigwig L.A. preacher with ratings up the wazoo and more money than God. He was there with his wife, some tight-faced bitch named Anne, and their daughter, Mary.

"What gives?" I asked.

"Seems the Reverend's daughter received an abortion from a doctor over on 6th," Edith explained.

I looked over at the kid; she seemed stone-faced—angry at being alive. "How old are you?"

She looked up at her father. He nodded. "Answer the lady, Mary," he said.

"Twelve."

Fuck! I was happy when I was her age. Mostly. And this girl definitely did not look happy. She looked like she didn't even know how to smile. Like if she did her face might crack.

"What do you want us to do?" Ralph asked.

"Put the man out of business," Edith explained.

Now, we both knew what *out of business* meant. It was what we did. But abortionists weren't our turf. "Why us?" I asked. "When there are cops who specialize?" A search-and-destroy team of goons who'd set fire to their mothers for looking at a vacuum cleaner the wrong way.

"We want to—" Edith began, but the Reverend cut her short.

"We need to keep this quiet," he explained. "And your commander here," he nodded towards Edith, "says you're the best."

"Compliments won't get you jackshit," Ralph said.

"There's a bonus in it for both of you," he said, nervously rushing the words.

Ralph and I exchanged glances. The Reverend had a reputation to worry about, I guessed. He couldn't have his little girl out having abortions while he's preaching about God and goodness and morality and all that shit to millions of the cash-donating faithful on cable TV.

I was about to ask Mary how she got pregnant, when Ralph spoke up.

"How much of a bonus?" she asked.

"Fifty thousand, in cash," the Reverend said.

"For each of us?" Ralph asked.

He nodded.

Fuck! I almost swallowed my tongue. That was a half-year's salary for a stinking job we could do in an hour.

"What do you say, partner?" Ralph asked me.

"What the fuck, right?"

She nodded.

And I said, "We'll do it."

We changed into something demure, then followed Mary's directions, ending up at this barely noticeable tenement over on 6th Street, near the Tar Pits. There was a small rusted sign that read, "Dr. Iscariot." That was the name the kid had given us. We shrugged and knocked on the door.

Now, I've got no personal use for an abortionist. I mean, fuck, I got no chance of getting knocked up. None whatsoever. But other women aren't as lucky, and something like a quarter million die every year from botched abortions, *in this country alone*. Back alley, they're called. Though I'd call them something else—like fucking hazardous to our health. So I have to ask, why not make the things safe and legal? It makes sense, right? There are already too many damn people. And why should a woman have to have a baby when she doesn't want to? Last time I checked, these were *our* bodies.

Ralph disagreed. She said that our bodies belong to whoever has the most money, or the most power, or both. A pretty depressing thought. She told me that abortions were once legal—done in hospitals and clinics, places like that. Then some religious types—"Funda-fucking-mentalists," she called them—got control of the Supreme Court. Laws were passed and next thing you know—*no more abortions*.

Ralph knows a lot about law. Her dad was a lawyer. She said that if men could get pregnant, abortions would most definitely be legal. "They'd be a Goddamn holy ritual." She believes men are afraid of the opposite sex, that they just want to keep women barefoot and pregnant. She says that all the time, *Barefoot and pregnant*—sometimes I wonder how she thinks that shit up.

The door finally opened and there's this old guy standing there. He's seventy at least, maybe older.

"May I help you?" he said, looking us over cautiously.

I was sure glad we dressed down for this one. A pretty flower-print dress for me, jeans and a shirt for Ralph. I mean, the motorcycle jackets would have probably given us away—would have definitely scared the shit out of *this* guy.

"We're here to see Dr. Iscariot."

"That's me," he said. "C'mon in."

We followed the doc into his office. It was clean. Lots of white. Real sterile. He took a seat behind his desk and motioned towards two chairs. We sat.

"I suppose one of you is in trouble?"

We exchanged glances.

"I'm pregnant," Ralph said, laying the trap. I kept hearing her say *barefoot and pregnant* over and over and over again in my head.

He sat back, folded his hands in his lap, then sighed. "I see."

"We're told that maybe you can help," I said.

"By whom?"

"Who told me?"

He nodded.

"Mary Bolton," I said, not sure if I should.

He looked away sadly, then nodded.

"What will it cost?" Ralph asked.

"That depends on the circumstances."

"Meaning?"

"How did you get pregnant?"

"Why should that matter?"

The doc remained silent. He just sort of stared out at nothing in particular.

Ralph looked over at me. I nodded, to tell her, like, it's okay. Tell the guy.

"I was raped," she said. Man, she said it so straight that for a split second I believed her.

"There'll be no charge, then," Iscariot said, softly.

"I beg your pardon?" Ralph said.

"I'm not in this to make money," he explained.

"Then why risk it?" I asked.

He gazed into my face. "I want to help," he said.

A lump formed in my throat. I shook my head and turned away.

What the fuck are we doing here? I thought. There aren't many people around who do shit for nothing—they're like one of those endangered species. And even though what this guy does is supposedly illegal, it's not wrong. Not at all. At least not to me. And I wasn't about to waste someone who's trying to help. Fuck! I stood up.

"What are you doing?" Ralph asked.

"I can't do this."

"No one will know," Iscariot explained.

I turned on him. Leaned in close, hovering over his desk. "We're PIGS," I said. "Hear me, PIGS!"

The old man turned pale—real fast. The word usually had that effect on men. He pulled back into his chair, as far from me as possible. "Please don't hurt me," he said. He knew men didn't come face to face with PIGS and live.

I backed off. His breathing was hard, he expected the worst. "Get lost," I said.

"What do you mean?"

"What are you doing?" Ralph said.

I looked down at the doctor. "Let's just say you're getting a second chance at life." I turned to Ralph. "I can't do this one."

"Then let me," she said.

"No."

"Think of the fifty thousand, Pandy," she pleaded.

I shook my head.

"Who offered you fifty thousand dollars to kill me?" the doc asked.

"Reverend Joe."

A single dread-filled chuckle squeaked from his throat. "That doesn't surprise me," he said.

"Why not?"

"That was *his* baby growing inside Mary's belly."

Man, I had to sit down on that one. Ralph just sort of looked at me. We each had these *holy fuck* expressions tacked onto our faces. I took a couple of deep breaths—felt like I needed to vomit, but there was nothing there. Nothing to heave up. I mean, what the *fuck* was going on here?

"Are you sure?" I said finally, after this long uncomfortable silence.

He nodded. "Yes. I'm sure."

"How do you know?" Ralph asked.

"The kid told me," he explained. "That's why she wanted the abortion."

"Did she pay you?"

"Be serious," the doctor said, standing, pacing about the room. I slapped Ralph's knee and stood. "We've got work to do."

She nodded, and removed a small packet she had tucked inside the top of one of her snakeskin boots.

"What are you doing?" Iscariot asked.

"Just go," I said. "Get out of here. You don't want to see this."

Ralph opened the packet, and removing a small container of yellowish liquid, she popped the top and began squirting it about the room.

Shaking his head in disgust, Iscariot took one last look at his office, and walked away. I watched after him, half expecting a *thank you*, or maybe a *fuck you*. Either would have sufficed. Or even some sort of warning that we were doing the dirty work of the fuckers who made abortion illegal in the first place.

Instead, he was gone, and Ralph was tugging at my arm. "Let's blow," she said, tossing a lighted match into the center of her piss-colored scribblings.

We sat in our car for a long while, sucking on Popsicles—mine was cherry flavored, Ralph's grape—and thinking. Thinking about what *we* should do, and how we should go about doing it. Then Ralph asked, "Where you learn to suck like that?"

I laughed. I mean, here I am speculating on how we can get even with this scum-fuck Reverend, and my partner's wondering where I learned how to suck down popsicles.

"You take the whole fucking thing down your throat," she said, flabbergasted. "If I did that, I'd choke."

"It's a long story," I said, starting to laugh.

"I got time."

So I tell her about my father. I was thirteen, and living with him. My mother had gotten herself caught in the middle of some gang-war gunfire when I was nine, and my dad had been taking care of me since. I mean, he did an okay job. Never really saw him. He mostly worked all the time. Then one day, he began freaking out—

seemed as if he was going to lose his job. So, he went to his boss, and told him he'd give anything—even me, his own daughter—if he could keep his job. And what do you know, the fucking guy accepted the offer.

Man, I was like ready to run away. But my dad pleaded with me. Just go live with the guy. Do whatever he says. Just for a little while. Please—he was begging. Crying and shit. I figured I really didn't have much choice. Funny how some things never change—no matter how old you get.

Now, his boss was this guy named Robert. Good looking, late thirties. Real rich. He lived over in Bel Air, in one of those old-style mansions with the big columns out in front. His wife had died a few years back, so he's all alone—no girlfriend, no maid, nothing—not even a dog.

"Lonely," Ralph commented.

"But posh," I explained.

Y'see, I got used to the circumstances real fast. This big bed, a twelve-foot TV—man, I was living in luxury. But something was weird. I was sort of expecting Robert would be using me for sex. I had seen it all on cable and figured I could fake my way through most of it. What I didn't know, he'd teach me, right? Wrong! The guy never touched me, hardly said a word. I did some cleaning, made dinner, but mostly wondered, what the fuck was I doing here? Finally after a week or two of being totally ignored, I asked Robert why he agreed to my father's proposal.

"Because," he explained, "if your father was actually willing to give you away, I knew I could provide you with a better home."

Man, I fell in love right then and there. I began wearing less and less clothing around the house. Hoping he would notice. I mean, I had developed fast—had already outgrown a B-cup bra, and was pushing five foot eleven. I was definitely big enough to fuck. And I had been practicing the suck twice daily on these gourmet popsicles.

"What flavors?" Ralph asked.

"Strawberry/banana was my favorite," I said, adding, "I was ready. Only problem, he wasn't."

A couple of very frustrating months passed, when one night I just said, fuck it, and went to his bedroom. He was sleeping, the latest issue of the *New Yorker* still clutched in his hands. I crawled into the bed, fumbled with the opening of his silk boxers, pulled out his cock, and began to suck—I mean, it seemed like the right thing to do. And though it was definitely bigger than any popsicle I'd ever seen, I improvised. He woke up, tried to pull away, but I wouldn't let him. I just started sucking harder and pumping faster until finally he came.

"You shouldn't have done that," he said.

"I wanted to," I explained. I mean, what was he going to do—make me go stand in the corner for giving him head?

I crawled into his arms and fell asleep. Later that night, he woke me up in much the same way I woke him. Man, he showed me how to do everything.

I looked over at my partner. She stared at me, all teary-eyed. "That's the most beautiful story I've ever heard," she said, sniffling.

I just sort of shrugged. It was the best part of my life, hands down.

"Why didn't you marry the guy, have lots of kids, and live happily ever after?" Ralph asked.

"Because he died," I said, the words scratching at my throat. "When I was sixteen."

"Fuck," she said.

"Cancer," I said, thinking, God took him away from me.

"Didn't he leave you anything? I mean, the house? Something?"

"He left me everything," I explained. "But his sister challenged the will in court and got it overturned. Said I was just some teenage tramp living with him for his money and the fucking judge believed her."

"Man," Ralph said. "Didn't the judge feel sorry for you, being sixteen and all?"

I shook my head. "The age consent laws had been taken off the books in California. After the governor was caught with that thirteen-year-old."

"Right." She grunted, half laugh, half disgust. "It's what happens when you give men too much power."

"Girl, America is what happens when you give men too much power."

"That's politics, right?"

"Politicians."

"But we've got power," Ralph said.

"Only until they take it away from us."

"Is that gonna happen?"

"Not if I can help it," I said. "But who the fuck knows? They could pull the plug whenever they damn well please."

"What would you do then?"

"Go down fighting."

"Chop off a few political cocks."

"That's your specialty. I just aim for the vitals."

"To men, there's nothing more vital."

"You got a point there," I said.

Ralph was silent for a moment, contemplative, or so I figured. Then she asked, "So, what happened?"

I shrugged. "The judge called me an opportunist. Said I deserved exactly what I was getting. A big fat fucking nothing."

"Man, how do you get over something like that?"

I began to laugh, then said, "I killed the motherfucker."

"No way."

I nodded. "Just walked up to the bastard as he was leaving his house and shot him in the head at point-blank range. Showered his fucking lawn with judicial guts."

"Didn't get caught?"

"Fuck no. Just another random shooting."

"But he was a judge."

"A judge who was fucking some senator's fourteen-year-old son."

"Out-fucking-rageous!"

"It seems I did the politicians a favor."

"Ain't that always the way," Ralph said, laughing heartily.

"Yeah," I said. "Great. So, what are we going to do about Reverend Joe?"

"I think I've got an idea," Ralph said.

"Did I just give it to you?"

"More or less."

I couldn't wait to hear this one.

We arrived at the Reverend's mansion—one of those sprawling Malibu palaces that overlooks the Pacific. Like the kind you always see in old black and white movies starring Orson Welles. A fictional home. Full of fictional people, plastic plants, and bone china.

We knocked. A butler opened the door and promptly informed us that the good Reverend wasn't there.

"How 'bout his wife?" I asked.

He frowned disapprovingly and said, "Follow me."

Anne Bolton was seated in a sun room, staring out at the ocean. She was sipping what looked like tea, but smelled like gin. On a small radio, the voice of Reverend Joe could be heard. He was speaking against sin and fornication. The word "sodomy" piqued my interest.

"We need to speak with Mary," I said.

"Why?" Anne asked.

Definitely gin.

"We need a description of the doctor," Ralph said.

That sounded good to me.

"She's in her room," Anne said, waving a crooked finger back over her shoulder. "You'll find her there."

"Thank you." We shrugged and walked off in the direction the crooked finger pointed us.

We found the stairs, and figuring the bedrooms were most likely on the second floor, ran up, taking two steps at a time. The hallway was a collection of oil paintings and antiques. Old shit—nothing that interested either me or Ralph. Except for maybe this big mother of a painting of the Reverend, wifey, and their kid. They looked so damn austere, like the artist forgot to say, "Say cheese," or "Smile, goddamnit," or some such shit.

We found Mary's room. Her door was open. She was seated on her bed reading a book.

"What are you reading?" I asked.

"Final Exit," she said, closing the book and placing it aside.

"Is it a good story?" Ralph asked.

I smacked her arm. "It's an old suicide handbook," I explained.

"Oh," Ralph said, then, lowering her voice, "I didn't know."

"Why you reading something like that?" I asked.

The kid shrugged. "Just reading it."

I looked around. Instead of rock star posters, there was a framed eight-by-ten of the fucking pope. Instead of teddy bears, there was a stuffed crucifix over in one corner, a stuffed Jesus hanging from small stuffed nails. Instead of comic books and *Sassy* magazine, the girl had a leather-bound edition of the Bible and fucking *Final Exit*—I guess those books sort of went together.

"What do you want?" Mary asked, looking back and forth between me and Ralph.

"To help," Ralph said.

"Who got you pregnant?" I asked.

The kid looked down. I could tell she wanted to cry, but was holding back.

"Go ahead, kid," I said. "Tears won't hurt you."

But she just sucked in her breath, and shook her head—shook off those tears. Man, what I wouldn't give to see this kid smile.

Ralph sat down on the bed beside her. "Tell us what happened. We can help. Really."

Mary looked into Ralph's face. She shook her head. "No, you can't."

There was an awkward silence. I stepped back towards the door and said, "Let's go."

Ralph stood.

"If you want our help, kid," I said, not bothering to finish.

"Bye," Ralph said, sadly.

Back in the car I put on the headphones and turned on the surveillance equipment. Clear as a fucking bell.

"What's she doing?" Ralph asked.

"Crying."

"Let me hear."

I handed my partner the other set of headphones. "Poor kid," she said.

"Where'd you put the bug?"

"Headboard."

I nodded, started the engine, and drove off.

Ralph removed the headphones, and watched the mansion get smaller as we drove away. "We'll be back soon, kid," she said. "Real soon."

"Sure you don't wanna just go to his studio and waste the motherfucker?" Ralph said. "It'd be a lot easier."

"I want to confront Reverend Joe with *his* sins. I want to hear what he has to say." I smiled in a way to let Ralph know what I was thinking. "Then we'll make him do penance."

"Three *Hail Mary*'s, four *Our Father*'s, and a .45 slug right between his beady little eyes."

"Something like that."

We drove back out to Malibu around nine, figuring wifey would be unconscious within the hour. That'd probably be when the dear Reverend would make his move. Mary went to bed a little before nine-thirty. We could hear her reading something, and wondered whether it was the Bible or *Final Exit*—then realized there wasn't much difference.

At ten P.M. on the fucking nose, Reverend Joe entered his daughter's bedroom. We could hear the distinctive click of the door being locked.

Mary's voice was but a whisper. "Daddy, I don't want to get pregnant again."

The bed creaked.

"I need you to carry on my name," Reverend Joe said. "I need you to give me a son. A holy son." His voice sounded so fucking solemn. "A son we'll name Jesus."

"Ain't nothing immaculate about that," Ralph muttered under her breath.

I exhaled loudly. This was getting more fucked by the minute.

"Please, Daddy."

There was a rustling of material, a gasp, the sound of a zipper, and a lot of wet slurping sounds. The bed creaked in a steady rhythm.

"Daddy, no please," Mary pleaded. "Put it in my mouth, Daddy. Please. Or put it in my other hole." She began to cry. "Please, Daddy, I don't want to have a baby."

The creaking rhythm stopped. The Reverend began screaming. "How could you?" he yelled. "My daughter, my holy daughter. Haven't you been reading your Bible? Don't you know those are deviant acts? Acts against God and nature. You're a pig. A Jezebel." There was a slapping sound. The creaking rhythm began again, only faster. "Jezebel," he yelled. Another slap. "Jezebel." Then a loud gasp.

"Motherfucker," Ralph said.

"Daddy, don't," Mary cried.

The Reverend's breathing was heavy. He began to make those about-to-come sounds.

"No, Daddy, please," she begged.

There was another slap.

Reverend Joe grunted, then groaned.

And all was silent, except for Mary's soft whimpering.

I put the headphones aside and checked the tape. Crystal clear.

"We should give this to the press," Ralph said. "Embarrass the son-of-a-bitch to death."

"Couldn't do that to the kid."

"Good point."

"Besides, they'd never run it," I said. "There's not much difference between them and him."

"That's a depressing thought."

"Yeah," I said, putting the car in gear, and driving away. "Real depressing."

The next morning, we had an appointment to see Reverend Joe at his office in Beverly Hills. Told him we wanted to collect on the fifty grand.

He let us in, instructed his secretary to hold all calls, and promptly locked his office door.

"Can we talk?" I asked.

"The walls are soundproof," he explained, taking a seat behind a huge mahogany desk. "Can never be too careful."

"Of course."

"I assume everything was," he cleared his throat, "taken care of."

Ralph nodded.

"No complications?"

"Not a one," I said.

He smiled a huge save-your-soul shit-eating grin. "Good," he said, stretching out the word into a few dozen syllables. "Then I believe I owe you ladies some money."

"Fifty thousand each," Ralph said.

Reverend Joe nodded. He swiveled in his chair and pulled open the bottom drawer of an old oak file cabinet. Fuck! Our eyes went wide. The drawer was packed to the hilt with cash. Not ones or fives. But crisp hundred-dollar bills, neatly wrapped in ten-thousand-dollar packets. He pulled out ten of the neat little parcels and tossed them onto his desk. Turning, he caught our wide-eyed look. "A little cash reserve for emergencies such as this," he explained.

"Of course," I said, in my most official PIG voice.

He slid the money forward on the desk. "Spend it wisely," he said, adding, "In the name of the Lord."

That's *exactly* what we plan on doing, I thought, grabbing the cash and shoving it into the backpack I had slung over one shoulder.

"Y'know, Reverend Joe," Ralph said, in her sexiest little-girl voice. "There is one other thing."

"Yes," he said, an eyebrow inquisitively cocked.

"Well," Ralph looked over in my direction and giggled. Shit, she was laying it on heavy—she loved playing these roles. "Ever since we first met you in the office the other day, Pandy and I haven't been able to get you off our minds." That was true enough.

The preacher cleared his throat and adjusted the knot of his tie—why the fuck do men always adjust the knots of their ties whenever they think they're about to get laid? "Oh, really," he said.

"We," I said, looking down, playing along with Ralph, "find you very attractive."

"Thank you," the Reverend said, a little more tie-knot adjusting.

Ralph walked around to where he sat, and leaned her butt back against the edge of his desk. Bending forward, grabbing his tie with one hand, touching his face with the other, she said, "Very attractive." She gave a yank on the tie, pulled his face to hers, and they kissed. Reverend Joe, wasting no time, stood and grabbed my partner lecherously. He squeezed her ass with one hand, fondled her boobs with the other. After a couple of those deep-tongue, spit-exchanging kisses, Ralph spun around, and still holding on to his tie, led him like a motherfucking Schnauzer on a leash to the leather couch on the other side of the office. "Let's get comfortable," she said.

"What about your friend?" he asked, motioning towards me.

"We flipped for it," Ralph said. "I get you first. I called *heads* and won."

"I *always* call *heads*," the Reverend said, stripping off his clothes. Ralph hiked her skirt up around her waist and peeled off her top. "The burning bush," he said softly, eyes glued to her twat.

I wanted to fucking roar—this guy was too much!

Ralph ordered the preacher to lie down on the couch. He quickly obeyed. Then, positioning her twat over his hardly significant but already stiff cock, she slammed down hard. The Reverend bucked and groaned.

"You feel so good, my child," he said, his hand fumbling with her boobs. They rode off together into the sunset of her bush. He grunted. She groaned. He moaned. She sighed. It was like some bad Z-grade Western written in coitus.

"I've got a special treat for you," Ralph said, after what seemed like a little too long.

"What's that, child?"

"Close your eyes."

Reverend Joe clamped them down shut, and Ralph went to work. Sliding his cock out of her twat, she pumped it a couple of times, heaped a glob of spit on it, then glided it into her ass. She leaned back and started riding the fucker like he was one of those bucking broncos—her pumped-up thighs lifting her up and down. Up and down. Man, she was slamming down so hard, I half expected her to crush his pubic bones.

"That's so tight," he whispered. "So tight."

"You can open your eyes now," Ralph said.

The look on his face was priceless. Here was his holy cock moving in and out of my partner's shithole. She fingered her twat and licked her lips. "Like what you see?"

"My Lord," he said, immediately losing control. "This," he said, his breathing becoming hard, "is," Chinese eyes time, "unnatural." And the Reverend came with a shudder and gasp.

Then it was Ralph's turn. Her hand furiously worked over her clit, as she squirmed her ass in little circles, tossed back her mane of red hair, and moaned, just slightly. She was quiet, when she wanted to be. But she always had to come—no matter fucking what. And she could always come on cue.

As he lay there, catching his breath, the Reverend smiled wickedly and said, "You're a bad girl. You shouldn't have done that."

Ralph smiled back and said, "You'll probably feel the same way about this."

Then, in the swiftest of motions, she spun around and positioned her butt an inch or two above his still grinning mouth.

Then she let loose.

Fuck! A tropical rainstorm of come and shit squirted out of her asshole into Reverend Joe's mouth and all over his face. It sounded like an Uzi underwater. Squishy, rapid-fire farts. And a lot of shit. I'm talking a foot-long turd. All soft and wet. A motherfucking refried bean chocolate milkshake delight. Ralph must have saved it up for days.

The Reverend started coughing and spitting and swearing. Ralph was laughing so hard by the time she jumped off his face to look back at her artistic masterpiece that she drowned out whatever it was he said. Would have liked to hear it, though—bet it was some killer line.

She picked up his discarded shirt and wiped herself clean, while I pulled the tape recorder from my knapsack and turned the sucker on full blast. The preacher sat up and just stared, all shit/come-faced. He looked mad, real fucking mean—but like he wasn't sure exactly what to do.

"Got anything to say for yourself?" I asked.

"Incest isn't illegal," he said, very matter-of-factly, as if he didn't give a shit. "Anymore."

Fuck it! I had had enough. Dropping the tape recorder, I pulled my .45 from the knapsack and aimed its barrel his way.

He leaned forward. "You won't get away with this," he yelled.

"What was that?" I asked.

"I have a lot of powerful friends."

"Fuck you, and your friends," I said, and fired away.

The first shot I aimed at his minuscule cock—blew it and his nuts to Kingdom Come. He'd need Saint Peter's help, if he'd ever want to piece together that hideous puzzle.

"You fucking cunt," he screamed, raising a hand towards me.

I blew the fucking thing clear off at the waist. "Slap Mary now, motherfucker," I said, not able to contain my laughter as I eyed the spurting stump.

He opened his mouth to scream, but no sound came out—just a lot of spittle and Ralph's shit bubbling out, a dark brown rabid foam.

"Say good-bye, Reverend Joe."

The next shot ripped into his chest. The one after that, the back of his head. His body slam-danced on the couch, arms flailing, thrashing about, what was left of his head spewing out multicolored ooze from a variety of openings. I kept squeezing off round after round, and must have pumped another half-dozen bullets into the fucker before I felt Ralph's hand on my arm.

"I think he's dead," she said.

"Fucking right, he is." I took a few deep breaths and tried to calm down. I realized how pumped I was, drenched in my own sweat—every muscle aching, my head pounding. Man, I was even crying. I wiped my mouth with the back of my free hand, and realized that even my lip was bleeding—must have bit down too hard in all the excitement. "Fucking right."

Ralph picked up the tape recorder and handed it to me. I tossed it into my bag along with the .45—the hundred thousand in there to keep them company. *A hundred thousand dollars.* Fuck! That suddenly didn't seem like enough. Not nearly enough. I looked over at my partner.

"You thinking what I'm thinking?" she asked.

We moved over to the file cabinet and emptied the contents of the bottom drawer into my backpack. Most of it fit; the rest we put in pockets—Ralph even stuffed twenty thousand dollars into her bra. As far as we were concerned, it was reward money. Payment due on an asshole wanted dead or alive.

"Think the kid'll smile now?" Ralph asked.

"I know I would," I said, taking one last look at the shithead before we headed out. Man, he stunk. "What the fuck have you been eating?" I asked Ralph.

"Beans," she said. "Lots of beans. I've eaten nothing but beans for the past two days."

"You crack me up," I said, smiling. Ralph could make me laugh no matter what. No matter fucking what.

I locked Reverend Joe's door on the way out and told his secretary that he was taking a much-needed nap and had asked not to be disturbed. She glanced up at Ralph, who was adjusting her skirt, giving it a little extra hike down, smiled salaciously and nodded her understanding—fuck, he was probably screwing her too.

In the car, Ralph turned and asked, "What now?"

"Man, it's over," I said. "I'm quitting. I've had enough. You know they're gonna come after us for this one. They'll say we stepped over the line." I snorted out a little laugh. "Like they ever told us where the fucking line was."

"We're supposed to know."

"Yeah, we know all right."

I slammed the car in gear and took off. Down Wilshire, over on 6th, and up the ramp. The Santa Ana Freeway South looked good to me.

"Where you gonna go?" Ralph asked.

I shrugged. "Just gonna drive. I'll know when I get there."

Ralph was quiet for a minute, then turned and asked, "Can I come?"

"What the fuck?" I said, never expecting her not to. "It'd be kind of boring without you. Y'know?"

Ralph nodded and smiled. She leaned forward and switched on the radio. Some oldies station was playing a Red Hot Chili Peppers' tune. She left it on, bopping her head in time to the beat. Personally I prefer music with an edge. These oldies seem so lame and dated. But Ralph was getting into it, so I didn't say anything.

I just listened, as she sang along.

Rockin' the Midnight Hour

ANYA MARTIN

The more I think splatterpunk, the more I hear rock 'n' roll.

Consider: The same sort of rebellious attitude which split rock off mainstream pop sheared splatterpunk away from traditional horror. Yet even those who accept this analogy tend to pigeonhole splat as the literary equivalent of grindcore or thrash, as screaming, obnoxious shit that JUST WON'T SHUT UP.

Uh-uh.

Because just as there are different forms of alternative rock— riot grrrl, death metal, industrial, goth—there are different forms of splatterpunk.

Here's ANYA MARTIN to tell you about that. Along with Skipp & Spector, Richard Christian Matheson, and David J. Schow. The one, the only, the original Splat Pack.

I first met Anya Martin at a horror convention in the Deep South in the mid-1980s. At that time I was a hired gun for film studios promoting genre pictures like RoboCop *and* Return of the Living Dead. *Anya was a petite woman with a shock of curly red hair. All eyes and ears, constantly watching, listening, taking it in.*

Since then I've discovered Martin is a rock critic and columnist who, as she puts it, "has penned more words on the subject of music and horror than she cares to remember." Said criticism has appeared in the likes of Iniquities *magazine and a number of others. Anya's currently working on a novel and nonfiction film book.*

"Rockin' the Midnight Hour" is Martin's attempt at explicating the rock/horror connection. Splatterpunks have always been aware of this link, of course. Indeed, the following essay records

how importantly the key splatterpunk pioneers—Dave, John,
Richard and the rest—tend to regard that connection.
Recommended background music while reading this piece?
Try Ministry. *Or* Napalm Death.
Or anything else that's loud, angry, and irritating to adults.

Horror is the rock 'n' roll of fiction. They share the same
sort of aesthetic qualities with each other, at least the
kind of horror that we're writing. It tends to have that
rock 'n' roll feel to it because it's very fast-paced. Even
the slow numbers are fast-paced. It's got a lot of energy
to it, it's got a definite beat, and it tends to go over the
edge.

—Spector

*T*he term "rock 'n' roll/horror connection" is apt to conjure up
three decades of monstrous melodies. Consider the number of rockers who've concocted songs with an often tongue-in-cheek macabre
tilt. Graveyard bop in the recording world goes back to rock classics
like Bobby "Boris" Pickett's "Monster Mash," Sheb Wooley's "Purple
People Eater," and Screamin' Jay Hawkins's "I Put a Spell on You."

Of course, some rockers got more into their ghoulish lyrics than
others. By the '70s, you had an entire rock subculture devoted to
the macabre, centered around performers such as Alice Cooper and
KISS, who actually decked themselves out in the wardrobe and
whiteface of the undead. Not to mention the king of the creepy
crooners, Ozzy Osbourne, who, allegedly, bit off the heads of doves
and bats with his teeth in concert.

Indeed, the whole heavy metal world seems Satan-obsessed,
with parents and child psychologists even now linking lyrics about
demonic spells and human sacrifice to the real-life growth of Devil-
worship among teens. This violent subculture—if you listen to
Geraldo Rivera and the cops—is spreading like a plague through
high schools across the country, along with the conviction that
Tipper Gore's PMRC might've been right after all: Dangerous rock
lyrics actually *do* cause unsavory behavior.

But metal did not create the only horror subculture in rock
music. Out of punk rock in the U.S. and Great Britain came the

"Goths" (short for "Gothic") or death-rockers. Rejecting the self-effusive glam look of the metalheads—something sure to scare parents, but sharing more in common with drag queens than Draculas—the Goths had a much more romantic view of horror. Taking Bela Lugosi and Lord Byron as models, they desired to emulate more directly the demeanor of the dead, or more precisely the undead—for every Goth's ideal nightmare was to be reborn a vampire. They dressed in black, lots of drapy fabrics and spiderweb netting; they dyed their hair jet-black, masked their faces in ghostly white, and lined their eyes with thick black liner.

As for their sound, though punk queen Siouxsie of the Banshees is credited as being the first Goth, the key band here was Bauhaus, a British band who composed hard-edged, somber songs. Their most famous hit, "Bela Lugosi's Dead," was featured in the film *The Hunger*, based on Whitley Strieber's vampire novel. Bauhaus broke up in the early '80s with lead singer Peter Murphy going solo and the rest of the band reforming first as Tones on Tail and then as Love and Rockets. Carrying on the Bauhaus legacy are such groups as Alien Sex Fiend, the Sisters of Mercy, Christian Death, Skinny Puppy and the Cramps.

And of course, none of this takes into account what seems to be a general fascination of rockers for death and darkness, from the teenage death songs of the fifties ("Teen Angel" "Deadman's Curve") to the black undertones lurking through works by the Doors, the Rolling Stones, Pink Floyd . . .

With all this supernatural rockin', it would seem like a natural twist for the supernatural story. Yet, how many examples can you name in which writers have set their horrors in the underworld of rock 'n' roll? Make that same list but include only stories or novels penned before 1985. Suddenly, despite three decades of horror-rocking, it's hard to come up with more than a handful. Why has it taken so long for the rock 'n' roll/horror connection to creep over into the written word, and why now? Add into the equation the fact that you now have at least two generations of horror writers who have grown up with rock music.

What seems to have happened is a slow build. Rock music certainly has been playing a marginal role in the field for some time, for example, in the pop-culture-embued works of Stephen King. No list of rock 'n' roll/horror novels could be considered complete

without reference to *Christine*, the tale of the demonically pos-
sessed '58 Plymouth Fury. King even included snippets of rock
lyrics at the start of each chapter.

As did George R. R. Martin in *The Armageddon Rag* (1983), a
book which resurrected '60s rock long before the much-touted
twenty-year anniversary of Woodstock. In fact, *Rag*, an early example of what seems to be gelling into a sub-subgenre in the field, may
be the best example of how it can be done, the blend of subject
matter and a distinct rock 'n' roll tone.

And then there's Anne Rice, who probably brought the notion
of a rock/horror connection more into the mainstream than even
King has. When she resurrected *The Vampire Lestat* in 1985, after
a ten-year hiatus, her suave, blood-sucking antihero rose out of
subterranean slumber to expose the secrets of all vampirekind as—
what else—a rock star through the medium of MTV videos. If Ms.
Rice's hand was on the pop-culture pulse, her actions were greeted
with loud approval by rock idols, such as Sting and Queensrÿche
lead singer Geoff Tate. Both have voiced aspirations to act in films
based on her novels. In lieu of any definitive contracts, Queensrÿche's *Rage For Order* album (1986) consisted almost solely of
songs focusing on the trials and tribulations of being a vampire,
while Sting composed "Moon Over Bourbon Street" (*The Dream
of the Blue Turtles*, 1985) directly in homage to the works of the
vampire mistress.

Still, rock 'n' roll wasn't at the core of any of these books—not
the kind of rock 'n' roll that ripped through your soul, the kind of
rock 'n' roll that parents accused of stealing their kids' souls. That
supernatural extension has slithered onto the bookshelves and magazine stands only in the last few years, thanks to a new breed of
writers whom nobody had ever heard of before. And it has influ-
enced them not only in terms of the characters and plots they
incorporate into their writing but also, as was hinted at by writers
such as King and Martin but never brought full swing, in the tone
of their writing—indeed, in the very process of creating their works.

At the head of the list of this type of writer must come a quartet
who are both friends and literary compatriots; David Schow, Richard
Christian Matheson and the duo of John Skipp and Craig Spector.
Other writers have danced with rock as topic and tone—Ray Garton
(*Crucifax Autumn*), the trio of Canadian lawyers who call them-

selves Michael Slade (*Ghoul*), Philip Nutman (*Full Throttle*), Mick
Garris, Poppy Z. Brite, Gregory Nicoll, and, most prominently, John
Shirley. And more will surely be added to the list after the publication of *ShockRock*, a horror/rock anthology edited by Jeff Gelb and
due out this year. Nevertheless, if one was searching for experts on
the topic, though Shirley gives them a fair run for their money, the
fearsome foursome of Schow, Matheson, Skipp, and Spector are
perhaps the closest core practitioners. Sometimes, rock is the subject matter of these writers. But more than that, what makes their
works rock 'n' roll is a certain bravado they exude in their writing,
a certain devil-may-care attitude that has sometimes pissed off their
parents, the older, respected fathers of the genre. It's in the rhythm
of their words, different beats but sharing a quality that rips through
your soul like a hard-edged guitar riff.

It is this sensibility that is missing, for example, in Rice's work,
or Michael Slade's *Ghoul*. While there are many other reasons why
these novels could be praised, the rock in *The Vampire Lestat* and
Queen of the Damned—no matter how many rock musicians it has
inspired—is merely the replay of "just one note," offers Schow.
Lestat may be a rock musician, but the novels just don't read rock
'n' roll; indeed, they have the tone of a classical piece, perhaps an
opera. According to Schow, his reaction was, "Here's somebody
writing about a rock singer who doesn't listen to the music."

The same criticism goes for *Ghoul*, where rock 'n' roll is treated
as the means to an end, not as an end in itself. Slade has produced
a psychological thriller and chosen to cast a rocker as the serial
killer.

But the rock 'n' roll/horror connection still doesn't end with the
writing style of these four and a gradually building community of
compatriots. Indeed, rock 'n' roll as a musical style that challenges
cultural taboos shares a number of characteristics with horror as a
literary style which at its best tests the limits of our sensibilities. A
case can be made for a multilevel dialectic. As Spector says in the
quote at the top of this piece rock and horror both share a quality
of danger, referring not to the mainstream of either field but to its
more experimental periphery. Artists who aren't afraid to take a few
risks, to tread into areas that the mainstream of our culture considers dangerous.

In the words of Skipp, "I think, with rock 'n' roll and horror, more than with their counterparts, they're designed to go all the way. They ask you to do the stuff your mom and dad wish you wouldn't."

"They're both not completely but fundamentally rooted in the gut," adds Spector. "It's the way you react to them. You feel good rock 'n' roll in your gut. You feel good horror in your gut. It's a real animal kind of art form."

Given such observations, then, it should come as no surprise that the rock 'n' roll roots of these guys does not lie in all that creepy crooning—what might have seemed the obvious connection. Though they are often spotted in black leather jackets and tend to wear their hair long, these guys are most definitely not diehard metalheads or Goths.

The influences that cut into these writers' works are found rather in the cutting edges of the rock 'n' roll they grew up with, what John Skipp calls "our tribal music. It's so much a part of the way we think that it couldn't help but flop over into the books." Skipp, Spector, and Matheson all are musicians; for Schow, the music is an inescapable part of his lifestyle.

Of the four, rock as subject matter has come up the most in the work of Skipp and Spector. They made their literary debut with the story of a punk vampire in the New York club scene (*The Light at the End*), and followed with a novel about a less-than-successful rock musician, offered the power by an "angel" to become the ultimate vigilante (*The Clean-Up*). As for 1988's *The Scream*, it was the ultimate rock/horror novel, in which the ultimate evil was provided by a Satanic heavy metal band called the Scream and their perverted manager Joshua Walker.

By coincidence or destiny, Schow's first published novel, *The Kill Riff*—another rock/horror story—arrived on the market just a few months after *The Scream*, raising questions as to whether there might be a certain timeliness to the subject. It was about a man whose daughter was trampled in a riot at a rock concert. He becomes obsessed with tracking down and murdering all the members of Whiphand, the now defunct metal band that played that gig.

Schow has also used rock music in short stories. "Red Light," his 1987 World Fantasy award-winning story, took its title from a song by Siouxsie and the Banshees. In his "Lonesome Coyote Blues," two guys on a long, lonely desert drive tune in a radio station that plays songs by greats such as Buddy Holly and Jimi Hendrix—only these are hits they never recorded.

As to why rock figures so greatly in his works, Spector suggests, first of all, simple logic; the age-group of their protagonists. "It would be culturally a part of their experience." While their upcoming novel, *The Bridge*, contains no main characters who are rock musicians, he and Skipp say that rock still figures in as the background music—what the characters listen to.

Schow ascribes the emergence of *The Scream* and of *The Kill Riff* as having a more direct relation to its topicality. Writers often find their subjects in the news. "You have people trying to bring lawsuits against Judas Priest or putting lyrics in songs that have offensively inspired people to hurt themselves or commit suicide or do drugs or whatever. You have people trying to sue Ozzy. You have the PMRC thing that went down a couple of years ago. The PMRC is still out there."

Still, as for the more general emergence of a trend towards rock 'n' roll horror fiction, Matheson is a bit skeptical. While he agrees that the high visibility of recent events such as the Tipper Gore/ Frank Zappa debate could have been contributing factors, he points out the long-running rock 'n' roll connection that slides the other way, that "Alice Cooper was doing this shit—albeit rather laughingly" two decades ago. Preferring to credit the odd coincidence rather than any strict causality, he acknowledges, "I could just as easily argue for it to have come out ten years ago."

And indeed, as said before, when one looks at the proliferation of horror rock and remembers how even the Beatles were supposed to carry messages from beyond the grave in the grooves of their records (played backwards, of course), he has reason. Perhaps, though it may cause chagrin for those seeking pat causal explanations, any sudden rise in rock as subject matter for horror tales is mostly an accident of time, albeit one that was probably inevitable given the tremendous influence of rock in the mainstream of American culture.

As for an interplay between rock music and the creative process of writing, Matheson, who was a professional drummer before turning full-time to writing in his early twenties—he's now thirty-nine— says that being a musician factors into his writing "everywhere." For him, writing itself is an aural experience. The basic relationship is "two-sided." First, there is rhythm; he is quick to compare the manipulation of language with the mixing of percussion instruments. The second component is melody and applies to the choice of words. "They actually have a musical tonality," he says. "Certain words sound beautiful together and other words sound cacophonous together. Being aware of that I think means writing that much better—it literally sounds good to the ear."

Matheson is known for his sharp-edged stories, tightly composed pieces that make up for their brevity in sheer emotional impact. His stories are not explicitly rock 'n' roll in their subject matter, though rock songs do come up, for example, on the radio dial in "Hell" (*Silver Scream*, ed. David Schow). As Jim Morrison's voice delivers a heavy assault of "Music is your only friend. Until the end," Lauren discovers that her VW rabbit is locked in on three sides by cars parked way too close for comfort; the nose of her car is facing a cliff.

And on another musical bent, Matheson has done a country-western horror tale of sorts called "I'm Always Here," for the Joe Lansdale-edited *Razored Saddles*, about a "Siamese-twin country western duo." According to Matheson, he has always been fascinated by the way that country-western husband-and-wife duos, like Porter Wagoner and Tammy Wynette, spend their entire life together "singing about their domestic crises. You get this entire marriage like a Swedish movie—like an Ingmar Bergman movie—in a country-western cooperation."

Nevertheless, even when they don't emerge in the text as the Doors' piece did in "Hell," specific rock songs are an integral part of his creation process. Indeed, Matheson reveals that each story he does often is composed with a song in mind. None of these songs become the title; they rather contribute an ambience that sets his creative juices in motion. "It's like if you're interested in someone, you feel an attraction to somebody, you lower the lights and you light a candle, put on some beautiful music. It fills in so that you have a perfect mood.

"So, if you have an idea for a story, by putting on a certain kind of music, it fills in the rest of it. It absolutely transports your mind to the perfect place. The music is like substance enhancement. If you listen to it the right way, it's very powerful, very transcendent."

As for a specific example, Matheson confesses that the bone-chilling enhancement for "Sirens" (also in *Silver Scream*) was Neil Young's "The Needle and Damage Done." When asked more generally about his musical roots, he cites the Beatles as his first big inspiration, what drove him into wanting to be a rock musician in the first place. Much of his musical taste was established during the years he was performing—Led Zeppelin, the Doors, the Rolling Stones, old Allman Brothers, Cat Stevens.

Skipp and Spector not only listen to other peoples' music while devising new books; they have created their own—full-scale sound tracks for *The Light at the End, The Clean-Up,* some miscellaneous pieces for *The Scream,* and most recently *The Bridge.* They stopped writing such extensive music, however, when they found they couldn't interest anyone in releasing the music commercially.*

"People don't release sound track albums for books," says Skipp regretfully. "It happens so rarely as to constitute never."

Which is one of the reasons, they add, that they would like to break into film, to have the opportunity to be able to integrate their musical and literary proclivities into one creative whole.

While Matheson has a song for each of his stories, Skipp and Spector associate certain pieces of music with parts of novels. For example, Spector recalls listening to a lot of Pink Floyd's *Momentary Lapse of Reason* album while working on *Dead Lines* and a four-day marathon of both the vocal and instrumental versions of Tina Turner's "We Don't Need Another Hero" during *The Clean-Up.* As to whom or what he listens to on a regular basis, he says that "it goes through phases. Certain artists or a given album will strike a resonant chord in the work."

As for what's on Skipp's self-assault agenda, when writing the current S&S novel *The Bridge,* he said he had been listening to lots of Oingo Boingo—"Oingo Boingo outnumbered everything else by about sixty percent." Other artists they are currently listening to include, for Skipp—Peter Murphy, Peter Gabriel, Kate Bush, Tin Machine, Treat Her Right, sound tracks to *The Thing, Cat People, The Dawn of the Dead*; for Spector—Pat Methaney, the Sisters of Mercy, Shriekback, Edie Brickell and New Bohemians, sound tracks to *Batman, Near Dark,* general Tangerine Dream.

---

*Skip and Spector's music for *The Bridge* was released by Dark Dawn Records in 1991.

Indeed, according to Schow, what a writer listens to while he writes, or indeed whether he listens to music at all, says a lot about the finished product. Schow had even contemplated placing a playlist at the head of his latest novel *The Shaft*, so that readers can get a tone for what he was listening to while composing the text. He, most definitely, like Matheson, Skipp, and Spector, writes with the music on. The first thing he does most mornings is turn on the stereo.

"One of the things I do a lot of day to day is listen to music," he says. "The stereo is on usually from the moment I wake up to the moment I go to bed. [It's] like clouds in the sky—sometimes all the music that you're listening to swims together and makes pictures for you and inspires you to do stuff. It helps the creative process along to hear other people indulging in their creative process."

While writing *The Shaft*, for example, Schow says that he listened to a "huge casserole" of musicians, from classical to jazz to rock. When he feels like writing to instrumental pieces—music with lyrics, he says, can be distracting—often it's Tangerine Dream, or various sound track music from Jan Hammer's *Miami Vice* track to his favorite, Wang Chung's *To Live and Die in L. A.* In terms of rock, he leans typically towards the alternative/progressive end, "almost everything by the Cocteau Twins," Sisters of Mercy, Shriekback, hard core/thrash bands like the Butthole Surfers, the Circle Jerks, T.S.O.L., Suicidal Tendencies. Or to the obscure, the 1974 incarnation of King Crimson, Japanese garage bands like the Mops (you know them—they sing "I'm Just a Mop"), Henrietta Collins, and the Wife-beating Childhaters. He even occasionally throws on some Screamin' Jay Hawkins.

Schow adds, however, that he finds Devil-oriented heavy metal "a crashing bore." "I think it's incredibly limiting in that biblical horror can be dispelled by waving a cross or a Bible at it. That's a pretty pallid horror, isn't it? I mean it's got a pretty established methodology for getting rid of it. It's not a problem in the way that bugs aren't a problem if you have Raid . . . And if you listen to the music, some of the better speed-metal and thrash-metal has nothing to do with it. I think bands are beginning to realize it, too."

Indeed, he modeled the sound of Whiphand—the band in *The*

Kill Riff—after his own musical preferences. "If there was a real band like that, it would be one of the more subterranean metal bands, and it wouldn't be as famous as Whiphand was in the book. They wouldn't be playing sports arenas."

But if Whiphand was on the periphery of bands who might become famous in our consumer-oriented culture, and Schow's musical tastes often run to the extreme fringes of the status quo of rock music, perhaps it is not so surprising that the work this music inspires has also been labeled as being on the edges of what is acceptable in horror literature. While it has for the moment died down, the Splatterpunk controversy itself that revolved around the loose group of writers including Schow, Skipp, Spector, and Matheson was phrased as an aural argument—quiet versus loud horror. The classicists versus the hard rockers?

The parallel is not lost on the writers themselves. "It was funny because I think that we all in our separate ways *did* do what the Sex Pistols and the Dead Kennedys were doing at the time," observes John Skipp in retrospect, commenting on the spontaneity with which their writing emerged on the professional scene, just as the Pistols rose to challenge the musical status quo. "And these were not a bunch of guys who were writing letters to each other, saying, hey, let's start a movement. They were just a bunch of bands who had the same kind of sensibility, and the next thing you know people had decided that it was a movement—nothing killed it faster than deciding it was a movement.

"Basically they had decided that things had just gotten a little too tired around here, a little too corporate, a little too regular and predictable, and they weren't addressing the things that they thought rock 'n' roll should be about. So they started going on stage and screaming and doing wild shit.

"And I guess that's sort of what Craig and I and Schow and Clive Barker and various other people have done. We were reading the stuff that was there and going 'yeah, this is great, but what if you went *this far* . . .' "

Schow agrees. "The whole idea [behind rock] is pissing off your parents, which we as horror writers seem to be doing to the wave of horror writers who came before us."

"It's as though we've done something and we don't know what

it is, but we sure pissed them off," he adds. "They're having the same reaction that your average '60s parent has had when you put on the average Dirty Rotten Imbeciles album."

What these guys are defending, however, is not loudness per se. In Spector's view, the key factor is not noise level, but rather a certain level of feeling: "Quiet horror can mask its inability to convey a message by simply being chilly and remote. [It can] hide behind that every bit as much as loud horror can hide behind the viscera. I think that what makes any kind of horror or music— whether it's quiet, loud, or whatever—good for us is this real feeling of emotional involvement, that the writer was going after something and got it."

Hence, he feels that in much the same way that punk rock today hardly pulls the same emotional triggers it did when it burst onto the music scene in the mid-'70s, too much loud horror can fizzle the fright. "There's also such a thing as a cyclical nature to this, cycles of desensitization and resensitization," he suggests. "If you do too much for too long, it becomes devalued."

Skipp returns to the aural analogy: "Then it stops being an alarm, and it just turns into a background noise."

As for Matheson, he agrees loudness is not a virtue in itself, but that part of the problem—and indeed where the analogy wears thin—lies in the different qualities and expectations of fiction and rock music.

"If we're talking about the fringe like splatter-horror, yeah, it's really like intellectually breaking the law. Or with music, it's aurally breaking the law. And at its worst, like every juvenile delinquent, it can just be an insolent punk, which does nothing. And at its best, it can be genuine revolution, genuine iconoclasm. It can be very exciting, but it can just be loud."

Actually, he feels that most of the loud horror out on the market is "pretty dumb. It just seems out-of-control in the worst possible way." Part of the problem, though, is that the sort of visceral anger that triggered bands like the Sex Pistols doesn't translate onto paper. "True angry teenage rock 'n' roll is very inarticulate stuff that relies on the most obvious phraseology, kind of a primitive way to get from A to B with an idea. Whereas any horror story has to be by its own construction so much more sophisticated than that. It cannot afford to be pure out-and-out angry. You couldn't have the Johnny

Rotten of prose because it would be unreadable, not unreadable because it would be offensive, but because it wouldn't be very interesting. There has to be more delicacy, and there has to be more maturity and refinement with prose writing, even with bad prose writing."

Indeed, one can find a literary parallel to this debate in the debates about rock music contained in *The Scream* and *The Kill Riff*, parts of the text derived straight from the news. While the fears of housewives and preachers may fuel the plotlines behind both books, the implication here is just as no type of writing is inherently bad, neither is any type of music. The real horror is censorship.

As for the thought of rock actually causing someone to wreak violence, Spector is skeptical. "Any dough-wad with a record player can sit there and say, I listened to your lyrics and they said I should go and kill my parents. Well, aren't we just a special child?"

As for what he'd say to Geraldo after that special on Satanism: "It's a theory. It's a piece of fiction. Have you ever heard of fiction before?"

Horror and rock 'n' roll are both something that many parents and educators seem to have a real fear of—they are genuinely scared that kids who are into the stuff will grow up to be mass murderers, drug dealers, rapists, or at the very least, sexually promiscuous profaners of the English language, damned to Hell. An article in *Omni* outlined numerous attempts used by those speaking for the child's best interest to remove Stephen King novels from school library shelves. The excuses ranged from foul language to the encouragement of Devil worship. Only pornography and evolution cause as much fury among God-loving Christians as horror and rock 'n' roll.

Which, of course, has everything to do with why kids like both horror and rock—the shock value that plays so well into the dynamics of adolescent rebellion. It is this teenage rock/horror connection that filmmakers, with their eye ever peeled onto the lucrative youth market, have cashed in on for much longer than the writers. Early examples date back to the early '70s and cult movies and cult movie musicals like *Phantom of the Paradise*, director Brian De Palma's update of *The Phantom of the Opera* to a rock-palace setting, and the more famous *Rocky Horror Picture Show*. As the '80s dragged on, more and more horror films incorporated rock stars (David Bowie, *The Hunger*; Sting, *The Bride*) into their casts and rock songs into their sound tracks (the *Nightmare on Elm Street* and *Friday the 13th* series, *Return of the Living Dead*). The culmination of this trend can be seen in the runaway box-office success of 1987's *Lost Boys*.

Still, the rock 'n' roll horror connection can be taken to the extreme. Obviously, there are a lot of similarities between rock and horror, but as Matheson points out, one is music and one is writing. While one can compare elements of the two, as in looking for rhythm and melody in text, the fact remains that while novels and short stories may be composed to a diverse and eclectic assembly of music, they don't come to the reader with a soundtrack (Skipp and Spector aside). Given this limitation, Matheson feels that writing is the "bigger accomplishment."

"The writer of horror who accomplishes what rock 'n' roll accomplishes is a very strong writer because he is providing invisible music," he puts forth. "He is making you hear as strongly and as loudly as a powerful piece of music."

But even beyond that, the fact is that rock music is typically produced by a team of different individuals, a band, while horror fiction—with the possible exception of Michael Slade—is the product of one person. This has inherently different implications for the process of creation. "In rock 'n' roll, it is very unusual to have an artist that is one person who plays all the instruments, who writes all the songs. In rock 'n' roll, if you can do that you're considered a genius. In prose, it is expected. It is expected that an individual have all the ideas. It is expected that you will write all the dialogue. It is expected that you will write all the descriptions. It is expected that you will handle everything, that you will orchestrate the entire thing. And it doesn't make you a genius or a savant, it just makes you a writer."

Indeed, Matheson adds that "a lot of what is attractive about being a rock 'n' roll musician is that it harnesses a very limited and primal part of your personality. It's like sex. On a certain wavelength, it's just the simplest thing you can do. It's so simple. To write beautiful scenes about lovemaking is difficult, to just fuck is simple."

Perhaps this is why Matheson left music to prospect the world of words. And this is why it would be terribly misleading to characterize all his work or that of Schow, Skipp, and Spector as simply the embodiment of a rock/horror connection. Such extreme reductionism would have the effect of distorting their work to fit categories that might not lend themselves to a perfect fit. Still, after reading their works and talking to them, it seems clear they wouldn't be writing the way they do if they hadn't grown up in an age of rock music and inundated themselves in its aural frequencies. It's become a cliché to say that writers write from their own experience, but these writers have experienced rock 'n' roll.

Embers

BRIAN HODGE

BRIAN HODGE is the author of five novels, including Nightlife *and* Deathgrip. *He's currently at work on* Prototype, *a "grimly existential look at psychosociochromosonal mutation." Approximately forty of Hodge's short stories have appeared in such anthologies as* Book of the Dead, Shock Rock, *and* Under the Fang. *His favorite stupid trick "involves the maiden from the Land O' Lakes butter box. I'm also an avowed gothic and industrial music enthusiast who's yet to beat an addiction to Ben & Jerry's Chocolate Fudge Brownie ice cream."*

The first thing you should know about "Embers" is that this melancholic novella radically departs from the female slant skewing its way through this book; chalk it up to a guy thing. Secondly, this sympathetic yet unflinching observation on youthful street life is characterized by "compassionate excess," and is supported by a sturdy subtextual foundation. "As in my allergic reaction to the Reagan/Bush years," sayeth Hodge. "Although I don't necessarily believe that a change in administration alters the fact that there are a lot of evil, greedy motherfuckers out there who see themselves as social engineers of some sort."

Fine. My sentiments exactly.

Problem is, Brian *doesn't think "Embers" is splatterpunk.*

A situation prompting this digression:

The first Splatterpunks *anthology included a clutch of authors whose introductions explicitly stated that they* weren't *splatterpunks. And after* Splat I's *debut, this seeming paradox was gleefully (and predictably) condemned by a few anal retentives more concerned with sharpening their personal axes than with any objective criticism of that book.*

So—let's set the record straight.

The real, the actual, the genuine reason why Splat I *contained stories by writers who insisted that they weren't splatterpunks was . . . professional courtesy.*

You see, prior to Splatterpunk I's *publication, a number of authors had been tagged with the "splatterpunk" label without being given a chance to respond to it. Therefore, simply to clear the air, I'd urged* Splat I *contributors to truthfully respond to the following:*

Are you now, or have you ever been, a splatterpunk?

Yea, said some.

No, muttered others.

Who gives a shit? answered the rest.

Having digested this information, the Splat I *reader was then supposed to move onto the primary, more important step of* processing the stories. *Raw, rude works that obviously trod on splatterpunk turf. Whether they realized it or not.*

Of course, I can already hear the nitpickers reply: "Arbitrary nonsense!" Well. Besides a hearty "Fuck you, too," try this response—

The best art is supposed to operate independently of whoever creates it.

And yes, maybe I should have pointed that out, somewhere in Splatterpunks I. *But it's still not the packaging that counts, folks.*

It's the gift.

Hope we're all clear on that now.

Anyway, this "splat by nonsplats" stuff never really came up this time around; most of the Splat II *contributors just didn't care.*

Except Brian Hodge. Whom I now quote again:

"Hodge is another of those ungrateful wretches who actively avoids the splatterpunk tag, considering it less a strata with membership requirements than a method occasionally employed. And anyway, aren't the emotional extremes the ones that matter most?"

Spoken like a true splatterpunk, Bri.

*T*he limo looked out of place, all polished Detroit gleam against stark brick, asphalt grime, stray trash. Newspaper wads blowing across the lot, the urban tumbleweed. Limo, *wrong* side of town.

No matter. Nobody messed with limos, at least nobody with self-preservation in mind. On the other side of the mirrored windows rode Power and Money, which by themselves inspired more resentment than respect. They rode, however, flanked by Muscle Executive protectors, the modern-day samurai. But *katana* blades had been exchanged for Uzis, Ingrams. It was the way of the world. Firepower won out over honor every time.

The limo circled once—can't be too careful—then cruised to a stop twenty feet away from the sagging loading dock, idled while Mykel and Russ watched. The message implicit: *You* will come to *me*.

"Hang back," Russ said. "My client, I do the talking."

Mykel shrugged, whatever, watching as Russ left the shadows of the overhang. He hopped down from the dock, wiry and straight, hands in pockets. His upper body did not move, tight inside and out, a compressed spring. Russ paced over to the limo beneath a sun nailed into the sky like a disc of brimstone.

One of the limo's back windows glided down to frame a man's head. Haddenton. A public commodity but Mykel had never heard his first name; newspapers were only something winos used for winter insulation. Maybe Russ knew, but he'd never mentioned it.

Haddenton. One of the ultrarich who gripped the city like feudal lords. Mykel didn't know which was more annoying: the man's relative youth or his steam-pressed good looks. Some guys would find either reason enough to gut him. Mykel couldn't do it, but Russ? Probably. But Russ wouldn't hack off the hand that proffered the golden eggs.

He'd shake it. And kiss it, if that was paid for too.

Mykel folded arms over chest, listening. There was no wind today, no relief. Sound carried.

"You're getting too careless, though. Sloppy," Haddenton was saying. "I've got people from the arson inspector's office in my pocket, but look: You can't leave a burned-out five-gallon gas can in the ruins and not expect *someone* to take notice. Use your brain next time, or I'll find someone else."

Russ nodded, leaning toward the limo, elbow cocked on the roof. "It's creativity you want, creativity you'll get. But . . . you know . . . you get what you pay for. I got worries, my man Mykel, he's got worries. Little extra cash, help free us up so we don't worry so much. *We* can think better for *you,* see what I'm saying?"

Haddenton smiled, lips only, no eye crinkles. "You get paid what you're worth. Let's see how you do tomorrow night. If you make me happy, maybe then we can elevate your fees a bit."

"Remember those words, then." Russ leaned in closer, flicked a finger into the interior at Haddenton's two bodyguards. "I got witnesses now, you know."

Haddenton laughed like royalty, turned to the nearer of the guards, from Mykel's angle nothing more than bulk in a suit. "A real pair of balls on this kid, huh?" Haddenton tossed out a fat envelope, which Russ deftly caught and jammed into a back pocket.

Russ pulled back, bounced his fist twice against the roof. "See ya," spinning for the loading dock while the limo's window slid shut and the machine rolled. Nothing more than a sonic wisp of engine when Russ hopped onto the deck and produced the envelope, sent it skittering away when empty.

Russ peeled through the cash, an even thousand at a 60/40 split. Mykel took his four hundred and didn't bitch. He'd asked only once for an equal cut, and Russ had laughed and asked what kind of blade and where he wanted the scar. Forty percent was fine. Russ could no doubt find accomplices willing to do it for twenty, even less. For fun. But thrill-mongers wouldn't be nearly so trustworthy.

"Where this time?" Mykel asked.

Russ was scrutinizing the slip of paper that had come with the cash, lips faltering soundlessly. He frowned, a familiar frustration boiling up in his eyes, fury contained and painful.

"It's not a number street. Fuck. Read it to me."

Okay, yeah, here was another reason Russ was so willing to cough up forty percent. Numbers he understood, monetary denominations, while much less adept at the written word. Mykel could read, but more important, never laughed, never gloated, never rubbed Russ's nose in it. Worth a lot, right there.

"West side, I think. Says 2215 Atchison. That's the west side, isn't it?"

Russ nodded, plucking the slip from Mykel's fingers. Out of

his skintight pants came a match, ignited by thumbnail, suave. He touched it to paper, which browned, curled, and he dropped it only when it started licking his fingers.

While blackened ash was caught and scattered by the day's first breeze.

They holed up the rest of the afternoon inside the ancient warehouse, years ago deserted, condemned, surrendered to vermin on six legs, four legs, two. Cockroaches, rats, street kids, all the same. It was no home, just a place to sleep, to nurse wounds, to escape the sun at its worst. Outside, the day broiled, but among the warehouse's dust and cobwebs and splintered crates, a musty cool could be found. You pack your bed of burlap and rags, and guard it rabidly.

Mykel and Russ shared strawberry wine, sickly sweet but it did the job. Shoplifters can't be choosers. For light, a few drippy candles sat jammed in the necks of earlier discards, a fire hazard, but that was life on the lost fringe. Shades of the love generation. Mykel remembered his parents, leftover hippie burnouts from a different geological age. A few snapshots of childhood were his only links to toddling days, dingy sad apartment made sadder by cheerless attempts at brightening it. Garish black light posters and hand-carved symbols: peace, yin and yang. His parents' friends made hazy by time, always there, communal property and communal lovers the rule rather than the exception. Resentments were bound to erupt sooner or later; human nature demanded them. Hands off, this is *mine*, I don't care what I said last year.

It made an impression.

Halfway through the second bottle, Mykel decided he'd better get the cash off his person. He wobbled to his feet, took a candle for light, then trod the creaking hallways. Soft echoing footfalls of his hightops, and always the lesser scuttling of more cunning creatures. Yellow eyes flashed in shadows, vanishing when he gave them a solid glance.

His stash was the ladies' room. Cash, gash, stash—mnemonics helped him remember even in the foggiest of stupors. Pebbled glass, fractured but intact because of inlaid wire mesh, allowed dusty yellow sunlight. Hotter in here; the sun took root, cooked into the walls.

He stood on the second toilet bowl, porcelain stained and clotted with evaporated filth, and reached overhead to wrest the tile from its frame. He retrieved a manila envelope filched from a drawer elsewhere in the building. He reserved twenty bucks for walking-around money, food money in case dumpster-diving turned up nothing edible, and stowed the rest.

A nine-thousand-dollar nest egg. There could be better days ahead, but everyone knew they cost; to the spender belong the spoils. Haddenton knew that; so did Mykel. He figured Russ did too, just that Russ did not care.

Mykel could no longer clearly recall a time when he didn't know Russ. The days were there, weren't even that distant. But yesterdays accumulated like so many expired coupons, essentially worthless; you could look at them but could do nothing with them.

Russ took curiously little pleasure in the accumulation of wealth, however meager. He had no plans for it; it just built up in whatever stashes he'd made. Russ had no dreams, nothing he hoped for, and Mykel figured it would be wrong to ask why not. The cash was the one goal in and of itself, as if Russ were continually reaffirming to himself that he could beat the system in his own way. Russ always worked nights, at one scheme or another. Sometimes wielding the torch on buildings Haddenton wanted razed for insurance profits. Sometimes selling streetside merchandise, hot watches or bootleg tapes or ghetto blasters for cheap. Sometimes Russ sold himself, hanging out on corners in the city's less savory districts, making the slim cocky stroll to cars which slowed, stopped to eyeball the goods. The sword swallowers, fudgepackers and bun boys, anal practitioners both insertive and receptive. The neon streets which never slept, a jolly Sodom whose morning survivors brought home wads of cash for having coaxed and dispensed wads of cum.

Russ wasn't even a fag, technically, that was the weird part. He just understood his market value in a free economy. It was how Russ had met Haddenton. Haddenton slumming on the wild side, bored with his wife maybe, out trolling for a fruit tart. He paid well, tipped better, recognized inner potential.

The cash secured atop the tiles, Mykel left the stall. Caught sight of himself in one of the mirrors, not *too* broken. The skinny frame, sallow face. Dirty smudges on his cheeks. He spit on his fingers and tried to groom. Hoped for rain. Could use a shower.

Back down the maze of corridors then, to rest up for tonight. Sundown was the universal signal, like a starter pistol. All the hustlers came pouring out of whatever holes and dank hovels had sheltered them during the day. Predators and prey and performers, all looking for quick scores, money that wouldn't get them killed.

Mykel flopped on his makeshift bed. Dust fogged, dry as bleached bones. "You awake?"

"Yeah." Russ's voice was thick but coherent.

Silence.

"Well? What do you want?" Sharper now.

"I was just wondering. How much money you got by now?"

"Why?" No longer sharp, just bored.

"I said I was just wondering."

Russ sighed, breath flickering one candle into a dance of shadows. "Maybe thirty thou. No big deal."

Thirty grand, Mykel mouthed to himself. Amazing. "What are you living like this for? Man, you could have your own place. Your own shower. Closets."

"I don't need 'em. And I can shower up at some of my tricks', when I want. I can always count on Haddenton for a shower."

"You got it made with him, huh?"

Russ shrugged. "I guess. Easy money. He likes my ass. He's a needledick, it doesn't hurt."

"He doesn't look like a fag."

Russ laughed, empty and mean. "What does that look like? Besides, he's not, really, not like some of the real queens you see. He just likes using people, anybody. Pretends he doesn't pay, makes him feel tough." Russ laughed again, then looked over. "Why, you interested? Want me to see if he's game for a threesome?"

"No." Very sharp. That scene wasn't Mykel's and Russ knew it. Just liked to tease him sometimes, get a rise.

"Try it. It gets easier after the first time. You wouldn't be so fucking poor compared to me."

Mykel snatched the wine and took a hit. "What's the money matter to you, anyhow? You never spend any, hardly. What do you want it for, if all it does is sit there?"

"I just do," Russ grumped. "I like to look at it. It's mine, I earned it. It's there, it's ... real." Russ raised onto one elbow. "What, you think you're better than me, just 'cause you think you got some big plans? Just 'cause you think you'll rack up enough money, and then you'll take your sow and—"

"Don't call her that!" Mykel yelled.

"Well, fuck, what is she, seven months along now?"

Mykel nodded, flexing a fist he wouldn't use. "Don't call her that, just *don't.*"

Russ's eyes, flashing, knowing he could drill that nerve whenever he pleased. "Okay, the *princess*, then, you're gonna take the princess and get away from all this, right? Where? Huh? *Where?* And what then?"

"I don't know." Mumbling, shutting his eyes.

"C'mon," Russ needled. "Where's the plan go from there?"

Asshole; Mykel hated him when he got this way. You could never be sure if it was the wine talking or just plain Russ, peacekeeping torpor peeled away to uncover the prickly soul beneath. The part that knew he was sinking into a quagmire and wanted to take someone else along, or torture them in the trying.

"I don't know," Mykel whispered. Damn him anyway.

Russ turned onto his back again, tugged some comfort into that tight crotch. "Go ahead. Dream your fucking dreams if that's what gets you by. Just don't let me see you cry when you realize that's all they are, and all they ever will be."

Let him have the last word for now, Mykel decided. Let him remember them. He'd eat them soon enough. Promise.

The next day, Mykel caught a crosstown bus, hopped off twenty-some blocks to the south. The rest of the way he walked.

The old brownstone down on Wright Street looked as comforting as a grandmother's quilt. St. Gerard's Home for Unwed Mothers. In this day and age it sounded like some archaic joke, but the place was literally a lifesaver. Gave her a place to stay, to be safe, to stay healthy.

Three stories of grimy brownstone and peeling windowsills. The windows wore iron bars, extra protection, for there were those who were not above preying on these women whose fertile bodies had slowed them, left them more concerned about their bellies than fight-or-flight. Mykel was glad she was here.

His name was on the guest list, as he regarded it, and he got buzzed in through the heavy outer door. The lobby was like that of a cheap hotel, with mismatched furniture, but it smelled better. Smelled clean. Girls and young women in various stages of pregnancy sat around, most watching a TV whose color was tinted a queasy green. Some afternoon soap opera; escape, plus commercials.

Mykel faced the nun at the lobby desk, would get no farther. She would see to that, Sister Constanza Immaculata. Her habit framed a little face, brown and wrinkled as a walnut, and her hands were veined and strong-looking.

Mykel smiled at her. "Could I see Angie? Angie Melendez?"

She buzzed up to the third-floor duty sister, told her Angelina had a visitor.

"Will you be taking Angelina out this afternoon?" she then asked. Eyeing him through no-nonsense glasses, unblinking.

"I thought we might go out awhile."

Sister Constanza nodded. "You have her back in two hours, and don't you be late, or you'll have *me* to answer to."

Feisty old gal. Mykel smiled, had always liked her a lot. She put up with no bullshit, but he could never imagine her in some parochial school, whacking knuckles with a ruler.

"And no funny business," the nun went on. "And if you bring her back with the smell of liquor on her breath, you're off the visitor list until the birth."

"Yes, ma'am. Can we bring you something back? Rum ice cream?"

Her mouth pinched tight in the corners, a stern mask fighting a little grin. She swatted playfully at his arm, then wagged a stiff warning finger.

Angie was down a minute later, delivered by a clanking elevator. All big dark eyes and big belly, and that careful stately walk of a young woman great with her first child. Unplanned or not, there had never been any doubts as to going ahead with it. The nuns had welcomed her with open, reasonably nonjudgmental arms. Angie was seventeen, a year younger than Mykel, and they saw too many her age taking the quick way out, stirrups and suction. Mykel had no love for the Church, but no real hate either, and you had to give the local Order of St. Gerard its due. The sisters at least put their effort where their dogma was.

Mykel hugged her as gently as if embracing a large egg. Her thick dark hair smelled of baby shampoo. They kissed, linked hands.

"I miss you," Angie said, and he nodded.

"Two hours, you," Sister Constanza called to his back, and he turned to smile, nod. "Or it's this." She smacked a balled fist into her palm.

And winked.

They sought no afternoon matinees, no dinners for two, no walks in the park. These were jokes, for people with normal lives and idle time. Solitude was all they craved. The sisters surely knew what went on during these dates, with the mothers-to-be whose partners hadn't vanished.

The hotel was close, only three blocks, convenient. Hourly rates, very considerate.

They undressed hurriedly, then drew together, Mykel taking care to fit himself around her swollen form. Stroking the rounded mound, kissing it, nuzzling his cheek against it while she reached down to run fingers through his lank hair.

The lovemaking was always slow, as if delicate china lay beneath them. Angie balanced on knees and hands while Mykel entered from behind, her distended belly hanging heavily. He would clutch her hips, this teenage Madonna who had given him renewed purpose for caring whether he lived or died, and reason to look to the future with tenuous optimism. He let her control the pace of exquisite thrust and parry, taking no chance of hurting her. Until they both were sweat-slick and trembling with the exertion of holding back, holding back. Slow, tenderly torrid, until Angie bit the pillow and cried out, and reached back along her belly to cup his sac. *Squeeze.* He shuddered, and released in a lavish flood, and they sank to the bed in a moist tangle.

Mykel brushed wet locks of hair from her eyes as she lay on her back beside him. "Don't ever think you have to do this just for me, if you don't want to. You know that, don't you?"

She held his hand and smiled. She had a cute tiny double chin now. "I know. I won't if it's too uncomfortable."

"Umm . . . how long you think you *can*, though?" It was a weasely question but he was dying to know.

"I don't know, it just depends. This one girl there I told you about, Lavonda? She told me she did it the night before she went into labor, last time she was pregnant. But this is her third time, she knows what she's doing."

Mykel tried to imagine making it with Angie two months along. No—*no*. There was always the fear that the act would pull the trigger of delivery. That his kid would come out with some unexplainable, deep-seated hatred of him; repercussions of an amniotic turf war.

He promised this: a better childhood than he remembered. Wouldn't *ever* let the kid have occasion to see him sharing its mother with friends. Taboo.

So they lay, they talked, they stared at the ceiling. A brown water stain marked it near the window, shapeless, its layers an arcane map of the topography of some new land. Way far away from *here*. Mykel found himself drowsily imagining its hills, trees, grass. Its air. He wanted to breathe country air, had sucked in so much city exhaust his lungs probably rated eighty-seven octane.

They would go, the three of them, someday. When the money was enough to get the task done properly.

"We got another job tonight," Mykel said.

Angie stiffened. "You and . . . Russ?" The name tasted bad.

"Uh-huh."

"I hate him. I really hate him. He's an awful human being."

Mykel shrugged, disagreeing without wishing to make an issue of it. "He's just sad, more than anything. He doesn't believe in anything. That's all. He always pays me."

Angie squirmed in hot discomfort. No A/C in this place; you were lucky if you had clean sheets. He rose to soak his T-shirt in the sink and drape it over her torso. It didn't soothe the look in her eyes, though.

"Don't get caught, ever," she said. "That guy, the one that hires you?"

"Haddenton?"

"Yeah, him. He wouldn't do a thing for you if you got caught. You know he wouldn't. He'd probably press charges, just so he wouldn't look guilty too."

Mykel shook his head. "Nah, nah, never happen. The buildings we burn out for him? It never looks like he owns them. That's why nobody gets suspicious about him. Russ says he uses things called dummy business fronts and holding companies. I don't understand how it all works, but I guess it does. He never looks worried."

Angie took the sodden T-shirt, held it over her face and wrung it, let the excess drizzle onto her cheeks. Replaced it.

"How much longer? When can we leave?"

"What do the nuns say? How long'll it take you to rest up and heal after the baby?"

"A week, maybe two. That's if I don't have problems, or need many stitches."

Mykel nodded. "Maybe then. We'll see what the money's like."

Angie beamed, eyes sliding shut in weary silent thanks. "But where? Really, where to?"

"Montana."

"Montana?" Giggled disbelief. "Why *there?"*

"I saw this cigarette ad on the subway. I swear it was Montana. It looked so . . . open. Montana. I just like the sound of it."

"Mon-tan-a," she said slowly, trying it like a new last name.

Forty minutes later . . .

"We have to be going soon. If I'm late I could lose TV privileges."

Angie pouted a moment. "There's not much else there."

"How's your back feel now?"

"A little achy, it's okay." Coy, now, shy beneath tousled bangs, beginning to dry. "Do you, do you want me to do you with my mouth?"

He glanced at her, sideways. "No, no, I wasn't thinking that. Just hold each other."

And so they did, his watch on a bedside stand slicing off the minutes one by one, the ticking of an unfriendly clock.

"Montana," she said again, this time more palatably. "It'll do."

Nighttime, later than late, when all folks decent and smart were behind locked doors.

Mykel and Russ vaulted the subway turnstiles and boarded before some gargantuan sexless drone in the token booth could sic a guard after them. The train whipped through the tunnels like an eel, clattering, and spit them out on the west side. They mounted the steps up from the graffiti-coated platform, to street level. The air still wasn't fresh, just a different kind of toxic.

"C'mon, what's in the bag?" Mykel asking again, not the first time.

Russ sighed, appearing to finally tire of secrecy. Hefting the small cloth bag and shaking it. Soft metal clunks, muffled.

"Sterno cans." Russ grinned, red neon from some pesthole bar pulsing across his face, his blond butch brushcut. "Can you believe winos drink this shit when they're really on the skids? Is that pathetic or what?"

It was starting to make sense now. Haddenton had said not to make things so obvious. Russ had gotten to thinking earlier about their target. Real skid row district, human wreckage shambling about, last place to go before they died. One foot in the gutter, the other the grave.

This is where he'll end up someday. Mykel's latest revelation on the subject of Russ. *Just burn himself out and not care at all.*

Onward, until they found it, 2215 Atchison. Once, perhaps decades ago, it had been a short office building. Now it was as distressed as the local populace. Wino central; plenty of rooms, no waiting, hot and cold running piss. The place stank of defeat.

"Work time," Russ said.

They crunched around back, alongside the building, close in. No grass grew here, no concrete stayed intact. Everything broken, crumbling, malignant. Russ found a back door hanging cockeyed from a shattered hinge, took it as an invitation.

Russ flashed a penlight around the room, perhaps an ancient shipping and receiving zone. Dry boxes jumbled high, wispy with cobwebs and gelled dust. Around and around, the small circle of light, Russ . . . seeking, seeking.

They heard a soft grumble and Russ quickly found its source. A heavy shuffling as the wino sought deeper shelter.

Russ nodded toward the door. "Keep watch, just in case."

"Russ?" Nervous fingers twittered in Mykel's stomach. "We gotta get him out of here first. We gotta check this place out."

Russ nodded again, impatient, waved him to the door. "Don't worry, don't worry."

"Whozzat?" coughed a voice from the floor. Thick and horrid, wet and fuzzy. *"Whozzat?"*

"Santa Claus." Russ smiling, stepping closer.

Mykel twitched a nervous leg, trying to watch two directions at once. Not liking this at all, watching as Russ approached the wino, a shadowed jumble of rage huddling on the floor, pitifully defiant, protecting his final domain. And then Russ pulled out the first can of Sterno, uncapping it, holding it out like a peace offering, saying, "Drink up, it's free."

Mykel watched a ghastly hand reach into the circle of light, an unsteady hand, dry and scaled and scabbed. It pulled back from sight, greedy. Then a wet slurp as the Sterno went down hard and fast and unheeding. Thick gulping, then the chime of an empty can striking the floor.

"Mmmmmmm, good, isn't it?" Russ asked, and received a soggy snorting laugh in reply. He fed the wino a second can, producing still more as the man drank. Russ opened the cans and stuffed them uncapped into the wino's pockets, layers of crusted clothing, Russ talking all the while:

"Mom used to make me go to Sunday School. How 'bout yours? No, don't answer that, drink up. Happy hour, you see what I'm saying? They told all us kids those Bible stories, you know? Jonah and the whale. Noah and the ark. Three little pigs. But Samson, he was the coolest."

"Russ, man, what are you doing to that guy?" Mykel asked.

"Nothing! Now shut up and watch that alley!" Back to his drinking buddy. "Samson, yeah. Killed like a thousand motherfuckers with a donkey's jawbone, right? But there was this other time, he gets pissed at these guys and wants to burn out their crops, see? But it's a big job for one guy so he gets help. My man Samson, he catches some foxes, and he gets some torches, and he ties 'em to the foxes' tails, and turns 'em loose. And they run tearing through the fields and set 'em right the fuck on fire. Pretty smart, huh?"

Mykel sagged against the doorway. You couldn't stop Russ, not when he got like this.

Russ uncapped the final Sterno can to sprinkle it over the wino in reverent libation, then gave him the remainder. "Chug-a-lug. Christmas comes just once a year."

"Aw, no, Russ, don't, *don't*—"

Russ wasn't listening, instead grabbing a husk of yellowed newspaper and twisting it into a torch. Flicking a match with his thumbnail and setting the paper ablaze. The room danced with yellow light, orange light.

The wino belched, groaning, and Russ thrust the torch into his sloppy wet face. Sunburst. The rush of flames was hot and hungry, while Russ stepped back to admire: "And just think, I told Mom Sunday School never taught me shit."

The flaming wino had surged bellowing to his feet, batting wildly at the air with windmill arms. Clumsy twisting steps, blundering into stacks of boxes while the Sterno cans in his pockets erupted like small time bombs. He shrieked, wasted lungs giving their all for one last roar of rage at the world.

Russ backed away, and now the room was bright indeed, and still the wino would not go down. He was, incredibly, gaining a full head of steam as he lumbered ablaze into another room, where other cronies apparently slept, unseen, rudely awakened. The cries and flares in the dark could only mean chain reaction.

Mykel clung to the doorway, trying to hold down the bottle of wine drunk earlier, knees gone rubbery. *No more*, he thought. *No more of this. I don't care what he pays me. I don't want any more of this at all.*

Russ collected him at the doorway. Behind them the rooms blazed brighter. Success. Russ slapped him on the shoulder to get him moving. Mykel stumbled alongside, trying to keep up, maintain that oft-practiced nonchalant fadeaway into the night.

Russ spat into the alley and grimaced.

"Fucking winos," he said. "I don't know when they stink worse."

Mykel didn't go home that night, such as home was; *couldn't* go. Russ was hot, Russ was horny, figured that the passion might be worth extra earnings, so they parted company. Still, it didn't matter. The warehouse was where Russ lived, if he could be considered to live anywhere, and so it was tainted, its atmosphere toxic. Flopped there on his burlap and rag mattress, Mykel would risk the poisons seeping into him as he slept, to later awake as hollow inside as Russ.

He opted for rail-riding the night away, paying his token without complaint, finding a seat in the back of one car to call his own for a few hours. One hand in his pocket on his blade for security.

Nodding off into nightmares with his head wedged against the window, the soot-grimed train whipping along its endless circuit, wearing deeper into the rut that was its lot in life.

The clatter, the rocking motion, the ebb and flow of starts and stops: these were his night's companions. Soothing in their own way, rock-a-bye baby, in the subway. Until the inevitable crush of morning commuters. They invaded, these business travelers afraid of the night people, driving them out nonetheless, victory won not through courage but by sheer numbers.

Mykel trudged off the train, up the platform, into the new day and humidity thick as boiled wool. He squinted into the sun.

And how it burned.

"Well, well. Look who didn't come home last night." Russ's way of greeting Mykel when he finally did make it back that afternoon.

Mykel grunted, then, "And *you* did, I guess?"

"Least I was working."

Working. Mykel said nothing. Sometimes he wondered if Russ wouldn't do it anyway, prowl the streets, his pants slim in the leg and tight in the crotch. Those random collisions of body parts and bodily fluids, like Russian roulette with diseases that may or may not have cures. Russ, tempting fate, maybe a part of him hoping for death, its sordid drama irresistible, saving him from the despair of watching his own body wither, a wretchedly useless castoff by age twenty-five.

"I saw Haddenton today." Russ was sprawled back on his bed, wearing only loose shorts. Must have been a heavy night. He only wore those when he was sore. And stolen wine helped his mouth flush the salt taste of too many encounters, too few names.

"So?" Mykel didn't even like hearing the name now. Once, its only implication had been money. Now it meant worse, some angel of death. Wall Street meets Heinrich Himmler.

"He was impressed with last night. Said he heard it looked great, you know? Winos and rotgut, smoking in bed or whatever." Russ laughed and swilled more wine. "He's got another one for us tonight. I figure you'll want in on this one for sure—"

"No!" Mykel cried, suddenly galvanized, the rejection nearly biological. "Not anymore, no. Not if it's gonna be like that was last night. Didn't that bother you at *all?*"

Russ hunched his shoulders, slack and bored. "Winos. Dirty stinking fucking winos. That building was insured, you get what I'm saying? Where's the profit in winos?"

"That's *all* it's about to you, profit?"

Russ gazed flatly at him, eyes heavy-lidded. "It's not about anything. I don't know what it's about. What's the use figuring what anything's about?" When Mykel didn't answer, Russ twisted one corner of his mouth, sour, knowing what was coming. "You're out of this, aren't you?"

Nodding. "Buildings are one thing. People, that's another."

Russ sneered, bowed an imaginary violin. "They're all the same. They all burn." The violin was forgotten. "So go, then. You're getting the fuck out of here right now."

"That's how I want it." Mykel started back into the corridors toward office space, the ladies' room. Stopped again. "You already knew it'd go down this way before I ever got here, didn't you?"

"Yeah."

Mykel pointed down the musty corridor. "My money better be there. I figure you knew where it was all along."

"Yeah, I knew." Russ glanced at the floor a moment, shook his head, mouth still soured. "I didn't steal your money, Mykel. It's yours, you earned it. If I took it, it wouldn't feel like *mine.*"

Two minutes later, Mykel counted it twice, just to make sure it was close to a tally he remembered. It was. Russ. Odd sense of priorities; you could just never tell with him.

Russ said nothing, half-watching Mykel gather the rest of his belongings, a meager collection by any standard. Good-byes were useless, a silly pretense to civility in some other world. Mykel merely nodded as he left.

And saw a single flash of panic burn through Russ's eyes, one simple glimpse of genuine humanity. There, then gone, as Russ twitched an indifferent shoulder, closest thing to a wave he had.

Mykel thought he understood what it had meant: *But who'll read to me now?* Mykel felt privileged, one rare peek at a part of Russ that must have cared about something, that still feared.

Before it was snuffed out.

*   *   *

It was a new problem, heretofore unknown: too much on hand to feel safe toting it around. Seemed as if he'd had the warehouse as a drop zone for years, longer than it truly was, probably.

But rail-riding no longer seemed a sensible way to pass his night, not with nine thousand on him. To get hassled on the subway was rare. Some predator takes one look at him, his clothes, the whole sorry package, and figures there's nothing worth taking. But there was always the chance. You could, at any moment, cross paths with the one crazy with your face on his mind, who saw the world with different eyes, and you did not fit his agenda. You were simply there, occupying space, and that was trigger enough.

The nest egg needed a new nest. Banks were out of the question. They'd take one look at him and summon the guards.

Mykel rode well into the night, then realized he had been overlooking one fundamental refuge, the only person in the world he trusted. Too late to expect the nuns to roust her now, but tomorrow he could give it to Angie, let her stash it beneath her mattress. She had just as much stake in it as he.

Tonight he would splurge. The hotel three blocks from St. Gerard's would be safer than any street cubbyhole or public transit. He'd get the money to Angie first thing in the morning.

He rode the B train until he could transfer and get close enough to St. Gerard's neighborhood to surface. A crescent moon tonight, murky through a muddy haze of airborne venoms. It made for some oddly lovely sunsets, though. Even poison had its beauty.

Wright Street; his footsteps always felt comforting here, all his hopes embodied along this stretch of concrete, the fleeting togetherness this path allowed. It brought him his happiest days.

Until . . .

Tonight.

It was a glow in the sky from blocks away, smudged orange, brighter the nearer he got. Too close to St. Gerard's for him to dismiss outright, and as he broke into a panicked sprint, he prayed, *No, God, no, please no nonono. I'm sorry we did the wino—*

He was screaming openly by the time he got there and saw the blaze. A conflagration, total loss. The rest of the neighborhood had turned out of row houses and other brownstones to watch, to wail, to wring knuckles. A few lone heroes who'd braved the flames now had scorched hands to show for it, or were doubled retching on the sidewalk.

No fire trucks in sight. Sirens sounded in the distance, but there were always sirens; like winds, they promised nothing. Mykel collapsed to his knees, watching raging flames consume the place bottom to top, all three floors, and so few residents appeared to have gotten out. Lax building codes, whatever the cause. All those antiprowler bars over the windows, solid as a prison.

He dared look at the third floor, soul cleaving in two, only to halve again and so on, and he focused on Angie's window. Hell, with bars. Someone up there, trapped, shrieking, just as there were in a few other windows. He was blind to all but one. Angie had a roommate. Which of the two this was he would never know.

He could only imagine her looking down at him, small soft hands cooking against hot iron as she wrenched at the bars, maybe seeing him kneel, slipping toward breakdown . . .

With that tiny, tiny life within her belly . . .

Roasting.

Subway, last refuge of the damned, to whom remaining stationary was tantamount to mad surrender. He must keep moving, if only in circles, with legs weak-willed and rubbery. Around and around the city, stop after stop, wretched refuse of the night piling on, off, avoiding this hollow-eyed boy in the back. Haunted eyes, crazy eyes. Hair triggers on these freaks, best avoided.

Russ, earlier: *He's got another one for us.*

If he had entertained that conversation for two more minutes, what would he have learned? Would Russ have warned him, get her out? Give them all a few minutes for evacuation?

To damn Russ to hell was a joke. There was nothing left inside to make the trip worthwhile.

Mykel looked past his own little circle of misery into eyes which averted once contact was made. Two ships that rebound in the night. His gaze settled on a cigarette ad high on the wall.

Montana. Wide open and free. Clean. Montana.

He drew his blade and raged, and left it in hanging tatters.

*   *   *

The next day he lay low for Russ, creeping back to the warehouse before dawn while his erstwhile roommate hawked himself on street corners. Concealment in the warehouse was easy; Mykel chose a crevice between two sagging crates a few yards from the small clearing in which they had built their nests of burlap and rags, belongings and bottles.

The footsteps that finally came were heavy, slow, weighted by a night's residue of nickel-and-diming himself to all comers. When Mykel saw him shuffle into range, he sprang.

Locked to one another, they rolled across the floor. They tussled, the dust of decades boiling around them. A tightness in Mykel's throat, his chest, burst into a wild sob. It had all focused to this, mad swinging rage, so uncontrollable it left him shaking and jittery. Shrieking accusations, lamentations.

He tagged Russ twice, a third time, glancing blows that had at least some measure of impact. The rest were wild, ill-timed—the tables were easily turned and Russ's fist opened his nose into a fountain.

Trembling, Mykel drew his hands up and Russ pounded into them, past them. Straddled him, sitting on his chest, a bony knee pressed to each shoulder, pinning him as his struggles feebled.

Russ, above him, gulping stale air, blurry through tears and blood. Mykel twitched, and Russ punched him again; he felt a tooth unhinge, tasted the bitter tang.

"You . . . you . . ." It was all Mykel could get out. "Fuck . . ."

"I should kill you," Russ wheezed. "But I won't."

". . . kill *you* . . ." Mykel choked out.

Russ whacked him again. "I won't . . . 'cause nobody oughta die as stupid as you are."

". . . fucking *kill you* . . ."

Russ wearily shook his head. "You? *You?* Nah, not you. Somebody will, probably, someday. But not you. Gotta be somebody worth doing it, you hear what I'm saying? Never you."

Mykel bit his lip, then probed the loosened tooth with his tongue. Russ was right in that awful way he sometimes was, right without thinking; instinct maybe. He probably didn't really want to kill Russ anyway, not deep within. The blade was still in his pocket.

Had he meant business he could have waited for Russ to sleep, sliced his throat in one deft stroke. No. He'd just wanted to pound on him, make him hurt, make him *feel*, but even this was flawed thinking. Hitting Russ was like pounding on a razor strap.

"Don't cry, stop that fucking crying," Russ said in disgust. "Told you before, I didn't want to see you crying when you got it through your stupid head that dreams are just shit."

"I *loved* her!"

"I did you a *favor*, you dumb shit! Did everybody a favor. You're free again. She won't have to worry about the little piglet anymore." Russ bore down harder to quell the struggles.

Mykel snuffled, twisted his head to wipe on his shoulder. "Haddenton . . . I didn't even know he . . . he owned the house."

"He doesn't!" Russ finally relaxed enough to ease up on the pressure. Looking down, mildly battered but not enough, his expression bordering on tender. "Open your eyes, Mykel. You're so fucking dumb. There's no more profit in unwed mamas than in winos. But you think it ends there? Think again, hear? Wise up. There's a whole different order going on. Even I didn't know about it until after I did the winos. But then Haddenton saw I had it in me, to do the kind of work *needs* doing. Haddenton and his people, mostly business guys, government guys. All so sick of shelling out their money to help leeches. All the welfare bums, all the sows that get knocked up again two months after they drop the kid. It doesn't get any better, it never gets better. You try helping leeches like that, get 'em back on their feet again—shit, most of 'em don't care if they stand up or not."

Mykel was shaking his head, no, no, unable to argue, only thinking that Angie, at least, hadn't been like that. She wanted to be useful, to be no burden, wanted *someone* to need her.

Russ knew he had no fight left and slid off to the side. "I'm at a whole new level, my man. I am *in*. Haddenton explained it out, told me about places down in Central America, South America, these governments that ran death squads. They had their reasons, political shit I don't care about. But no reason why the same thing can't work here, only for money. It's always money here."

Mykel crawled away, clutching aching ribs, ready to gag into the floor if needed. While Russ held up a wad of money, fatter than anything Haddenton had ever forked over before.

"All mine, this. And plenty more to come, too. Guess I can kiss this shithole good-bye. You can have it if you want."

You could've done that before, Mykel thought, an anemic flicker. *You already had the money.* It had to go deeper than that, some-thing different in Russ this time. Finding, perhaps, something to believe in after all. A cause that blended cash and thrills, belonging and self-interest.

Let Russ live. Hopefully for a long long time.

For as he limped away, Mykel wondered if it wasn't true after all, there *were* worse things than death. Like finally becoming what you always hated, the only reason you despised it in the first place because you were forced to look at it from outside.

Everything was a matter of perspective.

Amazing what money could do, a few thousand, when long-term pictures were no longer looked at. Just short-term improvements.

If Russ could upgrade, so could Mykel.

Once he had healed from Russ's beating, he continued to remake the outer man. Soap and shampoo and deodorant, daily applications. Fashionable haircut. New clothes, sharp and trim and well fitted to his frame. A downtown hotel room, safe insular existence while he turned his attention to the daily newspapers; and to the local city magazine, all bright pictures between glossy covers, the publication choosing to portray less than half the full story.

The dailies, though: Once you knew the pattern it was frightfully simple to recognize:

A mysterious gas explosion in a soup kitchen. A new predatory mutation christened the Skid Row Hacker. A flophouse collapsing on destitute inhabitants after an unexplained typo on a demolition order altered the address. A nursing home poisoning its residents with bacterial meat.

And always, always, the fires.

Death squads. It made sense, a logical extrapolation of the atti-tude. that advocated trickle-down economics. And while the press may or may not have been free, thank God for it, regardless. One must know his enemy.

Mykel finally learned Haddenton's first name: Andrew. There was much else to be learned for the student of media, though Mykel was sure they barely scratched the surface, these flattering articles, puff pieces, profiles that always caught the man's best angles. His favorite wine? Rosé. The world trembled at such a revelation. Fluff, but sometimes it's all you need to know.

Hot summer night, a Friday, August, people dropping of heat strokes across town. And Mykel, sharp and spiffy, taking a cab to the financial district, tipping generously as the driver let him off at one of its grandest buildings, a financial flagship, forty-eight stories of curtainwall glass and anodized steel. When the sun caught it just right it could blind you, like Saul on the road to Damascus.

The caterers arrived at a utility entrance just after dusk, a small elite army to minister to the whims of those scheduled to arrive on floor forty-two. One of Andrew Haddenton's famed office penthouse parties. To be invited was a passport to near-royalty. To work it was simply knowing how and when to kowtow.

Amazing what money could do, beyond the material. Such an inherent power to persuade.

"Say *what?*" asked the kid who had arrived in one of the catering vans. A straggler with an armload of sealed containers.

"You heard me right," Mykel said. "Two grand to trade clothes with me, and you take the night off. Go see a movie or something."

Narrowing eyes, too good to be true. "Let's see the bucks."

Mykel showed him, and it was a done deal. The switch was made hurriedly in the back of one of the vans, Mykel fretting with a loose waist of the formal black slacks until the kid showed him how to adjust the sides and take them in a bit.

"Hey, you even brought your own wine," the kid noticed. "Rosé's his favorite, I hear."

And off they went, the switch made, prince and pauper each going his separate way. One deeper into the city . . .

The other above it.

He caught a few peculiar glances from some of the other white-shirt-black-tie caterers, in the freight elevator and the sprawl of suites on the forty-second floor. But there were over thirty of them, all told, to insure everyone stayed fed and watered and fat and happy. None of the staff could have known *everyone* on this detail. Though a stranger, he looked the part; he *must* belong.

As the night wore on, Mykel had ample opportunity to study

the elite in their element, the wealthy and the beautiful. Movers and shakers, power brokers all. The glitterati, poised with champagne flutes and wine glasses and canapés, backdropped by plateglass windows. A skyline of lights, showing only the bright and gleaming—leaving the filth in shadows, as they preferred.

Fed and watered. Fat and happy. They fiddled loudest while, below, Rome burned.

Among them, Mykel was invisible, a utensil. He had expected nothing more, and so was content to serve, to bide his time, until the hour came for all good partygoers to go home, for the caterers to return to oblivion. At which time Mykel truly became invisible. Nobody ever checked the closets, not with this crowd on hand.

Much later he emerged to dimmed lights, to that solitary aftermath of any successful party. Strange silence, the echoes of conversations profound and banal, and everywhere the dregs of a fine time. He hoped the maids wouldn't be in until tomorrow.

Mykel paced the suites and offices with his bottle and a pair of elegantly simple cut-glass goblets. He found his quarry in a boardroom, alone, a conqueror overseeing his kingdom. Standing at the window bank, tux jacket shed, tie loose, shirtsleeves rolled. A silver ice bucket sat on a meeting table, its half-empty bottle listing at a jaunty angle.

Mykel cleared his throat.

Haddenton turned, saw him. Wobbled fractionally, as if uncertain whether or not to lurch for a phone, call security, the high-tech samurai. He did neither, finally, simply watching as Mykel set down the rosé bottle, the pair of stemmed glasses.

"Your wife go home already?" Mykel asked. He knew what voice to use, the inflections, had heard Russ use it all a few times when zeroing in for a libidinal kill.

Haddenton, bleary with late hours and champagne: "Who the hell are you?"

Mykel spread empty palms, malice toward none. "An admirer."

Haddenton plucked the champagne from the bucket with a wet slosh, tipped it to his lips, then pointed at him with the neck. "Oh. Right. You were serving earlier."

Not missing a trick. How long had it taken him to simply notice the clothes.

"They're all gone, your people. An hour ago. Did you get lost up here? Fall asleep somewhere?" His speech slurred minimally; he maintained well enough. A picture of dignity with only faint corrosion.

"I stayed behind for one reason," said Mykel, a step forward, hand reaching to undo his top shirt button, one, two, the seduction feeling bizarre, alien, somebody else's body he was commanding. Perhaps it was—he had never looked like this before, wasn't even sure he liked it.

He knew only that he was still the same inside, secretly.

"Now . . . your wife?" he tried again.

Haddenton gazed mournfully out the window, lifted a hand to gesture, some half-wave, finally a weak flip of dismissal. The spouse, public duty exercised, now over the hills and far away. Some unfamiliar bed, perhaps; Mykel needed to know no more.

He uncorked the rosé bottle, poured each glass three-quarters full. He lifted one, and this was where the final focus came to. The fumes alone nearly made him ill. Steel resolve. He gulped, and the pale, faintly pinkish-tainted liquid was in his mouth, down his throat, his head swimming already. The second gulp went down easier.

"I'll probably lose my job for not leaving with the rest of them tonight, you know." Mykel, maintaining the charade.

Haddenton smiled, for the first time, and shrugged. "For some people, losing a dead-end job can be the best thing in their lives. But they have to be smart enough to recognize it was an opportunity. Not a loss."

Another horrid swallow. His stomach was beginning to boil.

"And how about you?" Haddenton's challenge. "Just how smart are you?"

"Smart enough to know that if, say, I do certain things for you, you could do certain things for me."

Haddenton's smile was ancient, practiced, as old as the first deception. How many had he chewed up, spat out, under the guise of mentorship? "You've already learned the first lesson."

Mykel smiled, terribly difficult now, and showed him the bottle's label, tapped it. "This was the first lesson."

Haddenton's smile, now smug, confident. "Good lad."

Mykel was hard at work on his second glassful. Watching the man approach, remembering him from weeks back, framed in the limo window. The man would never recognize him now; Mykel was wearing a different face, different clothes, different body.

A different soul, too, come to think of it. It had still lived and thrived that day. There had been reason, hope, something to care for. All gone now, ashen, gone in heat and sorrow. At Haddenton's mandate. All that remained was fit only for martyrdom, it seemed. A final bid for sainthood, a pathetic savior keeping company with Jude, patron saint of the hopeless. There was worse company.

In fact, it stood before him.

Mykel smiled, pushed the second glass along the table into Haddenton's reach. Tipping his own for one last terrible swallow, nausea's trigger, then keeping a final mouthful in reserve.

Haddenton reached, eyes on Mykel's, a new hunger building . . .

He lifted, drank even before his nose detected something wrong, and then he flung the glass in shock, spraying the remainder of his first sip, eyes so wide—

"That's gasoline!" he cried.

Mykel pitched his goblet aside, lunging, hand rising from his pocket. The lighter swung up even as he pressed his face to Haddenton's, the man's mouth open and spluttering.

He thumbed the lighter to life, between them, seeking the mouth for a first and final savage kiss.

Eruption.

Flaming faces held one to another, Mykel spewed his last mouthful into Haddenton, following with the greater gush of his explosively risen gorge. Like Ahab to the white whale, bound to it even unto death and beyond: *I spit my last breath at thee.*

Mykel latched on, all rushing flames from gut to gullet to mouth, the stench of burned hair, the agony of scorched lungs, and the shared peeling hide with this man who had been dealt too many cards, and played them all badly.

Fused at the mouth, skin steaming and crisped together, they tumbled to the floor. Fortunate, in one sense: Most people burned out long before they actually died.

They were discovered near dawn, maids arriving to wade through the rubble of the party and consign it to waste. A dead boss, a dead stranger; there was no mourning. Tears were best spent closer to home. They simply phoned it in, let the police take over—*they* were not involved. Let Haddenton's bought-and-paid-for blue machine grind him through processing, autopsy, burial.

And good riddance.

Dawn already looked a little brighter, over this city of hollow hearts, empty souls, pauper's graves.

And gutted buildings.

Headturner

KEVIN ANDREW MURPHY AND THOMAS S. ROCHE

Featured throughout Splatterpunks II *are strong, complex women. Tough-minded femmes tackling abusive fathers. Crazed serial killers. Religious fanaticism. Death.*

But hey—maybe we should lighten up a bit. Kick off our shoes. Settle back with some titillating entertainment.

Like this little number, starring melancholy transsexuals and Filipino folklore.

But first, a warning; I'm about to reveal an important plot point here. Or at least allude to it. So those who don't like such surprises should skip this introduction and get to the story. Right away. Come back when you're through.

All done? Good.

"Headturner" coauthor KEVIN ANDREW MURPHY contributed the loopy "I'm Having Elvis' Baby!" to my recent The King Is Dead *anthology; his novelette "Cursum Perficio" recently appeared in the George R. R. Martin–edited anthology* Wild Cards: Card Sharks. *THOMAS S. ROCHE is the author of "The Beast with the Blood Red Eyes" and "a number of porn bits which I don't really talk about."*

As for "Headturner"—and for those wondering how such collaborations are worked out—this story's sex scenes originated with Roche's pen, while the gore came from Murphy.

Its outlandish beastie, however, is the real thing. Or at least based on actual Filipino mythology.

Eliciting this parenthetical, autobiographical aside:

I was raised in the Philippines, and occasionally heard about the weird creature Murphy and Roche herein describe. Usually from a Filipino adult trying very hard to scare the coconuts off a kid.

I also heard of other, equally nasty critters. Like the demon known as a mananangal. *This nocturnal charmer likes to hide in bedroom roof rafters waiting for its intended victim to fall asleep. Then it sucks out your liver with its tongue.*
Cheerful, no?
Here's a second Philippines memoir.
The now-defunct American military bases on which I grew up were surrounded by Filipino towns like Olongapo and Cavite, crazy-quilt communities whose main industry was catering to the vices of drunken sailors. This meant numerous bars, whorehouses, nightclubs, and strip joints. Hardcore pleasure pits whose raw salaciousness made the donkey acts in Tijuana look like Best of Breed kennel shows.
So—you have now been primed for "Headturner."
And you're welcome.
Wasn't it Woody Allen who said sex is dirty only when it's done right?

*T*rona hated the bar, but it was somewhere she could go. They'd laughed at her everywhere else, so this was the only place left.

The Grey Mare was tacky and seedy, but she'd learned to cope. The others in the bar could tell that Trona was not a woman; in fact, she was exactly what she appeared to be: a very poorly constructed transvestite. But it was protective coloration—she wasn't the only one.

Trona looked at Valerie, across the bar. Valerie was one of those ridiculous drag queens who resembled a woman not so much as she resembled a mannequin. Her hair was right, her dress was right, her makeup was perfect—but altogether, it gave the impression of being fake.

And Trona hated her for it. Because as fake as Valerie appeared, she was still more believable than Trona would ever be. Trona looked down at her hands: large, hairy, and ridiculous on the stem of the mimosa. She had tried shaving them; she had tried depilatories; she had tried plucking the thick red hairs off the backs one by one with tweezers. But the lotion had irritated her skin; the hair grew back. She didn't even know why she tried. Her face might have passed on a different body; but on her body, never. No one would ever believe her.

Trona watched with contempt as Valerie threw her arms around Mickey, the bartender. Mickey pushed Valerie away, looking uncomfortable. He was a college kid who didn't belong here any more than anyone else did; he was just trying to make some money. Nobody fit here, and they hated each other equally.

There was a sudden hush over the bar, and Trona followed the stares of all the other outcasts. There, at the entrance, kissing the doorman on the cheek, was a vision of androgyny—beauty, even—and Trona recognized her. It was Bobbi Rodriguez, the most beautiful Filipino drag queen who ever existed. She was a San Francisco legend, the female impersonator who had actually done what Trona and the others didn't have the guts or the money to do. Bobbi had become a woman.

And what a woman she was. Bobbi wore her trademark scarf and a revealing minidress. She was thin, frail, but with large enough breasts and enough curve in the hips to pass without a hint of doubt in anyone's mind. And her face was beautiful.

Even back when Bobbi was preop, she had been a headturner. Straight men had forgotten themselves when she'd done her act at the Option Club. But now that she had changed, she danced at the Mitchell Brothers' Theater. She appeared nearly naked, and the straight men went crazy stuffing twenty-dollar bills into her G-string. None of them ever doubted that Bobbi was a woman. And Bobbi *was* a woman. A woman like the one Trona would never be.

Operations and electrolysis could do their share, and pills would help, but Trona would never be small and petite like Bobbi. She had a man's frame and a man's muscle and a man's voice that some men were stupid enough to envy.

She would trade it in a second. If she had Mickey's body even, just a little surgery and a few pills would make her a woman that men would admire. But no one would ever love Trona, or want to be with her.

She lowered her head, staring into her cocktail and trying very hard not to cry. She'd given up her marriage, quit her financial-district job, and taken a position as an underpaid clerk in a Tenderloin leather store, all in the forlorn and ridiculous hope that she could somehow make herself pass as a woman and recreate herself into something she wouldn't be ashamed of. And it had all come to this: sitting in a sleazy transvestite bar on Polk, crying into her fucking mimosa.

What did it matter if she cried? No one would notice, not for a fucking second. The people around the bar had become used to Trona's repulsive presence, and they had taken to ignoring her.

She felt a soft hand on the skin of her neck. Somehow Trona wasn't startled; the touch seemed to meld with her flesh.

"You okay, honey?" The voice was soft and cool, like a silk scarf, and Trona looked into the rich brown eyes of Bobbi Rodriguez.

Trona was shocked that anyone was even speaking to her in the Mare—least of all Miss Bobbi.

Trona began to speak and found that her man's voice caught in her throat. She shook her head.

"No," she finally said, in a hoarse whisper. "I'm alright...."

Bobbi laughed a little and looked at her. There was something in those eyes that made Trona speak again.

Trona swallowed and felt the tears trickle down her cheeks. "You're just so beautiful...."

"You're not the first person to say so." Bobbi was quiet, like a fawn, and a space cleared for her at the bar immediately. She sat down next to Trona and placed her hand on Trona's knee. "But you're very beautiful, too."

Trona didn't hear any mocking in the tone. "What's beautiful about me?"

Bobbi reached up and patted the curls of Trona's hair. "Your hair. It's lovely. Red is such a rare shade to get, and I can tell that yours isn't dyed. I always wanted to have hair like that."

Trona felt a soft blush steal over her cheeks. "Thank you. But it isn't much good by itself."

"There are all sorts of beauty. I think the finest sort of beauty is the beauty you find within yourself."

Trona felt her gut knot inside her. How dare a woman like this tell her about inner beauty? It was fucking easy for *her* to say.

Trona tried very hard not to start crying again. "What if the beauty inside yourself is at odds with what's on the outside?" She looked up at the lovely visage of Bobbi Rodriguez.

Bobbi's face grew soft, gentle, and Trona felt the hand on her knee travel up, from her thigh to her belly to the curve of the falsies beneath her sequined top, finally coming to rest on her face. The fingertips were like a kiss.

"Do you honestly think I don't know what that's like? I understand. You must know that I understand."

Trona bit her lip. How could she hate Bobbi like that? She felt herself softening and collapsing against the other woman's soft, real breasts. Bobbi put her arms around her, hugging her tight. Trona knew Bobbi did understand. But Bobbi had made the transformation—a transformation that Trona couldn't make. The surgeons in the Philippines had worked their magic for Bobbi, but her case had not been beyond all hope. Trona's was. No matter how skilled the doctors or radical their procedures, there was no way they could turn an ox into a doe.

Trona began to cry again and looked down. She didn't want Bobbi to see. She felt pathetic and miserable, and abjectly unlovable. Certainly a real woman couldn't have sympathy for her.

Bobbi's hand snaked its way through Trona's hair, and Trona felt the warmth of Bobbi's body against her as Bobbi got off her barstool. Then there was a kiss on her neck, and Trona's hackles stood up. Something else stood up, deep inside the padding and the lace panties, beneath the loose, long skirt, and Trona felt a violent wave of self-hatred. But she couldn't deny that this woman turned her on. She felt a familiar desire, a desperate longing, and Bobbi's hand was under her cheek, lifting her head gently.

"It's too loud here," said Bobbi. "Would you like to go somewhere?"

Trona's eyes grew wide. "With . . . with you?"

Bobbi's lips broke into a smile and she nodded. "With me."

Trona closed her eyes, letting darkness swallow the bar and all the ugliness of her life. "Yes, I'd like that very much."

Trona marveled at the beauty of Bobbi's apartment. It was large and spacious, with bromeliads and trailing vines everywhere, like an aviary for some rare jungle bird. Orchids bloomed, and the air was thick with moisture and the sharp tang of tropical soil.

Bobbi came out of the bedroom, her perfect body naked except for a white silk shawl and a red velvet ribbon around her neck.

Trona looked over Bobbi's lovely body and felt a pang of jealousy and a thrill of amazement. Nowhere on the perfect olive skin could she see a scar or the mark of a surgeon's knife. Bobbi was as perfect as a woman born into her sex.

"Welcome, beautiful one," Bobbi said, spreading her shawl wide like the wings of a forest moth; she whipped the cloth once round her head, then with a dancer's flourish wrapped it over Trona's face. All Trona could sense was white light through the silk and the spicy scent of Bobbi's perfume.

Bobbi laughed lightly. "The gardens of paradise are not to be seen before one is ready. Are you willing to enter paradise?"

Trona felt her traitorous body aroused in a man's way, but didn't let that spoil the mood. She sank back deep into the satin cushions of the couch and let Bobbi's silky thighs caress her legs as she came to straddle her. "I can never have paradise."

"Miracles happen," said Bobbi. "Let me be your guide."

Trona leaned back, wanting so much to believe. "Please." Just to be so close to the perfection that was Bobbi might be enough.

Bobbi slid free; then a moment later Trona felt silken bonds being wrapped around her wrists and ankles. "Pleasure can be frightening and paradise is often feared," Bobbi breathed softly in her ear. "Let me tie you to the mast so you may hear the song of the sirens, Odysseus. This will be the longest journey of your life. . . ."

Bobbi's nails then reached down the front of Trona's top, pulling hard, and she felt sequins fly free before Bobbi's tongue traced the way from her shaved chest down to her navel. Her traitorous male organ strained against the lace and silk below. Bobbi knew the curves and fasteners of a woman's clothes; Trona closed her eyes and let the real woman take over. Bobbi slipped Trona's skirt over the long, heavily muscled legs, slipped off Trona's flats and tugged down the panties to her ankles—and then, Bobbi's glorious, naked body was against Trona, and the soft breasts, the smooth thighs, slid against the sweat of Trona's skin as Bobbi's hands went gently around Trona's throat.

Trona stifled a moan; she responded to Bobbi's touch as if Bobbi were a sculptor and Trona a hunk of clay. Bobbi began to growl like an animal as her thighs snuggled down over Trona and their crotches pressed together. Bobbi's nails dug into soft flesh. Trona bit at the shawl, unable to stop herself from reacting to the violence.

Her excitement heightened as Bobbi pressed against her and rubbed sensuously.

Suddenly Bobbi let out a wild screaming howl, the howl of a beast seizing its prey. The piercing sound turned Trona on even more, and she responded to the warm fluid dripping over her with panting groans of ecstasy.

Trona didn't have time to wonder for more than a split second what the droplets of warm liquid were. At first she thought Bobbi was spitting on her, and that turned her on. But there was too much liquid, and she realized that Bobbi was pouring warmed massage oil over Trona's chest and face. It soaked through the shawl and dripped down her neck. She felt a warm sucking at her nipples as Bobbi tore off the lace bra. Then Bobbi's glorious body slid off, and Trona was left writhing and exquisitely tormented on the couch.

In a second Trona's panties were ripped from her ankles. Warmth was everywhere, and she felt a juicy wetness pressing into her groin. She could not feel Bobbi anywhere, except for the luscious mouth and the wet feeling all over her upper thighs and hips. She heard a wild screaming again, and her excitement mounted.

The massage oil ran down between her legs, running in between her buttocks and onto the couch.

"Arch your back!" Bobbi screamed at her, the perfect dominatrix. Then Bobbi's mouth slowly traveled down Trona's crotch, her tongue sliding into Trona's ass.

There were long, luscious seconds of gentle, arousing sucking. Then, Trona felt the pressure at her opening, and something long and supple was penetrating her. She began to twist in ecstasy as Bobbi entered her—but those could not be Bobbi's fingers! Trona didn't have time to think about the kinkiness of getting fucked by a dildo in her lover's hands, as the supple form plunged to the hilt into her body.

Then, with a dull ache starting deep in her bowels, Trona realized that Bobbi was going in too far. Once again, her voice caught in her throat and she started to choke. She tried to push her body back against the couch to stop Bobbi, but she found that she couldn't move. Bobbi was in control, and Trona couldn't communicate.

The ache became a howling pain, and Trona tried to scream. The agony bored into her, as if her entire intestine were being ripped out. Then her paralysis broke and she thrashed wildly against the silken bonds, desperate to get away. With a final, gut-wrenching scream, Trona felt the long, snakelike wetness plunging into her belly and pulling back out. Just like a fishing line with Trona's insides on the hook. Bright stars flashed in her vision, and she felt her anus evacuating, like taking a shit. She was empty.

The shawl fell to one side and Trona looked up, through the exploding stars of agony and terror. It took a second for her eyes to adjust.

Her mind was gone. She didn't comprehend. Trona tried to look away, but couldn't, caught in the grip of a horrid fascination, like the first time she had seen a woman who had once been a man.

Bobbi's beautiful face, covered in blood and shit, with a long tongue snaking out of it fully two feet long, a supple muscular organ flexing in the light from the candle.

The head had detached itself from the body. It floated above Trona, a mass of flesh writhing underneath. The tentacles of Bobbi's entrails reached out as if in supplication.

Trona froze. The tendrils twisted above her, slowly, and drops of blood fell down onto her bare thighs. She stared, her eyes wide. Acid spasmed into her throat, cutting short her scream.

Bobbi's tongue flexed in the dim light; a dark lump at the tip glinted in a silver shaft of moonlight from the window, and Trona found her voice to scream. For there, impaled on the end of Bobbi's forked, rasp-edged tongue, was something that could only be Trona's heart.

Bobbi's long, dark hair stuck out like the fronds of a sea anemone, writhing and curling and twined with the air, keeping the at once horrid and beautiful visage suspended in space, like Medusa on the shield. Trona was transfixed, and watched as the long tongue slowly, luxuriantly, curled around the heart, drawing it back into Bobbi's mouth. The head swallowed, and Bobbi's sweet lips smiled in satisfaction as the lump that was Trona's heart slid down the creature's throat and lodged in the obscenely dangling stomach.

The creature floated closer, the long organs hanging down like jellyfish streamers, and with an awful horror Trona realized that the oil she thought she'd been rubbed with had truly been the creature's blood and oozing juices.

It floated closer, the organs dangling, until Bobbi's own heart hung but an inch from Trona's lips, glistening with slime. "Bite it, Eve," Bobbi's sweet voice floated down in a whisper. "Take the apple, or take death."

Trona felt the wetness and bleeding within her chest and the blood flowing out her anus into the soft recesses of the couch. The foul creature above her smiled like a twisted mother at a child, offering a favorite treat stuffed with razor blades, but Trona knew if she didn't accept, she would die.

With the sharp decision born of fear, she tilted her head back and opened her mouth, closing her eyes so as not to see the thing slipping in between her lips. It detached, like a sun-rotted plum, and Trona could hardly swallow before she felt it slide down her throat.

It passed through her rib cage, then slid, inside her, to the spot where her own heart had been. Trona felt the alien heart take root, then felt Bobbi's rasp-edged tongue encircle her neck.

There was a brief pain, like a leash jerked too tight, then Trona felt a parting as her own head lifted from the neck of her body and floated towards the ceiling, her own dripping organs dangling below her like Halloween decorations, pulsing in time with Bobbi's rhythmic laughter.

The Bobbi-thing shook with hideous mirth, sliding downwards and letting its organs slip into the empty hole in Trona's neck. The long, rasped tongue lashed out then, severing the silken bonds that held it to the sofa.

Bobbi/Trona stood up, running her fingers down the powerful chest, then reaching below to fondle the blood-covered male organ, obscenely still erect through the whole ordeal. She laughed in pleasure and fell back onto the gore-encrusted sofa.

Trona felt herself floating about, helpless and unsure. Bobbi, still smiling, looked up. "Think of sliding yourself back into my old body, Eve. It's easy once you understand."

Trona, not questioning, found she could move her writhing organs and found herself sinking to the floor like a bouquet of birthday balloons left for too long. The organs snaked into the hole in Bobbi's corpse, and a second later Trona felt a wet slipping sensation as her head went like a cork into a bottle and she could suddenly feel sensation in Bobbi's gore-covered body.

She sat up, and Bobbi, still fondling the obscene male organ, smiled at her. "Welcome, Trona. Or should I call you Bobbi? These things get so complicated, you know."

Trona slowly sank to the floor, her bare knees sinking into the blood-soaked carpet. She began to claw at the blood, sobbing as she realized that it was hers. She groped desperately at Bobbi's naked body, trying to understand what had happened. She heard her old voice laughing, deep in the throat of the man's body standing above her, and she looked up, terrified.

Bobbi stood over Trona, huge and powerful. Trona desperately got to her feet and tried to move away, but Bobbi had her cornered. Trona looked down at herself, unable to comprehend.

"What have you done to me?" choked Trona, and her voice had the same light, feminine quality that Bobbi's had. She felt a wave of nausea as she realized that she had become a woman—at long last— and somehow she didn't want it, didn't want it at all.

Bobbi moved closer, put his hand out and touched Trona's face. "Have you ever ... been to the Philippines?"

Trona didn't answer. She tried to push Bobbi's hand away. Bobbi laughed and slid his fingers into Trona's hair, gripping it roughly.

"They have a legend there. Of a creature called the Buso. You will find out what it means to do what I did to you—but it's so much sweeter when you steal the victim's liver instead and watch him die!"

Trona felt her stomach contracting in revulsion—but then a hunger began to come over her. Bobbi laughed.

"You'll understand," he said. "You will feed, soon, and you'll understand. But for now, darling, you don't have to understand anything. It's been ten years since I was a man, and the first time in a new body is always the most fun."

Bobbi gripped Trona's hair and put his lips close to hers. He spoke slowly and cruelly.

"I'm sure you will agree, Trona."

The crowd was howling before Trona even took the stage. She swayed with the thundering music, singing along to Black Sabbath's "Lady Evil." She grasped her crotch through the black G-string and stroked her bare breasts as she slid down to the edge of the stage and began to accept dollar bills from the men; the pounding beat of the music almost overwhelmed her.

She saw Bobby in the corner, watching her, his dark face hidden by his sunglasses. His teeth were bared in an obscene smile as Trona felt a bill sliding into her crotch.

She tugged sensuously at the studded collar she wore, sliding along in front of the crowd. Her money collected in a pile near the back of the stage.

Trona could see herself in the mirrored walls. She was beautiful. The bright-red hair looked strange and enticing on a Filipina, even if her jaw was a bit hard and her face a bit wide. The body was what counted, and it was the body of the most desirable woman in New York City. All the men thought so; that's why she brought in hundreds of dollars a night. And only Trona and her lover and manager, Bobby, knew that the olive skin of her face was nothing more than bronzing powder.

Trona felt herself becoming aroused as she caught sight of the man that Bob and she had agreed on for tonight. She licked her lips, touching her ass for the man to see. His name was Teddy. He was one of the hangers-on at the club; he was here every night and he had a thing for Trona. He had never been married and he lived alone, so no one would miss him.

Teddy always drank expensive Scotch. Trona smiled, knowing how delicious his liver would taste.

Teddy was a big tipper. He made his way up to the edge of the stage, holding a crisp bill.

Trona envisioned the delightful feeling as her beautiful female body slid against him, and as she performed the detachment . . . and slid into him.

She smiled, her near-naked form throbbing with the music.

And she looked over her shoulder, licking her lips for Teddy to see as he very, very slowly slipped the five-dollar bill into the strap of her G-string.

He would be a big tipper, all right.

Nothing But Enemies

DEBBIE GOAD

Here's all I knew about DEBBIE GOAD before she sent in her biography:

That she was one-half of the second husband-and-wife team to contribute to this book (the other being Melanie and Steve Tem), and that she co-edited ANSWER Me!, *America's most misanthropic magazine. With her husband Jim Goad.*

Here's what I now know after receiving that biography:

"Debbie Goad grew up in Coney Island, Brooklyn, New York. The product of a stifling, suffocating Jewish family, I dispel my anger in antisocial rants against society. In the seventies I was involved in the punk rock scene, but now I clash with these people as well. In fact, I'm capable of finding fault with just about everybody. Although I'm full of hate on the outside, I do confess that inside there's a heart of gold. But due to the way things are, this will remain a mystery to the world at large.

"When not at work doing data entry in an office and working on ANSWER Me! *with Jim, I'm at home in Hollywood playing with my cats Bjorn, Egbert, and Flavia."*

"Nothing But Enemies" most assuredly operates within the rant mode Debbie mentioned. Yet this isn't the work of a flip poseur. Beneath the lacerating invective is a fiercely held philosophy, one unimpressed by sham or hypocrisy. A blowtorch honesty that's as merciless as a sniper's Heckler & Koch.

In other words, Goad really means it.

Glad you still like cats, though, Deb.

I look out the window and I see them—I close my blinds. I turn on the TV and I see them—I pull the plug. The phone rings and I hear their voices—I hang up on them. The mail comes and I rip it up. But in my mind, I still see them.

So I turn on the computer. I'd rather glare into its icy screen than their cardboard faces. Unfortunately, sounds seep into the room from outside—cars passing, people talking, children screeching, alarms going off. It's futile. There's no escape. They're swarming beyond my walls like cockroaches.

But I must go outside to get food. War zone. Mankind. No one's kind. Everyone's an enemy. No immunity. Nobody's a friend. I don't want to breathe their air. If they take a step towards me, they get a knee to the groin. Opponents eternally. Foes forever. It's pretty simple—I'm right, they're wrong. They can argue with me until their arteries explode. I know the truth.

They don't think like I think. They're blinded by happiness. They're too dull. They don't learn. They need support from others. I'm above their shallow chitchat. They talk and talk and talk and talk, but no words come out of their mouths. They brush up against my mind like steel bristles. They expel repellent scents. They're mobile sacks of lard. Pathetic pus puddles. Walking heaps of foul meat.

I instantly dislike them. I reject any advances they make in my direction. If they get near me, that old violent feeling squirts to the top of my head. I am not a part of this. We clash.

Lying, two-faced cocksuckers. I see through them like an X ray. Their existence is a crime against me. They can't face themselves, so they play their stupid head games. They fail the test. Their plastic smiles mask hideous secrets. They puff themselves up like they're works of art. But behind the facade stands a pillar of shit.

I tremble, consumed with the nausea that human faces induce. The horrible specter of their hollow personalities awaits me. I shake with anticipation, knowing that I'll inevitably see someone. I shake, realizing that I'm smarter. I shake, realizing that they have nothing to offer except dead ends. I shake, realizing that my space and freedom shrink when they're around me. I'd like to choke the life out of them.

Strange to see a chick who's so angry, isn't it? I've got on my battle fatigues. I'm also packing Mace, a stun gun and my Ruger MKII. So don't expect a sweet hello. I won't ask how you're doing. I won't talk about the weather. I'm not interested.

Anyone who's moronic enough to bother me will get a quick education. Better stop staring if you know what's good for you, motherfucker. Did you hear what I said? You're fucking with the wrong person. Though I may look as sweet as a cupcake, I'm filled with cyanide. Get out of my way, or I'll plow you down. Don't dare look at me. Don't talk to me. If you do, here comes a bullet.

Feel a chill? You'll get no warmth from me. No smiles here. I don't care whether it's cool or not. This isn't an act. If you think it is, I'll start popping caps and knock your ass flat on the ground.

Here comes someone. I feel my heart slamming against my ribs. My eyes flare red and bloody. Heat sears my body. No words are exchanged, but there's poisonous tension. The knot in my stomach pulls yet tighter. My teeth grind into dust. I'm ready to pounce. I'm just waiting for him to say the wrong thing. Try calling me stupid, a cunt, a whore, or a bitch. Yeah, I've been called a lot of names. But now try "executioner."

My hand slips into my pocket. My fingers curl around the stun gun. Eighty thousand volts will jar anyone who wants to play. I'll jolt my enemy until his skin bubbles and his head smacks the cement. I'll trample him. Oh, it would feel so good to finish the job, to stick the Ruger up his nose and start gunning! I'd hear him whimper like a baby. I'd see the blood trickling from his head like juice from a lime. His lifeless hulk would just lie there. I'd kick his dumb face up and down, back and forth. If this stranger knew what I was thinking, he'd run across the street. He'd evaporate into the crowd. Good—he looks straight ahead as he passes. He knows better.

I'm stronger than all my enemies. If you lay one finger on me, I'll blow your head off your neck. No one fucks with me and gets away with it. If someone annoys me, their fate is sealed like a manila envelope. It only takes time. They *will* suffer. It may be subtle at first, but their problems will spring up like blades of grass. Their lives will crumble. I'll get justice in the end. They'll crawl back to me with wet cheeks, pleading for me to stop. They're wasting their time. I hold the grudge for life. I savor my grudges. I decide when, where, and how my enemy's demise will be accomplished. Dead, dead, dead.

My list of enemies could fill a roll of toilet paper. Their tragedies are my successes. When one of them dies, I quickly find a new enemy.

I slam my door. Home again. Out with the bad air. Now I don't have to see anybody. No more problems for now. I walk into the foyer and stand between two full-length mirrors. I raise my gun under the light bulb, letting its black steel reflect back and forth into infinity. There are hundreds of me lined one after another, our movements perfectly synchronized as we wave our pistols. We were too nice today. We allowed the enemy to squeeze through unscratched. We cock our hammers and wait for tomorrow.

Boxer

STEVE RASNIC TEM

Here's another one for youse guys out there.
STEVE RASNIC TEM needs no introduction to connoisseurs of the fantastic. The author of more than 200 short stories—some nominated for Bram Stoker and World Fantasy Awards, others appearing in such important anthologies as Book of the Dead, Metahorror, *and* Cutting Edge—*Tem recently collected most of that fiction under the title* Dark Shapes In The Road *for the French publisher, Denoel.*

Steve also has a Master's degree in Creative Writing from Colorado State University. It was there that he studied poetry under Bill Tremblay and fiction under Warren Fine. None of this will prepare you for "Boxer," though.

Two thoughts kept buzzing through my head when I finally got around to talking to Steve Tem about his story. The first regarded "Boxer"'s bizarre metaphor for sanctioned bloodsports. The second was admiration for the economical manner in which Tem had indicted said sports.

Then Steve asked me why I'd picked "Boxer" for this book.
The real reason.
"Uh—mainly 'cause it's so damn weird," *I blurted out.*
See for yourself.

Joe noticed the kid right off. It wasn't just that he was a new face— they got new faces in Chunk Willy's Gym all the time. Pretty boys, mostly, just wanting to build up a little. And fat guys who'd decided for maybe the tenth time they just had to lose that flab.

But those types never lasted long—a couple of months, three, four tops. Because Chunk Willy's wasn't no goddamn spa. It was a serious gym for serious meat. Boxers and wrestlers, a few weight lifters, and types like Old Paco, who had always just built themselves up because they liked it—it wasn't meant for show.

But the kid didn't fit any of those types. Too skittish. Sweating like a boiled pig even though he wasn't working out. Tall—he might get himself a pretty good reach someday—but skinny as hell. All gristle and no meat. Punch him in the belly and he'd fold up tight as a preacher's asshole.

The kid had been hanging around the fighters all morning. It was the boxers he wanted, looked like, although sometimes it seemed he couldn't tell them apart from the wrestlers. He'd go up and talk to a wrestler like Bingo Butane or Gator George and they'd just laugh at him, put one arm around him and squeeze one of their blubbery titties with the other and laugh some more.

Finally it looked like he'd learned the difference and he started hitting on the boxers. Going up to them one at a time and chewing at their faces like he was begging up his first meal in a week. Most of the guys looked at him like he was talking dog shit, and if he didn't leave them alone they were gonna have to scrape him off their shoes. A couple of the guys—the ones who'd had their noodles powdered pretty good—listened to him, at least, but like they didn't understand a word he was saying, which they probably didn't. But Joe guessed they made the kid feel encouraged some, because he'd reach into his back pocket and pull out his wallet for them. Then he didn't look like a beggar—he looked like a salesman. But the guys just stared at his money like they didn't know what it was, which they probably didn't.

Joe was the last guy in the gym the kid hadn't tried. And Joe listened. Joe had paid attention to all that money the kid had and Joe knew what money was. He never saw much of it, but he knew what it was.

"You're a boxer," the kid said to him.

"How'd you guess? Musta been the shorts."

The kid didn't smile, just looked a little red. "I want to hire you."

Joe didn't answer right away. He'd just noticed the scar on the kid's face.

Joe hadn't seen a face wound that ugly since the Etchison-Wagner bout. At first it looked like it hadn't healed: red and raw-looking, the skin spread a good half-inch, maybe even more. It ran down from the kid's hairline past the bridge of his nose, cutting his forehead in half.

"You oughta get that looked at, kid," Joe said.

"I'll pay you fifty dollars," the kid said.

The kid raised his eyebrows a lot when he talked. Joe watched the edges of the wound wrinkle and fold when the kid talked. In the gap between the two lips of skin there was pinkish, soft-looking skin, like the skin on the kid's cheeks, like a baby's behind.

"Okay, I'll go seventy-five," the kid said.

Joe stared at the kid. He'd never talked anybody into a raise without opening his yap before. It made him nervous. "What's worth that seventy-five?"

"Sparring. I want to box with you."

Joe started laughing. "You're kidding. Fellow like you? Might as well pay me the seventy-five to stick a gun in your ear."

The kid got red, looked pretty mad. Joe watched the wound. It was sweatin' a river.

"Fellow like you must surely need the money," the kid said in a snotty kind of way. "Don't tell me you're *afraid* of a guy with my build."

Joe didn't like that, but then he figured maybe the kid was crazy. "Keep your money, kid," he said, slow and careful. He turned away.

"Make it a hundred, then," the kid said behind him. "You turn that down and then I'll *know* you're afraid."

The kid said that last part loud. When Joe turned around the others were looking at him. "You got a big mouth, kid."

"A hundred twenty-five." The wound was soaked now, shining under the big gym lights. The crusted lips looked like they jumped a little, and suddenly Joe was thinking about something they used to do when they were kids—throw big fat earthworms into a campfire. Just when they started to burn, just before they started melting, they looked just like the kid's wound. Joe could feel himself sweat, and that made him even madder.

"Your funeral," he grunted, unable to look at the kid's forehead anymore. He grabbed a towel and headed for Willy's ring.

He didn't know the kid was walking along beside him until the kid leaned over and whispered in his ear. Joe went funny all over, like cold water was dripping down his back. He could feel that burnt earthworm of a wound just inches away from his own face, the kid whispering into his ear like some dainty little girl.

"I want you to concentrate on my scar," the kid whispered. "I want you to beat hell out of my head."

In fury Joe grabbed the ropes and jerked himself up into the ring. What the hell kinda freakin' shit pile was this kid, anyway? Freakin' kid. Joe turned around and danced a little, stomping his anger into the mat. The kid pulled off his jeans—there were pale green trunks underneath—and climbed into the ring.

Joe jabbed the air in front of his head. "Fifty more and I'll punch anywhere you like. I'll pound you to bloody hamburger you pay me enough, you fuckin' freak."

The kid smiled a thin line. Joe thought he looked constipated. "Sure," the kid said. "Fifty more. All you have to do is tear my face off, you big stupid prick!"

Then the kid waved his gloves around in the air like he was some kind of dancing puppet. He waved and made a little kissy face at Joe like he was making fun of him, like he was accusing him of something. Joe stood there watching that silly shit until he couldn't stand it anymore. Then he waded into the kid.

The kid just opened up his arms like he was going to hug Joe, and that made Joe want to punch him all the harder. But the kid didn't step any closer, just held his arms out like he was some kind of Christ, that awful worm jiggling on his forehead, and Joe gave that worm all he had, and the kid went down like a bag of wet laundry.

"You had enough, kid?" Joe was breathing hard, but it wasn't because of the effort. He was so hyped-up his head was swimming.

The kid looked up, his head greasy with blood. The worm was fatter, longer. Joe stared at the wound. It was still growing; the space between the crusted lips was broad and newborn pink. And moving.

"Christ . . ."

"Scared of a little blood, big boy?" the kid simpered. Then he blew Joe a kiss. Joe picked him up under the arms—grabbing him tighter as his gloves started slipping on the kid's slick skin—and put him back on his feet. Joe smashed the worm a couple of more times and when it looked like the kid was going to fall over again he propped him up against the ropes. The kid smiled through blood-crusted lips, coughed, then leaned over and tried to kiss Joe. Joe went after him again, jack-hammering his face.

And all the time the kid kept egging Joe on, pleading with him to hit him some more.

"Smash my face off, big guy!" the kid shouted through bubbled lips. And Joe did his damnedest to oblige. The worm jigged and wriggled, grew fatter and longer, stretched up into the kid's hair, down the kid's nose and across his lips.

Suddenly the kid screeched and stood straight up away from the ropes, blood spraying from his face, his arms reaching up over his head.

Joe backed away. The kid's face folded, loosened, and began to fall. Torn at the eyes, the ears. Like an old, rotten T-shirt, Joe thought. Or like a snake shedding its skin. Or like a baby being born. The kid's face fell off. And underneath there was another face: sharp, pink, a little bloody, and a little different from the one that now lay in a sloppy pile of skin and liquid at his feet.

"Hit me," the kid said, spitting out the blood and stray bits of skin that still filled his mouth. "Hit me *harder* this time. I'll pay another two hundred. Dammit, I'll pay you as much as you want!"

Joe just stared at the mess on the mat, his gloved hands hanging limp at his sides.

"Can't you see, you ape?" The kid started scratching at a spot on his forehead. "You stupid ass." Joe could see the new skin on the kid's forehead begin to split a little. "You moron. You *afraid* to hit me some more?" Joe stared at the beginnings of another wound, another worm. "Can't you *see,* you motherfucker? Hit me! Bash my face away! Can't you see there's *more?*"

Xenophobia

POPPY Z. BRITE

One of the brightest new stars to ascend the horror heavens is stamped with the unlikely moniker of POPPY Z. BRITE.

Born May 25, 1967, Bright's biography is studded with the eccentric job résumé of a true writer: gourmet candy maker, artist's model, cook, exotic dancer, and mouse caretaker (??). Her first published stories appeared between 1985 and 1990 in such respected small-press magazines as The Horror Show.

Since then, Brite's short works have seen print in Borderlands, Still Dead: Book of the Dead 2, Women of Darkness 2, *and other anthologies. Her first novel, 1992's* Lost Souls, *was nominated for a Lambda Award for outstanding gay fiction. Bright's also worked as an actress, in "John Five," a short erotic film by Athens, Georgia, artist Jim Herbert, who's directed several videos for the band* R.E.M.

All this by the age of twenty-six, too.

Sigh. Makes me wish I'd spent less time partying.

Poppy's fortune is her style; she's clearly in love with the English language. Her grammar is lustrous, sensuous. Emblemized by shimmering cascades of beautifully modulated prose. Bright's a classic decadent, too—lush textures, a melancholy tone, and a twilight sensibility are all constants in her work.

Or, to use a rock analogy—

If Poppy Z. Brite were a musician, her morbid romanticism and street-savvy attitude would peg her as a Goth. Something like a cross between Peter Murphy (of the old Bauhaus*) and H.P. Lovecraft (the dead guy, not the band).*

Yet "Xenophobia" is atypical Brite. Here's a story marked by an unusual playfulness, a lighthearted air of charm. A touch of giddiness, even, that's at odds with Poppy's usually more somber voice.

Although you'll still encounter street people, drugs, and corpses.

Not to mention a baroque twist on that old dirty joke about the sex of a Chinese woman . . .

I hated Robert. He thought he was a Punk Rocker. He wore one pink hightop sneaker and one yellow, and he never washed his hair, so it stood up in filthy little twists all over his head. When I took him down to Chinatown, I was hoping I could get him drunk and sell him to some unscrupulous Chinese chef for big money. It's said they use dead cats. Why not Robert Foo Yung?

He talked so much on the bus (about uninteresting things like the book of poisonous recipes he was writing) that we got off at the wrong stop and found ourselves in the porn district. The light of the setting sun was as red as desire. X's paraded across every marquee. The poster girls' nipples and lipstick had long since faded to a dusty orange. The signs and lampposts and even the square of sidewalk we stood on seemed to vibrate silently in the hellish glow, as if some enormous city-machine thrummed far below the pavement. "You've gotten us lost," said Robert, licking his lips nervously, and then we rounded a corner and saw the pinnacle of Chinatown's first gaudy pagoda rising above the city.

The streets of Chinatown thrilled me, but my excitement was spiked with a vein of clear unease. I sometimes wonder whether my large Caucasian presence was merely tolerated on the exotic streets, perhaps even found secretly amusing. At night the lights of Chinatown turn the sky bright purple, and the banners hung from balcony to scrolled balcony crack in the wind like shots, their messages unreadable (Good Health? Long Life? Get Fucked?). There seems always to be a smell of gunpowder and hot sesame oil in the air. The neon runs together in a blaze of colors, red and white and green and gold and azure, and if you should happen to arrive after dropping a nice hit or two of acid, all the spiky Chinese characters will jump off the signs and race round and round at a giddy speed, laughing into your mystified, unslanted, unblack eyes.

We stopped in front of a restaurant and considered having Dim

Sum, but the menu was written in Chinese, all up-and-down. "Fried lice," Robert translated, putting his sticky fingers all over the window glass. "Monkey brains in syrup. Eyeball pie." He giggled. I noticed a crust of old lipstick in the corners of his mouth. Why had I brought him? Could I drag him into the shadowy serene interior of some temple, leave him sacrificed before a smiling golden Buddha?

A river of people flowed around us as we stood waiting for something to happen on the corner of two inscrutably marked streets. Most of them wore neat black clothes and neat black slippers, and were a full head shorter than Robert or me. The darker of the two streets was lit mostly with blue neon—the blue light is a universal advertisement for Chinese food, and a native far from home knows that where he sees it he will find the rice lovingly steamed, the pork pickle well braised—and the glossily bobbing heads flickered with highlights of unearthly blue. I felt immense, pale, bloated. Robert was worse. He shifted from foot to pink-shod foot, muttering under his breath, twirling a matted lock of hair round his finger. His eyes had taken on the color of the night sky over Chinatown. One look into them and I knew tonight would be a hideous adventure that might never end. He had that wild empty glare he got sometimes, like his soul had gone out to party and left him behind and he was determined to catch up with it. Once when he had gotten that glare in New Orleans, we woke up three days later in a motel room that reeked of ash and sour vomit, wearing nothing but dirty underwear and beaded Mardi Gras masks.

But right now he only wanted ice cream. We huddled in a sweet shop, eating vanilla because the other flavors—lychee, almond, green tea—sounded too Chinese. Even the vanilla had a peculiar aftertaste, faintly oily but too delicate to offend. Beside us was a display case full of strange dusty-looking pastries: thousand-year-old eggs in sugared nests, squid jellies piped full of cream. The shop was lit by a single weak lamp behind a paper shade. In its dimness I made out only one other customer, a lone old man nursing a cup of tea.

Robert wanted to drink, but had spent our last money on the bus fare and the ice cream. We sat at the table trying to think of a way around our poverty, or straight through it if need be. "We could find some girls," I said.

The very ends of his hair trembled. "Chinese girls? I heard that their, you know, their, you know ..." His voice was loud and babyish.

I lowered my own voice almost to a whisper, hoping he would copy me. "Cunts, Robert."

"... that they open sideways instead of up-and-down."

Most of Robert's babble slipped past me, but not this. I stopped eating my ice cream and became lost in trying to visualize such an intriguing possibility. In my mind I could see the tantalizing orifice, but it remained maddeningly vertical; I could not make it turn sideways. Only when Robert poked me in the ribs did I notice the old Chinese man standing silently before our table.

He might have been three hundred years old. He might have been a Biblical king come out of the desert, with cold stars gleaming in his long black eyes. He might have been a bonsai tree, shrunken and gnarled, with skin the color of old wood. But he was well dressed, I saw: a neat and sober black suit, a shirt so white it took on a faint silver glow in the dim light. A little beard grew under his chin like a goat's, waggling when he spoke. "If I may disturb you?" He paused, then added, "Gentlemen?"

Robert was beyond speech; he just stared, his mouth open a little, a last trace of vanilla on his lips. The moment stretched out long, punctuated by the blinking of neon outside. On—and the inside of the shop was bathed in garish night rainbows. Off—and there was only the lamp behind its faded paper shade, and the soft web of shadows. At last my manners came back to me and I pointed at a chair. "Go ahead. Disturb us."

He sat neatly, his hands folded before him. They were like old ginseng roots, I saw: long-fingered, tapering, dry. The beard waggled again. "You were saying you needed money for the night's ... ah ... festivities."

His perfect English suddenly annoyed me. I became tough, but suave; all I needed was a snap-brim hat and a pencil-thin mustache. "You want to give us some?"

His eyes seemed to burn a hole through my facade. "Not *give* ... not exactly. I am a businessman, you see, and I require a service. If I were to offer you five dollars each, might you be able to perform a service for me?"

"Five dollars!" Robert snorted. "We wouldn't wash your chopsticks for five dollars."

"I see," said the old man. "And if I were to add that you might have unlimited use of a bottle of good cognac?"

Before Robert could say anything I leaned across the table and put my face right up next to the old man's. "Just what business are you in, mister?"

The man paused. I saw neon flickering across his eyes. On—and they exploded with a thousand firework colors. Off—and they were flat black, the color of dynasties long fallen to dust, the color of Mystery incarnate.

"I am an undertaker," he said.

It turned out that the man wanted Robert and me to keep vigil over the corpse of a middle-aged woman while he slipped out to drink with another undertaker. His apprentice was ill, he explained, and his parlor had already been broken into twice. Bandits came through the window and robbed the corpses of rings, watches, even—on one occasion—an artificial foot. I wondered who had wanted the foot, and why, and if the other undertaker was also abandoning his charges to go out drinking. At the back of my mind was still that disquieting image, the one I could not quite visualize.

Robert looked sidelong at me. It would be an easy ten dollars— if the old man's story was true. Why would he trust us to watch over the corpse of a stranger, and a Chinese one at that? At worst the man might lead us to a secret slaughterhouse where we would be hung on hooks, bled dry by tubes of bamboo shoved beneath our skin, and sold as cheap sides of pork to the less reputable restaurants. At best, he might lure us to an opium palace where we would be used like other, choicer cuts of meat, kept blissfully stoned every hour. But if the old man was telling the truth, his cognac would give our evening a fast start. Robert stared at me: he would not refuse, so neither could I. "All right," I said, and we followed the old man out of the sweet shop.

It was getting late now, and a party had begun in Chinatown. The street was a dazzle of lights, a feast of smells. Neon ran riot. Traffic signals stayed red or turned green, and cars inched along the narrow street flashing their headlights impatiently. Slabs of pork sizzled on a grill, oiling the air with the tender red scent of meat. I saw a row of ducks hanging in the window of a grocery, skinned, their eyes scooped out and their beaks tied shut with dirty bits of string. Below them was a porcelain bowl filled with what looked like thousands of tiny dried-up human hands.

The man led us down an alley, along a steep unlit back street where tough Chinese stood on the corner passing a pint of wine. We entered a high vaulted passage, then wound through a maze of corridors that opened onto a courtyard made of moonlight and stillness. Here flowed a small stream over rocks of luminescent alabaster. Here grew trees that seemed carved all in jade, each leaf, each twig. I looked up. The square of night sky above the courtyard was a deeper purple than we had seen earlier, a velvet hand cradling a cold slice of moon. We came upon an iron staircase that spiraled up into darkness. The old man beckoned to us, then began to climb.

We went down a long hallway lit by votive candles in wall sconces. The tiny blue flames flickered sharply in one direction, then in the other, though I felt no draft in the hall. We passed a line of tightly shut doors and were admitted into the last one.

"This is my parlor," the old man told us.

The room was wrapped in shadow. The darkness didn't recede much when the old man pulled a silk cord; the only light in the room came from a lamp with a shade of heavy red paper, as dim as the one in the sweet shop.

The object of our vigil lay on a long red table near the window. Through the thick draperies I saw the neon of Chinatown still blinking, playing over the shroud. On—and each fold of cloth was full of a different color light. Off—and it was only wrinkled linen again, bone-white and shadow-gray, wound tightly around each hill and lump of the woman's body. I stared at the blinking rainbow shroud, transfixed. Then I glanced up and saw Robert staring just as fixedly at the large bottle of cognac the man had brought out from a hidden cupboard.

"Enjoy," he said. "Gentlemen. And if the lady should become restless, you need only give her a sip of this."

Not until he was five minutes gone did we realize that the undertaker had cracked a joke.

I kept vigil beside the shroud, swigging from the bottle of cognac whenever Robert offered it to me. I was already well along—a warm amber fire smoldering in my throat, a puddle of brains swimming pleasantly inside my skull. Robert sucked down twice as much cognac as I did. He roamed around the room looking at everything. He tried to peek under the shroud and see the woman's face, but the cloth was tucked securely beneath the heavy head. The shroud molded the shape of the body precisely. After my fifth swig of cognac, an uneasy impression began to nag at me: the idea that there might be no corpse at all under that shroud, that the cloth might be like a decayed mummy's wrappings, cradling only the memory of a body. Robert had once taken me to visit his parents' house. He caught a big spider and put it in his mother's microwave oven on a setting of 1 MIN—HIGH. When we took the spider out and broke it open, whatever innards it might have had were cooked away—not even a gummy residue of viscera remained. The body was only a dry chitinous husk. This was how I pictured the shroud— an empty shell wrapped around eternity.

Robert found a cache of morticians' makeup in a drawer. The rouge came in a little gold compact with a vanity mirror inside, which I found obscenely funny. Robert began to smear the makeup on his face: yellowish pancake base heavy enough to cover knife wounds or the purple discoloration of asphyxia, white eyeshadow that made his eyes seem to bulge out of their sockets, shocking pink lipstick. Then he reached into the makeup case again and pulled out a more interesting object: a porcelain pipe with a long slender stem of silver. It was empty, but the bowl was blackened with a sticky, sweet-smelling residue.

"An opium pipe," I said.

"I knew what it was." Robert dipped a finger in the gummy black residue and sucked at it. "But it's empty. Wait, what's this?" From the depths of the makeup case he pulled out a crumpled plastic bag.

"Something in here—" He shook out several shreds of what looked like leathery dried skin. When he stared at me in alarm, I said, "It must be some kind of fungus."

"Mushrooms?" Robert's eyes gleamed; he might have been a child gazing upon Willy Wonka's wonderland of magic candy.

"Could be," I said. "He was a pretty trippy old dude. Maybe we found his stash."

Without further debate Robert crammed the leathery fragments into his mouth and chewed noisily, then smiled at me. I saw dark shreds caught in his teeth. "You'll have some too, *won't* you?"

At the implicit dare I stuck out my hand. Robert shook a generous amount of the fungi into my cupped palm, and I munched them thoughtfully. The taste was a little like psilocybin mushrooms, that same dry dead redolence that coats the tongue, but the texture was different—like trying to eat tanned hide. If Robert had not still been chewing, I would have spit out my mouthful. Bitter juice trickled down my throat. After swallowing, we rinsed our mouths with cognac.

I pulled back a curtain and stared down at the faraway carnival of Chinatown. The bright streets seemed impossibly distant from this room, this dim red parlor where we kept vigil over a corpse without a face. It seemed sad that there was no one to watch over the woman except two strangers looking for a cheap drunk. I wanted to be back down on the streets, back where the endless party of the living held sway, back there dancing with the city night. Not until Robert spoke my name did I realize that the neon had begun to swirl more vividly than ever among the folds of the shroud. On . . . off. On . . . off.

"We could *look* at her, you know."

"What?" With an effort I tore my gaze away from the rippling colors. I had no idea what Robert was talking about until I saw his sticky pink smile.

"You're fucked up," I told him. So was I, I realized. My voice reverberated from the ceiling. The room seemed smaller than before, shrunken by the enormity of the shroud's mute presence. I fixed my eyes on Robert. He, at least, was warm flesh. "We can't do that. Even if I wanted to look at . . . *that* . . . the old dude would know. He'd see where we unwrapped the shroud."

"We'd only have to unwrap her legs and hips. We could fix it so he wouldn't see. He'll be drunk when he comes back."

"Robert . . ."

"Don't you want to know if it really *does* open sideways?"

The bad thing was, I did. Ever since Robert had mentioned it in the sweet shop, that tidbit of pornographic trivia kept returning unbidden to my mind. I tried to picture it, failed, and tried again. Privately I had always found the territory between women's thighs a little frightening anyway—the pink fleshy ruffles like those of a deep-sea creature, the soft dark opening like the valve of some mysterious heart. To imagine that beneath the shroud might be a thing such as Robert described—

"Unwrap her," I said. I had to see; suddenly both of us did. The air of the room became tinged with dark excitement, like ectoplasm flowing out of us and bathing the thing in the shroud.

Robert tore at the brittle cloth. It came away easily, exposing the feet and lower legs. The flesh looked dense and waxy, as if nerve and blood vessel and bone had fused into a single mass, as if the legs were solid all the way through. Robert kept unwrapping. From the knees up the skin was smooth and nearly translucent. Robert prodded the thighs, leaving fingerprint-sized dents in the pale flesh. I caught my breath when I saw the black triangle shining from the juncture of her thighs. It might have been a hole cut through her body, a tunnel leading to forever.

Robert couldn't get the legs apart by himself. I took hold of one thigh and Robert clutched the other, as if we meant to break the woman in half like a wishbone. We pulled, and her legs came ratcheting open with a painful noise. *Only shrunken ligaments stretching*, I told myself, *only bone-ends rotating in dry sockets*. For a moment I thought I could see myself from above, as if I floated in a shadowy corner watching Robert and myself pry open the thighs of a corpse. But I could feel the tightness of my eyes, the neutral flesh under my fingers, the low ache in my crotch that throbbed with every beat of my heart.

"There," breathed Robert. "Now we can look at her. Now we can *see*—"

He dipped his fingers into the black nest of hair, smoothed it aside, and exposed the dark pink lips of the woman's vagina.

Which, of course, opened vertically. Like that of any other woman.

But Robert was not satisfied. Maybe he had never seen one at all before. His fingers probed further, slipping inside the fleshy lips and parting them, exposing what was *inside* . . .

. . . a single eye. An eye with two dark pupils like twin polliwog eggs in jellied embrace. As it rolled moistly up to look at us, time turned viscous, syrupy. The night seemed to contract to a shining point, a point contained in the crystalline, impossible orb that stared at us from between those two lips like the petals of pink anemones. I heard Robert scream first, ripping the thick silence open ...

... and then we were running. There was one awful moment when I thought I would not be able to get the door open. Robert clawed at my back. Behind his panting I thought I heard the dry rustle of the shroud. A picture came to me: the woman sitting up, the dry cloth falling away from her face, eyes sliding open both with that same jellied double pupil, staring blindly after us, not understanding why she had been left alone ...

... and then I wrenched it open and we hurtled down the hall. The flames in the wall sconces burned clear blue as we passed. The hall seemed longer now, the house bigger and more convoluted. Surely we had not passed so many doors coming in, nor had the doors been so tall and ornately peaked. I thought I saw rooms with marble walls like chocolate and vanilla, rooms hung with tapestries of jewels and pearls and golden thread. A rampant lion carved in jade lunged at us from a niche in the wall, and I screamed like a child. Robert dragged me on.

All at once we ran through a door and found ourselves in the moonlit courtyard. Its tranquility seemed sinister now, as if it were waiting for something to happen. The moon had disappeared. We found our way through the maze of corridors, clutching at each other, trying to catch our breath. At the street entrance we met the old man coming politely home in his sober black suit. Was he drunk? I couldn't tell: his eyes were as flat as ever, his little goat's beard sparse but neat. He folded his hands and let us pass.

"Did you enjoy the refreshments?" he inquired.

"Refreshments?" Robert's voice quavered.

"The cognac, of course." The old man seemed to bow to us slightly—but maybe he was just swaying. Maybe he was drunk after all. "I believe I owe each of you five dollars." He produced a ten and offered it to us, folded between the first and second fingers of his withered hand. I could not make myself reach for the bill. Robert hesitated, then grabbed it.

"Mister—" he said. "Mister—did you have some kind of mush-rooms in the drawer upstairs? In that makeup case?"

"Mushrooms?" The old man smiled at Robert, and this time I was sure he did bow: a slight ironic inclination of the head, nothing more. "Gentlemen," he said, "all of the mushrooms in Chinatown are poisonous. Except to the Chinese."

He was gone into the shadow of the corridor. Robert stared up at the building. I followed his gaze and saw a curtain twitching in an upstairs window. Neither of us wanted to see what face, if any, would look down at us.

As we began to run again, back toward the neon streets of Chinatown with the purple sky pressing down on our heads and the psychedelic night wrapped around us, I started to feel faintly sick.

Dripping Crackers

MICHAEL RYAN ZIMMERMAN

Shit.

> *Feces. Crap. Poop.*
> *We all do it, we all know it.*
> *So what's the deal?*
> *The hypocrisies surrounding bodily excretion are almost equal to the taboos concealing it. Americans routinely treat the elimination of their wastes as a secret shame—then just as quickly reinvent ways to free themselves from that disgrace.*
> *Consider: today you're relaxing on a nice private commode. Join the military, though, and tomorrow you're squirming on a lidless pot. In a wide-open, barn-sized room, under a naked two-hundred-watt light bulb. Rib-to-elbow beside twenty other straining grunts.*
> *Yet this abrupt relinquishment of privacy is considered perfectly acceptable behavior. Normal, even. It's also all right to walk into a public toilet and urinate next to a stranger. Pay that same stranger twenty bucks to piss on you, however, and it's a crime.*
> *Go figure.*
> *Anyway, some people seem remarkably un-hung-up on this doodoo thing. Women, for one. Must have something to do with their periods. Or birthin' all them babies.*
> *Then there's MICHAEL RYAN ZIMMERMAN.*
> *A twenty-five-year-old who's been writing since he was seventeen, Mike hails from Orwigsburg, PA. He enjoys "drinking in the sun, the Philadelphia Phillies in any form, running, skiing, golfing, and the usual creature comforts. The rest of my activities are as wide open as insane eyes."*
> *Zimmerman's stories have been printed in* Iniquities *and* Grue. *He's written four novels. "But I'm only shopping the latest since*

the first three suck donkey dingus," Mike continues. "The fifth and sixth books are currently under simultaneous construction, and the seventh is stewing in the brainpan. None possess the traditional trappings of horror. I don't know what they could be classified as. Black-eyed fiction, I suppose.

"That doesn't matter. The bottom line under all this man-behind-the-words stuff is killer writing. Nothing more. Nothing less. No rules, no excuses. KILL. That's writing."

"Dripping Crackers" kills. This smart, tough dissection of pop-culture decadence, of stand-up comedy, and reality TV (shows like A Current Affair*) has a lot more moving through its bowels than a crass entertainer hitting the big time by making feces funny.*

In fact, Zimmerman's shitty saga gives rise to an idea.

Next time you flush, think of something amusing. Try to laugh. Or giggle. At the very least, crack a smile as you button up.

Imagine the results!

A world of happy crappers.

Have a nice *day.*

*B*olt siphoned smoke into his lungs with a thick sound. His attention was rapt on the screens before him, and he barely noticed Tom's grimace from his right. The smoke was itchy and tough in the cramped editing room, in their mucous membranes like soap, and if Tom and Lydia didn't like it . . .

"Cue my intro," Bolt ordered. Tom coughed in reply and punched a button.

Bolt's image came up, holding a microphone while standing in front of a modest brownstone.

"Ham," muttered Tom. Lydia cleared her throat mindlessly from behind them.

Onscreen:

"I'm Bolton Marston, and welcome to *Media Fog*. Tonight, we'll probe the twisted yet frighteningly original world of Neddy Stuart, who police think murdered his live-in girlfriend, Jennifer Jacobi, and then killed himself. However, proof of his suicide is sketchy. If Stuart—a controversial experimenter in the broad lines of dark comedy—indeed committed the crime, what caused this torrential slash-and-burn comic mind to snap? For now, no one seems to have any explanation. All we can do is try to find one of our own. Join me, Bolton Marston, tonight on *Media Fog*."

Tom punched a button, holding Bolt's image frozen on-screen.

"Good enough?" Bolt asked.

"Good enough," replied Lydia.

"I can't be more poetic about this fascination," said Bolt.

"Say *huh?*" asked Tom with a scowl.

Bolt smiled. "That's what Neddy said to me when I interviewed him last year. I asked him what his muse was, and that was his reply."

"I remember," said Lydia. "Why not run part of that now?"

"Already planned," said Bolt. "This will be a great episode, Lydia. The stuff I have here ... I can't be more poetic about this fascination."

Tom snickered. "You're in love with a murderous perverted shitburger."

Bolt regarded his editor loosely, licking in the silver wisps of smoke by his mouth. Tom was just a rat-kid, long hair, a past geek who was now simply well paid. Bolt remained tensely silent, and Lydia put a hand on his shoulder. He felt the red nails resting against his Arrow cotton. The steadying hand of the producer. "Really, Bolt," she said. "Don't you think this piece on Neddy should be *lighter?* He was a comedian."

Bolt sucked the ember back into the filter and stubbed it out in the ashtray on the panel. He closed his eyes until the smoke scorched his bronchials black. He sighed a cloud. "Lydia," he began, so aware of her belt line just behind his head. Chunky as she was, he'd still fantasized of her dark skin behind masturbation doors. Her body, all wise and full and wet to be sucked. "Neddy was not about 'light.' The laughter was not necessarily out of humor. Just back off creatively on this one, I mean it. Make sure I'm technically perfect like you always do, but leave content up to me."

Her hand was gone. He chanced a look at her face, her full blackness and tempestuous eyes. They'd been working late, and she was now only in a T-shirt and jeans. He'd breathed deep and sent out peristaltic power waves; she'd backed off, slowly nodding. Not wanting to be sucked.

"Fine," she said. "You've run with things before, so you'll have this one. But if that's the deal, I'm not going to just sit here all night and watch you paste it together."

"Go do the Woolite thing, Lyd," said Tom. "We're stoked."

Bolt turned back to his screens. To him, she was already gone.

"I want to see this first thing in the morning. Then we'll talk changes."

Grunt. Bolt was chewing another coffin nail.

Tom had mumbled something, smiled at her, and she said something back, something offhandedly pleasant. She was gone. Bolt punched a button, and the sudden absence of female entropy sharpened him all the keener.

"Let me see the cop," he said.

Tom moved in the smoke, grunted coughlike, and they hunched over their work.

CUT TO

Captain Raymond Klecko, Berkeley Police *(Klecko is an old, big man, and he reads from a prepared statement):* "At approximately two forty-three this morning, Officers John Spolski and Frederick Black arrived at the residence of comedian Neddy Stuart at the request of a neighbor. They found the bodies of Mr. Stuart and his live-in companion, Miss Jennifer Jacobi of Berkeley, in the basement of the house. Apparently both had been dead for at least sixteen hours. Cause of death has not been ascertained, but we are not ruling out foul play."

"Overdub," said Bolt, and Tom obliged. As footage of Neddy's body being removed from the house rolled, Bolt's voice cramped into the airspace.

"The only foul play seems to be by Neddy himself. As the public now knows, Jennifer was found soaked in a cast-iron bathtub full of human waste." *(A photo of Jennifer, a twenty-year-old California blond, fills the screen in a gradual close-up.)* "Her throat had been torn out as if by an animal. But the animal was Neddy, and the basement was filled with manifestations of his own waste—feces, urine, vomit, semen, and blood. The coroner says Jennifer's mouth was full of a concoction of the five, and that she'd suffocated before the throat wound had been inflicted. Neddy" *(Neddy Stuart's face appears, a happy press photo of him out on the town, curiously with another woman)* "was across the room, naked and painted with waste, hanging by his neck on the basement steps in what appears to be an attempt at autoerotic asphyxiation, that is, oxygen deprivation at moment of climax to intensify the effect. Officer John Spolski, a four-year veteran, agrees."

CUT TO

Officer John Spolski, Berkeley Police:

(*a lean man with a trim black mustache*): "It was a suicide. You just don't see a thing like that and think accident."

Bolt wiped a drop of gritty sweat from his temple, rubbed at the yellow stains between his fingers. "Now," he said. "Cue Neddy."

CUT TO

Neddy Stuart, from *Dripping Crackers: Live at the Ritz:*

(Neddy is sweaty and crew-cut, stocky but not fat, a man always ready to laugh): "Approaching and handling my sneakers is an exercise in nineties barf therapy. How many of you've ever actually barfed from a bad stench? Feeling brave, lady? Here, c'mere and smell this." *(He lifts a sweaty armpit to an attractive woman in the front row.)* "Come on, don't be afraid of it. Good clean sweat from the bod of me! Oh, you want the shoes." *(He sits on the edge of the stage and pulls his shoes off. He tosses one into the lap of the front-row lady, who screams and brushes it away. Crowd screams, laughs. Neddy smells the other shoe, deeply.)* "Nothing like your own ferocious fungoids. I toast my toes!" *(And, to the crowd's groan, he pours cheap wine into the shoe and drinks it. Crowd roars, Neddy exults through purpled, drooling teeth.)*

Bolt froze the frame, Neddy grinning with his shoe and the wine bottle. So many teeth, all stained. Eyes bloody and inflated, nostrils blasted open. Bolt saw the face, saw the madman, saw it, saw it *clearly*. Framed. Fucking *nailed*.

But . . . Bolt's head registered a negative.

"Damn it," he growled, and sucked his butt.

"What?"

"It's not clear to me."

"What's not clear to you?"

Bolt huffed. "Shit. Like you'd . . . ah, do you *feel* what this guy is, Tom? Is there anything in the eyes?"

"Dude, I'm no more than a secondary-smoked-out feeble mind right now. If you want me to look at this footage and see broad

philosophies about mental illness, let me drink a beer, smoke something real, and I'll wax. Short of that, he's just a sick dead fart."
    Bolt reeled in silence, barfing smoke. He was doing it again, the
death trip, the excess trip, the revolted deep strikeout journalist.
Journalist as snuff-film obsessive. Journalist beyond journalism. Just
too much for it.
    "Maybe," replied Bolt.
    But lines were meant to be read between. And Bolt's glands
thrived on the nonlinear, on the pit in the peach.
    "Overdub," he said.
    CUT TO
    (Bolt's voice accompanies a newsreel of funeral footage; several
famous faces appear): "They came in droves to pay respects.
Neddy's actions in his basement were forgotten at the closed-casket
funeral, and only his devotion to his art was embraced, his mace in
the eyes of fear, his act. Ace Arlington's brief eulogy summed up
the congregation's sentiments."
    CUT TO
    Ace Arlington, dark glasses, dark day, bright tie:
    "We feel the tremendous loss of Neddy, the loss of life, of his
laugh. His laugh was a blast of fresh, unlocked self. A wake-up call
to every comedian content trying the true. You cannot trade for
Neddy's realistic aura, or his sensibilities. You can only live them
in honesty."
    CUT TO
    Bolt, interviewing Richard Appleseed, stand-up comedian and rival:
    "Would I call him a genius? To put it in Neddy's words, the same
way I would call my toilet a throne. He was fearless, therefore
flawless. He did his scatology with so much glee, people laughed at
the honesty of it. Scary as he was, comedy needed him."
    "Your feelings about Neddy are well documented. Are you glad
he's gone?"
    "That is a s----y question. Just low class, man." (A pause, and
then sudden close-up.) "I'm ecstatic he's gone. We needed him, but
the need evaporated. We'd seen enough."
    CUT TO
    Bolt with Theresa Angelino, Neddy's ex-lover and fiancée:
    "Did he make you laugh offstage, too?"

"Rarely. He'd joke, but mostly self-deprecating stuff. Onstage he could make me shiver. Offstage, even his turn-ons were darker, and life was just harder, you know?"

"Sexually?"

(Chuckle.) "Hmm, sex with Neddy. He made the earth shrug."

Bolt noticed Tom grinning. "This guy was a winner with the chicks, wasn't he? Talk about getting your shit banged out.

"Bring up the next clip," said Bolt, grappling with focus. Tom was distracting no matter how much smoke he blew at him. But Bolt couldn't do the machines alone.

CUT TO

Neddy, from *Feel the Bowels Move*, Yuks Comedy Club, San Francisco:

"I've taken pictures of some of my more perfect poopies." *(He brings out a series of five-by-eights and starts passing them into the audience.)* "Check them out liberally. There's length and girth info on the backs, as well as location. This one's from the Port Authority, New York City. Someone once told me it was a nice place to piss but I wouldn't want to shit there. Well, I cranked one of my best into that hairy tan toilet. Here, check it out. Notice the anal curve right here. Come on, lady, not even for the novelty of it?" *(Man with lady grabs for the pics—the crowd explodes.)* "YEAH! See? *He's* not afraid. Why are you all so afraid, so disgusted, so *polarized* by manifestations of bodily function? Lady, you won't have it, but this guy you're with scoops up those pictures with the aplomb of an *expert*. Mister, if you don't mind my asking, what's your name? Greg? Okay, great Greg. How many times a day do you go pinch one off? What's that? Four and a *half*?" *(Crowd roars).* "What's wrong, you have a butt-cheek removed? A half, you gotta be—what?" *(A dim, unamplified voice pipes: "Greg used to take poop pictures in college!" Neddy howls and falls to his back. The crowd bursts like an extended flare at the improvisation, and Neddy sits up, applauding.)*

CUT TO

Richard Appleseed:

"He just wanted us all to *understand*. He told me once that he would s--t himself onstage, but not let on to the audience. And if you look at the Fillmore show, like the last five or ten minutes" *(quick clip of* Fillmore Halloween Freak Show) "and we see that, indeed, he's picking at the seat of his pants."

"I'm now officially loving this," said Tom dryly, sucking down more coffee.

Unprecedented, thought Bolt. There it was, frozen in effigy before his eyes—Neddy Stuart's fingers digging deep. "There's more where this came from, Tom. More adrenalizing footage, compiled at request. Miles and miles of shimmering tape."

"Lick me wet," replied Tom, slumping in his chair.

CUT TO

Neddy, from *Feel the Bowels Move*:

"I went for a walk today in Golden Gate Park, a pleasant little constitutional to relax my glands. Check out some of the neat stuff I found." *(Giggling, he pulls a large Ziploc bag onstage and proceeds to snap on a pair of rubber gloves; the audience is abuzz and curious.)* "A syringe! Another syringe!" *(Items begin hitting the stage and members of the audience cringe as they clatter by.)* "What's a matter? You don't like getting close to your own garbage, you sick slobs? Whup, a broken syringe, a tampon, another tampon, four soiled condoms, and a wet mound of *stuff* that I believe is a puked-in, balled-up Burger King bag. I'm curious. Are all your parks active over-the-counter pharmaceutical volcanoes? San Francisco is a very tolerant city." *(He yanks the gloves off and tosses them with the rest of the garbage. The audience is muffled.)* "But I think the best features of your park system are the hairy unshowered bipedal vending machines that come up and ask for change. I stuck quarters in seventeen of the suckers before I realized I hadn't gotten any smokes."

CUT TO

Richard Appleseed:

"He only did his act maybe once a week. He was very careful ... more like *fearful* of burnout. He was very smart. The act was always fresh, if not to the crowd then to him, and that may be more important. He was a hobbyist with a gimmick that caught on. That's rare."

CUT TO

Neddy, a year earlier with Bolt:

"We all live in mortal fear of the rebellion of our own bodies, from the first helpless classroom erections of puberty to the terrified confusion of a young woman finding out she may be a lesbian in a heterosexual world. From the darker forgotten corners of sickness, and aging, to the doomful day you find you cannot do something you once could. Maybe after my show we're all more aware the rebellion's coming."

SPACING FOR SCENE BREAK

"There's our teaser," said Bolt. "Break for commercial after that." He sighed, again stuck on the frozen image of Neddy in midword. He sipped cool, thickening coffee, stared at Neddy, then closed his eyes. Everything in him was moving, the coffee down his throat, pulsing towards his stomach, into burn, into acid and heat and fallout. How had Neddy ever come to love this process? "Nothing is created but waste," Bolt mumbled.

"Say huh?"

"His shit obsession, his body rebellion. All the processes depend on chemical breakdown. Waste."

"Real deep, Bolt. Jesus." Tom shrugged at Bolt's glare. "Sorry, dude, but why buy into this dog? Let's get it done."

Bolt shrugged. "I dunno. I'm into it."

Tom laughed. "Well, any half-ass born with decent public-speaking ability can make his material sound like art."

"Even me?"

Tom laughed again. "Ratings were up last week, right?"

Bolt nodded and finished the coffee.

"Fuck, man," said Tom. "I gotta take a leak."

Deep, raspy sigh from Bolt. "Me too."

"Time check?"

"10:42."

"Bagel shop is still open. I'm gonna go whack it. You want anything?"

"Yeah." Bolt fished two bucks from his wallet. "Onion with butter. No cream cheese."

Tom scurried out, and Bolt lit another cigarette. Silence, and a frozen image of Neddy. Neddy the Killer. The Shitter. The Artist. Bolt couldn't help calling him that over and over.

He set aside his notepad and opened the folder of police photos he'd obtained from a friend downtown. Photos of the crime. There's one of Jennifer Jacobi hardened into a few inches of waste, her head lopped to the side against the rim of the tub, her mouth stuffed with a divot of feces, her throat like burger. One of the basement. Newspaper was spread all over the floor, soiled as if by an entire kennel. And one of Neddy. Comic, manic, irrepressible Neddy, his body inert and prone halfway down the basement steps, his neck corded and puffy, his face gray shades of anger. The rope ran taut to a dowel rod in the door, your basic towel rack, but reinforced for one ulterior reason—the prolonged orgasm. Neddy was nude, and hairy as a jackal. His hands were in his crotch.

Bolt had to suppress himself, and swallow the revolt. The coffee boiled in him, wanting its own chance at a second cup. *Damn.* His bladder cried wanton compression. He had to stop this, for now.

He went to the bathroom gnawing on his tongue.

At the urinals, Bolt moistened the ricochet sprays into his flesh and clothing, thinking of the blue tile in front of him, absently rubbing the underside of his cock. Lydia was going to give him holy-mother-hellfire in the morning. No matter. Shows like this one sent ratings through the proverbial roof, shows of fame gone bad, of art gone arguable, art gone dead, taking the artist with it. Lydia would look into his eyes and begrudge him small profanities and testy content. She would look sexy doing it.

His empty bladder now allowed for arousal.

The deserted bathroom echoed droplets, strokes. And Bolt's mind, simmering in the musk of Lydia, echoed police photos. Shit divots and hamburger, ropes and sewer gas. Lydia's brown flesh in bondage, Bolt in flames, and bloody ruptures through tight trusses.

Bolt went limp, and lamely traded for a cigarette in his fingers. He lit it without washing his hands.

SPACING FOR SCENE BREAK

Tom returned with a small bag o' bagel, and they rewarmed their seats. "What's next?"

Bolt sniffed bagel, took a distant, crunchy bite.

"The dark stuff."

CUT TO

Ace Arlington, stand-up comedian:

"Neddy hit a point where the success cramped him. He suddenly was pigeonholed in shock-comedy and had a lot of trouble being funny after that. The glee left his act, and that was the only thing keeping his material that one inch above credibility."

Bolt nodded. "Good." Fresh coffee, fresh smokes, the world was turning. "Now, do the fart with the voice-over."

Tom paused. "You sure? Didn't Lydia give you hell about that?"

Bolt grunted affirm.

Tom shrugged. "Whatever, dude."

CUT TO

Neddy, from *Dripping Crackers*, with Bolt's voice-over:

"Neddy's material corresponded with his decline. Many fans and industry people agreed this particular onstage stunt was the beginning of the end."

(Neddy onstage.) "Got a good one, oooo, oooo, got a good one!" *(He rolls onto his back with his feet up by his ears, eyes glittering down to the lighter in his hand. He puts the flame up against his crotch and a sudden puff of blue detonates. The crowd goes nuts, and Neddy is hysterical.)*

Tom chuckled. "This guy . . . Lyd's gonna have your ass."

Bolt blew smoke, tapped ashes. "It's a dream I have, Tom. Next clip."

CUT TO

Neddy, Keswick Theater, Philadelphia:

"Oh, my loving b---h. 'Put the seat up, put the seat down, the toilet paper should come over the top, and do you *have* to leave those dirty books on the counter?' Couldn't she understand that that bathroom is my bread 'n' butter? My truest revelations have come while in the throes of excretion. That *push, that stretch,* that extended moment of *body.* I told her. She didn't buy it." *(Mild laughter.)* "So I said, 'Why don't you go douche or something,' which was a dumb thing for me to say since I know full well feminine hygiene jokes peaked and were exhausted five years ago." *(Nothing from crowd.)* "Come on! HA! LAUGH!" *(Some men in the crowd hoot)* "Oh, I get it, the douche thing isn't politically correct, right? Now I'm politically *impotent* as well! No, no I'm not. It happens to a lot of men, *but not to me!* It's the slut's fault, my slutty wench! Her hairy c---h tastes like chewing tobacco and she

refuses to let me smell her s--t. What? What? F--k you, slut, you f----g semen squirt, you cruel mewling c--t! Eat bran! Eat it! F-----g EAT IT, it'll make your s--t float! You know you're getting enough bran when your s--t *floats!" (Abruptly he leaves the stage; the audience is buzzing, but confused. Neddy never comes back out.)*
CUT TO
Bolt, outside brownstone:
   "Neddy's material intensified, went further, and as a result, his personal life became enflamed."
CUT TO
Theresa Angelino:
   "Of course he did drugs. Who doesn't at that level of success? His favorite was acid because he giggled so much. It made his gross spells funny to him, and ... well ... he would drop acid and take half a box of chocolate Ex-Lax. Then he'd lock himself in the basement for hours."
CUT TO
Ace Arlington:
   "Drugs kill comedy, and just saying that anymore is a cliché. Ask anyone involved. Get on drugs, you're dead. Get off drugs, you got clichéd material. Talentwise, it's an all-around loss."
CUT TO
Neddy, from *Dripping Crackers: Live at the Ritz:*
   "I love chemicals. The all-natural jet-set people crack me up because they're so obsessed with purity of the body. What a losing battle those people fight. The air is the equivalent of a radioactive fart and they eat stuff with names like Nutri-Sack or GrowGland that they put in the blender with a mess of Chemlawn clippings to brew up a dinner that's a healthy snot-clot green. How 'bout a real dinner? Chicken McNuggets are deep-fried earwax, but after dosing on acid you can even dip those badboys in Vagisil and they'll taste pretty good."
CUT TO
Neddy, a year earlier with Bolt:
   "What is your muse? How do you channel this mostly ugly material into comedy?"
   "I just walk out there and do it. There's very little transition involved for me. I simply *like* it, and maybe that comes over in the

translation. I can't help it. I think about the weaponry of it ... the peristaltic strokes inside me that suck nutrients and leave behind stinking clay ... I dunno ... I can't be more poetic about this fascination."

CUT TO

Officer John Spolski:

"I must admit, when I was in school he cracked me up. But maybe I got too serious. Stuart even said it once in his act: 'You know you're getting old when *Playboy* no longer excites you to erection, and sick twisted comics no longer crack you up.'" *(pause.)* "After finding that girl, I doubt I'll ever laugh again."

CUT TO

Theresa Angelino:

"He chased me with it. Chased me with his f-----g turd all over the house. I was screaming, but he wouldn't stop laughing, and his hands were covered like he was baking fudge or something ... God." *(She covers her face.)* "I sound like him now. You see? You see what I mean? You see how he invades you?"

CUT TO

Neddy, a year earlier with Bolt:

"Put simply, we experience a moment of ultimate *vulnerability* during orgasm, bowel movement, regurgitation, and urination. Our bodies are at the mercy of the function at that moment, with total commitment to the act. We wish we had control, because that's what we're about. *That's* why these things are so private and somewhat embarrassing to us. We're stuck in time, open for the world to see. My body freaks out on me, so does yours. I just want to beat my body to the rebellion. I want to fire the first shots, and most times there are people around to see it. *F--k* my body. I will not be paralyzed by embarrassment, I will not let my body shut me up just because there's an uncertain chemical reaction going on inside me. No way. No way. Never."

CUT TO

Bolt, outside brownstone:

"And that last statement would serve as Neddy's defense against questions about his art, the whys. Unfortunately there will never be an answer to the whys of his downfall and death. We can attribute only so much to art. Yet, through it all, the poetic fascination was contagious, and whether you are a fan or not, it

becomes hard to deny that Neddy in the news was a hard thing
to put down."
CUT TO
Richard Appleseed:
   "No doubt, the bum crawls under your skin. I can't take a dump
without Neddy ... Boy, *that's* scary."
CUT TO
Theresa Angelino:
   "He'd purposely eat boiled onions in cheese sauce after a night
of drinking beer just because he knew it would stink the next day.
Finally, after all the s--t chases, all the Ex-Lax acid trips, I decided
I'd had my head held under the covers for the last time. That's when
I left him."
   "Do you still think of him, other than while doing interviews?"
   (Laughs.) "Going to the ladies' room is like visiting his tomb-
stone."

SPACING FOR SCENE BREAK

   Bolt stretched, felt the wet pickles of his armpits, the sticky
chew-toy between his legs. He felt so *loaded* with fluid, so ready to
flesh up and release it all. ...
   Tom cleared his throat, blinked pulpy eyes.
   "One last movement," said Bolt.
   Another cigarette would finish the night. Bolt scorched his fin-
gertips on the flame, and growled.
CUT TO
Neddy, *Dripping Crackers, Live at the Ritz:*
   "And now, finally, I leave you with a montage of advertising
hell. You've seen the commercials. You know it's not your father's
Oldsmobile. You know it's not your mother's tampon. But the world
around us and within us is much larger in scope. It's not your
grandma's denture cream either, and it's not your grandpa's colos-
tomy bag." (CUT TO *quick clip of Neddy belching into the mike.*)
"It's not your brother's coke habit, it's not your sister's dildo. It's
not your brother's girlfriend's middle-of-the-night moans, it's not
your sister's boyfriend's dripping coat hanger." (CUT TO *quick clip
of Neddy farting into the mike.*) "It's not your aunt's plastic surgery,
it's not your uncle's ruptured hemorrhoid. It's not your cousin's

cancer, it's not your second cousin's excited p---y even though you wish it was." (CUT TO *quick clip of Neddy vomiting into a bucket.*) "It's not your best friend's mother, it's not your girlfriend's mother, and it's not anywhere close to your own mother." (CUT TO *mix clip of fart-burp-puke.*) "It's not your son's bed-wetting, it's not your son's wet dreams with you in them. It's not your daughter's attractive mouth, it's not your daughter's panty drawer." (CUT TO *mix clip of four separate shots of Neddy's manic laughter.*) "It's not your wife's discharge. *(Manic laughter, belch.)* "It's not your husband's rape trial." *(Manic laughter, fart.)* "It's not me." *(Belch.)* "And it's not you." *(Fart.)* "It's not knowing anything except what comes out your end." *(Strutting across the stage with mike jammed down the back of his pants, alternately farting and belching.)* "And barring that, it's not your comedian's microphone. I only rented it and I gotta give it back. Good night." *(Neddy leaves the stage to final, roaring applause, and the screen fades to black.)*

SPACING FOR SCENE BREAK

The pregnant compression in the tiny editing room ruptured when Tom sighed and rubbed his eyes. "I just edited the life and times of Jabba the Hutt."

Bolt was nodding, but not at Tom's comment. "Yeah, I think we just may have nailed this one perfectly. I think we got him."

"Twenty-two minutes of shit noises," said Tom. "Christ, man, I don't think I want my name on this one."

"Let's wrap it up, Tom."

Tom kept shaking his head, shaking his head. Bolt blew smoke at him, but Tom had already fogged himself from view.

FADE IN

Bolt with microphone, in front of Neddy's brownstone:

"Neddy Stuart is gone, taken from us through violent and mysterious circumstances. His was in a consummate love-hate relationship with his fans, his friends, his women. We can only see what he offered each of us, and learn from that as best we can. To reiterate Ace Arlington's eulogy, Neddy Stuart's laugh was a blast of fresh, unlocked self. We cannot trade for his realistic aura, or his sensibilities. You can only live them in honesty." *(Long, emotional pause.)*

"I'm Bolton Marston. Thank you for joining us for this special edition of *Media Fog*. Good night."

FADE OUT

SPACING FOR SCENE BREAK

Tom stood and stretched.

"You're not done yet, Tom."

"Say *huh?*"

"One more thing you have to do."

"What the hell's left? You're not taking off, are you?"

Bolt scribbled a note, stopping twice to regrip the pen and wipe away grit and sweat.

> *Lyd—*
> *I want the credits to run white on black, in total silence. It's ridiculous, it's beautiful, it's everything Neddy was and if you fuck with it, I'll hurt you.*
> *—Bolt*

He handed the note over. "I want you to go back and restore every curse word below 'shit' level. All the bitches, sons of bitches, bastards, asses and holes, pussies, dicks, cocks, goddamns, and damns. All restored."

"Come on, man." Tom shook his head. "It won't wash."

"Fuck the wash, okay? Just do it. Then put the tape on Lyd's desk with this note. I'll see you tomorrow."

Bolt was at the door.

"Yo, Bolt," said Tom.

He turned.

"You're beyond prick."

Bolt scowled, regarding rat-Tom as if he were as pink and veiny as a pornographic erection.

"So die."

SPACING FOR SCENE BREAK

The drive into Berkeley was short, the air warm and the windows open to stereo pulse. The breathing was clean and once in the hills he slowed to take in the lights. Below him was the city. Far to his right, burnout. There was no smell. Only the pleasant fatigue that came with putting another show in the can, a heavy, useful show. One that made him bloat with want, with obsession and excess. One worthy of being his last.

Neddy, he thought, *oh God, Neddy.* I've fucking *digested* you.

SPACING FOR SCENE BREAK

His ego-armored bowels moved within him as he downshifted and pulled up to the brownstone—notoriously close to the design owned by Neddy.

Ouch, he squirmed. A belly cramp. Livid, his innards. Endlessly, everything endlessly. The intestinal sexual cycle never stopped, like breathing, like some red-flesh photosynthesis. This would go on forever. He caught the first tendril of himself in his nose, like the loose thread of a suit jacket. He was foul, oh God, sometimes he wondered how he was able to generate something so foul even in a breeze. Something must have died inside. Bolt thought of Neddy then, and smiled, a truer manifestation of the comedian possessing him sudden as climax. A clip of unused footage Bolt once thought extraneous.

CUT TO

Neddy from *Dripping Crackers: Live At The Ritz:*

"Think, women. For what is the True Man, but the Ugly Man. His drool like blood, his teeth clogged with chomped intestine. His cock hard, wanting to scoop his food and his women, wanting more than God for his crackers to drip dip. Over his fingers, down his wrists, into his sleeves. For my sanity, *I, Ugly Man, MUST FUCK!*"

Neddy ate it all, Bolt knew. Died with a clean plate. Lived for the bloat of gorged satisfaction. For the tribal manbeats, the up and down, pounding, pounding, pounding like a fist on the family table, beating up, in, and off. Smashing, demanding, *taking.* Neddy's Ugly Man: Appetite, teeth, maw, belly, and shithole. Balls and fucktool. Cursed forever to suppress hunger . . . a terroristic turnabout misleading instincts and detaching phallus. Scaring, scaring real bad. TO NEDDY: You think I'm fucking scared?

Moist and drippy. Tasty.

What men want.

The brownstone appeared dark, but Bolt rang for apartment 3. A moment passed. His head slumped against the security cage as he felt into his front pocket, moving the contents aside so he could grab hold of himself, sport some hardness, utter some fuck chants.

"Hello," came the voice from the speaker.

"Lydia," he mumbled. "It's me." He gripped the cage for delirious support. He scrunched his butt cheeks and began to shake.

"Bolt?"

"Yeah."

"What is it? I hope this isn't a desperation call. The show's done, right?"

Her voice was stuffed with crumpled sandpaper. Sweat was coming on, his cock was responding well to his hand. "The show's fine, Lyd. I just . . . need to talk."

"It's late—" Then her voice softened. "What's wrong?"

Genuine concern, indeed, like a rash, like affection, like working-partner trust.

"Just a rough time . . ." The pressure in his nethers suddenly eased thanks to some gaseous restructuring, and he sighed. "Just wanna talk."

There was a sigh from her end. Then the gate buzzed. Bolt moved in, opened the front door, and went to the far end of the hall, where Lydia's door creaked open as he approached. He was shuffling, trying to unbuckle without falling. Trying to hold his crotch and his wicked sphincter at bay.

"Lydia," he croaked.

"Bolt?"

And the door was punched wide, Lydia agape at Bolt's flopping trousers falling to his ankles. Her shock froze her. Bolt kicked off his shoes and stepped out of his pants, stepped on the contents of his inside-out front pocket: a crumpled box of chocolate Ex-Lax. His sweat-yellow briefs came next, and his erection bounced free between his shirttails. For a moment Bolt thought for sure Lydia was about to laugh behind her hand, so sure that he saw her teeth. But then he closed and locked her apartment door.

"Bolt?"

Lydia took three steps back and hugged her T-shirt, and now, suddenly now, she was scared. But Bolt couldn't care. She was clad for bed in shorts and shirt, clad in a chocolate-colored flesh Neddy Stuart could only dream about. Bolt's bowels gave way then, spraying violent and healthy down his legs, across the floor, on Lydia.

The rest was a magnificent party. Tribal manbeat was in his ears, in his loins, his stained socks in her mouth, and all at once it wasn't his parents' cars or hygiene products; it wasn't a comedian's favorite routine; it wasn't his salutation to a dead artist; it wasn't his producer's sticky, trembling hands stroking him at knifepoint; it wasn't his ambition; it wasn't spite; it wasn't relief.

It was full body commitment. Wondrous. Slathered. Potent. Fragrant as burnt muscle. A deep need he finally grasped and splinter-pulled from himself like gristle from a healthy womb. Natural and unnatural. Comedic and evil. An emptying of a human male. Flushed tubes. Clean systems. New meat. Fresh crackers.

Death in a bathtub.

SPACING FOR SCENE BREAK

When the puckery dilation subsided, and Bolt's heart stopped for a while, thoughts could wander to darker lust. He wiped his mouth and fingered his cock. He lifted the twisted, saturated sheet from the tub and stared at Lydia, her eyes open and tempestuous.

For the benefit of the audience, he looked deep into her camera: "I, Ugly Man, cannot be more poetic about this fascination."

Standing O.

Bolt fingered, fondled, twisted his reality into wet and tongueful gasps. He felt himself growing fatter, hairier, twisting like a jackal into a palm-stiff erection and, to his shuddering anticipation, a Lydia-soaked noose.

As the fabric tightened around his neck, Bolt started laughing. Neddy Stuart was suddenly diminished, a simple has-been. The revelation smacked him with tenpenny nails and his erection came full circle:

Neddy never dared do *two* shows in one night. To imitate the master was to become the apprentice; to be more prolific than the master was to become the *god*.

COMMERCIAL BREAK

Intimates

MELANIE TEM

Having suffered through the 1992 L.A. riots and the nonstop coverage of same, you can believe me when I tell you that the two words most often used by our local media were anger *and* fear.

However, when describing the emotional texture of this city, those selfsame newscasters were curiously reluctant to use a third, equally important word:

Loneliness.

So MELANIE TEM's written a whole story about it.

Melanie's short fiction has appeared in Skin of the Soul, Women of Darkness, *and* Best New Horror. *Collaborations with her husband, noted fantasist Steve Rasnic Tem, have seen print in anthologies like* Post Mortem *and* Chilled to the Bone. *Two of her novels (*Prodigal *and* Wilding*) were published by Dell Abyss;* Making Love, *a collaborative novel written with Nancy Holder, and the first of a projected "demon lover" series, was also released by Abyss in 1993.*

"Intimates" has Tem tackling a favorite splatterpunk theme— the horrors of urban life. It's a sad, poignant effort. One which acknowledges just how difficult it's become to give of ourselves.

Most of the time, anyway.

*J*oyce dug her nails into the man's back and twisted her head passionately against the arm of the couch. Her neck hurt. The romantically dimmed light was in her eyes. The tape of love songs had ended, and in the silence his panting sounded ludicrous.

He was working at the zipper of her jeans. She ran her fingers through his hair. It was dry; she didn't like the feel of it. "Stop," she moaned. "I'm a married woman." He paid no attention. Letting one arm dangle off the edge of the couch, she whimpered, "Oh, I shouldn't be doing this."

He passed a hand over her breasts, which were still confined by the bra he hadn't yet unfastened. In a husky voice that almost made her laugh, he murmured, "This is awful hard for you, isn't it, honey?"

It wasn't. He wanted it to be hard for her, but it wasn't. He wanted to be having an affair with a woman who felt guilty, but Joyce didn't.

The small excitement she'd managed to work up evaporated instantly, but they went ahead with the sex anyway. As soon as she could, she got up to rewind the tape.

The man lay on her couch with his heavy white legs spread and his brown socks still on. She averted her gaze from his pink and wrinkled penis. He didn't say anything. He was breathing normally and looking at the ceiling. She might as well not have been there.

"I want to show you something," she said, as she'd planned, and went to get her photographs from under the clipped coupons and folded paper sacks in the bottom kitchen drawer. When she came back into the living room she said again, "I want to show you something," and switched on the gooseneck reading lamp. The man flinched and shaded his eyes. She spread the pictures out on the carpet. "These were taken a long time ago," she explained. "Before I was married."

He glanced at the photos lined up across the linty rug. She could see that he wasn't much interested. Somehow, she'd thought he would be. She straightened the pictures, her fingertips just grazing the edges.

"Not bad," he yawned. "Your hair was longer then." He sat up and pulled on his pants. "Well, I guess I better get going."

Joyce nodded. She gathered up her pictures and slid them safely back into their envelope. She let him kiss her good-bye at the door, having decided that she wouldn't be seeing him again.

Joyce and her husband had given up trying to have children years ago, and at about the same time they'd run out of things to say to each other. Their lovemaking had become infrequent and purposeless. There wasn't much for Joyce to do during the long days while he was at work, and when he was home he was always interested in other things. This was the most intimate relationship she'd ever had.

She sat at the kitchen table and laid the manila envelope of photographs in front of her. She centered it, smoothed it. She slid out one photo and looked at it for a while. She took scissors out of the drawer in the table and, bending close, snipped very carefully around the outline of her long straight hair in the picture. Then she put the mutilated photo back in the manila envelope and slid the envelope under the bags and coupons in the bottom drawer.

She went into the bathroom and turned on the light. Carefully she adjusted the mirror. Leaning close, she snipped a lock of hair from a spot on the back of her head where it wasn't likely to be noticed. With a damp rag she wiped out the sink in case any hairs had fallen, and she put the rag under the dirty clothes that were already in the hamper. She settled the mirror back in its usual place and shut off the light before she left the room.

Carrying the slick loop of photographed hair between the index and middle fingertips of her left hand and the silky loop of real hair between her thumb and ring finger, she used her right hand to address an envelope to the man who'd just left. Both locks of her, the actual and the pictured, were parts of her, and she didn't have to decide which was real. She put them both into the envelope, sealed it, and put it out for the mailman to take, with no note and no return address.

Curiously Joyce let her fingertips linger over the soft nipples until they peaked and hardened. The woman in her arms sighed happily. "It's hard to believe you've never done this before."

"I learn fast."

"I knew you would." The woman took Joyce's face in her hands and kissed her mouth, then slowly slid down between the sheets, kissing as she went. Joyce waited. The woman's hands eased her thighs apart, and her tongue probed. Joyce willed herself to relax, and acknowledged a slight excitement, a small rising. The woman came up smelling pungently of her, and kissed her lips again before Joyce could turn her head away. "You're lovely."

"Thank you," Joyce said with some effort. The woman wasn't really talking about her. Joyce doubted either of them could describe the other when they were apart. "So are you."

"Now," the woman whispered, "you do it."

Lying on her back with her arm under the woman's shoulders, Joyce found herself thinking about the drive home and dinner to be served when she got there. This morning, planning ahead, she'd put chili in the crockpot. Her husband got home at six. "No," she said. "I want to show you something."

"Wait." The woman rolled over onto her stomach with her face to the wall and her fist between her legs.

"I want to show you something," Joyce repeated. She had set her purse beside the bed, so she would be ready. Now she snapped it open and withdrew the photographs. She lined them up on their envelope across her lap. Beside her, the woman gasped and groaned. Joyce glanced at her and decided she should say, "I'm sorry."

The woman turned onto her side. "That's okay," she panted. "You'll learn. I'll be the one to teach you."

"See? These were taken years ago, before I was married."

The woman raised herself on one elbow and surveyed the photos. "Oh, Joyce, you were beautiful. You still are." She touched one picture, brushing it a little askew but righting it before Joyce did. "That's a nice shot. The red of the wine in the goblet makes your breasts glow." She reached over and rested her hand lightly on Joyce's breast. "As though your blood is running hot, and close to the surface." She bent and kissed the slope of Joyce's breast. "Who was the photographer?"

"The father of a college friend. He was a frustrated painter. Some of the poses are pretty artistic, don't you think?"

The woman had stiffened, and her grip on Joyce's breast had tightened. "A man? You posed nude for a man?"

Joyce shrugged. "He had the camera."

"And there was a price, too, right?"

"Not really. We slept together a couple of times, if that's what you mean."

The woman pushed at Joyce's chest and knocked the pictures to the floor. "That's disgusting. That's real porn."

Joyce pulled away and crouched shivering beside the fancy bed. She picked up her pictures one by one, checking carefully to be sure that none had been damaged. "You don't understand," she declared under her breath, and began to put on her clothes as she left the room.

"You disappoint me, Joyce!" the woman shouted after her.

Joyce paused outside the woman's house to make sure the photographs were safely back inside her purse. Then, still buttoning her dress, she hurried down the long, wide, artistically curving white pathway between perfect hedges and planters, all the way to her car.

Her husband worked late that night. Joyce ate a bowl of chili by herself. It wasn't quite spicy enough. Her period had started, but she never had any symptoms other than the blood itself.

After she washed and dried her dishes and put them away, she got up on the stepladder and took down a clean, empty jar from the assortment on the top shelf. She took it into the bathroom and let her period flow for a few minutes into the jar. Though it seemed like a lot of blood on the pad, it hardly covered the bottom of the jar. Still, its red was rich through the glass. She screwed the lid on tight.

She hadn't written down the woman's phone number, but she remembered it. The answering machine was on. She didn't leave a message.

While she drove she held the jar between her knees, wedged against the steering wheel, so it wouldn't spill. When she went from the car to the ornate front door, she put it under her sweater, where it protruded like her own belly.

She rang the doorbell and waited. She knocked several times with the brass knocker, just to be sure. No one answered.

Her skin was cool where the jar had rested, and the ballooned-out place in her sweater didn't settle back flat. She unscrewed the lid, tilted the jar, and began to dribble her menstrual blood onto the flawless white path. The blood—her most intimate secretion, from as deep inside her as she could go—made a pale pattern, but she wasn't sure that anyone would know what it was. Moving steadily backward, she timed it just right, so that the trail of blood ended just when she got to her car.

Then she drove home, stopping on the way to throw the empty

smeared jar into a dumpster behind a grocery store. When her husband got home, she was watching the evening news.

The boy rolled off her and lay on his back with his knees drawn up, trying to catch his breath. Twenty years older, Joyce wasn't winded at all. "That's all there is," he gasped. "Jesus, lady, you're gonna wear me out!"

As convincingly as she could, she murmured, "That was nice."

"I'm gonna buy you satin sheets," he informed her, still breathless. "These damn cotton things are murder on the knees."

She laughed and switched on the bedside lamp. Her thighs were sticky and her pelvis ached. Otherwise, she felt nothing. "I want to show you something," she said.

"Just don't be showing the whole town," he snapped. "The curtains are open, you know."

"So?"

"So I want you to keep the lights off until you put some clothes on."

Joyce knew that this was part of the fantasy that allowed him to be with her at all: the lonely older woman who would do whatever he wanted as long as he'd stay. Deliberately she walked in front of the window that overlooked the street, pivoted, stood there.

"I should have known better than to try to tell you a damn thing," he complained. "Why do you always have to be in charge? Like paying for dinner. How do you think that makes a man feel?"

"I want to show you something," she said again, and bent to get the envelope of photographs from the secret compartment in the lining of the window seat. She heard him curse under his breath. "Look. These were taken years ago. Before I was married. When I was about your age."

The boy took the stack of pictures from her and looked at them one by one. His face reddened. "Porno shots," he said. "I could have guessed."

"Actually, the guy was a pretty decent photographer. A frustrated painter," she said eagerly.

"Well, it happened before I knew you so I guess it's all right." He snorted as a thought occurred to him. "Christ, it happened before I was *born*."

She reached to reclaim her pictures from him, but he wouldn't let her have them. "Some of the poses are kind of artistic, don't you think?" she asked.

"Not the word I would use. God, look at that. Unbelievable." She tried to see which one he was looking at, but he turned his back to her. He was laughing now. He was making catcalls and sounds like throwing up. "Oh, Jesus, what are you doing in this one? With your hand?"

He turned toward her then just enough that when she lunged for the pictures she got her hands on them. She felt at least one of them bend as she pulled them out of his grasp.

She didn't tell him to leave. She locked herself in the bathroom with her photographs. Her husband was out of town on a business trip. She would be alone for three days.

Using the manicuring scissors from the bathroom cabinet, Joyce cut the likeness of her hand out of the photograph the boy had mocked. Then she clipped the pink tips from the nails of the same hand. She emptied the Band-Aids out of their box and deposited the half-moon nail clippings and the oval piece of slick paper into it. Pieces of herself. But they didn't seem like quite enough.

When she'd waited a long time and was sure the boy was gone, she went down the hall from the bathroom to the kitchen. There she took the meat cleaver from the knife holder on the counter and precisely cut off her right ring finger at the first knuckle. It didn't hurt yet, but there was quite a lot of blood. She put the piece of finger into the box with the nail clippings and the piece of photograph and put a rubber band around it to hold it shut. She would have preferred to send her whole hand, but it would have been harder to package.

She used all the Band-Aids and some tape and gauze to bind her finger. It was hurting now.

She didn't have the boy's address. She didn't know his last name. But he'd told her where he worked, so she drove there, dropped the box anonymously in the overnight video return slot, and drove one-handed home.

*   *   *

"Joyce." Her husband came up behind her while she was making up the bed, clumsily because she could use only one hand. "What the hell is this?"

She knew before she turned around that he had her pictures in his hand. "My pictures," she answered.

"I thought I told you to throw them away."

"They were taken such a long time ago. Before I was married." She hung her head. He was every bit as outraged as she'd hoped he'd be, and she watched him from under her lashes as she protested childishly, "I just couldn't throw them away, honey. I just couldn't."

"I won't have those filthy things in my house. My wife, posing for some dirty old man with a camera for a cock! Just look at this trash!" He was waving her pictures in the air, bending them and tearing their corners.

She followed him into the hall. "I'm sorry, darling. I didn't mean to upset you." She had her face in her hands.

"I was willing to forgive and forget, Joyce, but you lied to me. You told me you threw these things away. Otherwise I never would have married you."

"It's been eleven years," she sobbed. "Our anniversary was last week."

That wasn't true. Their anniversary was in February. But it didn't seem to matter to him.

"Eleven years of deception!" He was roaring now.

One by one he tore up her pictures until small shiny pieces littered the floor. Then he stormed out, car keys jingling like a weapon in his hand. "Where are you going?" she screamed after him.

"I don't know. And I don't know when or if I'll be back. You just think that one over for a while."

Even after he was gone, it was hard to stop the tears. She finished making up the bed and then, still sniffling, got the broom and dust-pan and swept up the bits of her photographs. She saw her own eyes, teeth, nipples glistening in candlelight, belly glowing wine-red, fingers, hair, pubic hair.

She went out to the garage and pried open the trunk that held her wedding clothes. It was hard because of her hand. From among the folds of white satin and lace she withdrew her duplicate set of photographs, which she hadn't looked at since the day a little more than eleven years ago when she'd hidden them here. Quickly she riffled through them. They were all here, but she didn't want to think about them intact right now. She put them back and closed the trunk.

The garden tools were on their hooks on the wall. It was her job to take care of the lawn and garden while her husband was at work, but she hadn't been able to do much lately because of the injury to her finger. She considered the array for a moment, then made her selections.

The clippers took her hair easily. The scythe took the skin off her arms. The axe was heavy and hard to swing, but it sliced her toes and then her foot with single blows. Joyce acknowledged a small and rapidly dying excitement at the thought that if her husband ever came home he couldn't help but notice all the small shiny pieces of herself that she would leave in his path.

For You, the Living

WAYNE ALLEN SALLEE

WAYNE ALLEN SALLEE deals in pain. Physical and psychological. Certain moments from his life may explain why:
  Stabbed on a subway car in the late 1970s.
  Hit by an automobile (near-fatally) in 1989.
  Afflicted with ongoing cerebral palsy.
  But save your sympathy; Wayne doesn't need it. This tough, ironic writer long ago transcended personal roadblocks to produce an amazingly prolific body of work, one that's resulted in over seven hundred poems and eighty short stories.
  *Sallee's specialty is street-level terror. Disturbingly original fiction, sensitively observed. With ordinary people confronting all-too-real horrors. Characteristics best displayed in such compelling short stories as "Rapid Transit" (*Splatterpunks I*), the 1992 police procedural novel* The Holy Terror, *and the upcoming* Speck Behind Bars, *a nonfiction study of infamous nurse-killer Richard Speck.*
  Incidentally, Wayne hails from and still resides in Chicago. He often uses that sprawling, decaying metropolis as the backdrop for his fiction. In fact, Wayne tells me it was downtown Chicago's peculiar geographical isolation—as well as its ubiquitous snowplows—which inspired the following novelette.
  A heterosexual love story, told from the male point of view. Definitely a minority opinion in this *book.*
  "For You, the Living" might be chastised for bearing a certain resemblance to better-known zombie fare like Night of the Living Dead. *Just as I suppose there's some justification in mentioning the word "AIDS," here, particularly in connection with this story's loathsome, sexually transmitted disease.*

Both insights would be missing the point. "For You" isn't really about AIDS. And it's certainly not about zombies.

It is *about relationships.*

As well the struggle to reaffirm life within the direst of circumstances.

Not a bad comment on Wayne Allen Sallee himself, come to think of it.

For Rachel Drummond

with thanks to Bob Maddock,
for keeping track of the
body count in Milligan's 137.

*T*he most fortunate ones simply let the veins in their foreheads bulge until they exploded. Others saw this as a form of suicide and tried their best to monkey the attempt. With only a few it was good to go; the colder weather made it that much more difficult. Others, their spines slid out of their assholes or they just went mindfuck and tried to embrace anything in sight, including their own intestines.

Sherideen and I talked about the visceral aspects during the first days we met, after the plague made it to Chicago. Love among the viruses, we touched our fingers to each other's palms without worry of them splitting open like old lampshades. We took turns lying on top of each other in a Gold Coast apartment; the previous tenant was either dead, fled, or crazy in the streets thirty stories below. It's winter now; the only way you can hear them scream is if one of them makes it into the stairwell.

They don't last long in the stairwells. If they don't get shot right off by one of the Streets & San men, all the leg lifting makes the spinal cord sluice out that much easier.

No, the high-rises are safe. The view outside is that of the building across Guignol Street, but you can see the sun come up over Lake Michigan if it isn't overcast.

Romantic as hell with a woman in your arms. But now Sherideen's gone. I find myself frightened with the thought of my impending death.

They said it was politics that made strange bedfellows, but the same can be said for plagues. We never did get much information from the outside before everything went all to hell. But I met Sherideen MacLaren and that sufficed for me. A tender mercy in the last days of humanity. I know that things will never be back to normal. We will all be dead. This is the big time.

The virus was called Treats when it was big on the Southern coast. Like in trick or treat, as if it was AIDS and could be traced back down to one single entity, whether it be an African monkey or a twenty-buck bottle blond in the life on Bliss Street in New Orleans.

The damn thing evidently came out of a test tube in one of those underground Nevada bases, the kind you always read about in the tabloids. Little grey spaceheads at Groom Lake who love to eat strawberry ice cream. The things we got walking the streets now would love to power lunch on the nearest Treats-Negative's guts.

It has been suspicioned that the virus—which would have eventually involved inoculations—would be for anyone who tested HIV-Positive without showing the carrying signs of Acquired Immune Deficiency Syndrome. Yeah, I know we all call it AIDS. But what if this little journal goes unnoticed for decades or longer, and the remaining fringes of society have forgotten the luxuries of abbreviations. I guess they'd be S.O.L., huh?

Don't mind my delirium. It has nothing to do with Treats.

I want to tell you about some of the things I saw. And, after I met Sherideen, some of the moments we shared. Testaments of how hard it is to let go.

An aside here: remember that asshole saying, if you love something, let it go. If it doesn't come back, hunt it down and kill it. Treats affects the autoerotic system. Kind of the notion of people thinking with their dicks or gashes taken to the extreme. Either way, head shots take care of it good. Just like in those wonderfully spooky-scary zombie movies.

I'd like to think that this tale will have a happy ending. Thing is, you'll have to be the judge. I'm just the jury and the executioner right now.

"I'm terrified inside, Sher." I found out quickly enough that she didn't mind being called anything but Sherry, and that my early attempts at dialogue were like predictable lines in a low-budget movie.

"Of me, or of the plague?" Her sepia eyes, never blinking when she was listening closely.

"Both."

I think back to those words often. Hearing them echo in my head over and over, tumbling images like a hennaed woman in a yellow pillbox hat saying, "You'll just love Dallas, Mr. President."

Her voice heard over the sound of the rifle going off.

"Of me, or of the plague?"

"You'll just love Dallas."

So here goes. Typical day for me, I get up around dawn. Even if sleeping was hard in the summer months. Skittering screams like stupid bats, gunshots making head pops sound like cars backfiring. You get used to it. We never had any reason to change the clocks to reflect daylight savings time come October, but you can't help it; the sun comes up over Lake Michigan, even under a gauzy sky, and the *concept* of morning hits you like you're a vampire. On a sunny day, light bouncing off of a thousand Gold Coast windows.

For a while, back in the autumn, there were yachts on the lake. The owners afraid to dock. We shot up flares—I'm with what is called the gold team—the blue team works nights, natch—but they never came in. One morning in early October, they were gone. Maybe they tried crossing over to Michigan, though it is my understanding that the Coast Guard stations at Ludington and Grand Haven were shooting everyone on sight, signs of symptoms or not.

Treats started in the South, spread up through the Great Plains for some damn reason—maybe it was the Bible Belt's doing, who knew?—and into the Rust Belt. I have no knowledge of what is happening on the West Coast. Maybe this will be over quicker than I expected; some new and improved treatment to counteract this mess will slouch into Bethlehem to be born. Maybe Buddy and Jesus and Relling will get a chance to read these words.

There's always hope. Hey, if we can bomb the holy shit out of Iraq, who knows what the military can come up with under pressure. For right now, though, we're on our own. No help from Great Lakes or the Glenview Naval Station, if anyone is still out there.

The late February sky is the same color as the Treats-Positives' skins. Hell of it is, it's also the same color as my intestinal wall. I shot a hole in my gut a few minutes ago. Just before I started writing this.

And the only thing I feel is horny.

The last few weeks we've been headquartered in the 565 North Lake Shore Drive Building. When the shit went down during the dog days, we first thought that it was hallucinogenics in the water system that got people causing more trouble than welfare mothers. Then, when there were reports of gay men tearing up the grounds at Graceland Cemetery to fuck their dead lovers' corpses, the cops knew something worse was amiss. They actually used the word "amiss" in the papers, like in a crime novel.

It got worse right quick. We were lucky, being in the Loop. Good old Daley City. Bordered by the lake, the river, and a spaghetti bowl of interstate ramps. This being Chicago, the individual aldermen acted quicker than the National Guard armories. The 42nd Ward was us and we said fuck it. The city was fragmenting and we were getting little information. Unlike Baghdad, CNN wasn't sending anybody in to collate information on the weird outbreaks. Details were sketchy. The homosexuals around Diversey Parkway were being summarily executed. Most Northsiders fled to the suburbs; quick-thinking police in the high-income North Shore suburbs of Glencoe and Winnetka piled the to-be-expected corpses onto METRA trains and waited for the Treaters to climb aboard for their pathetic attempts at satisfaction. Switches were pulled at the train stations as often as those in the polling booths on Election Day— Cook County: Vote Early . . . and Vote Often!—and the Necrophiliac Express was back in Chicago to stay.

It is to City Hall's credit that we have lived this long. Since November, the Department of Streets and Sanitation has provided "martial law" to those of us stranded here in the Loop.

By the time the Treats-Positives were rolling into Union Station, hearty from eating out quite literally their companions and, in a few cases, themselves, the easiest thing to do was to run the brain-dead sexfucks into the ground with Chicago's infamous fleet of snowplows, then follow through and mulch them. Like on the commercial for the double-edged razor.

For weeks, all we could secure was the area within the North Branch of the Chicago River, Lake Michigan, and the Eisenhower Expressway.

Twenty blocks of office buildings and small shops. I was working in one of the latter, a comic book shop at Van Buren and Plymouth Court, when the first Treater rumors were hitting town. There were so many conflicting stories, and you can imagine how they would escalate amongst comic book-buying clientele.

There were tales of a space probe, even though the HTLV-4 treatment had already been introduced into test subjects at Pensacola Naval Air Base. It is the common consensus that it started there. But bring stories of the military into it and, well, there were space aliens with little grey bald heads who were causing it, tall blond Swedish aliens were equally to blame, as was a lizard race from Barnard's Star.

Customers big on reading the *Vietnam War Journal* and *Punisher* comics were equally big on saying that the virus was a result of the veterans returning from the Gulf War. Saddam's personal Operation Fuck You Right Back; the virus was what was really there at the baby-milk factory that got bombed the second night of the war. There was even an article in the *Trib* about blood donations that were tainted with a parasitic disease caused by sand flies, which is known as leishmania, and is treated by intravenous medication.

News reports were as hysterical as any single episode of Geraldo, and one of the last involved a reporter swearing up and down that the first Treaters came off a Trailways bus bound from Council Bluffs, Iowa. Streets & San said it was all bullshit; Caitlin Jurgens, the mayor's press secretary, said she thought it highly unlikely—a bus filled with a brain-dead driver and necrophiliac passengers had about as much of a chance of rolling down Interstate 40 as there was of a Republican getting elected mayor again. A City News Bureau staffer cut in and asked if anybody in the mayor's office had ever witnessed someone with Iowa plates hugging the median down Cicero Avenue.

That was about one of the last big laughs everyone shared.

Streets & San did a fine job of playing Eliot Ness and the Untouchables. Most of the Loop is under control, many of the corpses getting shoveled into the Navy Pier turning basin. Let Hammond, Indiana, fuck with them, which they probably will, come to think about it. We used to get all their piss water along Oak Street Beach.

So just before Christmas, S & S set up two teams to head north toward Yuppieville. Like I said, there always has to be hope. Blue team pulling graveyard, gold team day. If you know of Chicago's winters, then you know the city is damned proud of its Streets and Sanitation fleet.

My uncle, William Mamach, was a garbage man in the Twenty-Third Ward, twenty years until he died. I know the pride the drivers took. Also, it's common knowledge that a winter blizzard can make or break a mayoral reelection campaign. If civilization still exists when you read this, look up Michael Bilandic. Ask him about 1979.

There are two hundred and twenty-nine arterial routes covering just over fourteen hundred miles, according to a press release that is part of the information packets we all received upon enlistment.

So you're thinking, why the hell did I enlist, if that is the correct word to be using. For one thing, I can't leave the downtown area. I had been hoping to make a go of it—Sherideen and I both had—after it warmed up, maybe go down towards Louisville, Kentucky. We both have family from around there; Sherideen is from Cincinnati originally.

And there is a certain kind of adrenaline rush to doing this kind of work, I'll tell you. My dad was a firefighter out of the old Eggleston house, on the Far South side, and I could see how the job both frightened as well as seduced him. He was a twenty-year-old rookie in 1958, the year before I was born, worked out of LeMoyne Street when the St. Vitus Catholic School fire took a hundred lives. He loved it from that point on, the same way he loved the bottles of Kentucky Gentleman bourbon that eventually disintegrated his heart.

You can get jazzed on watching someone slouching under the elevated tracks, their pelvic bones tearing through pants and skirts like—and this is a strange image that always occurs to me—pita bread. Chunks of vertebrae falling from their pants legs like loose change. Holding a city-issued .38 firmly in my hands and aiming for the jawline. Because the impact made them spin around like stand-up circus animals in an arcade shooting gallery.

Most pragmatic: there were no jobs. The Board of Trade and the Merc were shut down. The restaurants had plenty of food stocked, but we didn't know how long that would last, so enlisting with S & S gave us priority of the muscle kind. All political. This, in a city where you get the mayor's birthday off if you are—rather, *were*—on the payroll of City Hall.

So, what was the point of working at the comic shop? Back when the occasional deadhead was a novelty, six months back, I was always having to call Capitol Distributors for relists on all the Herschell Gordon Lewis adaptations like *Blood Feast* and *2000 Maniacs*, the Anne Rice books on Lestat, Sid Williams's *The Mantus Files*, and necroerotic books like that. Right before the shit hit the fan, Eternity Comics had started a book called *Plan Nine from Outer Space, Thirty Years Later*. "Plan Nine" in the forgettable Ed Wood cult-classic involved raising the dead.

At least I knew more about books like those than ones involving characters with X's in front of their book titles.

Funny thing, though, how life imitates art.

Anyways, the mayor's office asked for as many volunteers as could be mustered. The city has nearly three hundred Navistar snowplows equipped to handle the spreading of three hundred tons of salt in blizzard conditions. This, again, from the press release. In addition to those, two hundred and twenty-five garbage trucks have been equipped for mulching up the mindfucks with their bone-dripping assholes.

Some of the guys and women I was working with were stragglers from the North Side. They looked to me for stories about the first days because I was in the Loop when it happened.

Plague stories, hey. I got a million of 'em.

* * *

The best thing about the whole mess was that I fell in love with the aforementioned Sherideen MacLaren, even if it was doomed from the start—the way writers feel about their novels and how they could be considered quick and torrid love affairs—and ultimately lasted only a few weeks. The worst thing I saw—to give you the big picture in a nutshell—out of all the atrocities, there was this high-priced call girl from an escort service out on Guignol Street. Rather, she used to be high-priced; there isn't much monetary value here anymore.

Anyways, a couple of Deputy Dawgs from the Sheriff's Department who happened to be at the Dirksen Federal Building when the city shut down caught up with the woman, Desiré Nix, giving herself up for food and/or toluene down by the Shubert Theater, Robert Morse playing Truman Capote each night for whoever the hell cared to see. They threatened to quote-unquote deport Nix out of the safe zones unless she gave head to one of the ugliest of the mindfucks.

The state cops killed her afterwards, but the most awful part was watching her give this brain-dead guy fellatio until she was actually sucking layers of the skin off of his dick. They videotaped both executions—the sex act and Nix with a derringer in the eye socket—and played it on the big screen at the corner of State and Randolph. Our own little Times Square. They kept the camera running, zoomed in on the man after his penis was a red, wet rag. Camera focused in nice on the guy wringing out the foreskin, still horny, the disease eating past his pain, squeezing deliriously until the veins in his forehead bulged and blood spurted out of his temples like he was a lawn sprinkler.

The last shot before fade was the Treats signature: the guy's spinal cord trailing behind him like wadded toilet paper. The drunk people in the crowd cheering. The county boys high-fiving and snubbing Streets & San and the Chicago P.D. Always a game between the law departments, even before Treats. The reason serial killers like Gacy and Eyler and Dahmer got off—if you'll pardon the pun—and got away with so much.

There are always victims, always sacrificial lambs. And on the night the video was shown on the big screen above Seno Formal-

Wear, what would have been rush hour on a Wednesday in September, there was all of a hundred people milling in the streets.

A few others were hanging from lightposts, winds whipping flags around the corpses: banners that once said that the Warhol exhibit was at the Art Institute through the new year.

The best and the worst.

I have, within the last fifteen hours, shot myself three times. Just to be certain that my fears are not unfounded. There are enough bullets left in the chamber that, after I have shot myself in the head, someone else can also kill him or herself, as well. I want to hope to God that that person will not be Sherideen.

But I have no hope left at all. I always wrote my best when I was low on hope. The delirium has made me forget to write earlier that I am/was/always will be a published author. I knew a lot of writers in different fields, but my tiny claim to fame was hard-boiled porn. Maybe you've heard of Mercy Fuck, Hollywood P.I.? Yep, those were mine. Are mine. Whatever.

I had given some thought to call my little narrative *Life During Gorktime*. The guys from Streets & San started calling the more stable Treaters gorks early on; seems some of the workers came of age during their tour with the reserves in the Gulf War and knew the word to be slang for anybody with a severe head wound. And the no-win situation here in Daley City is as much a lesson in futility for both sides involved as the desert war was.

Taking it further, if you will indulge me one of my last few indulgences before my suicide—the *greatest* of all the severe pleasures—one of my close associates, a brilliant writer by the name of Lucius Shepard, wrote a novel entitled *Life During Wartime*. This was several years ago, and the way the book chronicled a series of events in a man's life knocked me for a loop. Much more than anything Kerouac had ever done. Maybe this tale will do the same for someone.

The last time I saw Lucius, who is still among the living, I am sure, he was at Roger Williams College at Bristol, Rhode Island. After the writer's convention ended, he was headed for Borneo, of all places, to write a vampire novel. I often wonder about him, more so than my fellow writers in other cities like Mount Vernon or Detroit. Cities we lost track of early on. I think about whether or not the Treats virus will make it to Borneo.

And if it did succeed in crossing the oceans, I then wonder what Lucius is writing about now.

End of indulgence. I will do my best to keep this narrative from becoming disjointed. It is hard to concentrate in my current state. I feel like there is acid in my kidneys; that I have soaked my hands in Absorbine Jr. and aborted an attempt to jerk off. All I ever wanted to do with my life, all I ever felt whatever lesser gods there were expected of me, was that I just try to make sense of my time here. Not measure it with money or titles—hence, Mercy Fuck—not even justify it.

I suppose that I might have noticed the spasms and twitches sooner, but I chalked it up to the hypochondriac tendencies of the neurotic male. I was in love with a beautiful woman, she loved me in return, and that was enough to bunch my balls up and give me stomach cramps.

While everyone around me, both alive and dead, are cannibalizing each other, I continue to spit up my life in raw, undigested chunkages.

So here I am in the middle of February in a year that can't mean a damn thing to anybody anymore. Chicago's Loop continues on; we gain a little ground here, lose some there. No doubt about it, the Streets and Sanitation Department is doing a bang-up attaboy job of keeping us alive as long as possible. Sweeping Lake Shore Drive, Balbo, Grand Avenue ... downtown Chicago has always been surrounded by a spaghetti bowl of interstates.

All day long, we scrape the fuckers into Lake Michigan. I doubt if many other Treats cities have the advantages our geography allows us.

One of the leaders of the blue team, Mel Bland—he used to be with the DeKoven Street Fire Academy—swears that by summer we'll have cleared the mindfucks and headswells back to the Edens/ Tri-State spur out past O'Hare. Maybe so, but I sure won't be around to see that grand and glorious day.

It is so quiet in here. I can't believe that Sherideen wouldn't kill me, end my misery.

Sherideen MacLaren, the woman I fell in love with. How many times will I repeat that, like a litany? I can still smell the Chantilly in the air. That, and the coppery smell of my own blood.

But how could I have expected her to kill me when I'm too damn chicken shit to push my intestine back inside my body?

It was weird for a while, with only the occasional Treater shambling out of some far westside housing project. Soon enough, everyone was freaking. The aldermen north of the river and south of the Ike secured their neighborhoods like there would be no tomorrow. Gang crimes were replaced by sex crimes in the papers. Then there was no news from outside of the Loop.

Streets & San has done us well. We heard rumors that state cops out in the collar counties were shooting at anyone they damn well felt like. If you were in the Loop in August, well, fuck you.

Fuck me.

You hear a lot of stories out on the road. I wasn't the only one working the Loop on Treats Day. I started out by describing a typical day of waking up in the high-rise. We have a couple of men standing watch, but for the most part, we hear the Treaters before they've clawed open the doors and made it into the lobby stairwell. Sometimes, for fun, we'll dump buckets of shit on them, let them think it's some new anal gel from an upscale sex shop. Doesn't take much to fool a Treater into getting off. The plumbing in each building works erratically.

We head down to the lobby; the blue crew is waiting to cover us as we board the trucks. Mel Bland, the ex-fireman, was very fond of hunting out in Shelby County, and was able to blast a couple of heads off before the mindfucks could even move their hands towards their crotches and lunge forward.

Melvin was a good man, never let on to anyone that he had bone cancer. Found out about it by mistake, I did. Yesterday, my last full day, we killed a good hundred without losing one on our side. If you don't count me, that is. But I still wonder if it is all really worth it.

These salt spreaders we have are real cock-knockers. Diesel-powered, four-wheel drive, 240 horsepower, and three axles. Ten yards of galvanized steel in front to crunch and munch and crunch and munch the Treaters that cross their path. We flash the mars lights and they come shambling along; Mel's thinking is that the spinning lights create a perverse memory in their diseased minds of strip joints—he called them titty bars—and table dancers.

That's the thing. Most of them, I can understand. But the ones that keep wandering the streets, half-naked like it was the time of the apocalypse, I can't figure. I am completely unable to get into their heads. My only real suppositions are that the Treats virus operates on different levels of the subconscious. We all have our darkest dreams. Thinking in terms of how people react to your garden-variety delirium, whether it be based in the psychosis that little bald-headed grey men are monitoring your brain or the plain and simple fact that you watched your mommy fuck too many men with too little pauses while dear old dad was propping up the corner tavern with his elbow, it actually hurt my head to think about what fever beings were floating around in the heads of my once fellow men.

Submitted for your approval, I'm saying out loud in my best Rod Serling voice: here are a few things that happened to people before the Treats virus came along; some of this from the newspapers, a few from my college friend Mickey O'Malley, who worked sex cases out of Markham. Now this is supposedly normal men and womenfolk I'm talking about here.

There's the case of the man who sued his lover in district court for mental duress because he was forced to light bottle rockets and watch them shoot out of his aforementioned lover's penile shaft on the fourth of July. A street person was picked up, his arm and wrist in a fiberglass cast; the guy was jerking off so hard and furiously that his dick was cross-hatched with friction burns. He ended up dying from infection.

Our state's first woman-on-woman serial killer using a double dyke prong along Interstate 55 from Argo-Summit to Streator. This guy who had visions of vampiric immortality, going into the blind pigs behind the North Halsted gay bars, biting their ears off, trying just too damn hard to touch an erogenous zone. Hell, maybe he thought he was a fucking werewolf. Whatever floats your boat in that part of town.

Chicago was a sick enough place back when. Bars for epileptics with names like Seizure's Palace and Tourette Lautrec's; curio shop/trophy halls like Elviscera where you could buy the sperm or urine or you-name-it of dead celebrities, they took Visa, Mastercard, Amex, and Discover.

Rock bands that played Nolan Void's, right here in the North Loop, with names like Jeanne Splice and the Birth Defects, Renal Failure, and DeeDee Mau. There were about fifty autoerotic suicides or accidental murders in 1991 and we didn't even have this goofy shit showing up in our bloodstream.

How did you get it in the first place? Hell, I'm still not sure how I got it. Obviously, it backfired on the AIDS victims first; hence, Trick instead of Treat. Maybe health employees became the first invisible positive carriers; who knew where Treats Zero started out. Did I mention that some people think it actually came back with our troops from the Gulf? I'm sure I wrote that about three hours ago, back when I still had fear and my blood was warm. Truth is, I'm too damn weak to look back.

If I had a cuss box sitting next to me, it would be full of quarters. Remember: you can't get Treats from swearing. But you can get it from being passionate enough to close a dead Treater's eyes. One of the first guys out was a bit too compassionate; Joe Verve saw one girl lying there, with a sucking throat wound, and there would be no more oxygen to the brain. Her eyes were not staring wistfully like that girl in the closing scene of *The Grapes of Wrath*.

Verve tested positive in his urine sample seventeen days later. He chose suicide over mercy execution. Hung himself near the theater and we blowtorched the body down and scraped him into the sewers that don't connect to the pumping station near the DesPlaines fire station. Urine checks every Tuesday, Thursday, and Saturday. Blood tests on Monday, Wednesday, and Friday. For the seventh day, the Treats God rested. Probably played with himself and carried his bride Death by her nubbin like she was a six-pack of Hamm's.

Crimes of passion in a dumbstruck, libido-driven city.

I was writing about the plows: the only real down side about these babies is that the salt scrapers can't swivel worth a shit. They're hydraulically set, but some of the lead men have fun experimenting with the asphalt, curb, and gutter inserts.

Get those things going in tandem and you've got some great Treater-graffiti lining the Lake Street underpass. Crunch and munch. Like the commercial went, crunch all you want, we'll make more.

Actual graffiti that I saw and copied into my notebook a few weeks back, from the back wall of St. Peter's, bleeding over onto the Northern Trust Bank:

TREATS: A PLAGUE PROLOGUE

and so it was in that quick
breath of eternity which filled the gap
between Orwell's Year rotting forgotten
and the brimstone and stench of final
judgment, a plague and a pox hemorrhaged
from the bathhouses and tainted needles
of rust belts and scarlet garters, zippered
masks that held back bone chunks and skull
chinks, a grim shadow birthed in the veiled
past of Kilimanjaro and bred in the rectal
tissues and unsuspecting temple veins of
wretched hosts, and yes, as the living decayed,
Perdition's blind minions prayed thanks to
the God of Pain and his drink of antimony,
for his horrid boon, the Givers of Mutilation
and their bone-sawed visages, yet no one saw
Lovecraft's dreaming Cthulhu, the big kahuna
vagina dildo face hisself. Humanity's forsaken
gods witness not the blackness, and know not
that it is good

                              Positive Paul: 9/30/92

THE MAYOR OF PERDITION

in HIV streets floating mindfuck treats
beneath the moon of a severed seven
hunched, cross-legged, crashed

spewing black gouts from his ass
with a chant that would soon level heaven

11/11/92

Evidently, Positive Paul saw himself as some kind of emissary; it
was his corpse that covered the last words of his final poem. *His
home is closer than you dare dream, as close as a miniaturized
reaper's scythe, and you can get there faster than you can scream,
just two whores left, and one painfully slow writhe—*

Yea, poetry soothes the savage beast. Someone even took the trouble to quote e.e.cummings, though some of the poem was obliterated by fecal matter:

Babylon Slim
-ness of
_____

jolts of
lovecrazed abrupt

flesh split "Pretty
Baby"
to
numb rhythm before christ

Another; the author is forever unknown:

Her Treatongue an electrode
of elasticity, sparking
eyelids
and a zippered neck
with a gruesome grumble
of love

back to back and belly
to belly
at the zombie celebration

ball, he came
and the virus was his
forever to keep

in the windmills of his
    crime,
the Treats Man with his new
    bride
blundered, languored
and quite frankly fucked

he her nipples and it
was hard he
jammed his thumb

Ygor! It's alive! Alive!
they did the monster mash

I read that one in one of the subway tunnels. Part of the verse
was almost obscured by the person or persons who had been busy
painting the letter A in blood and brains along the walls.

The Scarlet Letter for the nineties.

But let's talk about monster mashes. I'm getting my second wind,
it seems.

There's this guy who strings the Treater's testicles around his neck
and tosses them to the gorks. They go after them like they were silk
scarves at an Elvis impersonator concert. The guy, nobody knows
him as anything but Beltram, sights in on the lucky gork who grabs
the grey nut, blows him or her away with a shot that goes through
the fist holding up the nut. Ba da boom, ba da bing.

So a few weeks ago, I'm shotgunning with this guy Hodge, used
to work as a messenger in the old Mandel building. He really got
into that kind of thing, he told me, racing his Miyata ten-speed
against the lights and the flow of pedestrians, hitting ice patches in
the winter and feeling the razor's edge of near death. Myself, I've
always thought the two safest kinds of people you could hope to

drive with were coppers and messengers. Reality-traffic was like a video game to them. No shit.

Hodge said it took balls to ride a bicycle in the Loop without a helmet or elbow pads; he used to tie a red bandanna around his forehead and let his long, curly brown hair flow behind him like he was a jumped-up Jesus in his own personal garden of Gethsemane, back in the days when there was real moving traffic to worry about. And there we were, rolling along Erie Street at a steady fifteen miles an hour. Rammed a couple of Treaters up against the drive-thru at the rock 'n' roll McDonald's, a 1959 'Vette still pristine in the front lobby.

Left them there, cut in two or pulped like roadkill, but still squirming. The new version of the planarian worm. One fellow's head flopping from side to side, his other head, the one attached to his penis, bobbing at half-mast with about ten feet separating the portions of the still-living corpse. Talk about sex drive.

Lust and death in the fast food lane, run down looking for their quarter-pounders and Happy Meals.

Radioed in for Melvin's team to follow through and give the Treaters their head shots. Onward and upward. Go to God, jerked to Jesus, laid a corpse, and all that happy shit.

America, the Beautiful. Oh say, can you scream.

Another guy I worked with, his name was Gomez. Looked like a young Jerry Lewis. Worked as a skip-tracer for this law firm, Lancaster & Frye. Dialing them digits, he referred to making the phone calls. One of the big clients the firm had was Freedom Military Sales. They'd offer GED and CLEP testing, Officer's Training Manuals and crap like that, get all the E-1s and E-2s to believe that getting reamed up the asshole was a good way to establish credit. The sales company was turning a sixty percent profit on the principal alone.

Crunch and munch we drive along scraping skinny asses off the streets, guessing the weight of the bigger ones by the sound they made when we run them over with the trucks.

Gomez told me how he called all these base housing units, to try and scam the serviceman's wife for possible assets in which to file a lawsuit. Pretend he'd offer her a Presidential Visa card or something. He told me that he was on the phone with this one skirt down in Rantoul, the armpit of Illinois, was telling him some cute thing like "God willing and if the creek don't rise," when this Treats-Positive from the Air Force base came out of her laundry room or someplace equally hinky and started chewing on her. I'm thinking, shit.

Now Gomez flashes this lopsided grin like half his face was in stroke position and says how Frye came into the main office—all the jazz about Treats was on the news at the time—and reached out to punch on the speaker phone. The fucker was getting off on it.

Reach out and touch someone. Hell, reach out and munch someone. Hey, I've got a million of them, and I'll sing "Danke Schön," too. Two, three, six, nine. Hit it, boys.

It kept scaring me the way Gomez kept smiling all the way down Ontario and back east on Huron to home base. Like a mass murderer recalling the frenetic, intimate moments before his capture.

Wild times. I like Gomez, though, because he doesn't mind that I slop on the Ben-Gay, more so now that it's winter. I guess I didn't mention that I have cerebral palsy. This time of year, the wind comes off the lake like a witch's tongue up my ass; I put a lot of the stuff on my back, where the spasms and throbbing are the worst. I still am surprised that I never knew that I was sticking my fingers through the skin over my shoulder blades for days now. Maybe the pain overrode the sex drive. Christ knows I never dated that much.

No, Gomez didn't mind the balm. But then, he was always putting Vicks VapoRub up his nose, so I guess everything evens out.

And he was working with me the day I met Sherideen McLaren.

Lying next to each other, touching but not stroking; there was more to this relationship. Whispering: laughing about weird graffiti; POP THAT COOCHIE on the Division Street viaduct, METALLICA SUX; old dog-eared ads for Club Lower Links and the Bop Shop. Gangbangers marking their turf with scrawls that identified the leaders as Chumbly the Great and L'il Pimple.

"Afraid of the plague, or of me?"

"Both."

afraid

It was during what would have been the middle of the holiday shopping season during normal circumstances. We were still laughing over an incident involving this old stewbum, Blackstone Shatner.

He used to sit under the Congress Parkway overpass and drink his Everclear out of a Dynamo measuring cup. Well, Shatner somehow tested Treats-Positive—blamed it on the damn Korean news vendors, because he "never shared his detergent cup with *anybodys*" and the weirdest thing occurred.

He had all the symptoms of a gork, as opposed to a mindfuck, the latter being quite a bit more violent and disparaging. The ultimate berserkers. Gorks more or less meandered around, exposing themselves or jacking off at appropriate moments.

Somehow, in some way I'll never understand, Shatner has turned into a self mutilating predator. Picture a fifty-year-old man with pepper hair and teeth blackened by survival in the streets long before there was any virus to worry about. He chews off pieces of himself; I guess it's similar to the symptoms of those with Lesch-Nyhan disease, where the muscular dystrophy causes the brain to act self-destructively. Never harms anyone else, like, say, a psychotic eighteen-year-old chihuahua named Tiny who would bite the hands, nose, and eyes of the hands that fed him. Thing is, no one with L-N ever lived past the age of thirty. I worked with a few at a summer camp at Bessemer Park, on the far South Side. Their knuckles were so swollen that they looked like they had tumors breeding beneath the skin. A black boy named Tommy had turned his skin grey; this other kid Richie actually laughed and giggled while he tore rinds of skin off of his fingers.

With Shatner it was much worse. Maybe the disease was in an early stage of mutation. That is a frightening thought; if Sherideen did indeed go positive because of me, then I hope to hell that she doesn't have to endure that bum's degeneration.

I hope to hell, because I don't hope to God anymore.

It is almost like Shatner is one of those stupid zombies you see in the splatter films. The S & S team knows this, but they let him live because, like I said, he doesn't harm anyone but himself. If you can call it harming.

The Streets & San team waits for those golden times when he drinks too much of his 'clear from one of the abandoned liquor stores around Van Buren, and he vomits up his guts, literally, ruined by the hooch long ago. Then he goes into a kind of feeding frenzy. Sits there like a kid with blocks and plays with his own internal organs before eating them again. Been doing it for weeks.

Gomez heard the yell, from somewhere above us. We were cruising down Chicago Avenue, the sun on its solitary way down past the Cabrini-Green housing projects a few blocks to the west. Lots of shadows stretching southwest across the street: a prize-fighter's broken grin. I flashed on some movement on the fire escape of the Lawson YMCA. All lime-green railings and wire stairwells, splashes of pre-Treats graffiti, gangs laying claim to turf. Gangster City. Vice Lords. Haddon Cobras. Dribbling down one wall, enigmatically, in neon orange: ALL LUSTRE IS BLACK, SIGNED PACO. The whole exterior like something out of a Klauba painting.

We hit the Mentor spotlights and bingoed in on a dark-haired woman five stories up, wearing a black raincoat. So close to the edge—geographically, not psychologically—that the thing was flapping over our heads like the Batman's cape. But, dammit, she *wasn't* cowering at the gorks in the window, reaching out towards her grabbing like it was a meat show in Vegas. No, sir and ma'am, Sherideen MacLaren was defiant. I later saw that she put out one of the gork's eyes with the heel of her shoe.

Sherideen Leigh MacLaren. I wonder where she will end up if she was lucky enough to be negative after her contact with me? Wonder, also, if she heard any of the gunshots. Or if she'll hear the final one.

The one that will end my life . . .

Saving her was easy. Hell, she would have been able to do it herself, if we hadn't been cruising by. We radioed Mel Bland a few blocks over, he picked off the gork Treaters in the windows, and I helped Sherideen down the five flights of the fire escape. One gork did try to follow, but his foot went through the space between the steps and he was caught dangling there.

Mel shouted out from his truck, "I've fallen and I can't get up!" like the gork was one of those actors in the commercials who faked being an invalid. I think that same actor was in the commercial for that wonderful device, the Clapper.

Anyways, Mel said this, laughed like a lunatic, and blew the motherfucker's head off. I think that even then the cancer was starting to eat at his brain.

Gomez was shouting at me to get back down so that we could

head back to base. I was too busy looking at a face that would make sane men drool. I suppose it was the cleft in her chin and a small birthmark smudge like mascara near her right eye that ultimately hooked me.

And my last days were changed, just like that.

I was totally dumbfounded when Sherideen showed interest in me. This is Chicago, after all, and I was used to everybody judging books by their covers. I wasn't quite a dog-eared paperback, but still. Sherideen was a Gold Medal original, I tell you. Sepia-brown eyes— did I mention that already?—with flecks of chocolate circling the nucleus, that fatal facial smudge, and this nose that looked like some artist had labored over it for weeks, a beautiful piece of flesh that surrounded two perfectly round nostrils. And she always smiled like she was mugging for the camera.

Besides the difference in our looks, all I had to mention was that, before the Treats virus, I worked in a comic shop part-time and wrote stroke novels on the side; my means at making a meager living . . .

In the old days, you tell that to a girl at a singles bar, you might just as soon say that you write splatterpunk horror fiction for a living. At least with the latter, you might get to go all the way with some ditz who thinks vampires are cool.

The first night together—not intimate, mind you—Sherideen told me that everything was fine in the area around the YMCA until a bunch of gorks came shambling up the stairs from the Dearborn Street subway. Trashed the abandoned Burger King on the corner before discovering the glass doors to the Lawson building. The subway line ran diagonal across the North Side, stretching west past Jefferson Park and O'Hare Airport. I could just imagine the ward aldermen coaxing the gorks onto the cutesy-titled Kiss 'N' Ride trains and pulling the switches Loop-bound. The el trains do run with some irregularity, so life does exist somewhere beyond our self-imposed boundaries. You can still take the A train, Mr. Miller.

Well, Mel Bland welcomed Sherideen and the handful of people who were staying at the YMCA, and holed up at the Salvation Army building across from Bughouse Square. The park John Wayne Gacy used to pick up his victims, back when serial killing was the most heinous of crimes. I'm trying to remember all the people who were there at the Y, but the only two I can recall were a couple of long-haired guys named Rory and Cousin Slick.

I spent as much time with Sherideen as possible. We joked with each other about our separate "factory defects," like scars from her bicycling and my 1989 hit-and-run. The other things like my receding hairline, and a number of scars that Sherideen received from working with iguanas at Lincoln Park Zoo the previous summer.

I think she might have made the observations about herself to ease my own insecurities.

Insecurity has *nothing* to do with my impending suicide. Let me make that clear right now.

The third or fourth week: the early morning sky an aqua color that only makes you more depressed because you are sharing the image with someone whose own beauty makes that near-dawn sky seem inconsequential. Does that make sense? What I am trying to say, I guess, is that it was a sky better suited in different times for walking down streets washed in clotted neon, thinking the long thoughts and maybe smoking a cigarette or seven.

Sherideen and I, more comfortable with our relationship. I touched her hair. The dialogue is easy enough to remember. I'm not writing a Harlequin romance.

"I'm terrified inside, Sher."

"Of me or of the plague?"

"Both." My mouth a minimalist sketch. "I feel like I'm in the glue."

"Huh?" Making an amused face, knowing I was embarrassed by what I was trying to say.

"Stuck . . . well, every time I find myself getting close to someone, I end up finding excuses for not staying in touch, for avoiding them. I felt that I'd end up getting hurt." Sherideen knew that I had never dated much; I had told her. "I think once, I was the one who caused the hurting."

She never asked me to elaborate, just as I never questioned her on past relationships when she lived in Cincinnati and Camden,

New Jersey. I was too concerned with the immediate future than with the now-distant past.

For me, the future wasn't Treats, it was Sherideen. Some born of the Compassionate Male Syndrome of the eighties might use a line like *I'm a cowardly drunk.* Well, I'm cowardly anytime. Dialogue time again. Me first.

"The more time we talk—"

"I feel like we've known each other for I don't know how long," she interrupted, in tune to what I was saying.

It had been less than thirty days . . .

"Sher, we've got so much in common," yet me still not comfortable with saying "hon" or "babe." Thank God for the latter. "The scars from our accidents; the way we each wrap a little shell around us to avoid being intimate." Trying to be flippant.

"Stop trying to be flippant," she said. "You flirt a lot is what you do." Seeing my expression, she added, *"Without* being obnoxious." And playfully punched my knee.

"Before we go off on another tangent of anecdotes, Sher, what I'm getting at is that I'm not"—I'm sure I was stammering at that point, like my old boss at the comic book shop had caught me using the old five-fingered discount on the *Flying Buttress and Gazebo Boy* graphic novel—"not . . . I, well, I don't want to let you go."

As close as we were, I knew that she was uncomfortable. I took a huge breath and exhaled, like the chiropractors tell you how to do.

"I respect every moment that I'm with you, and I'll stay by you as long as you'll have me around." Finished, I felt like I had beaten my face with my own fist. But Sherideen was smiling.

"You talk as if we are survivors of a great virus, and that we'll end up on a quest to Boulder, Colorado, or something. People are getting Treats every day, just like they were infected with AIDS in the eighties."

"Still," I told her. "I'm no optimist, I just see myself sitting here, more afraid of smelling your skin than trying to avoid being attacked by a Treater."

Somehow, that's exactly what occurred, but the conversation turned to more humorous things, like graffiti and what deep-dish pizza used to taste like.

*   *   *

We walked hand in hand through Washington Square Park and I told her how it was nicknamed Bughouse Square because of all the turn-of-the-century philosophers on their soapboxes, leaving out the sordid details about Gacy and his thirty-three known victims. It was relatively safer than a year ago, when gangbangers were killing anyone wearing the wrong colors, even if said colors were the store emblem of White Hen Pantry. We sat on Grover Hill, the new-fallen snow looking as pristine as it did in my childhood, when all the signs were written solely in English.

And stared into her sepia eyes, knowing I would do anything at all for her.

Love among the viruses. She told me jokes about her birthplace in Cincinnati; what was considered foreplay in Amberly and a two-dog town like Miamiville. I told her that we had the same yuks for our lesser-loved suburbs like Fallon Ridge and Cicero.

And on my days off, we'd walk through some of the secured neighborhoods. The Streets and Sanitation crews, by mid-January, had cleared things all the way north to Armitage Avenue and the Kennedy Expressway overpass. There was little loss of life on our side.

In Holy Name Cathedral, we saw a kid come off the street to talk with Father Malcolm. A gork coming in for confession? He was blond-haired, maybe fifteen or so. I'm sitting in back by the St. Vitus statue with Sherideen, looking over an old photo essay by Art Shay on Nelson Algren, and we see the kid go shambling up to the purple bunting which hung low over the nave.

He wanted the priest to kill him, pure and simple. Said that he had been autistic before Treats, and he wanted to be dead because now he understood things better. He couldn't deal with all the input his brain was getting.

Father Malcolm *didn't* kill him, even when the kid grabbed his chasuble and pleaded with him. The priest said, "My son, my son . . ." over and over, litanizing, and then wandered off, dazed, to give himself confession. The boy left and we never saw him again. But he was lucid, the Chicago River's north branch was only two blocks away, and the spring thaw always brings surprises to the surface . . .

Later that night, it was all but forgotten. The temperature was warming as we neared March; we were lying as close to naked as possible in a Murphy bed and making up lyrics to songs. Sherideen sang "Derby Geeks and the Thunder Chiefs" to the tune of "Dirty Deeds Done Dirt Cheap" by AC/DC. I made warm beer foam from her round nostrils and mouth by crooning "*Why are you shaving Rosemary's hair? Partly shaved, Rosemary is fine . . .*"

Why couldn't we have met under different circumstances? Like the Third World War?

It was eleven weeks since the incident at the Lawson YMCA. It seemed like eleven years. The days getting longer by slivers.

This is the hard part to write. Even after what I said earlier about my writing better when all my hope is gone.

The incident that rose from circumstance came crashing up into us as fast as the cancer through Mel Bland's brain stem. Sherideen and I were sitting at the window here at 565 North LSD, sharing a pleasant buzz of vertigo from looking out at the deserted street below. Talking, staring intently into each other's faces, concentration screwed into our expressions like we were watching the Challenger space shuttle explode or Ronald Reagan getting shot on television.

The famous final scene:

Maybe it was the adrenaline, the progress we were making. Myself, I was thinking about Mel. How, even in plague time, the first ways of dying are still around. Rape and ridicule, and the cancers of the body.

Sherideen brought it up first, and it ended up kind of like strip poker without the cards. Each of us removed an item of clothing, first tentatively, but never hurriedly.

We stared at each other like the whole idea of what we were doing was some crazy dream. I told her to make the first move; I didn't want to fuck things up by rushing at all, both of us remembering a conversation that seemed years old.

Do I write down what she looked like, her physical appearance in Tennessee Williams splendor? The way her every movement hypnotized me in the same way the Flatirons in Colorado mesmerized the Sedalia Indians?

I don't know that this is the reason you've read this far.

* * *

Should I confess even more about myself and tell you the pain and embarrassment of getting an erection every single time I was with her? Will the next order of civilization be so barbaric that my journal here will be spoken of as gospel because I described The Love Interest in microscopic and blunt detail?

Is that what is expected; was Sherideen's pussy shaved or did the pubic hair fan out like an untrimmed palm frond? Were her nipples sepia-colored to match her eyes, and was my penis erect enough to flop wetly against my navel?

What she looked like unclothed is of no concern; our relationship was based on common bonds and forced knowledge.

Never sex.

Never again.

She was massaging my back, I think to gratify me because I told her how much I liked the gentle touch of the scars she received on account of the iguana. We nibbled each other's chins. I'll skip over the part of the thrusting and the arching.

It suddenly felt as if Sherideen was raking her fingers hard across my back, and I felt my head spin. My fingers went numb as if frostbite was leaving them. We had been on our sides, Sherideen facing the door. She whimpered; I thought a gork had come up behind us by some fit of magic.

What had happened was this. Sherideen had pressed through the skin on my back; the reflex recoil made my spinal cord pull up and out of my skin. It wasn't severed; just humped out, pale like a sand spit. There was little blood.

I felt it as a vague throb, the way the doctors at Childermas Research long ago taught me how to zone out the cerebral palsy. Was I that good at masking the pain? No, it wasn't my spine, *I was still able to move my limbs,* yet it was like I was swimming underwater.

No. It wasn't my spine, it was a joke. It—

I reached over for the .38 that Streets & San had issued me months before. Sherideen didn't say anything as I shot myself in the kneecap. I'll always love her for that respectful silence. Her lower lip trembled when not a flinch of pain or shock registered on my face.

I shot myself again, avoiding the femoral artery. Nothing.

I still don't know when I was infected, when I became Treats-Positive. I thought of the autistic boy and of Blackstone Shatner. Was I another example of how the disease affected different people in various ways? Cripples have different sex drives than drunks and diseased children who were never taught any better.

There were two gaping holes in my leg and I was losing blood in huge pulses. And I never felt better.

I still had my erection.

Kill me, I said to her. Please. I can't do it myself.

Sherideen kissed me one last time and told me that she couldn't. And that she couldn't watch me do it myself.

I loved her even more for that. She never said a word about my infecting her.

That was a day and a half ago. I've spent these hours writing. It will be dawn soon, but the sky will be blue, not overcast. I shot myself in the intestine, back around two this morning, in a fit of anger.

I'll wait until the change of shift to do it because there will be less chance of my final shot being heard. I wonder what Sherideen will tell the crew, if she has told them anything at all yet.

There will be a pen sitting here on the last page, in case you who are reading this might want to add a few lines of small worth. I'm dragging myself away from the pages before I do the head shot.

And I'm leaving a bullet in the cylinder, if you want to use it on yourself.

A bullet for you, the living.

Calling Dr. Satan: An Interview with Anton Szandor LaVey

JIM GOAD

Judging by the revulsion with which splatterpunk is greeted in certain quarters, you'd think this stuff was written by the Devil.

Well, OK, I admit it. It is. Splatterpunk is nothing more than a diabolical plot by a cabal of warty Satanists to befoul the purity of Judeo-Christian literature.

We all masturbate over mutilated goat carcasses, too.

Having cleansed our filthy little souls, let's move on to a cozy chat with Dr. Anton Szandor LaVey, self-proclaimed "Black Pope" and founder of the San Francisco-based Church of Satan.

Younger Splat Packers probably recognize LaVey as the host of Death Scenes, *a gruesome 1989 video. This* Faces of Death *clone presents a half-century's worth of TrueCrime police department murder photos, with LaVey's early experiences as an L.A. crime photographer lending a depressingly detached patina to his matter-of-fact narration.*

But I remember first seeing Anton in the early seventies, on the old Joe Pyne *TV talk show. That's where a bald-pated LaVey (who'd already achieved underground notoriety by penning* The Satanic Bible*) so charmed his viciously conservative host that Pyne actually smiled, leaned over, patted him on the head, and praised Anton for being such "a good little devil."*

LaVey forms the centerpiece of "Calling Dr. Satan," which is unlike any Satanist interview you've ever read. An articulate, surprisingly intelligent conversation conducted by JIM GOAD.

Goad is the editor and publisher of ANSWER Me!, *a smartly realized, high-quality publication covering everything from poli-*

tically incorrect "celebrity" David Duke (plastic politician and former head of the KKK) to Mexican murder magazines and Vietnamese youth gangs.

Shining with solid writing and exceptional layouts, ANSWER Me! also radiates an intense hatred of humanity. Jim professes to a "boundless contempt for Homo sapiens," I believe him. Any issue of ANSWER Me! makes Splatterpunks I look like an excerpt from My Little Pony.

As for personal details, Goad "is from Philly, undoubtedly the most genetically warped city on the map; I'm quite proud to be working-class Irish-Catholic trash. I graduated summa cum laude, at the top of a journalism class of 400. Although I'd say my technical linguistic skills could match those of any newspaper editor, my temperament renders a straight journalism job impossible. I've written for Playboy and scores of lesser-known publications. My experience writing for others is what led me to do my own magazine—I was always defanged at other rags.

"By the way, Debbie (my wife and coeditor) and I don't get along with anyone."

Except, perhaps, "Dr. Satan." Who's about to spring some major surprises. Not the least of which are philosophical.

Who would have thought that a meeting between a misanthrope and a Satanist could produce such fascinating philosophies?

*I*t's a cool Friday night in San Francisco, and people are everywhere in their exorbitant ugliness. They're sprinkling their oblong bodies with noxious perfumes. They're stuffing their throbbing little gullets with hot, oily foods. Their faces slacken in cretinous simplicity as they chug-a-lug one martini after the next. They're cruising the city for a quick score, seeking to drain their genitals of mucilaginous goop.

We circle a restaurant district in a futile quest for free parking. Block after block, and not an inch of curbside space. Cars zip past us in a hellish stream of lonely red taillights. TOO MANY FUCKING PEOPLE!

A thumbnail-sized spider scuttles across the windshield. Its moonlit body assumes the hue of white chocolate. Quietly effortless, its balletic presence rises above the depressing humanoid muck.

So does the glowering aura of Anton Szandor LaVey, whom we meet in a French restaurant after throwing up our hands and paying for parking. Accompanied by biographer/sidekick Blanche Barton, LaVey cuts quite the figure in his black suit and gangster hat. His severe Transylvanian features compensate for the innocuous, pasty-faced nobodies who fill the dining room. Unlike most neo-pagans, he's charming and doesn't smell bad.

Over appetizers, we discuss the global clump of human mulch, serial killer Carl Panzram, self-fulfilling surnames such as 'Goad,' and how to get rid of one's enemies. While lapping up onion soup, I make a passing remark about my boundless contempt for Homo sapiens.

"I can see we're going to get along," he says with the faint tremors of a smile.

Why the fuck not? A friend of the devil is a friend of mine, and Anton Szandor LaVey might as well be Satan's press agent. More than anyone else, he brought Satanism out of the closet. Blending what he called "nine parts social respectability [and] one part out-rage," he founded the Church of Satan in 1966. The self-proclaimed "Black Pope" has counted among his followers Sammy Davis, Jr., Kenneth Anger, and Jayne Mansfield. He also penned *The Satanic Bible*, a lean, nasty tome first published in 1969. But most people, since they can't read, would probably know him as the guy who played the devil in *Rosemary's Baby*.

The details of his past have been disputed by lettuce-smoking navel-gazers, but I'll accept his version: He was born April 11, 1930, in Chicago. An only child, LaVey sensed that he was innately differ-ent from his peers. Genetically Satanic, he had a "vestigial tail" surgically removed during adolescence. In his teens, he worked as a lion tamer and keyboardist. While pumping the ivories as a tent-show organist, he noticed that the same pious-faced men who at-tended revival meetings also drooled like apes at strip shows. Later, while working as a crime photographer, LaVey toured the grisliest, basest nooks of human depravity. He concluded that if there were a God, he was indifferent to human suffering.

LaVey came to believe that any religion which denies man's carnality was doomed to fail, describing Christianity as "getting people to feel guilty for breathing and charging them for the oxygen they breathe." Declaring that "life is the great indulgence—death, the great abstinence," he crystallized a philosophy which rams a hairy fist up the clenched sphincter of all "white-light" religions. While other belief systems deal in the ego's dampening or annihilation, Satanism attempts to nourish it, preaching antimystical rationalism and creative vengeance.

Acknowledging that humans have a Jungian need for ritual, LaVey melded applied psychology with appropriately dark theatrics. He doesn't accept "Satan" as the persona is understood in Christian theology—it would be rather stupid to worship a fallen angel whose damnation is sealed at an omnipotent creator's hands. For LaVey, Satan *is* the creator, or at least a convenient symbol of nature's dark, randomly brutal forces. The devil's a lusty archetype, a superhero of the liberated id.

As leader of the "Alien Elite," LaVey promotes a pruning of the gene pool through "bright supremacy." Far from espousing noble savagery, he advocates strengthening the police to keep all you assholes in line. He yearns for a future of android slavery and self-contained environments. In a statement which won our hearts, he claims that "population is the biggest problem facing us now."

After chowing down on frog's legs and chocolate mousse, we were directed to his black Victorian mansion, a harsh edifice which nearly recoils from the houses around it. As we settled into his parlor after feeling our way down an unlit, tomblike entrance, *Herr Doktor* indulged us an hour-long taped interview. I expected him to sound like Bela Lugosi, but he spoke in the measured tones of a Midwestern barley farmer, an accent subversive in its unassuming normalcy. He closed his eyes as he retreated within his pinkish dome to fetch his answers, raising his lids at the end of each soliloquy.

He then wowed us with an organ concert featuring "Yes, We Have No Bananas"; "Mister Jack and Missus Jill" from the all-midget epic *The Terror of Tiny Town*; Bach's "Toccata and Fugue in D Minor"; Wagner's *"Die Walküre"*; sundry circus ditties, Sousa marches, and spaghetti-western themes; and Nat King Cole's "Answer Me."

An unscripted conversation went on until five A.M. As I sipped coffee from a pentagram-emblazoned mug, we covered such occultic topics as the pyromaniac film *The Flaming Urge*, miniature-pony farms, and SCTV's Shmenge Brothers. Basking in LaVey's genteel misanthropy, I found him to be keen-witted and palpably repulsed by a devolving, illiterate populace. I realized why he's considered a threat—beneath his shaven pate lies a formidable brain.

But you can't trust anything I'm saying, because when I wasn't looking, LaVey slipped some demons—thirteen or fourteen of them, I'm not sure—into my soul. Every Friday night since the interview, after ordering out for Thai food, Debbie and I perform ritual murder. So far, we've bagged six preschoolers, two metalheads, and a pregnant woman who was waiting at a bus stop. We recite the Our Father backwards at midnight, and Satan appears to counsel us. He even got us cheaper car insurance!

I'm brainwashed, you see, hoodwinked by the Great Liar. I'm a Satanic zombie, a Mephistophelean marionette controlled by dark angels I never should have fucked with. I started out as a journalist, but now I'm the devil's mouthpiece. To all ye who dare tread this perditious path, take heed: Satan ensnares minds with his seductively flawless logic. You MUST close your eyes and ears to logic, or it will DEVOUR you!

Why does Satan get so much bad press these days?

Well, because, I would say a lot of it is the *threat* of Satanism is coming closer and closer to the surface. And it's nothing that can simply be vanquished as a paper tiger, as a convenience, or a theological need, or some kind of entertainment device, but it's becoming now a very real force, philosophy, concept to be reckoned with. It's something that holds a mirror up to not only collective identities, but what people like to think of as individual identities. And it's overlapping, naturally, into many areas of endeavor that people never thought something called "Satanism" could. By that, I mean music, aesthetics of all kinds, literature, popular culture, and it threatens to become something that is, in fact, very threatening to not only the present economy, unless it modifies its machinations to fit, as well as to the social order as we have known it for many, many years. Probably centuries.

Comment on the concept of equality.

Well, naturally—I say "naturally" as a Satanist—I don't believe in equality. I don't believe there's anything equal. If you're going to dissect it or analyze it, even in the sense of quality control or something that's seen under a microscope or if a spectrographic analysis is made, there are going to be tiny differences in everything, even if they're rubber-stamp-type things or mass-production things. Nothing is really equal. And it might be quite similar, but when we're dealing, as I assume you're asking, in human beings, very few human beings are equal. The most equal of human beings, I would say, would be on the lowest level. Because there are, I mean, God must have loved them, 'cause he made so many of them. But when you get higher up on the evolutionary scale—or social order, whichever you prefer—you're going to find more differentiation in human beings as you ascend. And then, of course, the higher you go, the more *un*equal you find those from the ones at the bottom. What is usually meant by "equality" is really "common denominators."

But I feel that the question that would normally be put to me would be, "Well, who are you to say who is equal and who is not equal, or who's superior and who is inferior?" And my only answer to that would be simply based on the product or the impact that these individuals have on the cosmology as we know it, our world. And the contrast between the performers and the audience—those who are the performers in life are certainly not equal to the audience, who occupies a much vaster space than the performers on-stage. That isn't to say that everyone has to be a performer, but certainly, as far as inequality is concerned, the performer, or the stimulator, as I like to call him, is someone who does deserve a little more, if you want to call it, subsidizing, than the person who needs stimulation and gains stimulation from that performer. As far as I'm concerned, the greatest need of human life is stimulation. That allows these spores in this great yeast mold to know that they're alive, that they're actually functioning. They *feel* something. The stimulation is sort of like a cattle prod or a mild shock. Anything will do to give these people an awareness that they are indeed alive—they have a functioning nervous system. I call them people because, to me, the word "people" is not a positive thing. It is very much a derogatory expression.

And the second-most-vital need would be identity. Obviously, collective identities—that is, herd mentalities—seem to be in the majority. And of the herd mentality, people in the world—and again, I use that derogatorily—*people*—there are very few, or fewer, certainly, that are not collective in their identities. In other words, they haven't gotten their identities from something that's been prepackaged or mass-produced, but they've found something a trifle different to get more of a *personal* identity. And this is not to say that it's less important to them than it is to the people, but it still, to me, is probably the second-most-important human need.

And getting back to equality, or staying with equality, rather: The whole concept, the entire concept of equality is simply one of wishful thinking or flight of fancy that, very much like the concept of reincarnation, will allow the lowest to feel that they are equal to the highest. And the concept of equality, with that in mind, is designed to keep the lowest satisfied, to serve as pap, or serve as a sort of cosmetic indulgence or enticement to the lowest so that they, too, can feel that they are of the same stuff as the highest.

We've been talking for a while, and you seem well mannered and reasoned. When are you going to rip my heart out and eat it?

Oh, about sacrifice and that sort of thing? Well, I believe in sacrifice, but not necessarily on an unlawful basis, or one by which you would be apprehended, convicted, tried, and prosecuted or executed. This isn't to say that I'm against human sacrifice; it's just simply that I'm against the entanglements or the punishments or the social *inconveniences* that [laughs] performing human sacrifices might entail. So, when I talk about symbolic human sacrifices, I say it with the awareness that we are living in a world that frowns upon a Darwinian sort of thinning-out of the species, so there *are* ways of sacrificing, performing human sacrifices, without necessarily going out with a butcher knife and killing people.

One of these would be to demoralize or to, in some way, fragment the potential victim or victims into feeling their worthlessness or becoming aware of their own uselessness. And by demoralization and the ensuing, I guess you could call it, *breakdown* of these kinds of people, then you are in fact performing some sort of human sacrifice. But not cutting the hearts out of people, and if there's any of that sort of thing to be done, it would be certainly ill-advised to boast of it or to speak of it.

I would say that every society has its anger and hatreds, boiling rages, either individually or collectively. War is a perfect example of that, and that's an area that intrigues me and perhaps titillates me, even, because it gives entire countries a chance to advocate, if not cutting the hearts out of human victims, certainly shooting them down in wholesale lots or blowing them up. And yet, one need not feel any pangs of conscience when there's a convenient enemy during times of war by doing this sort of thing. So, when we are drawing comparisons about human sacrifices on a personal scale and on a mass scale, we certainly realize, or must realize, that if these sort of things are done on a grand enough scale, such as war, they're perfectly acceptable. So it's, as I assume you mean, on a personal level that we're treading on a little more, uh, controversial ground [laughs].

Based on what you can glean from the New Testament, give a psychoanalytic profile of Jesus. What type of human was he?

Yeah, that's a question that I find interesting in that it changes as far as the needs of the believers are concerned. And if, for example, we're living in the eighteenth century, the psychological profile of a Jesus type of divinity would be different than the psychological profile that would be analyzed in the twentieth or the twenty-first century. The current trend—I say trend—is to accept a Jesus type or a Christ figure as having some sort of strong drives, a great deal of anger and perhaps rage, and the "New Jesus," in the sense of the Second Coming type of Christ, would, in all probability, be the kind of guy that would go out and kill a lot of people rather than one who would die on a cross. And that would simply be because of changing needs, changing myth-needs and needs that fit, of course, the social order as it stands. I think the name would not necessarily change, just as often it remains the same throughout the centuries, but there is a distinct possibility—and that's why I use the term "the Second Coming"—there is a distinct possibility that the need, the myth-need for a new Christ will be transferred to one name that is more conducive to outrageous behavior, or anger, or revenge, or retaliation, or justice in the old sense of *lex talionis* [the law of retaliation], and that would be Satan. And that would provide the Christ figure, but in an updated version by a different name. So really, it's just a question of finding a need and filling it.

I guess the gist of the question is, a human being who would say, "Do unto others as you would have them do unto you," somebody who would say you have to give up all worldly goods and put on sackcloth—give your opinion of the driving forces in a person like that.

I can only see that as an extreme form of masochism, whether it's self-realized or unrealized. To me, Christianity as it has been practiced or advocated is a life-denying, rather than life-affirming, thing. It has been said before, and I'll say it again, reiterate, that wearing a cross around one's neck—the cross being the object of the execution or the destruction of the godhead or the spiritual leader—is no different than wearing an electric chair around your neck if he had been electrocuted or a gas chamber around your neck if he died by cyanide eggs. So, venerating the object of one's hero's or role model's death, to me, is rather silly. It always has been. And as far as Satanic "atrocities" go, there's nothing that can match a child's first impression when it walks into a room or becomes aware for the first time that what it is seeing on the wall is either a painting or a plaster statue of a man with his chest ripped open, with his entrails coming out, and with his brow torn by what appears to be barbed wire or thorns, that sort of thing. That's the stuff of which hack-and-slash movies are made. So, I don't ever want to hear anything about Satanic horror flicks, or any kind of supposed atrocities that are poisoning the minds of young people, because these kind of horrors have been presented by Christianity for centuries to young people, and it's probably the only *taste,* as a matter of fact, they've got of these kind of things for a long time, until Hollywood.

So, I guess, would you be saying that Jesus had maybe a *sexual* need to be crucified? He got off on the humiliation and torture?

Oh, of course, yeah. I feel with that kind of masochist, rejection, destruction, I mean, self-destruction, and punishment are definitely the things that he would get off on. And the jokes that we hear and we have heard pretty well sum all that up.

Like, one of my favorites is: The guys are standing in the doorway of their little house watching Jesus being whipped and beaten with a big cross on his back up to the hill where he's going to be crucified. They see his lips moving, and one of the guys says to the other, "What's he saying?" And he says, "Well, I don't know." He says, "Why don't you go up to where you can hear him?" He says, "I don't know whether I should go up there or not. I don't want to get hit myself." And the guy says, "Well, go on, it's not gonna hurt. Maybe you can get an idea. He's saying *something*. I don't know what he's saying." So finally, the guy goes up and sort of quickly sticks his head in front of Jesus before he gets completely past the row of houses, and he hears him singing, "*IIIII love a pa-rade....*"

It's one of those sort of things. And it's like the other one, where he's up on the cross, and he's motioning to Peter and trying, mumbling, to get Peter to come to him. And Peter's out there in a crowd of centurions, and they're throwing rocks at Jesus, and they're trying to torment him as much as possible. And finally, Peter inches his way through the crowd and gets to the foot of his mentor. And he says, "What, what, my Lord? What? What is it you have to say to me?" And Jesus looks down at him and he says, "Peter, Peter—I can see your house from here."

And so, there was no great problem Christ had, I mean, if you're talking about psychologically. His only problem was what the rest of the world saw in his problem and subsequently took as a role model for their *own* masochism. But I don't think he, if he was as he is portrayed, felt that he was unjustly put upon. He probably felt that without this martyrdom, without this kind of masochistic satisfaction, it wouldn't have all been worth it. Of course, that's not what we find in latter-day interpretations, psychological interpretations, of Jesus. And I can understand the reinterpretation, because it is essentially to create a more humanized man out of Jesus, one who is not a masochistic martyr, but one who was really put upon and unjustly maligned, and as in the case of some figures of history, like Wilhelm Reich, really crucified. And I think it's more of a convenience to psychologically see him as that after the fact. It's not like we suddenly have discovered psychoanalysis, because Freud has been around a long time now. It's taken a while to sort of catch up to the fact that maybe—or the supposition, it's not a fact, certainly, but the supposition—that Christ may have been a real ballsy guy and really was struck down in the prime of his life. Or somebody that was essentially Promethean and went against the grain. That could well be. Of course, I don't accept the reality of Christ as a living man. I accept only the reality of a myth-need, and the Christ figure to me was something that just sort of fit at the time it was promulgated, and he has been historically accepted sort of as a given, contrary to historical evidence that he never even existed.

Let's clear up one of the biggest misconceptions about the Church of Satan—by "Satan," of course, you mean an anthropomorphic being with horns and a tail, right?

To us, Satan is not an anthropomorphic being. Satan is certainly an anthropomorphic *image,* though, which is a little different from an actual being. And the anthropomorphic image of Satan is pretty well fashioned in that it is bestial as opposed to ethereal, or cherubic, or patriarchal, or avuncular. Satan *is* seen as somewhat of a dashing, or rakish, or, perhaps, feral-animal type of image. And, obviously, these depictions are something very much like talismanic magic conserved to reinforce the concepts of the philosophical ideas behind Satanism. So, I wouldn't do anything to dispel that image. Satan as a divinity or as a deity with a pitchfork and a tail and cloven hooves and a beard and all that is certainly more viable to imagine than Satan as a guy that looked like a bespectacled accountant that was sitting behind a desk, even though there have been deviations in the public image of Satan.

Sometimes a Satanic figure has been depicted as a very heavy,

CALLING DR. SATAN   363

or corpulent, individual with lewd sort of features—the kind of appearance you might associate with one of the Caesars. And other times, Satan has been seen, certainly *many* times, as a woman, or in the body of a sexy woman. And other times, Satan has been seen as a sort of grey or wizened old wizard with little hairs sprouting out of either side of his head, the sort of alchemist look about him. So, there have been other interpretations that are anthropomorphic that do work. And yet, the one we keep returning to, anthropomorphizing Satan, is the guy that looks like the devil, as devils are known. But this isn't a person, we believe, that's out there somewhere just sort of waiting to be called forth and appear in a puff of flame and smoke, but rather someone that walks among us and perhaps even walks *with* the person who is dedicated to the concept of Satan, so that when someone would ask, "Have you ever seen Satan?" that person might be able to say, "Yes. Every time I get up in the morning and shave and look in the mirror. Or every time I fix my hair or put on my lipstick," [laughs] or something like that, if it happens to be a woman. And that would be just as valid an answer for the anthropomorphic concept.

One of the most profound things that I read that you said was that truth never sets you free, that doubt is much more likely to at least *lead* to freedom. Can you say why that is? 'Cause when I interviewed Tom Metzger, the White Aryan guy, he said, "I don't believe in equality. When they say all men are created equal, I laugh, because nobody in power believes that." And something just clicked. And the same thing happened when I read that, that doubt is—

—That's right. I agree completely with that, that no one in power believes that. *No* one in power believes that. They would never be able to admit it except to their cronies, perhaps, in closed rooms. If they were all to get together, I know pretty much what kind of notes they would compare. And believe me, there would be some across-the-board similarities, and one of them would be that there is no such thing as equality. And their constituents, their disciples, would not necessarily be told what they are in public interviews for an audience.

About doubt setting you free . . .

Yeah, as far as the truth setting one free. Truth is very much a subjective thing. Because there are different kinds of truths, just like there are different kinds of love. I believe truth and love is, or are, words and terms that can almost be used interchangeably, because they bear this attribute, or this quality, of, "Which kind of love do you mean?" Or in other words, you could say, "What kind of truth do you mean?" There's the kind of love that's romantic love, maternal or paternal love, filial love, love as an aesthetic expression, like I love a particular object of art or a painting, a design of an automobile, or something like that. And truth is very much to me the same sort of commodity. Truth is able to be seen as the facts as we know hard facts to mean—applied, hard, demonstrable evidence can be said to be the closest thing to the truth. At least, to me it is.

The Nine Satanic Statements

1. Satan represents indulgence instead of abstinence.

2. Satan represents vital existence instead of spiritual pipe dreams.

3. Satan represents undefiled wisdom instead of hypocritical self-deceit.

4. Satan represents kindness to those who deserve it instead of love masted on ingrates.

5. Satan represents vengeance instead of turning the other cheek.

6. Satan represents responsibility to the responsible instead of concern for psychic vampires.

7. Satan represents man as just another animal—sometimes better, more often worse than those that walk on all-fours—

who, because of his "divine spiritual and intellectual development," has become the most vicious animal of all.

8. Satan represents all of the so-called sins, as they all lead to physical, mental, or emotional gratification.

9. Satan has been the best friend the Church has ever had, as he has kept it in business all these years.

© Anton Szandor La Vey, 1966 c.e.

Then there is, of course, more subjective truth, which can be altered or manipulated according to the dictates or the needs of what truth is supposed to be. Propagandists are experts at that sort of thing. So, if we are to believe the truth as we read it in print, or in factual evidence supposedly given by vested interests, should we really accept that as truth simply because it is put down by experts? We're getting to a sensitive area with me, because I detest experts, or so-called experts. I distrust experts. Anyone that has the word 'expert' after their name immediately, to me, conveys the impression of someone who has just sort of hung out his shingle and become self-styled, whatever. And I feel that the truth coming from these kind of people is absolutely invalid.

But I should get to this other definition of the truth, and that is that the real truth that matters is the truth that matters for *you*. That fills, or fulfills, your particular personal needs. And that could be very negative when we're talking about masses of people or humanity in general, because what their needs for truth happen to be are fulfilled in the *National Enquirer* and TV. That's as much truth as they need to know, and, of course, that *is* truth to them. And if it works, then that's true enough, as true as they need it to be. But it's a rather important point to me, being a Satanist, looking at these things like truth from a Satanic perspective. Do we *really* want to give these people the truth, because if they had the truth, what would they do with it? How would they react or respond to it? Would they be able to *live* with the truth? I don't think they would. So, is it really fair to say that the people that print things like the *National Enquirer* are fogging people's brains? What they're really doing is dealing in fogged brains and brains that are scrambled to start with, and they're telling them the truth according to the gospel of what their particular role models seem to put forth.

The meaning it had for me, too, was that it seems like the people who are most convinced that they're right are frequently, or almost always, the dumbest people. Maybe the beginning of intelligence is the ability to question what you believe in.

Yeah, and the most righteous, the most self-righteous people, I have found, are not only the stupidest people, but the people who want to believe as the truth what most likely isn't the truth, but simply the truth that fits their own needs. Now, their needs generally are to destroy anything that's beautiful, anything that's fine, anything that's of quality, anything that's Promethean or pioneering, anything that's worth preserving—in short, they're a pretty loutish crew, and anything that's of value, they really want to rip apart. They will elect a person to office that in the first place is a Hobson's choice—who is, perhaps, the lesser of two evils. And in the second place, once they have elected that person into office, then they'll spend the rest of the time, the remaining time of their attention span with this person, trying to destroy him. So I can't speak too highly of the discriminatory powers of the masses, because they have their own idea of the truth, and they have their own idea of what's right and self-righteous. And what makes them feel good, or better, or more right, is what they're gonna opt for in every case.

And as a Satanist, I prefer to attract or to draw out the kind of people that don't have to wear the mantle of a good guy or self-righteousness but are willing, as you expressed in your own editorial views, willing to stand forth and say, "Look—you know, I'm *not* a nice guy. I'm not Simon Pure. I'm not trying to save the world. I don't want to be a messiah. I don't wish to pin any good-guy badges on myself. I just want to say things the way I feel it, and the way I want others at least to give me a chance to say them. And if they don't want to, they can tell me I'm full of shit or whatever, but at least I've had the opportunity to express these views without the sanctimonious, hypocritical whitewash or varnish or sugarcoating of trying to say, 'Well, I'm trying to build a better world by saying these things.' "

Isn't the fight against stupidity a losing battle?

Yeah. To me, I've written my list of the seven deadly sins—how many of them were there?
Blanche: I think there were nine of them.
Anton: Nine. Yeah. I sometimes forget myself. It's like the old cliché, "I only work here [general laughter]." But the Nine Satanic Sins—the first one, the top of the list, is Stupidity. [*Note: The others are Pretentiousness, Solipsism, Self-Deceit, Herd Conformity, Lack of Perspective, Forgetfulness of Past Orthodoxies, Counterproductive Pride, and Lack of Aesthetics.*] To me, stupidity is the stuff that is needed, obviously, in the world, and the Christian concept would be to say, "Well, we're all sinners. We are all born or conceived in sin." To me, I would say, *"You* are all sinners by Satanic standards. You are conceived in sin, and you are able to plod through your lives in sin, and you will always be sinners." But to me, the great sin is stupidity. So, you could just, instead of the word 'sin,' substitute it with stupidity: "You are conceived in stupidity, you're born into stupidity, you live out your lives in stupidity. So, therefore, you *are* sinners." And I would accuse them, just as a Christ figure would accuse the minions, his minions, of being sinners, I would accuse these minions of being sinners, too.

That's a better concept of original sin, I think: You're born stupid.

Yeah, I think that's very well put. That's a much better concept of original sin, that it's stupidity.
Blanche: Yeah. Born into ignorance and work from there. If you *choose* to.
Anton: I mean, I've been quoted as saying, "The world is full of stupes," and I only started saying that after I sort of got tired of saying, "The world is full of creeps." And there will *always* be stupid people. There's a *need* for stupid people. The stupider, the better. When Nietzsche said that man, or the overman, must be evil*er*, I would say, "If that's the case, then the common man must be stupid*er*." Constantly stupider. And this degenerative process is what we're seeing right NOW, more than at any time in the history of the world, and if it is allowed to run rampant without an alterna-

tive or two or three to at least run interference for it, then it's going to envelop the planet, and we're going to be a dead planet. But that's not going to happen, because natural law will always prevail, despite man's efforts to quash it. So there will always be something like a Satan or a Satanic concept to run interference for this raging overabundance of stupidity.

We've already seen that Satan dresses better, dances better than God—uh, is he funnier than God, too? How does humor aid the Satanist?

I think a Satanic figure that would be humorless would be intolerable. The old adage that "I laughed that I might not cry," I think [laughs] applies to Satan, or the image of Satan, or the concept of Satan. Because, concerning the sorrows of Satan, his dismay at seeing this fucked-up kind of world, would necessitate that he *had* to have a sense of humor or some kind of concrete outlet for his dismay or for what would be devastating to him. Because how could such a figure or figurehead be able to live in such a grim world?

I've been accused of being an unhappy person deep down inside—a miserable, cynical, misanthropic person. I admit that I'm misanthropic. I admit that I'm cynical. And I do admit that I'm often rather miserable, perhaps, to other people. But if I am miserable at times, it's only because, as Sartre said, "Hell is other people." Because *they* make me miserable. And I'm actually a very happy person. I want to be a life-loving, happy person. I just happen to be living in a death-seeking, misery-loving world.

I've found the most superficially happy-go-lucky people seem to be in a constant state of denial of reality.

Blanche: Yeah, there's also that sanctimony if you compare the images of the white-light religions with Satanic images. Satan never allows himself sanctimony.

Where does this need to deny the way things are come from? Is it that if people admitted how

shitty things were, they'd just fall apart? I have trouble understanding that myself—what's this need to gloss over things? If you know deep down that it's fucked-up, why do you need to think otherwise? What's the motivation? Is it just an elaborate defense mechanism?

Blanche (to Anton): On the part of most people: Why do they watch Oprah Winfrey and forget about what's happening to the rest of the world, hmm?

Anton: Because I call it "masochistic America." Or you could say, "the masochistic Western world." It varies in some degrees from nation to nation—not much anymore. It's because their lives are so barren of any personal meaning that the surrogate lives of these shows, of these ongoing digressions, become as real to them, or more real, than their own lives could possibly be. And so, the nature of the show, the nature of the program says it all. Their lives wouldn't be complete without the stimulation. Again, I use the word "stimulation": of chaos, and disharmony, and problems. There is no way that they could possibly be happy unless they were miserable. And, of course, their miseries are small miseries. Tiny miseries. That still gives them plenty of time to make *other* people miserable. Which is, of course, what they do. So, if they had big enough *real* problems, then they wouldn't have time to make other people miserable. And they wouldn't, perhaps, be as misery-loving.

But they just get stimulation in doses that are palatable. Just enough to satisfy them. By that, I mean eustress, rather than distress. Fun fear, rather than real terror. I think that it would be fun some-times—I mean, not fun for *them*—but, certainly, it would be stimu-lating for me occasionally to see how these people react under true distress. Because I think that's the only thing that takes them away from their soaps and their theater of disturbance that they seem to crave. And when something really happens, like an earthquake or a plane crash or a disaster or a catastrophe, then it's no longer eus-tress. It really gives them what they want, but double or triple in spades. And they can't deal with that. And that's when you really see them for what they are, the frightened little creatures that they really are. They want so badly to live in this gradual decline, this gradual imperative to die, but on *their* terms, sort of like the epicurean masochist that says, "Hit me here. No—a little higher. Not quite so high, a little bit further down than that. But no, no, that's too hard." And that's the way I sort of feel most people are—they crave eustress, fun fear. And when they get into real *dis*tress, it's the sort of thing they can't take. They might be able to dish out to others, but they can't take it themselves.

The only thing people generally respond to in the state of distress that, they seem to crave, but not be able to cope with when it finally comes, is fear. And pain. Now, I don't mean fun fear, but I mean TERROR. I mean real fear. And pain—by pain, I mean physical pain. I mean pain like TORTURE. And I believe that most people need periodic doses of fear and pain in order to sort of reinforce the meaning of life for them. They even have coined the term, "No pain, no gain." And, "The sale begins when the customer says, 'No.'" And the whole concept of business procedure, where you're fighting these interminable odds at all times, and if the door slams in your face, it's a victory, not a defeat. And all success courses and the aggressiveness seminars.

Blanche: Yeah: *Winning Through Intimidation.*

Anton: And winning-through-intimidation techniques are proof of this. That most people really respond to what is most abrasive and what is most painful and what is most inconvenient. And here's the real, to me, the blow-off on the whole thing is, without these things—like, these inconveniences, these pains, these turmoils—there'd be no security. That is, verily, their security. It is their habit, it is their security. So, take those things away from them, and you do them a disservice. From time to time, give them REAL pain, and real distress, rather than eustress, and it will be like a rejuvenation for them, a shot in the arm. That's why wars, catastrophes, disasters, are necessary from time to time. Speaking as a sort of devil [laughs], if I were in that position, I would say, "Well, we've gotta have a catastrophe here, a disaster here from time to time, an earthquake, a tidal wave," whatever it is. A war. Something to really get people shaken up.

I'd like you to comment on what we were talking over dinner about seeing a paradox—that what

society would consider the most evil outcasts are invariably the most considerate type of people. For instance, Debbie's boss is a guy who has a business called [SELF-CENSORSHIP! SELF-CENSORSHIP!], and he speaks in this real glazed voice on the answering machine: "I hope this finds you in a happy and healing place." And he's a ruthless bastard! What is the principle behind that, that the most seemingly good people are often the most ruthless—evil in a truly negative sense? And Russ Meyer, yourself, and other people that society in general might consider evil are the most considerate and accommodating type of people. How does that work? I want to understand the physics behind that.

Because they don't have to cover up their meanness or their pettiness or their insecurity or their true *dastardly* nature. Because it's all up front. I mean, somebody like Russ Meyer—obviously, he's putting out material, putting out a product, that makes no pretense about being enlightening or redeeming or in some way a form of salvation, unless you want to say it's salvation for poor, repressed souls that need to be released. And, obviously, people who are not wearing good-guy badges are more up front, and they can *afford* to be nicer, because they're getting this meanness out, right out in the open. They're wearing it on their sleeves like an armband. They're sort of like the black widow spider with the hourglass on its abdomen, saying, "Look—you know, don't mess with me, because I'm really a pretty mean customer." Or the rattlesnake when it rattles.

Blanche (to Anton): You always talk about sleeping on the floor, too.

Anton: Yeah—I always felt that if you sleep on the floor, you never have to worry about falling out of bed. And when you get yourself in this exalted position of self-righteousness, then it's very easy to drop down a notch into what could be called degradation or disfavor. And so, the pretense has to be kept up even stronger than ever, lest you slip. And that's why there's a bigger smile, a more mellifluous voice, and a more godly or saintly approach in a public sense. And it's failure insurance, really.

What pisses you off more than anything else?

A lot of things do, and I don't deny it. I'm not trying to say, "Oh, these things just roll off like water on a duck's back," and all that sort of thing, like I don't pay any attention to these things. I think if you don't pay any attention to any of these things and they don't get to you, you don't get that concentration of energy or that controlled adrenal force or energy that can make magic happen, if you want to call it magic. It has to be for real. You have to really get worked up. It might not be too good for your system—stress is pretty bad for you—but, I mean, let's face it, it gets things done sometimes if it's controlled and contained, and this conservation of energy translates. Sometimes a bottling-up of rage and hate, bad feelings about things, anger, is often very powerful, very potent. Because you let a little of it loose, and it's like a lightning bolt.

And if you're going around waving your arms wildly and punching at the air like a punch-drunk fighter or raging all the time, that's not going to really accomplish anything, either. That's just as bad as taking the self-righteous approach. Like the frothing-at-the-mouth kind of guy with nothing to say but vitriol about everything and anything, that has no sense of aesthetics, that can't appreciate beauty, appreciate anything in life, that is just totally, "Whatever it is," like Groucho used to say, "I'm against it."

Let's see—what pisses me off? I think the Nine Satanic Sins cover what pisses me off pretty well. Generally, I have my list that would be on a scale from one to ten. Of course, I don't like shit-disturbers. That would be right up near the top of the list. That would be people who do not have direction or who take the individuals, the institutions, the objects that *should* be venerated or should be given consideration, and again, as I said earlier, try to tear these worthwhile things down just simply because they're better than who the shit-disturber is. And they can't be allowed to live or flourish, even as simple as their wants may be. Because, however

simple the wants of the superior person may be, it's still the stuff
of which resentment is made from the person who wishes to destroy
it. . . .
   What pisses me off? I don't like blaming leaders for everything.
Leaders are really not anything more than sounding boards for the
people that either vote them in or follow them. And when people
say, "I was only following orders," or, "I really don't feel this way
myself, but I was sort of led into this." People that blame leaders. I
don't care whether the leader is someone like Stalin or someone
like Hitler or someone like Manson or someone like a guy that
happens to have a group of followers that will just simply—like,
Tom Metzger is a perfect example—be blamed for what the knuckle-
heads or the dunderheads or the stupes do to, perhaps, overextend
what they have said. EACH LIVING CREATURE, whether it's human
or otherwise, should be held responsible for ITS actions.

OK. I'm sure you've been blamed for what the knuckleheads have done.

   Of course. And I probably will continue and never, never cease
to be blamed.

What do you think about anarchists?

   The new self-conscious "anarchists" are humans of little or no
value who have turned ineptitude into a movement. They are writers who have nothing worth saying, musicians who have nothing
worth playing. Yet they think themselves to be the "cutting edge,"
when invariably their blade is a butter knife. I've yet to see one
with real talent or ability. They resent anyone with plan, purpose,
or direction—especially aesthetic discipline and harmony. They're
like the hippies who considered any of the aforementioned "hang-
ups." If you happen to be on their team, when you shit, it's
"performance art." If you're otherwise, you could spend a lifetime
perfecting a skill and go unnoticed. Anarchists wear their badges of
aimless disarray well, though, and silently proclaim, in that manner,
how they really want themselves to be. If they want to wear rags,
let them toil the fields. Put them in a slave-labor camp for the benefit
of the elite.

Are animals really more noble than people?

I wouldn't squash a spider, but I could kill a human being. A spider is being the best spider he can be. He's fulfilling his purpose as a spider. He meshes perfectly with nature's overall scheme. Nothing in nature is wasted and I can't say the same thing about people.

Red Shift

SHIRA DAEMON

SHIRA DAEMON is a working actor and director who lives on Manhattan's Yupper West Side. A reviewer for the New York Review of Science Fiction, *Shira has also sold stories to* Tomorrow Magazine *and Jane Yolen's* Xanadu III. *Moreover, she's appeared in legitimate theatrical works and had her "fantasy plays for puppets and actors" produced at King Richard's Renaissance Faire. Psychotronic film fans probably know Shira best. Since she's acted in a number of direct-to-video titles like* Banned *(playing a drunken lady cop) and* Prime Evil, *where Shira's role as a coven witch landed her on the videocassette box art.*

"Red Shift" isn't an example of "loud" splatterpunk. What we do get here is a slightly phantasmagoric puree of domestic violence/human rights abuse, one that links America's still-too-common sexism with torture and imprisonment.

A connection some of my divorced female friends probably feel isn't that much of a stretch . . .

There's a black man in the mirror. I want to scream, but that would wake Charlie, and if he couldn't see the man then he'd think I was crazy. I don't want him to think I'm crazy. It was so much work convincing the doctors to let me out the last time that I get prickly all over just thinking about it.

I have to pass by the black man if I want to get to the toilet. If I don't go pee right after sex then I'll get another one of those infections and I'll have to go to the gynecologist. I don't want to take any more drugs from doctors, even if it's only antibiotics. Antibiotics make my water turn funny colors, and infections leave me feeling like snakes are climbing up inside me, trying to twist themselves around my female parts.

I would be okay if only Charlie didn't want to have sex all the time. But he's so proud of me, being here and better and all, and he thinks it's important that we renew relations a lot, even if it's real late by the time he gets home and I've already gone to bed.

Charlie really loves this condo, 'cause he designed some of the fancy features. Like having skylights all over the place, and having a mirror over the door of the built-in closet that's in the hallway right in front of the bathroom. I don't want to tell Charlie how the skylight hits the mirror funny. When the lights are out the stars are so bright they make shadow pictures inside the glass. Charlie wouldn't know nothing about shadow pictures. He always turns on the overhead before he goes to the john, even if it does wake me up.

I'm just going to run right by the mirror and into the bathroom. The black man doesn't seem to see me, but I'm still real glad that I put on my blue T-shirt before going to the loo. It's my safe T-shirt, so long that it covers my butt. Charlie told me the blue goes with my eyes, and I was real happy when he brought it to me in the hospital. It helped me get well quicker. It would be awful if the black man could see me and I was naked, him being a stranger and all.

I don't really want to, but while I'm sitting I keep sneaking peeks up at the skylight. It reflects the image in the mirror, and I can see the black man backwards against all those teeny stars. His room shines even bluer than my shirt. He looks so sad, sitting on the edge of that cot with those bright little pinholes behind him, and I wonder if maybe I shouldn't be afraid, but his hands are so big, and his face is all puffy.

Anyway, I don't really want no black man watching me in the john. Not even in my safe T-shirt, which covers most everything I'm doing when I squat or wash up. I run by him real quick, and when I get to the hallway I look back up at the skylight. My running by didn't seem to make no difference to him. I wonder if maybe it's me who's not all here, and that's why he can't see me.

Charlie's all warm and furry. I pull his arm around me and count the red hairs on it till I fall asleep.

I've almost forgotten about the black man by the time Charlie drops me at work. It's so much better when Charlie can drive me, 'cause I hate taking the bus. People stand so close, but they don't ever say nothing. I don't really like my job much. The only thing that's good about it is that Charlie lets me keep most all of my salary. That's 'cause he believes a girl should have some "mad money" of her own. I don't think he knows that I've been saving it up, 'cause he's always talking about how expensive stuff is, and how you have to "spend money to make money."

I guess I should be grateful that I've got a job, and that I'm working at such a nice firm like Goldberg, Blatt, Firkel and Strep, even if it does sound funny whenever I answer the phone. I tried to answer calls just "Goldberg and Blatt," but Strep caught me and made sure I say all the names.

Once I drew a really funny cartoon, pretending Strep was a germ who flew into a mouth to make it say his name. He looked all harmless as a germ, not tan and tensed up, like somebody who'll only play tennis if he knows he can win. Maude laughed so hard at my doodle that I thought her coffee would come out her nose, but I was afraid that Susan would see it, 'cause I had scribbled it on a carbonized message sheet. Now I use steno books to do my drawings in, that way I don't have to worry about people finding the yellow carbons.

I'm always drawing pictures, in between waiting for the phone to ring. I showed some of the doodles to Charlie, and told him that the doctors had said I might want to go to art school. But he doesn't want me to go to school. He likes me just the way I am.

Then he showed me the fancy blueprints that he works on. He's doing a shopping mall that he says they are "reapportioning," and he's so excited about it that I tried to be, too. He really liked redesigning his condo, only I wish he would move that mirror. I guess I haven't really forgotten about the black man, 'cause he's showing up in my doodles. No matter what I set out to draw he keeps creeping back in. The cuts on his face look deeper and meaner in normal light.

Mr. Strep comes back from lunch, and he smiles at me while he picks up his little white and blue paper scraps. He's the younger partner. At least he doesn't smell bad. Not like Mr. Blatt, who smokes a cigar, and always comes in from his lunches with the divorce ladies stinking of smoke and perfume. But I don't like it when Mr. Strep comes around the desk, pushes my hair off my shoulder, and bends over to look at my drawings.

"That's very good, Lisa," he says.

"Lucinda," I whisper, but I don't know if he hears me. He plays with my hair while he flips through my steno pad. I wonder if he's got a thing for blondes. Charlie always says yellow hair looks like gold, or at least money. Mr. Strep's secretary is a Haitian woman named Celeste, and she's got shiny black hair and wears lots of silver earrings and pretty little hoops. My fake pearls hit my bitty breasts and I squirm a little, trying to get away from his hand.

Mr. Strep stops even pretending to look at the pad, and I wonder if it's looking down my blouse that makes his mouth stretch like that. I know he wouldn't grin so big if he had really seen the last couple of pictures I drew. I hunch forward a little, and he quick-like tells me that my unicorns are "commercially stylish." Then he jokes that he'd like to meet the girl who "modeled the flowered hat."

I giggle so I won't have to actually say nothing, 'cause he's got to know the girl in the flower hat is mostly me.

His teeth are real even, and I think that only sharks can have so very many teeth. It isn't until the phone really starts up ringing with the after-lunch flurry that he finally leaves. When Susan comes to relieve me for my break she looks angry about something, but I don't know what.

Somehow, no matter how much I try to draw roses or kittens, I keep on drawing dark brows, and bloody faces with white teeth all around them.

I fall asleep before Charlie gets home. He has to wake me so that we can do it. Then he rolls over and mumbles nice things at my shoulder for a minute before he starts snoring. I want to stay all snuggly under his arm where it's safe, only I still have to go to the john. I wish I didn't have to use the loo except in daylight, but I don't want no more infections. Charlie might keep sleeping if I turned on the light, but he's so cranky if he gets woke up that I don't want to risk it. It's only when he's drunk that it's safe to make noise or turn on lights.

Besides, if I wake him up and he yells at me, then I end up getting mad. I don't need no more snakes in my belly, or Charlie telling me I'm stupid, to remind me of how angry I was before I learned to be quiet and invisible. Charlie only sees me sometimes, like when I look specially pretty. I guess maybe Mr. Strep sees me then, too.

The black man is still there. The stars behind him look real hard. They seem to be just pouring all that ancient sunlight, or moldy moonbeams, or whatever it is that a dying star shoots out, right through Charlie's shined-up skylight and into the mirror.

I run into the john. While I'm squatting over the toilet I study the black man's reflection. If I squint I can see him and his blue room just a little bit better. His grey pajama top is all rumply and cut up, and the blankets on his cot look sticky. He just sits on the mattress and stares out the mirror at nothing. He's got eyes like some great big dog that you just get one flash of before the car runs him over, and I think his chest looks even worse today. I can see more of it, on account of his top's being all tore up. It's hard to tell if he's got bruises, since his skin is already so dark.

He looks so sad, I almost wish I could give him one of my comfy shirts. I guess it wouldn't be really big enough, but it's a shame he doesn't have something clean and nice to wrap up in. I can't understand why the room behind him is so bright blue. Even in the dark it kind of hurts my eyes. Maybe Charlie would understand why the color seems so fierce? It probably has something to do with track lighting.

I run back through the closet, but the man doesn't see me. If I wasn't so scared of him I'd wave. He looks real lonely and miserable in that bitty cell.

In the morning Mr. Strep comes by and stands around. He's pawing at the magazines and showing his teeth at me for so long that I get nervous and muddle all the names together on the phone. It sounds like I'm saying Goldblatt, Bergfuckel and Stupp, and then Mr. Strep gives me a look like he either has to leave or yell at me. So he leaves.

Susan comes by later and she spills hot coffee all over my drawings and onto my legs. I get an extra break to wash up, but it doesn't make the burn feel much better. There's a wet patch on my thigh that I hope doesn't stain 'cause the dress I'm wearing is the cherry-colored one Charlie made me buy.

Susan said she was sorry, but I bet she did it on purpose. I don't usually like thinking bad things about anyone, 'cause then it reminds me of how mean I could get when my mad was on me, but I'm glad that Maude is taking the rest of my breaks today. I don't know what would happen if I had to play-pretend at being sugar to Susan right after she hurt me. Maude's awfully nice, even if she does like telling me the plot of every Harlequin Romance ever written.

It takes me a long time to dry out my drawings. The black man is looking worse and worse, especially since the coffee made the pen sketches all runny and he's a dripping colored mess. I figure I've just got to tell Charlie about him. Maybe if Charlie sees him too, then we can do something to help.

When Maude comes to relieve me she says that "of course nobody would mind" if I went in back and took another steno book. So she gives me the key, and I go over to the supply room by the elevator shaft.

Maybe if I wasn't thinking so hard about the black man, wondering where he lives that the light is all blue and funny, I might've wondered why the supply room door isn't locked. I don't even notice the thumpy noise, louder than the humming coming from the elevators, until I walk in on Susan and Mr. Strep doing it doggie-style.

She's pressed right up against a stack of Pendaflex folders, and her skirt is hitched up around her hips, showing off her fancy stockings with their black lacy straps. I back out of there, wondering if they saw me, or if I can pretend that I'm just some ghost who was floating by.

When I get back to the desk I call Charlie and make him promise to take me out to dinner. He gives me some grief, but I sound so scared he's probably afraid I'll act crazy or something and he says of course we can go out.

At the restaurant I can't tell which I'm more afraid of, Mr. Strep and Susan, or that someone's going to kill the black man in the mirror. But even to me talking about the black man sounds nuts. So instead I ask Charlie why a light would seem so fierce blue.

Charlie starts out by talking about gels and wattage, but then he gets into showing off his community college degree, and he tells me all about physics.

"Wavelengths," he says, "can be blue or red. Something red means you're moving through the past, and something blue means that you're moving toward the future."

While he jabbers I wonder what kind of future it could be where a man is all locked up in a big grey cage and people hit him. It makes me angry. I never liked it when the doctors gave me drugs and told me to be quiet, or the nurses threatened to slap me around till I kept still. But Charlie doesn't like it when I remember that, so I try to be a good girl for him. Instead of talking about how it makes me all crazy again to see somebody locked up, I tell Charlie I'm afraid of losing my job 'cause I saw Mr. Strep and Susan doing it.

"See, the bad thing is," I explain to him, "that Mr. Strep's got these expensive oil portraits of his wife and his two little boys. And his wife calls him up all the time, especially when he stays late. Susan's got a little boy of her own, but his father hasn't called for a while. I think she saw me," I tell Charlie. "She might get me fired 'cause she'd be afraid that I'd get her in trouble if I told."

Charlie just thinks it's funny. "If the boss wants to grab some ass," he says, "it's his privilege. Just so long as it's not yours. Your pretty ass is mine." And then he laughs and runs his toes up the side of my stockings. His wine sloshes and spills, dribbling down the black stem of his glass like the ink that leaked out the black man's ears in my last picture.

Charlie puts down his wine and switches to whiskey, like he always does around about when he starts spilling things. When he gets to telling me how much he likes my cherry dress, and that I shouldn't worry 'cause he'll always take care of his little honey, I stop trying to talk about anything important. I really hate it when he gets dopey like this.

He seems more sober when we get home, and I want to explain to him about the mirror before we go look at it. Only by now he's too horny to listen. I've got to coax him over to the closet, and if the black man could see me he'd sure get an eyeful, what with my dress all open down the front. I try to explain why I want to turn the overhead off, but Charlie's too excited to listen.

"You never wanted to do it in front of no mirror before," he says. His breath smells like garlic and whiskey, and when I realize he's not really hearing me I try to lead him back to bed. Only he won't go.

"Let's set up some diffusion," he says, and he keeps hold of my dress with one hand while he fusses with cords and pullstrings. Finally he gets the glow of the bulb inside the closet to mingling with the starlight coming in through the skylight. The closet door is so thin that the glow leaks soft-like around the edges of the mirror.

The stars go showing me their other-place shadow pictures, and

I can see the black man again, only this time he's got guards with him. They're as tanned and strong as Mr. Strep, and they've got the black man's pajamas off. The only clothing he's got left on is this funny tie-up thing around his privates.

Each time the guards whip him they bend over a little and then jerk back up again, real stiff and quick-like. They make me think of some nasty kind of toy doll on springs. I think maybe they're asking him stuff, but I can't hear no sound coming through the mirror. "No," I say, "oh, no."

Charlie sort of laughs at me, and works harder at my dress. He's usually real gentle, explaining to me that if we don't have relations every night then we can't bond, and we need to bond or I'll just drift away to nothing. Usually that's enough to make me like him again, and most nights he throws in some sweet talk, so I feel like he thinks I'm special. But tonight he's got liquor in him, and he doesn't want to say much.

"It'll be more exciting in front of a mirror, honey," he mumbles. It's just that he's really talking to himself, not me.

Charlie doesn't look at the men in the mirror, but I feel like I'm hypnotized by the motion of the lash against the black man's back. It cuts really deep into him and when the strips crisscross his skin peels away in curly dark ribbons. Every time he leans over I feel like I'm staring at one of those anatomy drawings, the kind where you can see the muscles and the tendons. Only the pictures in those books don't end up getting all red and sticky-looking. I don't help none, but Charlie finally twists me up enough to pull the cherry dress off me. All the while he's tugging at my panties I just keep begging, "No, no, Charlie, look."

If he's glancing at the mirror at all, though, I guess what he sees are the guards' eyes, crinkling up smiley as they flick the whip at the black man. Or maybe he's following their perfect teeth, and the way their piggy little tongues go greasing up the outside of their mouths. It's like they want to eat up the ribbon candy that they're peeling off my black man. Only instead of chewing him up they spit out these stupid questions.

I know the questions have no answers. They are surely impossible things like, "Why aren't you happy when you have everything but what you really want?" They couldn't actually be asking him practical things like, "When is the bomb going to explode?" because they wouldn't twitch that whip so fast if they thought he could possibly tell them anything between the beats.

Then Charlie pushes himself inside of me, and we're doing it doggie, just like Susan and Mr. Strep. Charlie keeps fumbling his hands over my bitty breasts, and now he starts staring at the mirror. I watch the guards moving their arms up and down, and up and down. The black man jerks something fierce as they flick their whips over the little white tie-up thing covering his bottom. When the cloth finally drops off of him they let it just lie there, all awful on the floor. It looks like some used sanitary napkin. A really full napkin, like maybe one that got worn right after some bad miscarriage. There's little pieces of private flesh all stuck inside that rag and the guards' mouths are stretched up in a real wide grin. I think that they must know that they shouldn't, can't, be doing this. Like Mr. Strep grins because he knows that it's wrong of him to fuck Susan.

I decide that it's all right to hate Mr. Strep almost as much as I hate those guards. I don't know how I feel about Susan, though. Maybe she thought if I had coffee all over me I wouldn't look so good to Mr. Strep. Maybe she's scared of losing her job, almost as much as the black man must be afraid of losing his life.

Charlie is pounding away, and I think he might really be able to see the guards, 'cause every time they hit he grunts himself harder into me. I want to scream at him, but I know he won't listen. Finally, both guards are moving their arms so fast that the black man just crumples up and tumbles over. I have no idea how he managed to stand so long. Charlie moans, stiffens, and then finishes. I fall, just like the black man in the mirror, in a heap on the floor.

"You're the best, honey," Charlie moans all sleepy at me. He pats my shoulder, and his whiskey breath ruffles my hair. Then he lumbers off to bed. I lie there, quiet, but I can feel the mad take me up again.

It's like when I get crazy I can't help but see all the stuff I try to pretend isn't really there. Like that Charlie only wants me around when I'm a good girl, and how I can only keep my job if I don't never go and push Mr. Strep's hands away. I get so angry that I forget to be embarrassed that I'm naked, when I stand up and stare right into that mirror.

The black man has been dragged onto his bed. His hands cover the mess they made between his legs. I let the mad take me over, and it helps me raise up my fists and beat on the mirror. The glass cracks, and little chips of silver get caught in my hands. Blood leaks out of my palms and drips down the frame. Somehow the blue light in the glass changes to purple, and then it goes red. As I bleed over the mirror the black man starts moving in reverse, kind of like a speeded-up video rewind. My blood sprinkles all around him, and it fills up lots of the spiderwebby cracks I made. Days of him being locked up and tortured all seem to dribble away. He keeps looking healthier and more real every second. It's great seeing him turn into a whole person, and stop looking like some sickly ghost.

Just as he's running backward out the door of the cell, I think maybe he sees me. Some glimmer of recognition flickers in his eyes. I whisper a prayer for him as I tear pieces of glass off the sticky paper that holds it onto the closet door.

I manage to tumble pretty much all the glass to the floor. The tinkling sound it makes when it falls seems real hopeful. It reminds me of good luck wind chimes, or maybe of hospital walls being blown up. Perhaps my black man will figure out how to live, now that he's been given a second chance. I can't stand the thought of his blue future being replayed over and over again in starlit mirrors.

I pick up a big piece of glass and walk over to Charlie. He's lying there on his bed, all snoring innocence, with his red hair curling damp and sweaty on his forehead. I hold the shard up under his ear and listen while he breathes. My mad sees too much. It sees how little it would take to break the skin. To open up Charlie's veins and watch his blood spill out like my black man's pain.

My breath comes out fast and heavy as I watch Charlie and listen to my mad. My hands are shaking real bad, and the glass shines with flickers of light that come in from the windows. The light wanders over Charlie's face, and he mumbles something. I'm real scared he'll wake up and see me, my hands all drippy and ready to cut him, but then he rolls over the other way.

I listen to him snore for a minute, but then I drop the piece of glass onto the nightstand. It's so smudged and sticky that it feels real good to have let go of it. I go to wash and Band-Aid up my hands. I want them to be all dry and clean so I can pack. Since I don't have to be invisible no more, I guess I've got to try and be free.

That's going to be horrible enough.

Within You, Without You

PAUL M. SAMMON

PAUL M. SAMMON likes music, movies, literature, and sex. He hates hypocrisy, sauerkraut, and Republicans.

Sometimes he feels the need to turn up the volume and bring things to extremes.

Once upon a time Paul also liked nonstop partying and getting into spectacular amounts of trouble. Then he gave that up. Now Sammon quietly pounds keyboards or roams the globe working on films, generally behaving like a good little drone.

He still isn't sure he made the right decision.

"Within You, Without You" addresses another of Sammon's pet peeves—casual cruelty. He feels the world is a nasty enough place, thank you very much, without egotistical assholes picking on the shy, the socially maladroit, or the weak.

Unfortunately, Paul M. Sammon is also a realist; nothing that people do surprises him.

Perhaps this explains why he believes that the most dangerous human quality is innocence.

*I*t's like kiddie porn and snuff movies," Kurt said, passing the blunt on to Nick. "This ex-CIA spook, that guy I told you about, the one passed through receiving when the cops had me tanked down on Wilcox? You know, after the Palomino gig?

"He was wasted. Paranoid, too. Said he was afraid of being taken out by The Vikings, this secret white supremacist group that operates inside the L.A. Sheriff's Department. Motherfuckers are *bad;* wear little Viking tattoos on their ankles."

"Fuuuck!" said Nick.

"Anyway," Kurt continued, "this guy's totally ripped. On speedballs. Couldn't shut up. 'Got a habit, kid. A *bad* habit.' He kept saying that, over and over. Yammer yammer yammer, all fuckin' night.

"I wanted to hit him. But the trustees there, man, you start anything, they'll drag your violent ass to some empty cell and stomp the shit out of you. Later they'll play innocent, claim you slipped in the shower or something. Jailhouse cocksuckers."

Kurt paused. Snorted a minuscule heap of crystal off the small silver spoon he kept chained around his neck, the one that looked like a tiny metal dick with a flat head.

Firelight wavered on the puckered scar zigzagging across Kurt's forehead. Threw it into deep, ridged relief. Glinted off his huge, intense eyes.

Iceshards, Reba thought. *Splinters sheared from a cold, beautiful soul.*

"Anyway," Kurt continued, "all *I* wanted to do was sleep. So I tuned him out. But then this guy gets interesting. Like he'd started something he couldn't stop."

Reba surreptitiously studied the group sitting around the fire, thinking of ghost stories and summer camp. There were five of them: Kurt the lead guitarist, Nick (on drums), Suzi (Detour's left-handed bass player, bald-headed and buff), Joel & J.

Those last two—identical twins—played synthesizers. Reba thought of them as the Silent Siamese; Joel & J. hardly ever spoke. Mainly walked around aiming shotgun mikes at everything. Obsessive tech heads, grabbing samples for the band.

Not that J. or Joel mattered. No one did.

Except Kurt.

"First he tells me how he's been all over Europe and the Middle East," Kurt continued. "Amsterdam, Paris, Baghdad, Kuwait, you name it. That's where he'd picked up his habit. CIA found out and kicked him out. *Adios, muchacho, sayonara.* So now he's in the private sector. 'Security,' he called it. Bodyguard work, all over L.A. Corporate types, studio honchos, whatever.

"Me, I could care; when's this asshole gonna wind down? But then, honest to God, just when I'm thinking, Jesus, shut *up!*—he does. Right in the middle of a sentence."

"Freaky," Suzi said.

Kurt ignored her. "Except now he's staring. Buggy and crazed, like his eyes might fall out.

"That's when he told me."

Kurt paused again. Slowly raised his face, which had been canted, impassive, towards the flickering light.

He glanced around the sulfuryellow circle. Studied his rapt, captivated audience. The master showman, nearing maximum effect.

Reba was sitting to one side of the fire. Alone, her back against the band's pickup truck.

Kurt's gaze swept over her. She felt a shock. A distinct, delicious shock.

" 'You wouldn't believe what I've seen, kid,' " Kurt intoned, low and sinister, imitating the absent agent's voice. " 'The things I've done. Like snuff films. Ever hear about those? Lots of people think they're not real. Figments of the media. Yeah. Like wife beating and child abuse. Nobody used to believe in them, either.' "

Kurt cleared his throat.

"Here's where the guy looks nervous, like maybe nobody else should hear this. So he moves in, close. Real close. Right in my face.

" 'You think with all these camcorders floating around, people won't use 'em? That this recession's made money any easier to come by? Right.

" 'It all starts with kiddie porn. The producers, the guys who tape this garbage—and believe me, it's everywhere, you don't *want* to see the stuff comes out of Thailand or the Philippines—these producers have a problem. What they gonna do when their kids, their stars, are too old to pass for children anymore? Too old to turn tricks or wag eightyearold tail?

" 'I'll tell you what—they kill 'em. On video. Makes sense in a sick kinda way, when you think about it. Recycles the inventory. Keeps the product line fresh.' "

" 'Bullshit,' I said. 'How would you know?' "

" 'Told you I was with The Company, kid,' he shoots back. 'These weirdos think they're invisible, but the CIA sees everything. And it *hates* them; snuff movies offend The Company's sense of decency. Makes it look bad, too.

" 'That's why, back in '83, Bill Casey OK'd the Chicken Squads.

Hit teams exclusively targeted at the sick fucks who make this shit. Ever hear of them?' "

" 'No,' I said."

" 'See? They do a good job. Clean and quiet. Plus, they help John Q. Public sleep at night, since the average Joe never finds out how *really* screwed up things are out there.' "

"I'm thinking that one over when he says, 'And you know the funny thing about these videos, these snuff things? They're junk. Out of focus, bad lighting, no acting . . . I mean, we're not talking Schwarzenegger here. Never saw a good one yet. Sometimes I wonder what all the fuss was about.' "

The joint had worked its way back to Kurt. He took one last hit. Put out the roach with a drop of saliva beaded on the tip of his tongue. Swallowed it.

"That's when a cop came and got him, right after he'd said that. Somebody'd bailed this guy out. Never did see him again."

Kurt leaned back. Crossed scabbed, stickthin arms over his bare chest. "Weird, huh?"

The group's collective exhalation was a sigh.

"Whoaaa," Nick said.

Love welled up in Reba's throat, like tears.

She'd spent the past two weeks haunting the few clubs that would still let Detour play. But shadowing the band was a drag. An expensive one; the three hundred Reba had withdrawn with Esther's stolen ATM card, the money that was floating her on the street, was running low. Plus the police were looking for her. Or so Esther said.

The biggest problem, though, was the band's own notoriety. Detour was famous for its excesses, which meant lots of places wouldn't book them. Property damage, insurance, hassles from the cops—whatever the excuse, it all boiled down to most clubs being afraid that Detour was too hardcore.

Anyone who felt that way was an idiot, Reba had decided. How could they *not* see what Detour had become? That what had started as this ordinary thrash/industrial group had mutated, seemingly overnight, into a pack of beautiful young gods? Dark rock angels, screaming down death's highway. Blood in their eyes, white knuckles gripped *tight* on the steering wheel, howling, flying, stomping the accelerator flat.

Detour was the best band in L.A. No, fuck that. The *world.* Bigger
than Megadeath, bigger than Metallica. Bigger than anybody.

And all because of Kurt, who wrote the songs and fronted the
group. Kurt, who'd started by slicing his body with rusty razor
blades before killing puppies/taking a dump/fucking people/even
letting himself be *crucified,* live, onstage.

The night Kurt had had his tongue pierced for the audience
and the video monitors stacked around him, the night new lingual
jewelry was added to the other piercings adorning Kurt's nose, lips
and cheeks, the night blood gushed from his mouth as he wailed
the word "Transgression!," Reba—eyes blinded by tears, ears thundering with Detour's primal scream—had fallen in love.

But not just because she wanted to fuck him.

Uh-uh.

Kurt was an *artist.*

"Hey," Suzi said. "What's your problem?"

Reba started. The older woman was glaring at her.

"Sorry?" Reba said.

" 'Sorry?' " Suzi mimicked. "I said, what's your problem?"

Reba was confused. What had she done?

"No problem," she mumbled.

"Yeah?" Suzi answered. "Then what are you looking at?"

Reba fidgeted. Felt her back stiffening against the truck.

"Chill, Su," Kurt said.

Suzi turned on him.

"Yeah?" she spat. "Fuck you. *And* your teenage wannabe."

Kurt smiled.

Suzi scowled, hands balled into fists. The pressure made her
heavily muscled forearms swell and puff up. Corded veins snaked
across her scalp like twigs.

Kurt pursed gorgeous, ohsofull lips. Blew Suzi a kiss.

Suzi snorted. Turned away. Tossed a pine cone onto the fire.

Sparks whirled up, an incandescent miniature tornado.

Reba squirmed. Had she been unconsciously staring at Kurt?
How uncool.

Then again, maybe Suzi was still mad.

Earlier today Reba had heard rumors about a Detour gig in San
Pedro. So she'd dutifully trooped down there, down to the boats

and the docks, mostly by Blue Line and bus. She'd found the band in a local watering hole, a damp noplace for nobodies.

The club was almost empty. Reba had sat at a tiny table next to the stage. Close enough to see Nick leering at her breasts, which clung to the thin tank top she'd so laboriously silk-screened with the Detour logo.

After the second-to-last set, Nick had unstrapped his Gibson. Stumbled offstage and collapsed at Reba's table.

He was very drunk.

"I like your tits," he'd slurred.

Reba saw an opening.

Minutes later, Nick was fondling those tits. Out back, in the alley.

Kurt had materialized from nowhere.

"Showtime," he'd said.

Reba couldn't breathe. Ohmigod! He was here, right HERE!

Kurt might as well have been ordering a taco. He didn't notice Reba, didn't even glance at her exposed boobs. Just turned and walked away.

Reba was embarrassed. Totally mortified. After all, Nick was only a key, a way through Kurt's door.

Nick had jumped up and stuffed himself back into his pants. Stumbled along behind Kurt.

"Wait!" Reba had yelled.

The two young men paused.

"What?" Kurt had said.

For an instant, Reba was struck dumb. Good question—*what?* Then she'd had a rush of brains to the head.

"Know why I love your music?" Reba somehow stuttered, tugging the T-shirt back over her breasts.

Kurt looked bored. He'd shrugged.

"Cause you're the new Baudelaire."

Kurt cocked an eyebrow.

"Verlaine, Mallarmé, Rimbaud," Reba babbled on, "forget them. It's *you.*"

Kurt looked at her. *Really* looked.

"You've read those people?" he'd asked.

Reba couldn't meet his eyes. She'd lowered her head, cheeks flaming. Nodded.

"Cool," Kurt said. "Let's talk."

What followed was a dream.

After the final set, Reba had helped the band break down their equipment and load it onto their truck. Nobody talked much.

Nick, Joel & J. climbed in back. Kurt made room for Reba up front, between him and Suzi. Suzi hadn't liked that. She'd started to say something, but Kurt cut her off.

Reba's head was whirling. She and Kurt were *talking,* actually *discussing* poetry and the French symbolists.

As the truck clattered over the Vincent Thomas Bridge, zipped up the 710 and swung onto the 5 North, Kurt had slipped a special CD into the pickup's sound system.

Thudding percussion rattled the cab, followed by the wah-wahed sting of electric guitars.

"Brainticket," Kurt yelled. "Scandinavian group. Cut back in '71. It's still a big cult thing in Europe, especially Switzerland. That's where I picked it up."

Reba was impressed. Was there anywhere Kurt hadn't been? Anything he hadn't done?

The pickup merged onto the Glendale Freeway. Headed north, towards the mountains. The ones overlooking Pasadena and La Canada.

They were going to the forest. The Angeles National Forest.

All the way there, Reba silently thanked god for *Propaganda* magazine.

That's where she'd read about Kurt's fascination with the decadents.

The band knew about this old fire trail near Mt. Wilson, so the truck had pulled off the main road onto a dirt one. They'd rolled a couple of miles back into the trees. Stopped at a circular meadow, ringed in by pines and sandstone cliffs. The leafy bottom of a stony bowl.

Here they'd parked. Scavenged some wood. Started a fire.

Suzi vibed Reba the whole time. Snickered and made little cracks until Kurt pulled the bald-headed woman aside to say something, too quiet for Reba to hear. Whatever it was shut Suzi up. Still, she kept shooting Reba these nasty little smiles.

Things settled down after that. Some tweak and chronic got passed around. Then beer. A fat, full moon floated up between the peaks.

Reba hadn't had the nerve to join the group around the campfire. Instead, she'd hung back and listened. Legs tucked beneath her, resting against the truck.

She did want to keep up, though. So Reba took out the little gelid square of acid she'd been hoarding all week, carefully unwrapping it from its crinkled tissue paper. She washed it down with a quick gulp of the coughsyrup-like MD 20–20 that Nick had finally, begrudgingly passed on to her.

An hour later, blue trails of light streaked through Reba's head. Which prompted her to take those last two tabs of Ecstacy.

That's when Detour had started swapping conspiracy stories. UFO cover-ups, the Reagan White House running cocaine, who shot the Kennedys, whatever.

Detour loved conspiracy stories.

"And I love you," Reba muttered.

"Huh?" Nick said, bottle of Mad Dog paused halfway to his lips.

Reba smiled. Nick's face was wavering. Undulating, as if he were a deepsea kelp forest moved by surging tides.

In fact, everything around Reba was moving. Take that Ponderosa pine; its rough bark was expanding, contracting. Breathing.

"She's loaded," Suzi grunted. "I saw her drop some shamrocks and windowpane."

"No shit. Goddamn E-head, huh?" Nick growled. "Bet she's just as fucked up fucked up. Hey!" And he laughed.

Kurt suddenly stood. Firelight caressed the large tiger tattoo covering most of his chest. Turned the swaying rings hanging from his nipples into burnished hoops of gold.

"Let's do it," he said.

Suzi leaped up. Nearly knocked Reba over as the bald-headed bass player stalked past the pudgy sixteen-year-old and threw open a door of the truck.

Reba scootched sideways, made room. Nick and Kurt jumped onto the flatbed. Joined Joel & J., who were untying the tarp that covered their instruments.

Reba watched. Tried to concentrate.

This *light* kept blasting down from overhead.

She looked up.

The moon was a hole in the side of a silver furnace, belching pewter flame.

Reba stared and stared. She settled down, backwards, flat on the ground.

Grass shoots pinched the underside of Reba's thighs. She heard a faint *snick!*; Suzi had engaged the truck's CD player.

A humming Vox organ rolled through the trees. Was joined by the breathy exhalation of a flute.

Reba recognized the tune. Kurt had played it on the way up. Brainticket again, doing "Places of Light."

How many people in L.A. even know about this? Reba marveled.

A woman's voice segued into the music. She sounded anxious. Kurt had said that Brainticket fed some girl a lot of acid while they were cutting this album. Then they'd taped her rantings in the studio and used them on the record. That was the rumor, anyway.

Reba relaxed. Listened as the singer?/victim? chanted urgent lyrics into mellow, endless night:

> *Tread softly, walk on silent notes*
> *She will ask you nothing and tell you all*
> *And you, without thinking,*
> *Will lose your soul . . .* *

Reba smiled. Let herself flow with the music. Tipped back her head.

Silvery moonlight cascaded down the slopes. Picked out boulders, fissures, trees. On a distant peak, Reba could just make out the lone silhouette of a pine. It stood in stark, majestic relief, painted against an immense hovering moon.

Above and around Reba, the encircling tips of mountains were leaning in. But friendly. Protectively. Embracing her.

Reba's smile grew wider. It was all so beautiful!

Within and without her hummed a deep subsonic buzzing. This was an old, familiar sign; she'd be peaking soon.

Within and without me, Reba thought. Then, correcting, came *No—you. Within and without you. Like that old Beatles song.*

Reba loved the Beatles. Too bad they were so retro. People like

* "Places of Light" by Bryer/Kolbe/Muir/Vandroogenbroek. Edition Phonag, 1971. All rights reserved.

Kurt laughed at the moptops; Reba would have to keep her feelings secret.

But that was easy. Reba was good at secrets.

Like masking her love for unicorns and fairy princesses, bold knights in shining armor. Or hiding her own self-hatred, and the dull anger she felt towards her family, body, life. Or those melancholy yearnings to *belong* to something, to stop being the chubby smart girl who talked strange and acted weird, the one everybody dumped on. Or Esther pushing in through the bathroom door when Reba was a little girl, reaching down into the tub to press her thumb against Reba's slit and stroke and stroke and—

Wait a minute—where had *that* come from?

Oh, yeah.

The acid.

Reba took a deep breath. Slowly let it out.

Better stop, she thought. *Don't remember, don't recall.*

Reba conjured up the Beatles again. *Within You, Without You.* She silently mouthed the phrase. Watched it lazily somersault through her brain, trailing bubbles behind it.

Reba raised an arm towards the sky. Opened her hand. Began saying "Within you, without you," a little louder each time. Tuning out the other music, humming, singing, saluting her dear Fab Four as the stars pinwheeled across heaven and whirlpooled down her arm.

"Shut the fuck up!"

Something wet spattered Reba's mouth.

She swiveled her head.

Nick was standing behind her, hands crossed at his crotch. Between Nick's fingers was the shriveled pink-and-brown worm of his penis.

It was splashing a hot stream of urine down Reba's throat.

Reba gagged. Tried to scream. The piss clogged her windpipe, choking her.

Reba lurched up. Panic gripped her, sheer animal terror. She had to RUN! Take OFF! GET AWAY!

Nick's barking, drunken laugh rode Reba's shoulders as she dashed away from the truck.

Suzi's laughter joined Nick's.

"Told you to leave her alone," Reba heard Kurt say.

"Fucking Kurt, man," came Nick's receding reply. "He'll nail anything with a hole and a heartbeat."

Reba pumped her legs. Furiously picked up speed.

The moon winked out, wiped away by a cloud.

The landscape had turned hostile. Murderous. An enclave of hidden beasts threats monsters forcing her to run fast, faster, oh shit God please!

Then the ground dropped away.

Reba was actually airborne for a moment, back on her feet and racing a hundred feet down its face before she realized she'd run straight off a cliff.

Her fullthrottle fright had carried her over the lip of a scrub-and-sandstone canyon; Reba was now hurtling down a thirty-degree slope, racing towards wells of bottomless shadow.

Somehow, though, she'd stayed on her feet. Running like hell, maybe, dodging little bushes and totally unable to stop. But still on her feet.

The incongruity of this, coupled with her abrupt, unexpected plunge, made Reba laugh.

The sound icepicked her fright. Chipped away panic. Touched her inner child.

Wow! Reba thought. *I'm flying!*

She threw out her arms. Held them away from her body, like wings.

Wind poured across Reba's face. Lifted her hair needled her body scooped out her heart. Tossed it to the sky. Made it soar, dive, glide with the spirits of eagles, angels, doves!

Reba laughed again.

She was still accelerating.

Overhead, the cloud passed by.

A flood of moonlight suddenly poured down the slope. Spot-lighted a huge sprawl of cactus rushing up to meet her.

Reba's next move was instinctual.

She *jumped*. Tucked up her legs and used her forward momentum to twist her body frantically 'round in midair.

Reba was bending at the waist, reaching for her knees and trying to curl into a fetal position when she slammed into the cactus.

Something hit the back of her head. The blow *thumped!* out her breath.

Reba gasped. Waited for a follow-up impact, the one that *must* smash flesh from bones.

The jolt didn't come. Instead, thick pads of prickly pear cushioned her descent.

Reba was now lying, arms and legs flung wide, on a buoyant, succulent mattress. Yet her weight and awkward angle held the teenager pinned as surely and securely as an insect mounted on a specimen card.

Reba moaned. Vaguely registered the suspended moon, wavering behind thousands of tangoing dark dots.

She struggled. Tried to move. Couldn't. Reba's black leather jacket, the one she'd ripped off from Goodwill, was protecting her arms and back. But the fall had thrown her ridiculously short skirt over her waist; thousands of spines fishhooked her buttocks, exposed ankles, thighs.

The pain was horrible.

Another wave of panic. Reba writhed wildly, futilely. Tried to struggle free.

Suddenly, the night sky *rippled*. As if the moon were a monstrous white marble dropped into an enormous black pond.

Calm DOWN! her mind screamed. *It's the DRUGS! Just the DRUGS!*

Desperately, Reba focused on that moon. Clung to it for dear life, her cosmic life preserver. Studied its every shadow, crater, pore.

Wait. Those dark blotches. That curve. Yes! They almost looked like—

A face. A woman's face.

A wispy cloud bisected the moon's upper quadrant.

Hair, she thought. *Grey hair.*

Esther's hair!

Horror suffused Reba's body. *That's* who it looked like, *that's* who it was! *Esther,* her *mother,* she'd *found* her, tracked Reba *down!*

Now the moon was no longer a satellite, because the shadows on its face were moving—writhing—screaming!—in the same shrill voice, Esther's voice, which had screeched across so many aborted telephone calls home, calls that always left Reba crying sobbing bereft of hope as the echoes bellowed *don't come back, who wants you? you were only trouble, you were always trouble, worthless nothing more than nothing, a thief, a whore, always whining about poetry or music, your rock 'n' roll music, think you're smart? you're just a smartmouth, you'll never make anything out of yourself, never never NEVER!*

Esther's voice buzzsawed through her brain.

Reba screamed and passed out.

"Reba?"

Her eyes opened. The moon was still up, but repositioned. Lower in the sky, now.

Reba groaned. Why was her body aching? Why were all these needles puncturing her? Had she been bad? Had Esther caught her at something? Beat her and locked her in the closet again?

"Reba? You OK?"

Painfully bright light stabbed at Reba's eyes. She clenched them shut.

Memory came crashing back.

Nick's pissing. Her terrified flight. The plunge down the canyon. The cactus. The moon. Esther's huge, shouting face.

Reba's stomach twisted. Turning her head, she vomited.

"Jesus! Hang on, babe, I'm coming."

Who *was* that?

Reba's eyelids crawled open.

A bobbing light was carefully moving down the slope, picking its way towards her spiny bed. A flashlight, aimed by a thin shadow.

Kurt?

It was him!

The young man moved closer. Reba could see his tattoos, his concerned, worried face.

A cool breeze blew between Reba's legs. She remembered her exposed crotch. Involuntarily reached forward to hitch down her dress. Gasped in pain as stickles ripped her flesh.

"Don't move!" Kurt commanded. "You'll only make it worse. Wait for me."

Kurt reached the cactus patch. Gingerly worked his way down and around it, traveling back through the center of the mass via a thin path he crushed down with his heavy Doc Martens.

He stopped behind Reba's head. Pocketed his flashlight. Took hold of Reba's jacket.

"Try to sit up," Kurt said. "Slow."

Reba tried. The movement only pushed her backside deeper into the cactus.

"Easy!" Kurt barked. "I've got you. You won't fall."

Reba started to cry.

"It's OK," he soothed, voice low, caressing. "Just sit up. You might tear your legs a little, but that can't be helped. Come on now, baby, I've got you."

Through shame and pain Kurt's words licked at Reba's heart. *Me!* she thought. *He came for ME!*

Slowly, awkwardly, with Kurt pushing her back, Reba sat up.

The next instant he reached under her armpits and swung her to the left. Kurt let go.

Reba collapsed onto firm, dusty ground.

"I'm sorry," Kurt murmured. "Here."

He stretched out his hand. Reba took it. Kurt winced. Didn't complain as the thorns in Reba's palm bit into his flesh.

Kurt pulled Reba to her feet. She swayed, stumbled. Nearly fell back onto the cruel biting plant.

"Watch it!"

Rough hands, steadying her.

"There. Stand still for a second, all right? I want to look you over. Check out the damage."

Kurt picked up the flashlight. Reba felt herself blushing as the beam swept up and down her legs. While he studied her, Reba noticed a backpack slung over Kurt's shoulder.

Kurt set down the light. Unslung his backpack. Reached in.

"You're covered in needles," Kurt said. His tone was even, reassuring. The perfect bedside manner. "I'll try and pull them out. All right?"

Reba nodded.

Kurt removed a large object from the backpack. Handed it to her.

"Drink some," he said. "It'll help."

Moonlight revealed a fresh fifth of Jack Daniels. Reba took the proffered gift. Gratefully broke the seal. Twirled off the cap and took a shallow, tentative sip.

"More," Kurt commanded. He'd returned to searching through his pack.

Reba drank to a count of three. Coughed and nearly puked a second time. But the liquor injected tranquilizing shots of languor into her battered legs and butt.

Kurt's hand came out of the backpack, gripping a small plastic container. He opened it. Shook out a pill. Held it up for Reba to see.

"Swallow this."

Reba regarded the pill curiously. It was tiny and heart-shaped. Writing, too small to be read in the diminished light, was stamped across its face.

"What is it?" she timidly asked.

"Painkiller," Kurt replied. "Wash it down with some Jack—this could hurt."

Kurt smiled. Strong, pearly teeth went off like flashbulbs in the dark.

Reba's heart melted. She took the pill from Kurt and popped it into her mouth. Sloshed it down.

"Good girl."

Detour's leader carried a complicated Swiss Army knife in a pouch on his belt. He opened it, revealing a tiny set of tweezers.

Kurt shuffled. Knelt behind Reba.

"Just keep drinking," he told her. "Enjoy the view while I get these spines out."

A coolness on her fanny; Kurt had lifted the back of Reba's skirt.

His hand encircled her left buttock.

Reba felt herself grow damp with pleasure.

Kurt pressed down. Hard.

Reba yelped.

"Sorry," he murmured. The hand was instantly removed. "Let's try that again ... how's this?"

A pressure on her right cheek. Softer, this time. Tender.

A sudden unexpected tug.

One of the countless points of pain went away.

"Better," Reba said.

Kurt went to work. Silently, methodically, he cleared her right buttock and worked a path down her leg. Eventually, he started up the other one.

Reba drank and watched the moon. It was just a moon now, Esther's face a fading memory.

A delicious lassitude coursed through Reba's body. She felt calm and tranquil. More relaxed than she had in weeks.

The back of Kurt's hand brushed her inner thigh. She shivered. Wondered why this vision, this knight had come after her.

Was it her running away? Or had her obvious terror ignited some latent protective spark?

Whatever the reason, Reba had to speak. To thank Kurt for his kindness, for his bravery and love.

"Thank you," she whispered.

Kurt's reply was curiously flat.

"For what?"

"For saving me," Reba replied.

He didn't answer.

"No, really." The liquor made her bold. "Know what you remind me of? A paladin. That's a knight."

Kurt said nothing.

Reba tittered. The sound drifted away from her lips like smoke.

Minutes crept by. Comforting minutes, underscored by sighing winds and twinkling starshine.

Kurt abruptly stood up. Clapped his hands.

"That's it," he said. "Let's get back."

Reba smiled, dreamily. Sir Kurt led the way.

Time stopped. Did it really take them fifteen minutes to crest the slope? Ten minutes more to return to the truck?

Reba didn't know. By now, she was floating above her body, which allowed her to take in the unexpected spectacle waiting back at the meadow with detached, remote-controlled eyes.

The formerly meager campsite had been transformed by a roaring pillar of fire. A *bon*fire, thick and hungry, whose massive combustion scorched the sky.

Behind the flames, curving in a Stonehengelike arc, hulked a towering array of Peavey amplifiers and Yamaha synths. Guitars and oscilloscopes loomed there too, blinking and interconnected by a thick nest of cables plugged into two Honda generators chugging away on the truck's flatbed, farting blue clouds of smoke.

The band members stood evenly spaced in a half circle before the fire. They were naked. Whorls of paint adorned their eyelids and cheeks; feather tufts, applied in ovals, spiraled across their chests.

"Rings within rings," Reba murmured. "Circles within wheels."

"What?" Kurt asked.

"Too circular," she said.

Directly before Reba lay a king-size comforter, flung open on the ground. Heaps of pillows and piles of pelts were stacked upon it. The bed itself was surrounded by props from Detour's stage show: human rib cages, dried pig's heads, antlers, skulls.

A female mannequin hovered near the bed, dressed in black lace panties and bra. A black garterbelt flowed over the bizarrely inappropriate metal legbrace cinched around one thigh.

The dummy's head was pushed down. It stared at the comforter.

Reba felt dizzy. She swayed.

Kurt caught her before she fell. He stroked Reba's arm and murmured endearments, gently lowered her onto the luxuriously soft bed.

Joel & J. stepped forward. Reba watched their naked genitals wobble in the firelight.

Identical cocks, she thought, and giggled.

Each man held a dark shape in his hands. They raised them to their faces.

Tiny lights winked on.

Video cameras, Reba thought. Joel & J. were holding video cameras.

Kurt knelt beside her. Took Reba's face between his hands. Nuzzled her cheeks and kissed her mouth.

Reba went weak. Kurt was undressing her. Softly, slowly, careful not to touch her tender punctured flesh.

Kurt wriggled out of his jeans.

Reba was naked. A subterranean flash of embarrassment shot through her, shame at her exposed, pendulous breasts. At her pale, sagging thighs.

"Don't . . ."

Kurt pushed Reba's hands away. Raised the Jack Daniels bottle to her lips.

"The sacrament," Kurt said.

Reba drank. Kurt tilted her head towards the right.

"The cameras," he whispered. "Do it for the cameras."

Reba swallowed, trying not to choke. She was dimly aware of Joel & J.'s hovering shapes.

Kurt tipped the bottle; Reba drank some more.

Stop! a distant part of her shrieked. *Run!*

To what? another, closer part replied.

Kurt dropped the empty bottle. It hit the ground with a *klunk!* Suzi walked up.

"God, Kurt," Suzi said. "Look at her. She's so *gross.* Can't we—"

"Do it," Kurt snapped.

Suzi sighed. Dropped to her knees and wrestled open Reba's legs. Leaned over. Kissed Reba's sex.

Reba closed her eyes. Barely felt the woman's tongue flicking across her inner lips. There was only a curious numbness as Suzi moved up and down, laving, parting her with fingers and teeth.

Suzi touched Reba's clit.

Reba shuddered. Groaned. Felt a hot red flush blossom on her upper chest. She grabbed Suzi's head.

Her orgasm was a gathering tension, a curled congestion that tightened, tautened, and exploded. Reba's pelvis jerked wildly, convulsively. Smeared her sopping cunt against Suzi's moving face.

"The tuning," Kurt said, as J. moved in for a closeup.

Suzi sat up. Wiped her mouth and looked surprised.

"She came," Suzi said.

"Not good," Reba heard J. reply, muffled behind his camcorder. "Give her another pill."

Something was forced past Reba's lips. She gladly opened her mouth, sucked greedily on the small round object that nudged past her tongue.

Something else was nudging her, too. Down there. Something hard and wet, yet wonderfully soft.

Reba opened her eyes.

Kurt was levered above her, poised across Reba's body in a push-up position.

"For you," he whispered. "For me."

Kurt thrust forward.

"For music."

Reba felt every ridge and vein of him push past her inner folds.

Gently, considerately, not slamming it home. Millimeter by loving millimeter, so SLOW!

Kurt bumped her cervix. Withdrew.

Reba moaned in frustration. Threw her arms around Kurt's back. Shoved her mound up eagerly to meet his next downward lunge.

Tears dripped from Reba's eyelashes, ran scalding down her cheeks.

My prince, she thought. *My champion!*

Reba humped and pushed and sucked Kurt deeper within her, aware that, even as his thrusts became more urgent, the sensation of his penis was gradually slipping away. Fading, tuned out, a ghostly signal picked up on someone else's TV set.

That was fine. It didn't matter. Not about her. She'd had her come and now he was coming too, her rescuer, shuddering above her, mouth wet against her neck. Squirting and shaking as his unfelt seed jetted into the depths of her very soul.

Kurt collapsed. His weight was heavy, suffocating.

Reba didn't care. She could die here under him, stroking his shoulders and damp, panting back.

The pressure disappeared from Reba's chest.

Kurt had stood up. His eyes were dull, and a thin line of spittle drooled from his mouth. He rubbed it away with the back of his hand.

"She's ready," Kurt said.

J. handed Suzi his camera. The tall, silent keyboard player squatted beside Reba's bed. Withdrew some objects hidden there.

Out came a mass of curling black cables terminating in flat metal discs. These were followed by a roll of translucent tape.

J. laid one of the metal circles in the hollow at the base of Reba's throat. She vaguely realized she should feel something, perhaps a brief chill. Like a doctor's stethoscope. Yet her senses registered the pressure of the disc even less than they had Kurt's phantom erection.

J. picked up the tape. Ripped a piece off with his teeth. Pasted it over the disc on Reba's throat.

More of the discs were taped on Reba, quickly and efficiently. One on each temple. One on each wrist. One on the side of her neck, just below the right ear.

J. briskly slapped discs on Reba's thighs, near the junction of her legs. His fingers slipped up her cunt. A cable was left dangling between her lips, like the string from a black tampon.

Reba focused her eyes. Her nudity was festooned with grey metal, black cables, and brilliant yellow tape.

"Frankenstein," she mumbled.

J. gathered up the cords. Rose and moved behind the fire, carefully unspooling cables as he went.

The other end of the cables ended in gold-plated plugs. J. socketed these into numerous instruments and amps. He paused at a flat console, looked expectantly towards Kurt.

Kurt was wiping off his penis. He flicked his wrist. Drops of semen and lubricant sprinkled the air.

Then Kurt sat down. Stroked Reba's hair.

"It doesn't hurt, does it."

The words weren't a question.

Reba shook her head. Even her long-standing, deep-seated ache had gone away.

Kurt snapped his fingers.

At the mixing board, J. threw a switch.

White noise hissed between the towering peaks. Was joined by a series of *basso profundo* thuds and grunts.

All across the meadow, the night was submerged in an ambient sea of sound.

Joel stepped beside Suzi. Both musicians had their cameras intently trained on Reba's face.

"Sensors," Joel said. "From you. It's your heartbeat. Alpha waves. Lungs. Blood."

At the mixer, J. slid up a fader. Diddled some pots. The deep concussions and sibilant hissings gradually merged, became one. Were tuned, tamed, and modulated into a gorgeous fluid symphony.

It's beautiful, Reba thought. *Like whales or dolphins. But more complicated.*

"There's an old movie," Kurt said. "*Videodrome.* Ever see that? High weirdness. Television, hallucinations, The New Flesh." He slapped away an ant. "The director got it wrong."

J. had magically reappeared beside Kurt. Now he held what looked to be a long metal wand, connected to thin copper wires.

"People aren't turning into television or videos," Kurt continued, reassuring, reasonable. "It's music. Always was, always is."

The Swiss Army knife was back in Kurt's hand. He flipped out
its largest blade, which reflected a bright band of light across the
mannequin's watching, painted face.

"I love you," Kurt said.

His hand stabbed down. Thumped against Reba's breastbone.
Moved right, turned left, turned again.

The knife slid in a long, graceful curve between Reba's breasts.
Arced across her belly. Stopped at the top of her pubis, where Kurt
cut right.

Reba felt nothing. She was lost, melting in the music.

Suzi handed Kurt a pair of vice grips with thick serrated jaws.
Kurt bent forward. Grunted.

Reba's body shuddered as he worked the tool, *snip snip snip,*
through her ribs.

Kurt threw the vice grips away. Reached down. Pulled out a
large coil of intestines with both hands.

The meat was hot, pinkish-grey, and marbled with fat. It steamed
in the night.

Kurt lay the smoking pile on Reba's upper thighs. Took the metal
wand from J. and slid it through Reba's intestine, skewering her
flesh.

Kurt showed Reba his hands. They were clotted and red.

"Out of my way!" Suzi hissed.

Reba watched the bald woman step around Joel. Suzi was avidly
pointing the camera with one hand and fingering herself with the
other.

Kurt kissed Reba's forehead.

"The performance," he sighed.

Reba looked up at the moon.

Such a *big* moon, really. Huge. Lovely.

Growing larger, too, as Kurt reached into her body and rhythmi-
cally squeezed her heart. Played her lungs and strummed her guts,
as the thundering organic melody swelled into a crescendo which
threatened to engulf the forest, the mountaintop, and the world.

Reba smiled. Realized she'd been wrong.

It wasn't Esther's face up there, oh no.

It was Kurt's.

And now his shadowed, cratered features were expanding. Enlarging, getting bigger all the time. Reaching down to greet her as she rushed up to meet him, happy, laughing, watching her own body recede, wink away, she gaseous now, infinite, holding on to one last insight, one final thought, before she merged and imploded with the merciful planets and stars.

Esther had been wrong too.

So very, very wrong.

Reba had finally made something of herself.

—for Wildy Petoud

Epiphany

CHRISTA FAUST

"CHRISTA FAUST is twenty-four, ratty-haired, and underfed, with a ring in her nose and a profound inability to sit still. She is not exactly what you would picture when you imagine a professional dominatrix.

"She was created by New York City but home is where she's at. She has worked as a twenty-five-cent peep girl, exotic dancer, tarot card reader, performance artist, and panhandler. Currently she sings backup for Skipp and Spector's band Blood Brothers. *Throw in some underground comics, some weird flicks, and some loud raunchy music and you have Faust's literary DNA.*

"Christa cut her teeth on splatterpunk. Her momma put splatterpunk in her bottle. Schow, Skipp and Spector, McCammon, and Lansdale are her parents. Those guys gave the sperm; Brite, Koja, Lannes, Califia gave the eggs. Yet Christa is not so much a splatterpunk as a splatterbaby. Splatterpunk, The Next Generation. And she doesn't mind wearing the splatterpunk suit as long as there's a zipper.

"Finally, Faust has been a dominatrix for going on four years now, working out of dungeons on both coasts. She believes that it is better to be paid to have her ass kissed than to be paid to kiss someone else's. Bondage is her personal fetish and she often dreams of tying pretty girls to train tracks. She is currently plying the whip at Lady Laura's Dominion in Los Angeles and working on her first novel, a corrupt little love story set in the S&M underworld.

" 'Epiphany' is her first publication."

That, more or less in toto, was the biography sent in by Christa Faust.

I'm not sure I need add much else.

Except to note that the next time someone tells you women don't write splatterpunk?
Hand them this.

*F*irst, as always, the mask.

It is black latex, featureless except for a diamond-shaped opening for my nose and mouth. The scent of it brings wetness to the walls of my vagina like blood tears to the stone eyes of a weeping Madonna. Kneeling before my Mistress, I am filled with bad-girl expectation. It is a struggle not to squirm and fidget.

I watch her shadow on the stained carpet as it mimics her actions. Her long fingers caress the inkblot shape of the mask, holding it poised above my head. My heart is clenched tight in my chest and I know that I am irrevocably in love with her. As I am with each of them.

Her name is Lana. I met her at the Clit Club just the other night. I was very drunk and crying in the bathroom over seeing my ex with her new slave, a whining little boy-dyke with ratty orange hair. I wiped puke off my chin with a handful of toilet paper and prepared to give that bitch a piece of my mind. Instead of getting my ass kicked, I was snared by the woman who would become my new Mistress.

Can I describe her? No. It would be like trying to describe gravity. Instead, let me describe her effect on me.

I cannot meet her gaze. I don't even know the color of her eyes. When she is in the room, every sin I've ever committed rushes to the surface, undeniable evidence to prove my deserving of the severest punishment. I can hide nothing from her. Every moment of her attention is ecstasy and her disinterest, agony. I love her, but underneath I know that she is not my perfect mistress.

Soon, as always, we will tire of each other and I will be left with the woman of my most treasured nightmares. My real Mistress. The fiction that I create in my most shameful and terrifying fantasies. The woman with the power to take me all the way. To strip away the civilization and sink her teeth into the exposed meat of my soul.

Her appearance changes constantly. As I crouch, sweating, in the back of my closet with one hand between my legs and the other clenched around the chain that connects my nipple rings, I imagine her as a flayed and glistening demon with long skeletal arms and gnashing teeth chasing me down the corridors of Hell. Sometimes she is a multiarmed goddess with golden skin and a razor-tipped implement of torture in each delicate hand, creeping wide-eyed through the dark behind me. Sometimes she is a machine big enough to encase my entire body, ready to penetrate me with grinding pistons and pierce me with a thousand needles. Sometimes . . .

A sharp crack pulls my wandering mind back into focus. I blush darkly, feeling as though I have committed some obscure adultery. I stare at the braided red cracker at the tip of my Mistress's whip where it lies coiled between her spike-heeled boots.

"It's time," she says, yanking the mask over my head.

I feel a trickle of warmth on my thigh as the mask's security enfolds my senses. The mask is the key to my training, like Pavlov's bell. It is the signal to let go. The bridge between my ordinary life and my *real* life. I have been with many women, but the mask is mine and always will be. I am ready.

An angel stands amid forgotten winter coats with a cold eye pressed against the crack of the partially open closet door and one hand resting on the cut-glass doorknob. She is lusciously fem, a creature of no angles. Her curves are dusted with a hint of childhood freckles. For as long as she can remember, she has wrapped herself in ladylike cliché. Her perfume is subtle lavender and rose petals and her dress, watered silk with a pattern of tiny flowers. She inspires chivalry in even the most indifferent New Yorker and she accepts all she is given with a coy smile.

She has been in this narrow closet for almost fifteen hours, listening to the quiet music of domesticity and waiting for the slave to arrive. To pass the time, the angel draws on the walls with a soft charcoal pencil. Mostly self-portraits. She has no fear of detectives.

Here she has pictured herself with wings that curve back over her head like the wings of stained-glass seraphim. At her feet lie the lovingly drawn corpses of women in bondage, their chests open like books. In her hands, she holds clusters of ovoids like black eggs or some strange fruit. These objects are everywhere in her drawings. When rendered larger, they seem to have a jagged pattern on their skin, similar to the lines registered by an earthquake

On the wall to her left, she drew herself reclining, being fed the black fruit by eviscerated slaves. On the right, she is dressed in rags and pitifully thin, carrying a huge basket of the ovoids up a steep incline, towards a cloud of spikes.

Hearing the click of locks and the soft, wet sound of tongue against boot leather that signifies the slave's arrival, the angel has dropped the pencil in favor of an ivory-handled straight razor. She presses the blade to her babydoll lips as the scene in the room unfolds.

She watches impassively as the mistress leads the masked and naked slave to an eyelet-studded cross on the far wall. Using shanks of red and purple rope, the mistress binds the slave to the cross, tying and twisting intricate, geometric patterns.

The bright prettiness of the colors appeals to the angel, eliciting a smile of almost childlike innocence. The ropes are followed by colored clothespins and brightly painted weights. The angel watches with her head tilted to one side, her smile gone dreamy and unfocused. The whip licks between the clothespins, precise as a forked tongue, leaving pink and white welts behind it.

Sobbing, the slave is unfastened from the cross and forced to walk the length of the room with weights swinging from the rings through her labia. She takes tiny steps and mewling noises like the cries of a half runover kitten escape her parted lips. At the mistress's bidding, she lies down on the carpet and the weights are fastened to a low-hanging suspension bar. A winch bolted to the far wall raises the bar higher and higher until the slave's stretched labia begin to bleed. Pulling her leather skirt up over her narrow hips, the mistress lowers her exposed vagina onto the slave's open mouth.

The mistress's back is to the closet, so she does not see the angel slip barefooted into the room and stand poised behind her, the razor inches from her throbbing pulse. She is absorbed in her own ecstasy when the angel slits her throat.

My tongue aches at the root as I struggle to service my mistress. My senses are full of her. Her sweet-salt taste and the rich, animal smell of her sweat. My nipples burn and the pain and pleasure between my legs are as indistinguishable from one another as the teeth of a spinning buzzsaw. I feel her muscles clench convulsively and a torrent of hot piss drenches my eager face. I writhe and shiver beneath her, struggling to swallow every precious drop. In my head I repeat a mindless mantra of gratitude.

Thankyouthankyouthankyou

My love is stronger than it has ever been.

Her body goes slack against me and I continue to lap the hot fluid from her thighs and ass. Her piss has an unusual taste, metallic under the acridity. Almost like blood.

But then the soft flesh of her thigh drags across my face and she is gone.

I feel icy cold in her absence. I cannot measure time in my latex darkness and as the elastic minutes spin out longer and longer, I find that I am falling back into myself. My body clamors with a thousand hurts and I know that transcendence has escaped me again. The mundane hell of my daily life comes crowding back into my mind like a flock of carrion birds, momentarily frightened from their carcass by a gunshot.

I see myself at work. Serving coffee to yuppie drones. Smiling hard enough to crack my teeth.

I see my answering machine blinking with a thousand messages from my mother, asking when I'm going to meet a nice boy and settle down.

I see myself cruising the bars, brushing elbows with hundreds of empty lives.

Loneliness is a tighter mask beneath the one I wear. I will never be free.

The angel stands over the body of the mistress, unmoving, her head tilted to one side like the RCA dog. She has a face like a cherub from a Victorian valentine, but her eyes are grey and empty as the eyes of a shark. If it weren't for the trembling of the slave, the scene could be a tableau in a wax museum. Then, with slow determination, the angel reaches out a dimpled hand to touch the slave.

*   *   *

In the blackness, a touch. Silvery, almost, like a high note on a harp. I gasp and clutch at the sensation like a drowning woman, my tormented clitoris twitching. The touch seems to multiply, racing up and down every nerve in my body. The clothespins are plucked off one after the other, rapid-fire agony that burns through me like music. Then a pause. I am alone with my pain, flesh aching with anticipation.

Again a touch, skittering across my inner thigh. I groan uncontrollably. Arch my body to meet the elusive sensation. Breath, hot against my fevered skin. The wet flick of a tongue. Before this inexplicable pleasure can register, can penetrate my brain, teeth clamp down and fill my body with fire. Love wells up inside me, I can taste it in the back of my throat. I know Lana doesn't like me to speak, but the words tumble out before I can stop them.

"My life for you."

Silence. I am struck with a sickening fear. Fear that I have displeased her. My love feels crushed under the weight of sudden panic. Endless years go by while I wait for my punishment. I am convinced that she has left me and that I am alone, but I am afraid to move in case she is still there, watching. When I feel that soft touch on my clitoris, I come violently in fear and shock. Instead of drawing away, the fingers probe my vagina, working their way up inside me like living things. I feel myself stretching to accommodate her hand. Rock back and forth as I am hit with orgasm after orgasm. I can hear myself moaning like a slut, but I can't help it. There is a strange tickling sensation against my thigh that I can't identify; I am so wrapped up in orgasm that I cannot think. Her fingers open inside me like some strange, night-blooming flower and I feel that soft tickling again, brushing up over my hip.

Suddenly a supernova of pain bursts through my abdomen and I simultaneously realize what the tickling sensation is. It's hair. Long, soft hair. An image of Lana's butch-cropped locks flashes past my inner eye and I know that someone else is here.

It's *Her*. My true Mistress.

No martyr could ever come close to the rapture that fills me and swallows my consciousness. My body is reduced to a knot of agony at my core. I want to promise her my undying love and devotion, but I feel as though I'm falling away from myself, leaving my body behind like a paratrooper watching the plane spiral up and away.

I am finally free.

The angel crouches over the slave's still body. In her hand she holds the loops of intestine that trail from the slave's vagina. For a long moment, she is as still and lifeless as her victims. Then, slowly, life bleeds back into her face and she gets up, licking her tiny fingers. Standing over the slave with one foot on either side of her chest, she lifts up her bloodstained dress, exposing her hairless vagina.

She crouches over the dead woman's face and moans in parody of the mistress's pleasure, rubbing herself against the slave's cooling lips. Soon, her gasping gives way to giggles and she stands back up, covering her mouth with her hands.

Drops of iridescent fluid ooze from the angel's vagina and splash against the slave's solar plexus, hissing minutely as the skin chars and blackens. Laughing still, the angel throws back her head and extends a questing tongue from between the lips of her vagina. It moves slowly towards the slave, tasting the air, until it reaches the clammy skin of her chest.

The dead flesh parts with little blood under the sharkskin texture of the burrowing tongue, until the still heart is visible between the ribs, along with its shadowy twin. The black ovoid is still pulsing when the angel bends down and scoops it out.

Letting her dress fall and retracting the bloodflecked tongue into her body with a wet snap, the angel steps away from the empty vessel and turns her back. She holds the quivering ovoid to her ear like a seashell, listening to the whispering song of pain. The fruit is fat with the sugar syrup of the slave's despair. The angel finds herself tempted to press it to her lips.

She is still holding it in both hands when the piercing, dog-whistle voice of her own Mistress rips through her dreams of sustenance.

Bowing her head, she places the ovoid in the basket along with all the others.

Notes on the *Splat II* Soundtrack

True child to its raucous parents, *Splatterpunks II* was edited to a constant beat of background music. The songs, groups, and records which shaped this anthology were, in no particular order:

Seven Year Bitch, L7, Voice of the Beehive (*Let It Bee*), Fear, Patti Smith (*Horses*), The Pogues, Ministry (*The Land of Rape and Honey*), Mazzy Star, N.W.A., k.d. lang (*Shadowland*), The Cramps, Napalm Death, Current 93 (*Dog's Blood Rising*), Public Enemy, Buddy Guy, The Shamen (*Drop*), Bad Religion, Roxy Music, Peter Murphy ("Socrates the Python"), The Germs, Pink Floyd, Sheer Terror, The Ventures (*Surfing/In Space*), Anti-Nowhere League, Etta James, Richard Peaslee (*Marat/Sade, Music for Martha Clarke's THE GARDEN OF EARTHLY DELIGHTS/VIENNA: LUSTHAUS*), Katie Webster, The Surfaris (*Fun City U.S.A.*), Elmore James, Fats Waller (*Cincinnati Fats: Dick Hyman Plays the Music of Fats Waller on the Emery Theatre Wurlitzer*), Flat Duo Jets, The Astronauts ("Baja," their first three albums), The Shadows (*Greatest Hits*), Brian Eno, Lyle Lovett (*Joshua Judges Ruth*), Enya, Alphaville ("Romeos"/"Forever Young"), Patsy Cline, Nick Drake, The Trashmen (*Tube City: The Best of the Trashmen*), The Neville Brothers, Jimmy Dolan ("Hot Rod Race"), Commando Cody ("Hot Rod Lincoln"), Lou Reed, Miles Davis (*L'Ascenseur pour l'echafaud*), H. P. Lovecraft (the band, not the dead guy), The Lively Ones ("Paradise Cove"), James Brown, Carl Perkins, Roy Orbison, Dire Straits (*On Every Street*), Jefferson Starship (*Blows Against The Empire/Sunfighter*), many amazing Rhino Records compilations, Jimi Hendrix, The Cheers ("Black Leather Trousers and Motorcycle Boots"), The Swans, The Moody Blues, Yes ("Wurm"), Peter Schilling ("Major Tom"/"The Different Story"), The Residents, Love (*Forever Changes*), Shadowy Men on a Shadowy Planet, The Posies ("Flood of Sunshine"), The Ink Spots, Booker T. & The M.G.'s ("Behave

Yourself"), John Renbourn (*Sir John Alot*), Jerry Lee Lewis, The KLF (*Chill Out*), The Kingsmen ("Haunted Castle," the B-side of "Louie Louie"), The Rivieras ("H.B. Goose Step," the flip side of "California Sun"), 2 Live Crew, Vangelis (*Opera Sauvage*), Spiritualized (*Lazer Guided Melodies*), Nine Inch Nails, Ice Cube, *Jeff Wayne's Musical Version of THE WAR OF THE WORLDS* ("The Spirit of Man"), Frank Sinatra ("One for My Baby," especially), Fleetwood Mac (*Then Play On*), Skinny Puppy, just about anything by Nino Rota, Ennio Morricone, or Bernard Herrmann, Genesis ("The Carpet Crawlers"/*The Lamb Lies Down on Broadway*), Dead Can Dance, David Bowie (*The Rise and Fall of Ziggy Stardust and the Spiders from Mars*), The Space Negros, about two or three thousand sound tracks (particularly *Juliet of the Spirits* and *The Seventh Voyage of Sinbad*), as well as maybe a hundred or so classical works. Plus quite a few other rock, blues, jazz, rap, rockabilly, riot grrrl, punk, Goth, techno, grunge, R&B, industrial, hip-hop, DiY, and country albums.

And not one single fucking Madonna record.

—Paul M. Sammon
Los Angeles, CA
May 19, 1993

About the Editor

Paul Michael Sammon was born in Philadelphia. He grew up around the globe—mainly in Asia—where he was early exposed to the harsh Third World realities now affecting the United States.

Sammon's distinctive career is best described by the movie industry expression "hyphenate." His film production articles on classics like *Blade Runner, RoboCop,* and *Cocoon* have appeared in *Omni, The Los Angeles Times, The American Cinematographer, Cahiers Du Cinema,* and *Video Watchdog* magazines. His short fiction has been published in *Ghosts* (edited by Peter Straub) and *The Year's Best Horror Stories Series XIV* (edited by Karl Edward Wagner). Sammon also edited the controversial 1990 *Splatterpunks* anthology as well as 1994's *The King Is Dead: Tales of Elvis Post-Mortem.* He currently serves as film critic for *Cemetery Dance* magazine.

Paul M. Sammon is not only a writer, but a professional filmmaker as well. Through his company, Awesome Productions (which he founded in 1980), Sammon has produced/edited/directed dozens of documentaries for all the major Hollywood studios. He also provided publicity services for films like *Platoon* and *Blue Velvet,* was Computer Graphics Superviser on *RoboCop 2,* and has co-produced such Japanese television programs as *Hello! Movies, The 21st Century Theater,* and *Let's Go See Movies!*

Sammon's life was recently profiled in Stanley Wiater's 1992 book *Dark Visions.* Paul likes listening to *Ministry,* movie soundtracks, and surf music; he reads magazines like *Ecco* and *Psychotronic Video,* when not watching such videos as *Tetsuo* and *Kill Baby Kill!*

His latest accomplishment was completing the same training program Linda Hamilton used to buff herself out for *Terminator 2.*